Bright Spring

Bright Spring

EMMALINE STRANGE

For you, if you were the weird kid obsessed with Greek Mythology.

One

Ultimately, the head was to blame.

Alexios had received it three mornings before, delivered with its own honor escort, in a chest of fine, dark oak, chased with finishings of gold. It had been a lovely chest, and the head inside, nestled in folds of velvet, was lovely too. It was the bust of a young woman, carved out of white marble to capture her refined, delicate features. Alexios had set the bust on a table in his private apartments, hoping that it was a symptom of the medium that made her face so cold.

Alexios had posed for a sculptor, too. The woman had sketched his face, first, in charcoal. Then she had made the bust of simple clay, forming the raw, wet earth into Alexios's cheeks, nose, and lips. She used the clay bust as a model for the marble one, and after a month, it was delivered to the royal villa. Alexios's parents, the King and Queen, had praised the artist's skill in capturing their son's look so handsomely. Alexios had forced a smile, nodding and agreeing, all the while thinking that his own blank, sightless white eyes were unsettling, bordering on creepy.

But Alexios had acted pleased and excused himself as

quickly as he could to his chambers. He'd then known a few weeks of relative peace before the other head arrived, and now she stared at him while he slept.

The head had been carved in the likeness of Alexios's future bride. Nothing was official yet, Alexios tried to remind himself, the voice in his head growing feebler every day as the head stared at him. Her name was Dafina. He had not met her, would not meet her for some time yet. Her mother, queen of a neighboring kingdom, had been in negotiations with Alexios's parents for months, laying the foundations for their courtship.

It was not, what one might call, peak romance.

The head had sat upon his side table for three days, staring blithely at him, judging him with her milky stone eyes, almost as if she knew. She *knew* Alexios would not be a good husband.

Three days. It took three days for Alexios to crack under the weight of everything this fucking stone head represented. He had breakfast with his parents and feigned a stomach complaint. Once back in his chambers, Alexios paced for a while. He turned the bust of his intended to face the wall and made his escape plan.

There were a few ways out of the royal villa that Alexios was certain no one knew but him. He chose one, which deposited him on the roof of the stables. He jimmied the baked clay roof tiles and slid down inside, lowering himself to the straw-strewn floor. His favorite horse, Xanthos, had a spacious stall at the rear of the stables, and that was where Alexios found him. He saddled him, mounted up, and took off at a slow walk. It was mid-morning, the first day of spring.

The sunlight, the staggering blue of the sky, all of it mocked Alexios as he rode out from the villa grounds. He urged Xanthos through the northern gate in the imposing stone curtain wall, barely pausing long enough to hail the guards. It seemed to Alexios the whole world rejoiced in the start of a new season—the trees, the animals, the new green grass. The sun. All of it cheery and gloating.

As the Crown Prince of his kingdom, Alexios had responsibilities—things he had been born to, with no say in the matter. He had to carry on the family line. He needed to secure an heir of his own, lest their line appear vulnerable. Unfortunately, as with many things in royal life, appearances had a way of becoming prophecy. A line that *appeared* vulnerable often was. He had always known this time would come, the time when he had to put aside his own desires and get married, but it did not make it any easier to bear.

Alexios did everything that was asked of him. Always. But he did not know if he could do this. It wasn't that Alexios didn't wish to get married—it was that he did not wish to marry the woman whose head now haunted his sleep. He did not wish to marry *any* woman, frankly, and the head served only to remind him that one day, and one day soon, he must.

When he wished to escape the confining press of the royal villa, Alexios often took the southern gate and traveled the short distance to Papia City, where he could disappear amongst thousands of people. Other times, when the need for escape was not too great, he would simply take Xanthos riding in the expansive grounds claimed by the crown. The territory of the royal family went about two leagues into the forest that bordered the grounds of the royal villa to the north, which usually provided enough room for Alexios to roam or hunt when he felt restless.

Today, he knew before he'd even swung up into the saddle that type of escape would not be sufficient. He needed to flee; he needed to leave the trappings of royalty as far behind him as possible so that he could at last take a full breath. Alexios had a notion to travel as far into the trees as he possibly could within a day's ride. He had a bow with him, taken from the gamemaster's shed, thinking he could travel deep into the forest to hunt. Of course, Alexios did not need to hunt. Every meal was brought to him, prepared precisely to his tastes by cooks who knew their business, served to him on gleaming silver trays. Most days, that was fine.

But other days, like today, it left Alexios feeling abraded and foolish. There was nothing he truly controlled, not even his own breakfast. He was a modest archer, at best, but with enough time and patience, he knew he would not return to the villa with empty hands. Alexios would deliver his game to the royal cooks and feel like he had contributed something, feel a little less useless.

Xanthos whickered and pawed at the ground, as eager for a run as Alexios was. Alexios nudged his flanks and Xanthos took the rolling hills outside the villa at a hard gallop, but when they reached the tree line, Alexios saw the ground had already begun to thaw from winter's chill, leaving the game trails muddy and treacherous. He slowed Xanthos to a walk once they entered the cover of the trees.

While Alexios told himself he could make it back home to the royal villa before nightfall, he had brought with him some dried beef, bread, and a bedroll, just in case.

Just in case he was *forced* to spend the night outside, free beneath the stars and moon, as if he had only himself to answer to.

And what a pity that would be.

It was a fantasy he indulged often, though under the scrutiny of the stone head, he'd felt more guilty about it of late. Alexios could ride into the forest, find a river to bathe in. Naked, stripped of his crown, his toga, and everything else—Alexios was just a man. He always imagined some handsome, faceless stranger coming upon him as he bathed, someone who knew nothing of Alexios's birth and station, who just saw a man, and liked what he saw. Alexios shivered, as he imagined the faceless stranger ravishing him right there upon the banks of his imaginary river.

Alexios smiled to himself, patted Xanthos's neck, and continued north. After several hours' ride, he had left the border of the crown's lands behind him, and the forest turned truly wild. The going was slow, and Alexios felt an ache in his legs and between his shoulders—his sleepless nights making themselves felt.

He was determined to press on, however, and Xanthos certainly seemed eager to continue their trek. They rode on, along the unfamiliar winding paths, farther and farther away from the grounds of the royal villa. Up ahead, Alexios could see the trees start to thin, and he was as confused as he was disappointed. Had he reached the northern edge of the forest already? That didn't seem right. He had studied the maps in the Queen's private study and had estimated it would take far longer than half a day to reach the other side of the wood, especially at their current pace. He rode on, his stomach sinking as he realized he would not have an excuse to be gone as long as he hoped. The sunlight filtered through the thinning trees and created a fearsome glare on something just up ahead. He shaded his eyes, and when he and Xanthos finally emerged beyond the trees, Alexios gasped.

They had *not* reached the edge of the forest, but a clearing and an enormous, glittering lake. In the center of the lake sat a small island, and Alexios could see what appeared to be a collection of ruins on the island. He squinted against the light bouncing off the glassy surface of the lake, thinking this would be a lovely place to spend the afternoon, not thinking about princesses, or marriage, or judgmental stone heads.

So, overtired, distracted, and sun blind, Alexios did not see the horned viper as it slithered from the underbrush, directly in his path.

But Xanthos did.

He reared, dumping Alexios from the saddle before he could so much as react. His ass hit the ground first, followed by his elbow and his head in quick succession thereafter. The pain in his arm was blinding, and his last conscious thought was that if he died here in the forest, at least he would not have to get married.

There was nothing like the first rays of the spring sun, bright and innocent as a mother's kiss upon Auro's cheeks when he woke from his cursed slumber. Nothing like shaking the stiffness from his bones, awake at last. He climbed down from his marble plinth, stretching his arms above his head. Every single spring had been much the same since Auro had been cursed four hundred years ago. It had been four centuries of service, of solitude. There had been grief, of course. There still was, and always would be—but the passing of the years and the unending isolation had allowed Auro to bury that deep within.

The only joy Auro felt was in his work, the only joy that remained to him, one that even the passing of years in their hundreds could not dull. He was the God of Spring, but saw himself more as a shepherd of the season, a guardian. A servant. And he loved nothing better than to perform his duties to the earth and all of its inhabitants, year after year.

Until today.

Until he had woken for the first time in centuries to the acute feeling that he was *not* alone. Auro woke each spring in the same place he'd gone to rest at the previous spring's end— a temple on an island, in the center of a sparkling lake tucked into a northern corner of a wild forest. The only other occupants of the island and the temple were the statues of Auro's brothers, cold and unreachable as they had been for four hundred years. Each brother held power over one season, and only during that season did each walk free.

Most of the year, Auro slept. At the end of spring, he would transform once again into a statue, and wait, still and stone and lifeless, for spring the following year. He had three cycles of the moon to enjoy his freedom, to enjoy walking amongst his trees, and it would not do to waste those precious hours dwelling upon things he could not change.

His feet were bare, as always. It was important for Auro to *feel* the earth, to begin to know its needs straight away. He turned his back on them, the statues, and scanned the shoreline for signs of life, for something that would have raised the hairs on the back of his neck upon waking. Auro did not have to look for long. He turned toward the frantic motion out of the corner of his eye to see a horse taking off along the shoreline, leaving deep hoofprints in the mud. The horse was riderless, which was peculiar, given his fine saddle and the reins flapping in the wind as he ran. Auro shielded his eyes, and to his surprise, he saw a pair of legs sticking out from the shadows of the undergrowth, right where the leaf litter and moss gave way to sandy mud on the banks of the lake. It did not take much for Auro to put together that the horse's rider had taken a fall, and lay now, hurt on the forest floor. He watched for a few seconds to see if the legs would stir, but they did not.

Before his mind had caught up with what he was doing, Auro was jogging along the submerged stone path that led from his island to the shore.

When he reached it, he hurried up the bank to the pair of legs, dropping to the ground beside them. The legs belonged to a traveler. To be succinct, he was breathtaking, even lying in an undignified heap. To be more expansive, he had a fit, rangy body, long legs and arms tanned a deep olive brown, and a head of thick brown curls. He was young—perhaps around

Auro's own age. Or, at least, the age he had been when he was cursed. It frightened Auro, to see one so youthful and innocent lying so still, like a statue or a corpse. With trembling fingers, Auro probed the boy's neck, searching for any hint of life thrumming beneath the paper-thin skin of his throat.

A fissure of awareness shot through Auro, freezing him in place. The warmth of the boy's skin was so foreign it took him a few moments to realize why.

When Auro had first been cursed, he would creep every year toward the edges of the mortal realm, the city that was nearest to the temple where he and his brothers were bound. He would watch the people, and he would ache with loneliness, until after a few years, his heart decided it was too much pain to bear. Auro no longer had anything in common with the people of the realm, if he ever had. After that, it was only the occasional hunter or forester he would see, of a year. Whenever he revealed himself to them, the people feared him, so afraid of a god's might that they would flee the forest, leaving Auro even lonelier than before.

But still, he had tried.

Until one day, he hadn't. He'd seen a man hunting and decided to let him pass. *I'll talk to the next person,* he had thought, so tired. But he hadn't. He had never approached a traveler ever again, and after that, the solitude became his armor and the more used to it he became, the easier it was to bear. Besides, it wasn't as if Auro had no friends. The grass, the bears, the songbirds, even the trees themselves, not to mention their guardian spirits—he had friends enough who understood him and loved him. He didn't need the love, or even the attention, of mortals to be content. He did not need to be known by them to serve them.

Now, though, Auro sat there, his fingers to this stranger's throat, sitting close enough to smell the sweat of his skin, and tried to recall the last time he had touched another person.

Auro released a sigh of relief when he felt it, the barely-there pulse. It was faint but steady, and Auro found himself exploring the rest of the boy's face with his fingertips. His chocolatey hair streaked with gold, and he had a thin angular face, tiny ears. It appeared he'd struck his head upon a tree root. Auro gently probed the back of his skull, gasping when his fingers came away wet with blood. His skull seemed intact, however, and the wound shallow.

Initially, Auro had rushed to the traveler's side, some instinct overpowering the centuries of loneliness that had, somewhere along the way, transformed into fear—but now as he sat beside this young man, he found himself painfully aware of every little thing: the slightly parted bow of the boy's lips, the rise and fall of his chest below a creamy white tunic, the warmth that seemed to seep off his skin into the air between them.

Auro shook his head, hoping to clear it. This traveler needed help, not someone ogling him. The shore of the lake was as fine a place as any for a camp, so Auro got to work.

Two

The fluttering of moths brought Alexios from the fog of dream, brushing against his cheeks and his brow. Everything hurt, and he couldn't quite bring himself to open his eyes. He allowed himself to drift slowly toward consciousness, trying to take stock of his body and remember what had happened.

He'd been riding in the forest. Hunting? A few things swam in his mind's eye—a snake, a marble bust, and then a blinding white light. Not helpful. Alexios could feel the sucking sensation, like water draining out of a crack in a bowl, and the pain was great enough that he did not fight it.

The next time he wandered out of the blackness felt a bit better, a bit more present in his body. For a start, he was warm. Covered in something heavy. He could feel heat on his cheeks and hear the crackle of a fire. Perhaps someone had found him and returned his unconscious body to the royal villa. He tried to sit up but the effort was insurmountable, and as he strained himself a feeble groan slipped out.

Something cool, soft, and damp pressed into his forehead, dabbing the sweat from his brow, down his cheeks, and then down toward his neck. Groggy, aching, and disoriented, Alexios thought maybe he could at least roll over, toward the warmth of the fire. He tried to push himself up on one arm, and a lance of pain stabbed through him as he twitched his shoulder, but his arm did not respond. It took an undue amount of mental effort to arrive at the conclusion that his arm had been immobilized—not removed. He opened his eyes, and Alexios found himself face to face with someone he did not recognize—someone with sparkling green eyes and... pink hair? Alexios squeezed his eyes shut again, thinking perhaps he was still dreaming. When he opened them again, the man's face remained unchanged.

They blinked at each other in confusion for several seconds, and Alexios realized this bizarre stranger was sponging his forehead with what looked to be a bundle of something green—moss, perhaps? None of this made any sense, and thinking made Alexios's entire skull throb. Before he could open his mouth, the person dropped their sponge with a soft wet *squelch* and fled.

Alexios opened his mouth to call after them, but even the effort of moving his jaw was excruciating, so he closed it again. He waited for the blackness to pull him back under, and waited, and waited, but he remained present, pain and all. That was good, he thought. A good start.

With small, slow movements of his head, Alexios looked around and realized that he was still in the very same place where Xanthos had dumped him from the saddle—but someone had transformed it into a cozy little campsite. A whicker from somewhere behind him told Alexios that Xanthos had returned, which was good, because he did not relish the idea of walking all the way back to the royal villa in this condition.

His throat was parched, and his limbs stiff enough that it made him wonder just how long he had been lying there. The sun streaming down from the sky told him it was close to midday, but was it midday the same day he'd set out from the villa? Or midday the next day? He could not be certain, and the thought that he'd been missing for an entire day had his stomach swoop nervously. Alexios left the palace and stayed out all night from time to time, of course, but usually he was *aware* of doing so.

Alexios, as it happened, had a reputation. It was the sort of reputation that often followed young, handsome men of station. Alexios had heard the rumors, even encouraged them, of a day. They were a safe armor to wrap himself in: a young, lusty prince, sneaking away from the royal villa, absent proper escort—the story wrote itself, and it was far safer than the truth.

He must try to sit up. That was the first step. He clenched his jaw and summoned all of his strength, heaving himself onto his side. His balance was off because of his bound arm, and nausea swooped through his guts as he steadied himself. The pain in his tailbone made him gasp as he put weight on it, but otherwise, it seemed a successful venture.

Despite the effort it took to reach this point, Alexios savored his triumph in knowing he was not too badly injured to sit up, at least. The fire burned low but gave off plenty of heat, and soon enough Alexios stopped shivering. The heavy thing on his body turned out to be Xanthos's horse blanket, now pooled on the grass around his legs, and it was this that reminded him of the pink-haired stranger. He must have put the blanket on Alexios and...for the first time, he looked down at his bound arm.

What he saw took him so long to compute that he thought perhaps he'd fallen back to sleep. His arm, crooked at the elbow, was tucked snuggly against his body in a manner Alexios had seen the royal medicus set breaks before. However, unlike the thin planks of wood and sterile, sun-bleached linens the medicus used, Alexios's arm was wrapped in leafy green vines. Branches curled protectively around his arm, creating a cage of sorts, and a pair of branches braced his wrist.

Speechless, he probed gently at the wrapping with the fingers of his right hand, finding that his injured arm had been padded with soft, green moss, and vines wrapped tightly up over his opposite shoulder. He couldn't explain it to himself, but all of these components felt...alive. Somehow, Alexios knew they hadn't just been plucked from the ground and used—they had been coaxed into growing around his body, embracing his injury and protecting it. Marshalling his wits, gritting his teeth against the growing nausea that came with every slight movement, Alexios focused as best he could and looked closer at the elements of his impromptu camp. Everything appeared to have sprung up out of the ground beneath it, as if the forest itself had wanted Alexios to feel welcome. There was a short lean-to behind him of living saplings bending toward each other, their delicate branches tangled like lovers' fingers. A woven net of leaves and vines draped over it, keeping the worst of the cool spring wind off and trapping the heat from the fire. Beside him on the ground was his pack and the waterskin he'd brought with him, cradled in the ring of golden narcissus blooms and peony buds, too perfect to be anything but intentional.

He pinched his thigh with his good hand, trying to be certain he was truly awake, because this could not be real. Of course, pinching himself did not do much but add to his list of pains. Alexios twisted around, slowly, searching for a glimpse of the person who had done this. He thought he saw a flash of pink just out of the corner of his eye and heard the rustle of the trees.

"Hello?" he called out, his voice hoarse. "Hello?"

∼

Auro watched anxiously from the branches of a nearby tree as the injured boy awoke and observed his surroundings. He called out, his voice raspy, and Auro opened his mouth to answer, but no sound would come. Now that this stranger no longer seemed in danger of dying, the urgency bled out of Auro, leaving only fear to take its place.

He couldn't remember the last time he'd spoken to another person. He conversed with the dryads, of course, but they only spoke the language of the trees. Somehow, Auro did not think this young human man would be fluent in their whispery tongue. Rooted to the spot, clutching the branch of the tree he hid behind, Auro watched as the traveler turned to look around the clearing, searching for a sign he wasn't alone. It was like someone had stolen Auro's tongue, and no matter how much he wanted to reveal himself to the boy in the clearing, he couldn't. His feet were as rooted to the ground as the trees beside him.

But he stayed, and he watched.

The boy had still not recovered from his head injury, that much was plain, but he heaved himself to his feet anyway and made a valiant attempt at staggering toward his horse. His ungainly, lurching gait finally spurred Auro into action, and Auro lunged, throwing out his arms to slow the boy's descent as he went tipping to the ground. With an arm behind his shoulders, and one hand bracing his head, Auro was able to lay him gently back on the grassy bed of the forest floor.

Before Auro could say or do anything else, the boy rolled over to retch violently onto the dirt. Nothing came up, and Auro held him until the retching stopped, before easing him onto his back once again.

He noticed the boy's eyes for the first time, then, deep brown and rich. Warm—albeit quite dazed. Unfocused.

To Auro's great surprise, the boy reached up one of his

hands, weakly, and touched an errant curl that had fallen across Auro's brow.

Before losing consciousness once again, he said, "*Pink.*"

Auro sat frozen for quite some time, processing what had just happened. If it had been a long time since he'd spoken to someone, longer still since he had touched another person, he could not even *recall* the last time someone had touched *him.*

Gooseflesh burst across his arms, his chest, and a shiver ran down his spine. It frightened him, being touched. It had lasted half a heartbeat, maybe less, but it had sent curling tendrils of warmth down Auro's skin where this boy's fingers had connected. And now, he was unconscious. Never had Auro been so acutely aware of another human being—who may as well have been a thousand miles away for how aware he was of Auro. It was unnerving, as if the very air currents of the forest bent and moved around this fragile, human body. Making space for it.

Now that he was effectively alone once more, with his charge unconscious, Auro tucked the heavy wool blanket back around him. He retrieved the waterskin he'd found in the traveler's saddlebags and using some fresh springy moss, he dabbed water onto his cracked lips, just enough to get a few drops inside.

Soon, his long lashes fluttered open again, which Auro took as a positive sign—he'd regained consciousness more swiftly each time. "Don't sit up," Auro blurted, startling himself. His voice was a tiny, frail thing. A proper whisper would have drowned it out, but the boy fixed his brown eyes on Auro's face and managed to nod a fraction of an inch. Carefully, carefully, Auro eased his head onto his lap, propping him up a bit to try small sips of water. They stayed like that for a while, a long while, until half the waterskin was empty.

By that point, Auro's charge showed signs of coming back

to himself a bit. Auro helped him sit, and he was able to lift the waterskin to his own lips to drink. This allowed Auro to study him in profile, and get another look at those tiny ears, which he'd decided he quite liked, especially with thick caramel waves of hair curling around them, shining in the sunlight. Auro found he also enjoyed the gentle slope of the boy's slender neck, the cut of his jaw, and his pointed chin.

"You are staring," he said, and Auro jumped.

He could feel the heat rising in his face, and try as he might, he couldn't find the words to answer.

"I'm Alexios," he said, and Auro decided it was the most beautiful name, the most beautiful word he'd ever heard.

Just the sound of it warmed him from scalp to toes.

Alexios turned, slowly, and gave Auro an expectant stare.

He tried to speak around the tightness in his chest, but he couldn't. Instead, he nudged the waterskin with his hand. Alexios should drink more, if he was able.

Alexios sighed. "Alright," he said. And he drank, which of course allowed Auro to track the bob of his throat as he swallowed.

Since Alexios could sit, and drink, without immediately keeling over, Auro thought possibly it was time for him to leave. After a bit more rest, Alexios would be stable enough to determine when he could mount up to ride home, wherever home was.

"You did this, didn't you?" said Alexios, indicating his bound arm.

Auro nodded.

"Thank you."

Auro said nothing, but the corners of his lips tugged upward.

Alexios's eyelids began to droop, and Auro knew that sleep and rest were the best things for him. And besides, the sooner Alexios fell asleep, the sooner Auro could extricate himself from the campsite. Asleep, Alexios had been diverting. Awake, his presence was like a constant spark of static, prickling all over Auro's skin. He glanced over his shoulder, the quiet solitude of the temple beckoning him, urging him back into the loneliness that had grown so familiar it was *almost* comfortable.

When he turned back, Alexios was looking at him through heavy-lidded eyes, fighting a losing war with sleep. "Please tell me your name," said Alexios quietly, but the final words were mumbled as he drifted off.

"Auro," he whispered. "I'm called Auro."

He stayed to watch Alexios sleeping for several hours, watching the way his face relaxed, softening so much in sleep. He looked very peaceful. Before the sun rose, Auro slipped silently into the shadow of the trees and turned his back on the little camp.

The first few days of spring were a delicate time. Auro's brother Kryos, God of Winter, and his influence still lingered in the earth—the nights could still be cold enough to threaten the lives of the tender young things just beginning to awaken, and Auro's grace, his power, had only just begun to wax. It always took him a week or so to adjust to a new season, and he had already taxed himself sorely in his desire to care for Alexios. When Auro had been cursed, he had lost the lion's share of his power, leaving him only a fraction of it, leaving Auro a shell of his former self.

For now, though, Auro did not need to summon much more of his grace, which was a relief. The first day or two saw Auro covering as much of his home as he could, using the forest as an indicator of how the winter had gone. Kryos had left the earth not so ravaged as he could have. A mild winter required careful balancing in spring, too. Everything must be coaxed just so, and Auro would do well to remember that, in lieu of spending his time fixating on selfish desires.

By the time he returned to the camp after completing his work for the day, Alexios and his horse were gone. Auro felt a small pang, wondering if he'd ever see the young man again. He wanted to—more badly than he had allowed himself to want anything in years.

Overcome with his curiosity, Auro asked the trees for help to pick up the trail left by Alexios and his horse. The forest clamored to show him the way, the branches and roots and moss and even the birds in the canopy above all reported seeing a handsome young man passing this way or that. Auro followed their intel through the trees for hours until they began to thin up ahead of him. At the edge of the forest, he balked. A vast, fertile field sprawled over lazy rolling hills. In the middle distance, a stone curtain wall wrapped around a grand villa. Auro swallowed nervously, hiding in the shade of the trees' edge.

Auro wanted desperately to find Alexios, but the fear in him had rooted deep. He would have to do some planning before he ventured beyond his trees, as he could hardly blunder blindly through the human realm, without any direction or idea where he might even *find* Alexios. He retreated back, farther into the comforting dark press of the forest.

As he returned to his temple, Auro chastened himself for his foolishness. It was probably for the best if Auro never learned anything about Alexios. Auro had been put here to aid the natural world, not moon over pretty strangers. He vowed to put Alexios from his mind and continue with his work as always.

Three

Alexios woke at dawn with a foreign name on his tongue and a headache that had dulled to what might be considered manageable. He sat up without feeling the urge to vomit and decided that to be a victory. Xanthos still grazed happily nearby, all fear of interloping vipers apparently forgotten.

Alexios twisted around where he sat, searching for some sign of Auro, but the campsite had a definite feeling of coldness to it that had not been there the night before. His heart sank as he observed the dry listlessness of the roof of his shelter, the vines and leaves dried out and brown, crispy. The saplings threatened to straighten up, back to their natural position, straining against the tangle of brittle vines. He looked down at his arm, and the wrappings on it now appeared dull and lifeless—still holding his injured elbow secure, but no longer warm, green, and friendly. Had it all been a dream? Had the pink-haired Auro merely been a hallucination born of his head injury? He hoped not.

Shielding his eyes, Alexios looked out across the still, sparkling surface of the lake to the small island. The ruins still sat squarely on their island, and while that didn't necessarily prove he'd been healed by a magic, pink-haired stranger, he at least knew he hadn't imagined *everything.*

By the time Alexios managed to get home, his parents were beside themselves, especially given the state he returned in. They hovered over him while the medicus cut away the vines holding his injured arm in place, and Alexios could tell they were waiting for him to be medically cleared before they started in on him. As the moss and branches and vines fell away to the floor, Alexios felt a peculiar pang—like all traces of his encounter with Auro were going to be swept away.

Alexios had told his parents and the medicus a half-truth —that a compassionate young stranger had set his arm for him and made certain he had shelter while he recovered enough to ride home. The medicus probed Alexios's elbow, his skull, made him wiggle his fingers and count to twenty before he deemed him fit to leave the infirmary. His elbow was badly bruised, swollen, and stiff—perhaps fractured deep inside, but with a fresh splint and sling, the medicus was confident Alexios would heal up just fine in a few weeks. This was a relief, because all Alexios could think about was returning to the forest to learn more about the mysterious Auro.

A few days later, once he could be certain his royal parents would not send a search party after him for disappearing again, Alexios enlisted a groom to help him saddle Xanthos and used a stepping stool to gracelessly mount up. Riding with the use of only one arm was a challenge, but Alexios had always been a confident horseman and knew he would adjust swiftly.

He tried his best to recall the twists and turns of the path that had taken him to the lakeside, and Alexios was surprised to find it wasn't at all a challenge—despite the knock to his head. It made no sense, but Alexios got the strange, unsettling notion that the forest *wanted* him to find the way. The narrow game trail was smooth as a garden path, the errant roots one might expect were nowhere in evidence, and it seemed the brush and trees had converged into a dense, intentional tunnel for him to travel.

He reached the lake and felt a sense of relief. When Alexios had left the forest to return home, he had been afraid he'd never be able to find it again, or even that the place had vanished somehow, in his absence. But here it was. His stomach squirmed nervously as he faced the possibility of seeing Auro again.

The lake sparkled gaily in the light of the spring sun, and the morning was brisk and cheerful. Alexios dismounted clumsily and toed off his sandals to feel the sandy mud squelch between his toes. He shielded his eyes against the glare off the water to squint out at the island and its small ruin. Had he the use of two arms, Alexios could easily have swum the distance, but in his current state, the small lake might as well have been a vast ocean.

Instead, he walked the shore of the lake for a distance, wondering how best to get out there. Alexios had almost decided to give up and return home, at least until his brace was removed, when something caught his eye. There was a place where the sun hitting the surface of the lake shone strangely—differing from the surrounding water. He crouched in the sand, changing his eyeline to get a better look, and grinned. Beneath the water sat a path of stones, submerged and hidden. With his sandals tied together and slung over his shoulder, Alexios picked his way carefully along the hidden path until he reached the island.

The island was small, and the ruin was a single square room. The columns that made up its perimeter had once been white marble, Alexios knew at a glance, but they were grey with age, and some had cracked and fallen, pointing errantly toward the sky like broken teeth. When he stepped inside, the hairs on Alexios's arms stood on end, an immediate feeling of unease, of dread, descending upon him as he stepped into the shadows of the ruined building. It had been a temple, perhaps, once, though not one housing gods Alexios had ever heard of. His people did not put much stock in the gods of their ancestors. The gods had left the world centuries ago, retreating to their unreachable Godsrealm and taking any magic with them. Generations without evidence of their influence had allowed them to pass quietly into archaic legend. Temples still existed in Papia City, but most had been converted to tabernae, occupied with merchants who used the faded splendor of the carvings and statues inside to display their wares.

Inside *this* temple were three statues, and they alone seemed in good repair, which only served to make the place more eerie. The statues were tall and fine, pristinely maintained as if someone came regularly to polish the marble until each one shone, clean and glossy, every detail visible. Alexios spent a moment picturing Auro moving amongst the statues, quietly cleaning them as if it were his sacred charge. It did not compute, somehow—the still, crypt-like quality of the temple, and Auro's sweet, shy demeanor. There was one statue in each corner of the temple, except the fourth, which held only an empty plinth. The three statues were all different, but there was something about their features that called to one another, and all three looked familiar to him in a way he could not place. One was nearly naked, covered in carved jewelry, and sporting a mocking grin. One was tall and solemn, with a massive stone scythe in the crook of his arm, and a stone owl upon his shoulder. The last was big and broad, his face turned skyward, a bow and three arrows clutched in his marble hands. The empty plinth filled Alexios with a peculiar sort of dread, for reasons he could not place, so he turned his back upon it. So far, his search had turned up nothing but a feeling of deep foreboding.

There was nothing in the temple to indicate anyone had ever made a home here—even a temporary one. Alexios was just about to leave when a gust of wind disturbed the carpet of dead leaves upon the stone floor, and something dark and shining caught his eye. He squatted in the center of the room, brushing the leaves away to reveal a mosaic inlaid to the floor. It displayed a skull, attended by ravens, the pieces of enameled stone and ceramic glittering strangely in the sunlight, giving the skull's eyes a luminous, living quality, like the face was judging him. Alexios shuddered and covered the picture once again with leaves.

The trill of a songbird startled him out of his wits, and Alexios's heart pounded in his chest. Deeply unsettled, Alexios fled the temple, the island, and the lakeside.

When Auro returned to the temple that night, his body thrummed with an awareness that someone else had been there. Though he had a giddy notion of who it might have been, Auro sat cross-legged beside the entrance to the temple and plunged his hands into the sandy dirt, reaching out with his grace until the ferns nearby told him of the barefoot golden boy who'd walked out across the bridge and examined the statues of Auro's brothers and the mosaic on the floor, the epitaph, the reminder of all Auro had lost.

Auro brushed the dirt from his hands and entered the temple himself. As he often did when he needed to think, Auro boosted himself up onto his empty plinth, drew his knees up to his chest, and rested his chin upon them. He had tried his best to put Alexios from his mind, to focus his entire being upon his work, but it had been impossible. He may as well admit to himself that he was delighted—and, frankly, a bit terrified—to learn Alexios had not forgotten him, either.

What other reason would he have to return here, to poke about the ruins?

Before he could talk sense into himself, Auro summoned a charm of finches to find out what they could about Alexios. They were quick and clever and from the skies could cover vast amounts of territory in their search. Auro could not explain to himself why he even bothered, just that the encounter with Alexios had been a startling diversion to the centuries of monotony he had been living. It would be nice to know more of him, where he lived, if he spent a lot of time in the forest. It was a passing curiosity, nothing more.

The birds returned at sunset, all atwitter with what they'd found. This boy was a prince of men, the birds sang, locked away in a sparkling white palace, guarded night and day.

When Auro heard that, he expected to feel a sense of relief, to feel the matter was closed. Alexios was unreachable. Auro did not expect to feel even more intrigued. He did not expect to feel a muted pang of longing. Auro shook his head, trying to shake some sense into himself, perhaps. He was more convinced than ever that the wise thing would be to put this prince from mind, but knowing that and doing it were two very different things.

After a restless night's sleep, Auro rose at dawn and left the temple, making his way to the lakeshore so he could begin one of the most important parts of his work. Each spring, the trees would be coaxed back to life, to bud and bloom and fruit. Each type of tree had its sacred grove, and each grove had its dryad. It was for Auro to wake them each year, so they might disperse and wake the rest of the trees. His brother, Cedras, God of Fall, would tuck them into slumber before returning to rest himself. It was so, every year.

The gold of dawn had just become tinged with blue by the time Auro reached the willow's sacred grove. This was one of his favorite duties, one of the times he felt well and truly himself. His power waxed and mounted, his grace pumping through his body. It bubbled and boiled to the surface until Auro could feel it sluicing down his skin, warm and friendly and familiar. And his.

When he worked, he could almost forget the past. Trees lived so long they had no concept of what was past or what was present. Auro hoped that he'd live long enough to feel that way, eventually. For past and present and future to blur and fade. He placed his palms on the trunk of the ancient willow tree, felt its life dormant inside, and pulled. Tugged, coaxed. He whispered to the tree's heart, encouraged it, warmed it with his grace until it met him on the surface of the bark. It hummed with life as it woke, and a large knot in the center of the tree's ancient, gnarled trunk throbbed and twisted until a pair of deep-set black eyes blinked awake, and the willow dryad sat up, yawned, and stretched.

His eyes fell upon Auro and lips like tree bark pulled back in a feral but friendly smile. Rolling out his grey-brown shoulders, the dryad loosened up after months of sleep and slid from his nest in the crux of the tree's wide boughs. He knelt before Auro, who offered his hand, and the dryad bent his head to brush a dry, scratchy kiss to Auro's knuckles. "Come now," Auro said, gathering the dryad's hands in his own. "Rise. It is time for you to wake your siblings."

The dryad dipped his head deferentially and turned to leave the glade. Before he had traveled two steps, however, a twig snapped in the undergrowth. The dryad hissed and fled, melting into the trees as if he had never been there.

Auro wasn't *quite* as fast. He backed up a step until he collided with the willow tree, only to see Alexios, the prince, stand sheepishly from where he had been crouching in the bushes. "Hello, again," he said. His arm had been re-bound, Auro saw at once, in strips of clean white cloth. He didn't like it.

Words failed Auro, whose fight or flight response weighted firmly toward flight. He edged around the willow's trunk, knowing that if he could just slip from Alexios's sightline that the trees would conceal him.

"Wait—" Alexios called. "Please."

Heart hammering, Auro paused and turned to look back at him.

"I only wanted to..." he trailed away. He looked just as frightened as Auro felt. "What was that?"

"A tree spirit," Auro said, and his voice came out so quietly Alexios had to take a step closer to hear.

"Pardon?"

"A tree spirit," said Auro, a bit louder. He still stood on the balls of his feet, still poised to run.

"Truly?"

Auro nodded. He took another step away, but he could not break their shared gaze, could not commit to flight.

"And what are you?" Alexios blurted, reddening as he realized his rudeness. "I mean, who?"

"I'm no one," said Auro. He let his heels settle to the dirt and stopped edging away. "Just Auro."

Taking a cautious, slow step closer, Alexios said, "Then what were you doing, just now?"

"Nothing," said Auro, too quickly.

He narrowed his eyes suspiciously. "Alright."

Auro sighed. "Apologies," he said. "I was...waking him."

"Waking—the tree?"

"Yes."

After chewing on that for a moment, he said, "Are you a witch?"

"No," said Auro.

"A sorcerer?"

"No."

"Alright," he said. "I give up, Auro. What are you?"

Auro would normally not have answered, but he found he quite liked the sound of his name in Alexios's mouth and figured that he would have to give a piece of himself up to hear it again. "I am...a guardian of sorts."

"A guardian? Of what?"

"Springtime," said Auro.

"This is madness," said Alexios. "This is impossible."

Auro shrugged. He had heard all of this before. He resigned himself to the fact that Alexios would most likely leave the forest and its madness, fleeing from Auro. He could have told Alexios the truth, that he was a god, but he didn't. Instead, he found himself asking, "What are you doing here, Alexios?"

"I had to find you again," he said. "I had to thank you."

"For what?"

Alexios let out a light, startled laugh. "For not leaving me to die on the forest floor," he said. "I was hoping...do you live in the city?"

Even as the question left Alexios's mouth, Auro could tell he doubted the possibility. "No."

"Where, then?"

"Here. I live here."

Alexios looked as though he had not one idea as to what to do with that information. "Would you come back to my villa with me?" he asked, his cheeks reddening. "Apologies. That was forward. I just...I want to repay your kindness."

Auro's instincts had him shaking his head before he could even truly consider the offer.

Alexios furrowed his brow—not like he was frowning, more like he was thinking. Like he was trying desperately to figure Auro out. "Would it be alright, then, if I came back here? To visit you again?"

Something warm woke inside of Auro, and he couldn't stop the grin from breaking over his face as he gave a tiny nod.

"Very well," said Alexios, sounding pleased. "I will return tomorrow. And I plan on asking you to accompany me to the villa again, too."

"You can certainly ask," said Auro.

"I will. Goodbye, Auro."

"Goodbye, Alexios," he whispered. At first, he thought Alexios had not heard him, but he turned and smiled at Auro before disappearing over the ridge.

y the time Alexios and Xanthos left the forest, he'd almost convinced himself what he'd seen was a dream. He'd watched from the bushes as Auro had placed his palms against a tree's bark. The power had flowed off Auro in waves, to the point where Alexios could feel it on his skin as if he'd turned his face up toward the sun. It was mesmerizing. He'd had no idea what he was watching, and then part of the tree had shuddered and taken the shape of a young man. Alexios had watched in awe as the buds on the willow's stringy branches had swollen, looking ready to bloom before his very eyes—but it hadn't. Perhaps it was still too early, for that. The dryad had climbed down from the tree, with hair that closely resembled the tree's branches. It was remarkable.

And then, there was Auro himself. The man had pink hair.

Pink.

Pink as the soft velvet inside a rabbit's ears.

Pink as the dawn sky.

Pink as the petals of a peony, like the ones Auro had left beside Alexios's waterskin. Alexios found himself spending a lot of time wondering if the hair on the rest of Auro's body matched the hair on his head. His coloring was as alluring as it was peculiar, and Alexios could only hope he'd have a chance to encounter Auro again. He'd claimed himself a guardian, but Alexios had seen the way the tree spirit had regarded him, the demure way it had bowed before Auro, and the obvious power sloughing off his skin in waves. He was more than a guardian, Alexios was certain. But that begged the question, what on earth was he?

When Alexios returned to the villa, he trotted Xanthos into the stable and dismounted carefully, so as not to hurt his arm. Now that a few days had passed and the swelling had gone down, the medicus was certain that he hadn't broken anything, but Alexios had to wear the brace and sling for another fortnight to be certain. Alexios planned to put up Xanthos himself, brush out his coat, and then head straight up to his mother's library. He had about a thousand questions for Auro, but he had a feeling the man who called himself a guardian would not give up his secrets easily. Besides, Alexios was not about to accept the way Auro refused his invitation— not when he seemed so unhappy to watch Alexios leave.

Unfortunately, as soon as his feet touched the ground, he caught the eye of the stablemaster, beside himself with nerves.

"What is it?" asked Alexios.

The man twisted his hands over each other. "Their Majesties commanded I intercept your return, Your Highness. They wish to see you at once."

Alexios sighed. No wonder he looked so afraid; commanding one royal at the behest of another was not a position in which palace staff would ever want to find themselves. Alexios gave him a smile, a pat on the shoulder, and thanked him in advance for brushing down Xanthos.

A wide set of grand marble steps led up to the enormous oaken doors into the main vestibule of the royal villa where

Alexios had lived his entire life. When spring was further underway, the doors would be thrown wide, allowing the breeze to sweep in off the bay and freshen the entire place with tangy sea air. It was still too cold for that, however, though hardly colder than the reception Alexios anticipated from his parents. Two guards hauled open the doors at his approach and bowed him inside.

The royal villa of Papia had an ostentatious throne room, but King Nelios and Queen Clio more often than not preferred to receive audiences in a smaller, but richly appointed private chamber. It was less intimidating than the throne room, and Alexios's mother often said it inspired more frank discussion and less posturing. The audience chamber was warmed by a hearth-fire, and the cool white stone of the floor was piled with plush furs, many of which King Nelios had personally hunted from the very forest Alexios had just left.

It was there that Alexios found his parents, and a stern-faced man unfamiliar to him. The stranger had a hard, angular face, and was perhaps a decade older than Alexios, with long, dark hair swept into a braid. One side of his head was shaved, revealing an intricate tattoo of green vines curling around his ear. Alexios realized with a jolt that this stranger had on familiar, elaborately decorated bronze armor, with the crest of the royal guard upon a chain that hung over his breastplate. Which could only mean—

"Alexios, this is Leofric," said the King, direct as ever. King Nelios was tall, the tallest man in most rooms, whip-thin with a hooked nose, dark hair, and richly tanned olive skin belying his heritage. He hailed from the nearby desert kingdom of Sokol, where he once held position of imperator and commanded armies on behalf of *its* king. Looking at this Leofric, Alexios thought the man favored his father a bit. Perhaps he too hailed from Sokol.

"Your Highness," said Leofric with a deep bow.

"What happened to Baal?" asked Alexios, ignoring the newcomer.

Queen Clio pursed her lips. "We have allowed Baal to resign his post." The Queen was shorter than her husband and son, but that did not make her presence any less commanding. Alexios favored her more than his father, sharing her deep brown eyes and rich caramel curls streaked with gold.

Alexios blanched. It was hardly Baal's fault that Alexios had always been something of a menace—stealing horses, sneaking out, dodging him at every turn. "But—"

"Trust us," said his father. "We know you made the position a misery for the poor man."

"Yes," the Queen agreed. "We offered Baal an honorable discharge, as well as a severance package that would allow him to retire comfortably, should he wish it. He's certainly earned it."

"Fine," said Alexios, relieved. He jerked his thumb toward Leofric. "So, what's his story?"

"He comes highly recommended from the Sokolian army, and we're hoping he will be up to the challenge of keeping you reined in a little bit."

Alexios knew the Sokolian army's reputation, from his father's stories. He studied this Leofric, who seemed fit and utterly humorless. Not the type of man to cross, Alexios thought unhappily. Baal had grown indulgent after knowing Alexios for so long, and as such it had been easy for Alexios to charm him. Something told him this same strategy would not work on Leofric.

There was more to this, as well—the King and Queen had plainly sent for Leofric well before Alexios's misadventure in the forest. What made them so concerned about his safety, all of a sudden? He forced his face into what he hoped was a pleasant expression and said, "Congratulations," to Leofric.

"Thank you, Your Highness."

Alexios turned to his parents, watching their expressions closely. "Why is it that you think I suddenly need such careful guarding?"

His parents exchanged a look. Their marriage may have been a political one, but over the years the loving bond between them had grown fierce, unbreakable...and at times, infuriating. As now. To Alexios, it seemed as if they could communicate with just subtle movements of their eyes.

"You have a habit of coming and going as you please," said Queen Clio. "You often go without any retinue. After what happened to you in the forest, you can hardly fault us for thinking that you shouldn't take these...trips alone."

"I value my privacy."

"Kings do not have privacy," said King Nelios bluntly.

Alexios narrowed his eyes. "I am not king, yet."

"No," said Clio, resting a hand on her husband's arm. "You are not."

Alexios could tell there was something they weren't telling him, and he had the distinct impression of a trap closing in on him. He was acutely aware of Leofric standing stiffly at his back. His instinct was to babble, but he knew his father approached conversations as he might a battlefield—and it was often better to let one's opponent show their hand before one mounted their own defense.

"Where have you been going, Alexios?"

"Here and there," he said mildly, as though he had never done anything wrong, ever, in his life. He hadn't, not *really*, but something about being questioned had him on the back foot.

"Well," said Nelios, "Rumors follow you *here* and *there*, though your personal guard may not, and they are growing wilder, Alexios. It cannot continue."

"Queen Petillia is traveling here, from Neossós, so that we

might formally introduce you and the Princess and hammer out your betrothal agreement in person. Your galivanting must come to an end in advance of their arrival, or see all of our careful plans falling to ruin."

Alexios felt as though his stomach had filled with cold stones, but he forced a brittle smile. "I look forward to it," he said stiffly.

"You must begin laying the foundation for a strong marriage and a stronger alliance between our kingdoms. And that begins with your reputation."

"Alexios, you are the Crown Prince," said his mother. "You must begin behaving as such. Your father is right. As the sole heir to our line, you must secure your own heir to rule after you."

"The sooner the better," added the King.

Alexios's throat closed, which was all to the good, because it stopped him from blurting out something he could not take back. "Of course," he said placidly. "If that is all, I would excuse myself."

His parents dismissed him, but he barely heard it as he turned on his heel and strode from the room. He was halfway down the airy corridor when he realized he was being followed. He stopped and turned to see Leofric striding behind him, his face impassive, his hands clasped at the small of his back. For a moment, Alexios faltered. He wanted nothing more than to run to the stables and saddle Xanthos, injury be damned, and ride as fast and far as he could—yet somehow, he did not think his new wet nurse would hesitate to report such a thing to his parents, or follow him, or perhaps both. Fighting down a growl of frustration, Alexios turned abruptly and stalked off to his own apartments, where at least he could slam the door in Leofric's face.

～

Auro had, not once, ever, found himself so thoroughly preoccupied with another person. It had been only been a few days since he had encountered the dazzling Alexios, and every particle of Auro hummed with desire to lay eyes on him again.

The following day, Auro busied himself with his work, woke more dryads in their trees and some bears slumbering in their dens. He tried not to dwell on Alexios.

He failed.

For some reason, Auro's thoughts kept returning to the white bandage on Alexios's injured arm. He'd studied it closely during their brief conversation the day before, and he could not quite put his finger on why it bothered him so much. Surely, he wasn't upset that Alexios had received proper medical care—was he? He frowned, probing the recesses of his memory, trying to find some lingering trace of anything to explain this strange, uncomfortable feeling.

As a child, Auro had never broken a bone. He and his brothers were the sons of a god, more robust than mortal children—and healed more swiftly besides. His brother, Cosmo, had experienced more injuries than the rest of them put together—but nothing ever slowed him down for long.

Perhaps he simply misliked seeing that Alexios was still in pain. Auro did not like to see any living thing suffer, could hardly bear it, even though the cycle of the seasons involved a lot of death, a lot of pain. Death was as much a part of life as birth, after all, and Auro had witnessed the turning of the world for four centuries now. It should have lost its power to hurt him, but it had not. He understood it, but he never seemed able to accept it.

It had been one of the things his father had wanted to groom out of him, when he first started sharing his godly grace with his sons. He needed to be sterner and stronger, if he ever hoped to rule as a god, above mortals, above everyone.

"Mother is mortal," young Auro had said, but his father had only scowled.

As he got older, Auro learned to do a better job concealing the softer parts of himself—from his father at least, but he was never as strong as his brothers. As they grew to manhood, Auro, Cosmo, Cedras, and Kryos each inherited a portion of their father's godly power. They would share their father's burden and help him in his many, varied duties—working in harmony to shepherd the seasons.

And they had, for a while.

Until they hadn't.

Until his brothers all began warring amongst themselves, vying for control, for the right to champion their father's legacy. The power-mongering had consumed them all before the end, resulting in their father fleeing to the Godsrealm forever, cursing his sons, and leaving them behind in disgrace.

Auro swallowed around a lump in his throat as he remembered the events that led to that terrible time, the worst of his long life. Worse than after, worse than turning into a statue for three-quarters of the year. He shoved the thoughts away, as deep and as far down inside himself as he could.

An air of melancholy hung over Auro for the rest of the afternoon as he went about his duties. He tried instead to think of Alexios, and the fact that he'd promised another visit to the forest. Auro couldn't imagine someone like Alexios taking such an interest in him—until he reminded himself that it was most likely because he was an oddity. A novelty. A magical curio in the tedium of a prince's day-to-day life.

What was it Alexios had said? He wanted to thank Auro, for helping him, the day he'd fallen off his horse. It was a sense of obligation that had inspired him to track Auro down, nothing more. Auro should have assured him no such thing was necessary, but he'd been swept away, enchanted by the pleasurable buzz Alexios's smile sent through his veins.

The sun sank below the horizon line, Auro had almost convinced himself Alexios wasn't coming when a subtle tremor passed through the earth. It was no more than a blip, traveling from leaf to branch to root to fern, through the spores of mushrooms, traveling from living thing to living thing until it touched Auro where he waited by the lake. Suddenly, Auro was blind, blind and green and *feeling*, it was a split second, and a warm golden light moved through him. In the time it took for Auro to blink, he was back, on the lakeshore, staring at the stars reflecting on the water.

He barely had time to be bewildered before the sound of hoofbeats moving through the forest alerted him to Alexios's arrival. Auro scrambled to his feet, brushing sandy dirt from his tunic and turning to greet his guest.

The moon was high, and Auro had expected him much earlier. Even still, he could hardly contain the delight at having someone come to the forest expressly to call upon him. "You came," he said.

"I told you I would," Alexios answered, with a lopsided grin that made Auro's stomach swoop.

As if by some agreement, they began to stroll down the moonlit shore. "How is your arm?" Auro asked him.

"Hurts," said Alexios, but he sounded more annoyed than like he was truly suffering. "Makes riding a challenge."

Auro nodded, staring down at the bandage and sling. "You should be more careful."

Alexios followed his eyes and said quietly, "I miss the one you put on."

Auro stopped and looked up into his face, startled. Alexios looked surprised too, like he hadn't meant to say what he had. It was only then Auro realized precisely what he did not like about the sterile white cloth wrapped around Alexios's arm.

It wasn't his.

That realization unsettled him, and his jaw snapped shut.

He was unable to pry it open until it was time to say goodbye, but Alexios didn't seem to mind. He hummed quietly as they walked around the entire perimeter of the lake. When they reached the place where Alexios had hobbled his horse—all too soon, in Auro's opinion—Alexios turned to him and said, "I have to be heading home. Come back to the villa with me?"

Auro shook his head again, but this time he smiled.

Five

It had not taken Alexios long to puzzle out Leofric's routine, observing his habits as carefully as Leofric observed him. During the waking hours, Leofric was ever-present as a shadow. At night, however, the man did sleep, as all men must. The soldiers in the royal guard all slept in the barracks, a small outbuilding within the curtain wall of the royal villa, but detached from the main residence.

As the personal bodyguard of the Crown Prince, Leofric had been awarded his own private chamber in the barracks. The scant hours he spent asleep in his small cubiculum would be the only time for Alexios to slip free of his constant scrutiny. During that time, the entire villa was patrolled by groups of guards who walked the walls in trios—far easier to evade. Besides, the night watchmen expressed far more vigilance in preventing folk from sneaking *in,* as opposed to one young man sneaking out. Or so Alexios hoped.

As he rode into the forest, he thought about the stone head sitting on his table. Whenever the cleaning staff entered his chambers, they always spun it out from the wall, to face the center of the room, as if it had gotten knocked backward by mistake.

And every time he returned back to his apartments, Alexios turned her right back around again. There were some things he just couldn't bear to face yet.

The night after he'd met Auro by the lake he was especially eager to see him again. Alexios got the distinct impression that Auro wanted to see him, too. The way his round, pretty face lit up at the sight of Alexios, his cheeks glowing a soft pink that matched his strange hair...no one had ever looked at Alexios like that before.

Alexios had about a thousand questions for Auro, but he suspected they would not be welcome. On their second moonlit stroll, Auro took Alexios to another of the groves that contained a tree spirit. He watched from a distance, amazed that he was invited this time. Invited to see something so rare.

Alexios had never prayed before, but as he watched the power rolling off Auro, his eyes glowing like green stars as he communed with the tree, Alexios felt like he was watching something truly sacred.

The tree was an olive tree this time, the leaves slender and silvery in the starlight. The bark began to move, and while this might have been the second time Alexios had witnessed a tree spirit awakening, it was no less miraculous. It was no less astounding. Just as the first one had, this dryad knelt before Auro, crossing one branch-like arm in front of her chest in an unmistakable salute. The deferential way in which the dryads regarded Auro was not lost on Alexios, for whom the practices of royal court were second nature.

"If you please," said Auro, clasping her hands to draw her to her feet. "It's time for you to awaken your sisters."

The tree guardian smiled at him and stood on tiptoe to kiss Auro's cheek. She curtseyed before disappearing into the dark, shadowy world of the other trees.

When Alexios had to depart, he put to words something he'd been working over in his brain, like a puzzle. "You are no mere guardian," he said decisively.

"Oh?"

"The way she regarded you," he said. "You rule here, do you not?"

Auro's smile flickered. "For three cycles of the moon, perhaps. The rest of the year, I rest."

Alexios did not entirely understand what he meant by that, but a shadowy, haunted look had crossed Auro's face, so he didn't want to press too much. "Come back to the villa with me," said Alexios, as he did every night.

Auro sighed, no longer trying to hide his smile. But still, he shook his head no.

Alexios grinned back at him, knowing it would only be a matter of time. Auro was wearing down, he could feel it. Whatever fear kept him so skittish and shy, kept him concealed in the trees, beneath it was something else—a playful, curious nature that craved companionship. "I will figure you out, Auro, Prince of Springtime."

"I hope you do, Alexios, Prince of Papia."

Alexios didn't lose his lingering grin until he had slipped back inside the postern door, where it was wiped off his face with alarming speed. Leofric waited for him, standing just inside the door with his arms crossed.

Alexios wondered how long he'd been waiting. "What are you doing here?"

Leofric was almost apologetic when he answered, "My job."

Alexios was dying to know exactly how Leofric had found out, but he wasn't about to give him the satisfaction of asking.

The following morning, he awoke to the pink light of dawn and the singing of finches on the railing of his balcony. They drew a smile to his lips, because Auro had confessed the birds were his friends and emissaries. He sat in bed, stretching, and listened to them singing. As he rose and dressed for the day, Alexios made a mental note to fetch some dried fruit and nuts from the kitchens to lay out for Auro's little messengers.

His mood soured like old milk when he pulled open his chamber door to Leofric's somber face. He stood at attention with one hand resting upon the pommel of his sword of office, his hair neatly braided, and his uniform beyond reproach. Alexios wondered if Leofric slept standing up, like a horse. Without a word, Alexios strode off down the corridor, setting a brisk pace for Leofric to follow. Which he did, of course, his long stride all but silent on the marble floor.

Leofric followed him through the halls of the royal villa until they reached the doorway to the Queen's private library. If he wasn't able to sneak away to *see* Auro, perhaps Alexios could learn more about him. Besides, if the research hit a dead end, Alexios knew of a passage from the library down through the bowels of the building, through the kitchens, and out into the garden. Alexios turned and almost bumped right into Leofric, who'd stopped directly behind him. He summoned his most commanding demeanor and said, "I'll take bread, honey, and tea, please."

"Forgive me, Your Highness," said Leofric, raising one dark brow. "But you have mistaken me for a servant."

Alexios blinked. "I beg your pardon?"

"It is not within my duties to fetch and carry," Leofric explained, as though Alexios was perhaps a bit slow. "I am to remain by your royal person at all times during the waking hours."

With a roll of his eyes, Alexios flagged down a passing porter, requesting he go to the kitchens instead. He looked to Leofric. "Do you care to eat?"

Leofric was suddenly flustered, as if he was not accustomed to being served. Perhaps he was not as used to life at court as he first appeared. Good. If Alexios could set him off his footing, perhaps he could find a vulnerability to exploit. "Fruit," said Leofric at last. "Please."

When the boy returned, he carried a tray with bread, honey, fresh sweet plums, and two mugs of hot tea. Alexios thanked him and had him set the tray on the working table in the library. He took his food and indicated Leofric should do the same. Leofric dipped his head before taking one of the clay mugs and a plum.

Queen Clio's tablinum within the royal library was more of a converted eyrie, one of the highest points in the villa, airy and bright with many windows. A collection of busts of the Queen's ancestors filled the niches set in the walls. In the center, the largest display was dominated by busts of Alexios's parents. Looking at them gave Alexios a pang—they were just like the ones he and Princess Dafina had exchanged, but his mother plainly loved them so much that she displayed them proudly, prominently, so when she sat at her desk they were gazing directly at her. He fought the urge to turn them all around to face the wall.

Alexios was pleased to see the birds appeared to have followed him here as well, chirping merrily from where they perched on the window ledges. With his tea in one hand, Alexios strolled through the stacks and scrolls and bound ledgers, searching for the sections containing histories that predated Papia's founding. Its mother empire, Mykellia, had fallen centuries ago. Each of the empire's vassal city-states had formed its own kingdom from the ashes of the empire.

This much Alexios knew, having learned it from tutors as a boy, but the ancient histories were vague. His tutors had focused more on the history of Papia as an independent kingdom, *after* the fall of Mykellia. He found a few fragile, dusty documents and returned to the desk. When he'd seated himself, he began leafing through the scrolls, until the hairs on the back of his neck rose on end. Looking up, Alexios saw Leofric standing just inside the doorway to the study in much the same stance he adopted outside Alexios's bed chamber. "Must you watch me read?" Alexios asked him irritably.

"I am afraid it is my charge, Your Highness."

"There is only one door," snapped Alexios. "Could you not stand outside it? I doubt an assassin is likely to fly in through the window."

To Alexios's great surprise, Leofric smirked. It was the first time Alexios had seen him smile at all. It was unnerving. Without uttering a word, Leofric released his sword pommel and clasped his hands at the small of his back, walking sedately around the interior of the room. He paused a few times, nudging furniture with his foot, or examining a sconce. Eventually he came to a stop in front of a particular set of bookshelves. Alexios could not help his eyes darting to the piece, and away, and then back once again. Leofric threw his shoulder into the shelf to slide it a few feet to the left and then tapped the wall behind it with his fist. The hollow echo was unmistakable and damning.

There would be no escaping the villa that morning.

Seething, Alexios hauled a heavy sheaf of vellum toward himself. Alexios would find a way to shake this man, sooner or later. For now, he had things to uncover. He began to read about Mykellia, its fall, searching for clues about the ruined temple and its statues. The temple was linked, somehow, to Auro, Alexios could feel it in his gut, though he was not sure why. It was not on any current maps or charts, dating after the rise of the Papian kingdom—and if something was not found within his mother's records, it was usually a safe wager that thing did not exist. Unless, of course, that thing was a relic of a time more than half forgotten.

The morning was gone before Alexios had finished with the maps and his eyes were dry and itchy. Alexios had never been taken with scholarly pursuits, and would sooner be outside in the bracing breeze and sunshine than in the study, airy though the room might be. He had consulted every single one of the maps his mother possessed of the Papian region. Most of them did not even have the lake, and of the ones that did, fewer still had the island. Suffice to say, not a single one mentioned the temple or its statues.

Alexios picked at the bread crust remaining from his morning meal, frowning over the veritable mountain of aging yellow documents stacked around him. He wished to clear his head, bogged down by this poring endlessly over ledgers and histories. It was the sort of thing that delighted his mother, the Queen, but soon had Alexios fidgety and bored.

Perhaps there was nothing here. Perhaps Auro was no more than he said he was—and wasn't that enough? Alexios had seen the proof of his magic with his own eyes—did he really need to find its source? The suggestion to let the mystery of Auro lie sounded feeble even in his own mind. Alexios sighed and hauled another stack of documents closer and began to read through them.

He reflected on the ease with which his mother could probably help his search, but he knew she would be immediately suspicious of Alexios's sudden interest in scholarly research. After hours of reading, he found his first promising clue—a record of trade, which he wasn't sure why anyone would even keep for centuries. However, it contained evidence of a shipment of fine marble brought in from what was now the kingdom of Neossós, renowned for its rich and plentiful quarries. Much of the marble that made Alexios's home came from Neossós, he knew. Based upon the details present in the ledger, Alexios was certain that the marble had been shipped to Papia right around the time the Mykellian Empire had dissolved. That struck him as more than passing odd—why would a ruler be ordering vast quantities of expensive stone when their empire was falling down around their ears?

So, Alexios sought out other records present from that same year, and the few preceding it. Agriculture records, weather accounts, and personal histories. Between the lines of all these dry documents were the clues that something catastrophic had befallen the empire. Alexios was eager now to read on, that he appeared to be getting somewhere.

Finally, he found it.

As he had known, the ruling line of the Mykellian Empire ended with its final empress, Her Radiance Soli Bursio Lepidus, whose dynasty had perished with her. The histories with which Alexios was familiar simply moved on *after* her death. However, the fall of the Mykellian Empire had been preceded by disaster after disaster, from what Alexios read. Droughts, monsoons, blizzards, fires...and then, forty days where the sun refused to rise, if these personal accounts were to be believed. However, immediately following Empress Soli's fall, all of that had stopped.

One account claimed her final act had been to sacrifice herself to the gods, one last act of devotion to the empire she had loved so well. He frowned, wondering. Alexios had been certain all the gods had abandoned the human world by that time, but perhaps there was something else at play. At last, he unearthed a personal record of one of the empress's lady companions—and it mentioned that in the final days of the empire, Empress Soli had been driven mad by the death of her sons.

"*Sons,*" Alexios whispered to himself. None of the histories had mentioned the empress having sons. All of them indicated her line had died with her...

He raced to the shelf where he'd found the diary, searching for more. *Thank goodness someone preserved these,* he thought.

Lots of people, Alexios included, would have tossed the personal diaries of servants who had lived and died hundreds of years before Papia's founding, especially when many of the entries seemed to be comprised of what the empress and her ladies had worn and eaten on each particular day.

Alexios skimmed through most of them hoping something pertinent would jump out at him. It took him all afternoon before he found another mention of the young princes, and he stared in disbelief at the parchment as if he could will the words to change. No matter how long he stared, they remained the same. The empress of the Mykellian Empire had four sons before they all perished under mysterious circumstances: Kryos, Cedras, Cosmo...and Auro.

As if he were following orders, Alexios rose stiffly and gathered all the materials he'd spread out upon the worktable in his mother's tablinum and returned them neatly to their shelves. He had to fight the urge not to throw them in the hearth. When he'd begun the search, he had only been hoping to discover something about the construction of Auro's temple, and all at once he had stumbled on something very, *very* private. Auro *was* a prince, just as Alexios had suspected, but plainly he was so much more than that.

There was a chance, of course, that Prince Auro of the Mykellian Empire was only the namesake of his Auro...Alexios flushed, realizing he'd absently thought of Auro as *his.*

He shook his head, returning to the matter at hand. There was a chance these were two different Auros. Alexios himself had at least four ancestors who shared his praenomen, so it was not outside the realm of possibility. And yet, he didn't think so, somehow.

That would mean Auro was four *hundred* years old. This history said that he'd died. Was he a shade, haunting the forest, the temple?

What happened to his three brothers? Thinking of the

three statues in the temple filled Alexios with dread, and he fled the library.

Six

Auro's routine had remained unchanged for so long that the disruption of Alexios's nightly visits shone like a beacon fire in his day.

Each time Alexios invited him back to his villa, Auro declined—but each time, he considered accepting. And each time, the voice urging him to decline shrank. He waited eagerly for the forest to warn him of Alexios's approach and planned new delights to show him every time he came into the trees. It felt wonderful to have someone to share his work with, and he adored the look of awe and surprise on Alexios's handsome face as he performed his duties.

Auro was just thinking perhaps he was bold enough to accept Alexios's nightly invitation when he abruptly stopped coming. Auro waited and waited, waited half the night before he fell asleep on the shore of the lake, which had become their meeting spot. He woke at dawn, sad for some reason he couldn't place until he sat up and realized Alexios must not have come.

By the second night, Auro was cursing himself. And Alexios.

By the third night, he began to worry that something had gone wrong. Perhaps Alexios's head injury had taken a worse turn? He dispatched the finches, who reported back swiftly that they saw Alexios pacing anxiously inside the walls of his sprawling villa, guarded by a fierce warrior who never left his side, keeping him from making any more nighttime escapes to the forest. Auro spent the entire day working up his courage, edging closer and closer to the southern edge of the trees as he worked. When the sun had well and truly set, he took one tentative step out onto the grass.

He immediately took a step back. The rolling foothills that surrounded the villa on this side were just so...exposed. Auro took a few steadying breaths and told himself he was being ridiculous. If Alexios could brave the trees, he could brave the approach to the villa.

Auro's courage, such that it was, only carried him to the curtain wall before he was stymied once again. He considered the towering obstacle, walking back and forth, hiding in the safety of its shadow to evade the night watchmen. When Auro found a place where the mortar of the wall had aged, allowing an industrious vine of ivy to begin to take hold. He crouched on the ground and encouraged it, coaxed it, until it had formed a nice, leafy ladder for Auro.

When he landed on the other side, he slipped from moon-shadow to moonshadow until he approached the walls of the royal villa itself. The birds had been happy to tell him which wing of the structure held the Crown Prince's private apart-ments. As it happened, Auro had grown up in a palace much like this one, when he and his brothers had been young princes, the sons of an empress and a god. Untouchable.

He'd learned, shortly after they'd been cursed, that their empire had fallen in the wake of his family's immolation, and their villa had been torn down, brick by brick, until nothing of it remained. The stones had been parceled off, sent far and wide, too valuable to waste. Auro thought he'd never lay eyes on his home again. This new villa had sprung up, on different land, closer to the harbor city, on an advantageous hill, housing the ruling family of one of the new smaller kingdoms that had risen out of the ashes of the Mykellian Empire. As he looked now, from his hiding place in the shadows, Auro wondered if any of the bricks of his family's home had found their way into this one.

With another ivy trellis, Auro easily climbed the outside wall of the villa until he could haul himself up and over the railing of Alexios's balcony. Sheer fabric draped the window, allowing the breeze to enter, but also allowing privacy and perhaps some protection from the invasion of insects. Through the fabric, by the light of the moon, Auro could see Alexios at rest, soft and innocent and lovely, his face relaxed, his hair fanned out on a silk pillow. His lips parted with each sleepy breath, and Auro longed to trace them with the pad of his pinky finger.

He slipped unheard, unseen, into Alexios's bedchamber and sat upon the edge of his sleeping couch. His weight shifted Alexios, whose lashes fluttered, revealing eyes clouded with deep sleep. As his mind caught up to what he was seeing, his eyes widened, and Auro placed a finger to his lips before he could cry out. "It's only me," he said.

"What does *that* mean?" Alexios hissed. "I barely know you."

Auro furrowed his brow. "I had thought...you invited me."

Alexios let his mouth fall open, then closed it again, and scrubbed his hands over his face.

Perhaps Auro had made a colossal blunder. Perhaps Alexios had stopped coming to the trees because he'd tired of Auro. "I had wanted to see you again."

Alexios sat up, the blankets tangling about his waist. To

Auro's surprise and delight, he placed a hand on Auro's knee. "I had wanted to see you, as well," he said softly. "I just hadn't expected you to get in my—" he frowned. "How *did* you get into my bed chambers?"

"I climbed the wall."

"How?"

"With the help of some ivy."

Alexios knit his brows together. "There is no ivy growing on this wall," he said.

Auro allowed himself a small smile. "There is now."

Alexios stared at him in awe for several seconds, before a delightful flush bled up his chest from below the blanket. "Could you please, um..."

Auro cocked his head.

"Could you please allow me to dress?"

"Oh!" Auro scrambled to his feet and turned his back, granting Alexios the privacy to wrap some linen around himself.

"There," said Alexios when he was covered.

Auro faced him once again and said, "I had worried when you stopped coming to the forest."

Alexios's expression darkened significantly. "Unfortunately, my nighttime wanderings did not go unnoticed by my royal parents. And my new personal guard takes his job quite seriously."

"I can hardly begrudge the man that," said Auro. He spun on his heel, very curious about his surroundings. Auro wished to lay his eyes and hands on every part of Alexios's life—his secrets, his treasures.

"I can't believe you're here," said Alexios.

When he turned back to Alexios, Auro watched his eyes darting from one corner of the room and back to Auro's face. When Auro followed his gaze, his own eyes landed first on the stone bust of a woman, resting on the worktable in Alexios's chamber. Beside it was a stack of parchment, some scrolls, and a few ancient books that threatened to fall apart if one glanced at them too hard. "What's all this?" Auro asked.

Alexios sucked in a breath through his teeth, furtive. "Um..."

"'Um' what?" Auro asked, apprehension building inside him.

"I have been doing some reading since we met."

"Oh? About what?"

Alexios chewed on his lower lip. "You."

Auro blanched. "Me?"

"Yes," he said.

The silence between them grew as Auro waited for Alexios to reveal what he'd read. "You could have asked me."

"I know," said Alexios. "Apologies. I just...had to know."

"And? What did you find?"

"I am not even sure," he admitted, crossing the room to flip through some of the loose sheafs with one long-fingered hand. "I thought, maybe you could just tell me... What happened to you?"

Auro sighed, looking toward the window ledge. Coming here was a mistake. He had thought perhaps he could keep his history and his crimes from Alexios for a little bit longer, enjoying his company without strings and weights and ghosts, but plainly he'd underestimated Alexios's tenacious curiosity.

"Please," said Alexios, "Don't go. I just wished to know you a bit better, that's all."

"I wish to get to know you, too," admitted Auro.

"Well, alright then," said Alexios. "Tell me."

Auro hesitated a long while, weighing his words, trying to decide the best way to ease Alexios into the story of his past. Somehow, though, when he opened his mouth, he blurted, "I'm cursed."

Alexios blinked at him. "You're—I'm sorry, what?"

"Cursed," Auro repeated, wincing. He had not intended to be so blunt. Chance was, this conversation would scare Alexios off entirely, but perhaps it was better to do so sooner, rather than later. "My father cursed my brothers and me, a long time ago."

"How?" asked Alexios.

"He was a god," said Auro simply. "Still is, I suppose—though when we shamed him, he left this world for the Godsrealm."

Alexios staggered over to his sleeping couch and sat down heavily upon the edge of it, face rigid with shock. "You and your brothers are...*Gods?*"

"God-sons," Auro corrected. "But essentially, yes."

"I can't believe it," said Alexios faintly. "I had always thought there were no more gods in the world."

"As far as I know, my brothers and I are the very last."

Alexios stared into the middle distance, a look of extreme concentration on his face.

"I thought you had found out about my past," said Auro.

"Well, some," said Alexios. "But I never imagined...I thought you were a prince, like I am."

"Once, perhaps," said Auro. "Now though..."

"Yes," said Alexios, his voice rising to a slightly hysterical register. "Now, you're just a god."

He watched as Alexios scrubbed his hands over his face again, unsure of what else he could say.

"Alright," Alexios said at last. "Tell me the rest of it. Why did your father curse you?"

"When we were younger, much younger, our father began to share his godly grace with us. He was the last one, you see."

"The last what?"

"God," said Auro, "who remained in the mortal realm. The others had all left by then. He was lonely."

"So, he decided to just, make some new gods. Sure. Stands

to reason." Alexios appeared dazed, as if he'd taken another blow to the head.

Auro sat beside him on the bed and continued his tale. "He gave each of his trueborn sons dominion over one season, to share his burdens and perhaps one day inherit his legacy."

"'Trueborn sons,' you said."

Auro nodded. "We had another brother, Ozias. He was our father's...natural son."

"Was?"

Auro could hear the dread in the question. "Yes," he confirmed. "He—he died. His bones rest in the temple on the lake. After his death, our father cursed us."

"Why?"

Auro blinked rapidly. "Because it was our fault he died."

Alexios did not respond right away, and Auro feared that revealing this truth might have at last scared him off. And yet, eventually he pressed for more details. "How?"

"We were young, arrogant, with far too much power between us. Too much for young, rash men. All of us wished to be honored by our father, especially my brothers Kryos and Cosmo. They had never truly gotten along; they were far too different." That was a half-truth. Auro had always privately felt his constantly dueling brothers had been far too similar. "Ozias tried to mend fences between them, between us all, and was caught in the middle of Kryos and Cosmo's duel, and killed."

"It was an accident," Alexios said softly, resting a hand on Auro's knee once again.

"Yes," agreed Auro. "And yet, it was the direct result of our foolishness. Our father cursed us all, to stand vigil over Ozias, and awaken only one season a year to carry out our duties."

Auro could not watch as the meaning behind that statement penetrated Alexios's mind, so he stared down at his hands, twisting his fingers over each other.

"So, the three other statues, they are of your brothers?"

"You misunderstand," Auro said, though it squeezed his heart to do so. "The statues are not *of* my brothers. The statues *are* my brothers."

"So that means...the empty plinth?"

"Yes," Auro whispered. "Yes. I will return to stone in just over two months' time."

Alexios was silent for a long time, after that. "Can the curse be broken?"

"No."

"But—"

"*No,*" said Auro firmly. His father made sure of that. And Auro had dwelled on that enough in the first few years—he would not have Alexios dwell upon it now. Such things were fruitless. "It matters not. The penance we serve is just."

"But—"

"Hush," said Auro, wanting desperately to change the subject. He placed a finger once more to Alexios's lips. "Let us speak of other things."

"Such as?"

"Such as arrangements that will enable me to see you again," said Auro.

Alexios smiled, wrapping his long fingers around Auro's wrist. "For starters, if you wish to be companions, you best not be caught climbing in through my window, as a thief in the night."

"I do wish to become your companion," said Auro seriously. "Among other things. How am I to gain approval to do so?"

"I am not certain," said Alexios. "But I will think of something that will allow us to continue being friends."

Auro decided to let that lie, for now—though he was interested in pursuing something much more than friendship with Alexios.

"...and to that end, allow me to introduce your newest Aedile, Marcus Ajax Velius!"

The polite applause scattered around the cobbles like hailstones as Alexios bowed respectfully toward the tall, broad man beside him, who waved genially at the crowd. The pavilion stood at the center of town in Papia City, and today it was dotted with multicolored tents to shade Papia's nobility from the sharp spring sun. The rainbow of dyed linen cast multicolored shadows on the stone where the sun shone through them, illuminating the silvery flagstones like a prism.

The Aedile was appointed by the crown every two years to oversee the city, manage trade through the harbor, and act as paymaster to other professions that served the crown. Alexios gave the speech welcoming Marcus Ajax to office—though it wasn't like he'd had anything to do with his appointment.

Sometimes, that was all he felt he did—hand out laurels, christen ships, give oration before the summer games in the gladiatorial arena. Alexios attended court, sitting dutifully at the table of high counselors just below the thrones of the King and Queen. He did everything his parents asked of him and yet he truly felt as if he was no use to anybody—especially on days like today. By the time he had worked his way back through the crowd, his cheeks ached from smiling.

After his late-night talk with Auro, Alexios had found sleep difficult, and now, the sun made him sleepy and the words they'd shared left him uneasy and abraded. The revelation of Auro's godhood was shocking, but humbling, too. Even cursed, Auro did more to help the people of Papia—and the rest of the world—than Alexios could ever hope to accomplish in four lifetimes.

It gave Alexios a bit of a thrill to be so woefully outranked. Despite his reputation, Alexios was very inexperienced. He had exchanged hasty kisses at festivals, a few hurried, furtive touches, but Alexios always wondered if any of his partners actually *wanted* him. Perhaps they were simply afraid to tell the prince no. It took the savor out of such explorations and made Alexios feel slimy besides. Auro was different. Not only was he a prince himself, but he was a god. He could do anything he wished with Alexios, and Alexios could only pray that Auro's wishes might coincide with his own. The idea left his blood boiling beneath his skin.

"If your jaw were any tighter, your teeth would surely crack."

Alexios turned to see Gaius Ursus walking toward him. Gaius was the son of Papia's wealthiest consul, Festus Ursus, and his father had plainly told him from an early age that it was expected of him to befriend the Crown Prince.

Even as a boy, Alexios could see Gaius's father pulling the strings above him, but somewhere along the way, he actually had become Alexios's friend. Or at least—someone from the landed nobility with whom he could tolerate socializing.

"Yes," said Alexios with a brief, but more genuine smile. "I actually have a new set being shipped from the quarries of Neossós."

Gaius grinned. "Word is, that's not the only thing you're having shipped from Neossós."

Alexios turned to Gaius. "What do you mean?" he asked sharply.

"I hear our future queen is also being, as you say, shipped in from the Neossan quarries."

Alexios bristled. He had no idea how Gaius ferreted things out, but ferret them he did. It was said he could unearth a scandal before it had even happened. "You forget yourself," said Alexios. He wasn't even certain why it upset him; it's not like his future betrothal was a secret.

"Apologies, Your Highness," said Gaius, but he was still

grinning. "At any rate, it was a lovely speech. I'm certain it pleased your mother's brother, too."

Alexios rolled his eyes. It was true, Marcus Ajax was a cousin of his, technically third in line for the throne, after only his own father and Alexios himself. This was how the game was played—but it irritated him to pretend to be the player. Alexios was no less a pawn than his cousin, and it grated at him.

It also irked him for Gaius to mention it so uncouthly, but then again, that was part of what Alexios liked about him in the first place. You could tell straight away when he was not wearing a mask. Alexios's own mask, of magnanimous and tractable prince, remained firmly in place for the rest of the afternoon as he talked to the consuls and praised the honor of the Aedile elect and the wisdom of his gracious parents, the King and Queen, for their choice to serve the citizens of Papia City.

And Marcus Ajax would be fine, of course: clear-headed, able, and intelligent, with polished courtesies. But Alexios was certain there were other equally clear-headed, able, and intelligent men and women who were not already third in line for the throne. Who perhaps actually lived and worked within Papia City, who might more closely understand the needs of its people.

But no one has asked for Alexios's thoughts, so he kept them well guarded behind his teeth.

uro knew the only way into Alexios's world was through its front door.

To prepare himself for court, Auro had divested himself of his usual, more casual tunic, and summoned a spring breeze full of white snowdrop petals. Some considered snowdrops a mark of winter's end, but Auro always thought of them as a sign of spring's beginning. With a nudge from his grace, the petals became as one, floating around Auro and draping into a floor-length tunic like he might have worn to court before he was cursed. Unfortunately, he knew his clothes would not be the largest problem. His hair, of course, was not a color most humans would consider natural, and he doubted his ability to concoct a lie that would make pink hair seem possible. Instead, he crafted another swathe of fabric from petals and wrapped it tightly around his skull, and then covered the whole thing with a pointed cap.

Dressed and ready as he ever would be, Auro approached the grounds of the royal villa, his heart up in his throat. Instead of sneaking in under cover of darkness, this time he approached the front gate. Two armed guards flanked the entrance, and Auro approached them with as much false confidence as he could muster. "Halt," said one of the guards. "State your business."

"Hello," said Auro.

The guards frowned and leaned forward—subconsciously, it seemed—because Auro's words had been so breathy and quiet.

Auro took a breath, cleared his throat, and chastised himself. "Hello," he said, much louder. Well, measurably louder, anyway. "I would like to request an audience with His Royal Highness, Prince Alexios."

The guards exchanged a look before taking in Auro from head to toe as if skeptical.

Auro forced himself to keep his back straight, to meet their eyes, and kept his face a pleasant, bland mask as he awaited their answer.

"His and Her Grace hold court in three days' time," said one.

"You can request an audience with His Highness then," added the other.

Auro frowned. He did not want to wait another three days to see Alexios again. "Could you take a message to him? I am certain he'd see me."

The guards exchanged another look. "Alright," said one. "This way."

The man escorted Auro through the gate, leaving the other at their post. Auro followed his long, purposeful stride, willing his shoulders to come down from around his ears, as if he spent all his time in fancy villas and not hiding in the woods like a squirrel. The guard nodded to his fellows posted at the doors into the villa itself, and led Auro into a lush chamber to wait. Auro stood awkwardly with his hands at his sides, alone, for a few moments before a young woman with a tray entered the room. She placed the tray on a spindly table without looking at Auro before busying herself lighting a fire in the hearth. Once the tongues of flame were going, she bowed respectfully to Auro and left him alone once again.

The chamber was open on one side, facing a portico and the wide, shallow pool in the villa's central courtyard. Auro alternated between pacing, sitting, and watching the shadows in the courtyard grow longer as the hours passed by.

The longer he waited, the more foolish he felt.

His plan had seemed simple enough to work—but perhaps it was *too* simple. Here he was, in the middle of the royal villa, nothing but a woolen cap to conceal his true identity. He tugged the edge of it nervously, his fingers fluttering around his ears to make certain not one single pink curl had escaped. None had. Auro sat once again, twisting his fingers over each other in his lap, and waited.

Alexios rode back to the villa with his parents in their covered wagon. He would have preferred to ride out in the open air, but they'd mentioned having something to discuss with him.

Leofric rode alongside the wagon, Xanthos's lead tied to the pommel of his own saddle.

"Alexios," began the King. "You did very well today."

"Indeed," added his mother. "You comport yourself quite well in public."

Alexios tried to look pleased at their praise, but when his parents exchanged a look, he knew he hadn't fooled them.

"What is it?"

"I just...I wish there was something more I could do," he confessed. "My duties are all...ceremonial in nature. I'd love to help our people with something more."

"You do help them," said the Queen. "You give them a face

to cheer, and with Princess Dafina at your side, they will have even more faith in our rule."

Alexios must have made a face because his father sighed. "Alexios," he said. "You have always done what is asked of you—I am surprised to find you so reluctant when it comes to the matter of marriage."

Alexios looked between their stern faces, wondering how much he could share with them. They were his family, of course—but they were the King and Queen first, his parents second. "I worry about committing to someone I have never met," he said. This was a partial truth—even if his tastes ran toward women, he would have liked to have at least spoken with the girl before marrying her. "Someone I've never even had a conversation with."

"Well, interesting that you should bring that up," said the Queen.

Alexios's stomach twisted. "Oh?"

"We received a letter just yesterday from Queen Petillia," said King Nelios.

"A response to an invitation," said the Queen. "We have invited Her Grace and Her Royal Highness to come and stay, in advance of the equinox festival."

"The spring festival will be the perfect time to formally announce your betrothal," said King Nelios, with a frown. "Provided we can finish the betrothal negotiations by then."

Alexios sensed something in his father's tone. "What makes you think the negotiations will be so complicated?"

The Queen pursed her lips. "In her letter, Her Grace said she will be bringing her...advisor."

"Janus," said his father, deepening his scowl. "Or should I say, Lord Praetor?"

Alexios wondered what was so wrong with this Janus, that his appointment to a high political office would upset his parents so. Perhaps this dislike was mutual, and, even better, perhaps it was something he could use to delay the betrothal. Even as he thought it, Alexios knew he could not delay forever—but he also knew that he was hardly the only available husband on the continent. If Her Grace, Queen Petillia, decided Alexios's family wasn't one she wished her daughter to marry into, his parents would be back at square one in negotiating an advantageous match for their heir. Alexios made a mental note to ask Gaius Ursus what he knew of Janus.

His stomach squirmed at the thought of mentioning his impending betrothal to Auro. He'd have to tell him soon enough. It felt wrong to keep it from Auro, but part of Alexios feared that whatever time they had before Auro turned to stone would be ruined by the shadow of Alexios's impending marriage.

By the time they arrived back at the villa, Alexios was weary in more ways than one. Leofric requested the chance to visit the staff bathing chambers, and perhaps an evening off after standing in his armor in the sun all day, something Alexios was more than happy to grant. He relished the idea of spending the evening totally alone in his chambers, and even though Leofric usually posted himself outside the door to Alexios's apartments, his presence could be felt, seeping in through the cracks, reminding Alexios that his privacy was an illusion.

Unfortunately for Alexios, it seemed the trials of the day had not yet finished. No sooner had the guards bowed him through the villa doors but the royal herald accosted him. "Your Highness," she said. "There is a man awaiting you in the audience chamber."

"Tell him to return tomorrow," Alexios said.

The herald looked uncomfortable. "He was very persistent, Your Highness."

Something tugged at the back of Alexios's mind, and he allowed the herald to escort him into his parents' audience chamber. Standing at the edge of the room, examining an elaborate tapestry on the wall was a man in a peculiar floor-length tunic and pointed wool cap.

"His Royal Highness," began the herald, "The Crown Prince, Alexios Velius Papinus."

The man turned, startled by the booming voice of the royal herald bouncing off the walls.

Alexios did his best to contain a laugh when he saw Auro in the funny cap, which had been pulled down far lower than could ever be considered fashionable, to conceal his hair. The hat was brimless, but it still appeared Auro had to peek out from under it—as he had tugged it down past his eyebrows.

Alexios dismissed the herald and crossed the room, ready to pluck the cap from Auro's head. With a smile, he lunged forward, swiping at it when he heard his father's voice boom through the echoing atrium just outside. "Alexios!"

Auro's eyes were wide, round as coins, when the King and Queen entered the chamber and he grasped on to his hat so Alexios's hand wouldn't knock it askew.

"Hello," said the Queen.

"This is Auro," Alexios blurted because Auro looked as though he might never speak again. "He's the traveler who saved me when I was injured in the forest. I invited him to come and visit, if he passed through this way again."

Auro dropped swiftly to one knee, dipping his head to bow deeply before Alexios's mother and father. "Your Majesties," came the barely audible whisper.

Alexios noted Auro had not released his cap for fear it might reveal his secret. "Come, Auro," said Alexios. "You are my guest."

"Yes," agreed King Nelios, regarding Auro's strange garb skeptically. "If we have you to thank for returning our son in... mostly one piece, you are welcome here any time."

"Of course," said the Queen. "You should join us for evening meal, tomorrow night."

"I would be honored, Your Grace," said Auro with a small smile.

Alexios's parents excused themselves, and Alexios walked Auro toward the villa entrance himself. As he bade him farewell with the promise of supper together tomorrow, Alexios clasped Auro's arm. He leaned in after saying goodbye and whispered, "Come to my chambers tonight. We can figure something better out for your hair."

"You don't like my hat?" Auro whispered back, his lips twitching in a nervous smile.

"I just think you might be a little behind the trends of fashion," Alexios told him.

Alexios could not believe that Auro had even made attempt at such an extreme deception. He was plainly terrified to be out of the forest, to be confronted by so many strange faces. Alexios could not help smiling at the thought of Auro braving the villa, just to see Alexios in the daylight hours.

It would be wonderful to have a companion, someone to talk to, but he knew Auro needed something of a makeover, and soon—otherwise someone would surely figure out he wasn't as he appeared. Alexios wondered if Auro had even concocted a human history for himself, but his hair posed the most significant obstacle.

He realized that he did not relish the notion—Alexios rather adored Auro's unusual head of curls. But a new face around the villa would have been sure to have Leofric's hackles up—at the very least—and Alexios could only imagine how he'd react to Auro's true coloring, let alone his true history. After giving it some thought, Alexios realized he might already have something close to hand that could help conceal Auro's hair. The tunics of the villa staff were dyed brown, and the laundry kept some of that dye on hand, in case a tunic must be re-colored or replaced in a pinch.

After evening meal, he visited the laundry and managed to conceal a jar of dye within the folds of his toga without Leofric noticing—or so he hoped. Waiting for Auro that night, Alexios grew restless. He'd told Auro to come, but would he? Perhaps his terror at nearly being discovered today had frightened him off for good. The magnitude of the gesture was not lost on Alexios, who vowed that he should find a way to make Auro feel welcome, if only he were brave enough to return.

It was more than that, though. Alexios's heart squeezed when he thought about what Auro had told him last night. Auro had been alone for so long, punishing himself for the death of his brother. He told Alexios, in no uncertain terms, that his curse was unbreakable, but Alexios wasn't as ready to accept that. He refused to accept that a spirit as radiant as Auro was condemned to a lifetime of isolation and grief.

He returned to his mother's library, searching through the shelves. His mother was a practical woman, a scholar, who believed in things that could be explained empirically. However, she still maintained a small collection of books regarding arcane practices, higher mysteries, and magic...even if she didn't believe in them. Alexios would have agreed with her, before he met Auro.

He wasn't entirely sure where to begin, so he selected a few books at random and brought them back to his private apartments to peruse, wondering if there was anything to be found on the breaking of curses.

As he waited for Auro's return, Alexios paced around his chambers, occasionally crossing to his worktable, flipping idly through some books. He had no luck. Squinting at minuscule letters written in archaic dialects that made his eyes swim and his head ache. For books about spells and magic craft, they were surprisingly dull. Eventually, Alexios came to the conclusion Auro had changed his mind and decided not to come. The moon was high and he was exhausted, so he undressed and climbed into bed, falling into a restless sleep.

"*Alexios?*"

The bed dipped, and a whispered voice penetrated the fog of his sleeping brain. "Hmm?"

"Alexios."

He blinked awake to see a pair of huge green eyes staring down at him. Startled, Alexios sat up, and Auro jumped to his feet like Alexios was the one who'd snuck into *his* bed chambers. "I thought you had decided not to come."

"It took me some time to work up the courage again," Auro admitted, turning to give Alexios privacy to dress.

Alexios threw back the covers and pulled a tunic over his head. "I know that leaving the trees frightens you," Alexios said. "What made you come?"

"I wanted to see you," Auro whispered.

"Good." Alexios went warm all over as he looked at Auro, who had dispensed with his cap and the strange outfit he'd worn today for his usual short, one-shouldered tunic. He noticed for the first time that Auro had something clutched in his hands. "What is that?"

Even in the dark, Alexios could see Auro blush. "I brought you—it's just...something," he stammered.

"What is it?"

Mutely, Auro handed it over. It looked something like a cup, but a bit larger. It was made of roughly shaped clay, and it appeared to be full of dirt.

Alexios looked at it, puzzled. "This is...very nice?" He couldn't help the way his voice lilted upward at the end. Why on earth had Auro brought him a cup of dirt?

"Put it on your window ledge," said Auro. "You'll see."

"Alright," said Alexios, bemused. He crossed the room and

placed the cup on the window ledge by his balcony. "Come, I have had an idea about your hair."

He nudged Auro into the adjacent chamber, where Alexios had a private bath. Inside, Alexios had prepared a wash basin, a small table, and a chair. The chair had a low back, and when Auro sat, it allowed him to lean his head back over the lip of the ceramic basin. Alexios draped a towel around Auro's shoulders, to shield his pale skin and the fabric of his tunic from water and dye alike, and when his finger grazed Auro's neck, he shivered.

As much as Alexios did not wish to actually *frighten* Auro any further, he couldn't deny that he quite liked the way he reacted so viscerally to Alexios's touch. "Where did you even find that cap?" Alexios asked.

"I made it," said Auro, shifting his weight in the seat. "I used what I had at hand."

"You *made* it? How?"

"Spider silk and flower petals," said Auro, as if this were something completely normal to say.

"I suppose I should be grateful you did not take up residence here disguised as a tree in the garden." Alexios filled a small jug of fresh water from the bath and returned to stand behind Auro.

With his hand, Alexios shielded Auro's eyes and poured the water over his scalp, moistening the strands. Auro tensed as the cool water trickled down around his ears, down the back of his neck, but raised no word of complaint as Alexios filled the jug again and again, pouring it over Auro's head and washing his curls. Alexios could not help himself, letting his hands linger, cupping Auro's skull, and scratching his blunt nails over the skin of his scalp. Auro seemed to relax a bit, after a while. His tense little gasps and flinches mellowing into contented hums and shaky sighs, and eventually his eyes fell closed, the lines on his brow softened. Alexios wished that he needed another several hours to dye Auro's hair. It seemed the necessity of the act allowed Auro to accept it better, and Alexios was loath for the moment to end. He washed every lock of hair as deliberately and slowly as he could, reveling in it.

Too soon, Auro's hair was as clean as it would ever be, clinging to Auro's forehead and curling around his small ears. Alexios fetched the jar of dye he'd swiped from the laundry and returned to show Auro. "I believe this is made from walnuts," he said, giving the jar a sniff.

Auro didn't respond except for a nod, and his eyes remained closed, his face upturned toward the ceiling.

Alexios considered using a square of cloth to apply the paste to Auro's head, but decided stained fingers were a small price to pay for the chance to touch him again. Slowly and carefully, Alexios massaged the brown globs of dye into Auro's scalp, working it to the roots with his fingertips, combing it through every curling strand. As he worked, Alexios considered Auro's eyebrows but decided against trying to work the color into them as well. Without the staggering shade of Auro's head as a backdrop, one could pretend his brows and lashes were merely a ruddy shade of pale auburn. Almost. If you squinted.

"There," said Alexios at last, when he could not pretend to have left even a single strand of hair un-caressed. "I think it would be best if you leave it on through the night and rinse it in the morning."

Auro gave another jerky nod but didn't answer. Nor did he open his eyes.

"Are you alright?" asked Alexios, concerned.

Auro sat forward and lurched shakily to his feet. "Yes," he said, voice oddly thick. "Yes, I'm fine."

Alexios wanted to grab his shoulder, to spin him around,

and look into his eyes, but the smears of brown paste on his hand gave him pause. "Auro?" he said.

"It's nothing," said Auro, almost angrily. "Some of the color stinging my eyes, that's all."

Alexios let it pass, though he wished desperately to know what had Auro so upset. He'd seemed to enjoy Alexios's hands plying his hair, at the time. "Come," he said, instead. "Let me wash around your hairline before it stains your skin."

Alexios cleaned his hands and then reached for a soft clean cloth doused in fresh, warm water. Alexios stood before Auro, scrubbing errant drips of dye from his brow, his cheeks, the tops of his ears. Auro refused to look at him, his eyes cast down toward the floor, but he submitted to Alexios's ministrations and allowed Alexios to spin him about so he could cleanse the nape of his neck, his skin so soft and white it stole Alexios's breath. Alexios was close enough that he couldn't help but breathe in the scent coming from his skin. The smell of Auro was clean and subtle, the smell of fresh leaves, and earth after a good hard rain. He allowed his thumb to slide down the column of Auro's neck, to feel his pulse, just for a second, before drawing away. "There," he said.

When Auro turned back, his smile was back, and he, at last, looked Alexios in the eye. He appeared to have gathered himself a bit. "How do I look?"

Beautiful. Sad. Not yourself. "You'll do."

"Good enough."

"Perhaps I can loan you something to wrap yourself up," said Alexios. "Or else, the dye will surely stain your..." He frowned. "Where were you planning to sleep?"

"I found a likely hedge," said Auro, "Just at the edges of the trees."

"You'll freeze," said Alexios, aghast.

"I truly won't," said Auro, smiling indulgently, as if he

knew something Alexios did not. Which, to be fair, he most likely did. Many things, if Alexios were being honest.

"My mother keeps a glass structure on the southeast side of the gardens. She had it made to entrap light and heat to keep her more delicate plant specimens happy."

"Oh?" said Auro, with genuine interest. Perhaps he had never heard of such a thing before.

"The door remains unlocked," Alexios told him. "If you would sleep among the trees, at least do me a kindness and sleep in there, where I'll know you're warm."

"Thank you," said Auro. "I will admit my professional curiosity is piqued, as well."

Alexios smiled. "Good."

Eight

Auro found he rather adored the sleeping nook he'd created for himself in the royal gardens. He'd always loved flowers, of course, and they him. They represented a large part of his work each year. Auro woke their dormant seeds and tubers, nudged the branches of the trees to bloom, and he could do all of that just as well from his newfound hideaway at the royal villa as he did from the forest.

Alexios's mother, the Queen, had an extensive collection of rare plant specimens, and Auro found it hard to fall asleep that night as he stared at them in the darkness. He found a secluded alcove overgrown with vines, and the glass-domed building was just as warm as Alexios had said, and Auro found himself happily examining every plant in his range of sight. The other thing that kept Auro awake was the notion of dining with the royal family tomorrow. He was thrilled to have a chance to spend more time with Alexios but terrified that his parents, or his guards, would see through his deception.

While they had waited for his hair to dry enough for him to leave, Alexios had helped Auro come up with some alternate clothing to wear, something more in line with the fashion of the day, and a personal history that would, hopefully, not invite too many intrusive questions. The northern region of Mykellos had a kingdom called Aetós, and Aetós had a collection of inhabited, but remote islands. The northern climate would easily explain Auro's milk-pale skin and the way he was out of touch with the current city fashions.

As far as Alexios knew, neither of his parents had kin or other close social ties to Aetós, another bonus. He gave Auro a map and a book of Aetóan flora and fauna to study up on. The dawn sun shone bright and hot through the glassy roof of the Queen's botanical garden, and Auro woke, stretching. He concealed his few belongings behind one of the plants and snuck out of the glass gardens to meet Alexios for a walk around the royal grounds.

The dye Alexios had secreted from the laundry turned Auro's hair into an unremarkable, dull sort of brown. He would have to redye it regularly if he hoped to maintain his disguise. Auro wondered if Alexios would do it for him again, or if he would have to do it himself. He had very much enjoyed the feel of Alexios's long fingers combing through his hair, taking such care with how they washed his head and massaged the dye into his scalp—though being touched still felt so alien. He hadn't realized how much he'd missed it.

Until he had, all at once.

It had been a miracle he'd kept himself together, the burning lump in his throat, the stinging at the backs of his eyes —he'd taken great pains to conceal that from Alexios. He knew he hadn't been entirely successful, but Alexios was far too polite to point out his erratic reactions to simple touch.

Auro would be more prepared next time, if there ever were a next time.

He met Alexios in the atrium of the royal villa, dressed in a calf-length tunic, a short, light half cape, and a pair of sandals Alexios had lent him. "Good morning, Your Highness," said Auro, with a bow.

Alexios's cheeks turned pink. "Good morning," he said, his voice stiff and formal, his eyes flitting around to the guards and others milling about the villa. "And please, call me Alexios."

Alexios's personal guard, Leofric, walked behind them as they stepped out into the grounds. Alexios toured him around the gardens, the various outbuildings, and the stables. When Leofric was a safe distance behind them, Auro said, "You didn't have to invite me to dine with your parents, you know."

Alexios held out an arm, stopping Auro. "What?"

"I just meant, I'm happy to be able to see you at all," he said, his own face heating. "I don't need to intrude."

"I'm delighted for you to join us," said Alexios earnestly. "I want you to know, it means a lot to me that you've come here."

"It means a lot to be invited."

The royal family had an enormous banquet hall, but tonight they dined in a more casual, private chamber on the second floor of the villa. A collection of low tables and dining couches clustered near the hearth. Alexios draped himself over one, casually lying on his side and patting the spot beside him. Auro sat nervously on the seat's very edge, hyper aware of the proximity of Alexios's knee, which barely brushed against his hip.

A servant entered, bowing, and filled the cups on the table with golden wine. Auro took a hesitant sip, finding it crisp and tart.

"The wine is from Órnio," said Alexios, taking a sip from his own cup.

"I could tell," said Auro. When Alexios gave him a

quizzical look, he added, "They were renowned for their vine-yards even when I was..."

"When you were...?"

Auro took another sip and cleared his throat. "*Before.*"

"Oh," said Alexios. "Sorry, I didn't mean—"

"It's alright," said Auro with a small smile. A memory surfaced, and Auro's smile grew. "Once, one of my brothers told me Órnian wine was for children, and it wouldn't get you drunk."

Alexios grinned. "How did that go?"

"Not well," said Auro, laughing. He'd only been about thirteen years old, and he'd drunk enough wine to float a ship. "I threw up at the dinner table."

Alexios laughed, too.

It had been Ozias who told him the lie about the wine, he recalled with a pang. When Auro had gotten sick, their brother Cosmo had decided to match him cup for cup, so he wouldn't be sick alone. They'd spent the entire evening puking in the garden before they'd collapsed on the grass, staring at the stars and waiting for the world to stop spinning.

Auro jumped when he felt a hand resting on his shoulder.

"Are you alright?" Alexios asked him.

Auro realized he'd been silent for some time, staring into the silver goblet in his hands. "Yes," he said. "Sorry, I was just remembering..."

"Their Majesties, King Nelios and Queen Clio of house Papinus." The herald's voice drowned out the rest of Auro's words, but he was grateful—thinking about his brothers was always painful, and he couldn't remember the last time he'd allowed a positive memory to surface. It left him feeling untethered and confused.

Auro summoned a smile and rose with Alexios to greet the King and Queen. Alexios clasped his father's hand and kissed his mother's cheek while Auro bowed deeply. Once everyone was seated, the Queen summoned a musician to play for them. He stood quietly in the corner, plucking the strings of his lyre. The sound was so enchanting, Auro found himself closing his eyes to listen.

It was hard to know what to focus on. Alexios and his parents discussed the newly appointed Aedile's plans for Papia City, the musician played, and servants filtered in and out, replacing dishes and refilling the wine. King Nelios refused to drink Órnian wine, Auro noted, though the Queen teased him about it good-naturedly.

"Auro?"

Auro startled. He lowered his goblet to see Alexios and his parents staring at him expectantly. "Pardon?"

"I was just wondering what brings you all the way from Aetós," said the Queen. "It must have been quite the journey."

"Yes," said Auro. His mouth ran dry, and he reached for a cup of water, taking a long sip. "Sorry, yes. I had never left home before and decided to make a tour of the continent."

"That's rather ambitious," said King Nelios.

"This sort of thing is something of a tradition from my town—travel and study, before returning home. My father is a consul in Aetós, and he wishes for me to become more worldly before I inherit his title."

"Study?" asked the Queen, and Auro turned politely to her.

"I had hoped to use the travel as a chance to observe and study plants that don't grow up north, where I'm from."

"You simply must visit the glass gardens," said the Queen. "I have accumulated many rare specimens there."

"I would enjoy that immensely," said Auro, wondering what the Queen would say if she found out he was already sleeping in there.

Alexios nudged him with his knee and Auro turned to see him smiling encouragingly. Auro was happy to spend time with Alexios and get to know his family, but the meal was long and tiring, and he couldn't deny he was happy when the servants brought out dessert, knowing he'd be able to retreat to the quiet solitude of the greenhouse soon. Perhaps Alexios would accompany him for a nighttime stroll. His mind was half under the stars outside when it was summoned back to the dinner table with an unpleasant yank.

"You know, Alexios," said Queen Clio suddenly. "Princess Dafina is said to have a fondness for candied dates, such as these."

She nudged the dish toward Alexios, and he stared at the small platter of salted dates, stuffed with crushed pistachios and baked in honey, as if they were poisonous beetles. Auro heard him gulp nervously, and the tension in Alexios's body beside his was immediate, vibrating in the air between them. "Oh," he said.

"Perhaps you should arrange for there to be some at the equinox festival," the Queen continued.

"It would be a sweet gesture," added the King.

The rich food turned to ash in Auro's mouth, and it was a massive effort to swallow his current mouthful. Somehow, he found the courage to ask, "Who is Princess Dafina?"

Auro should have known—and perhaps he did, on some level, once the young lady was mentioned—but it still felt like a punch to the gut when Alexios said quietly, "She's the Princess of Neossós. And...my intended bride."

"Ah," said Auro. His voice had gone high and brittle. "Well, best wishes on your betrothal, Your Highness."

"Thank you," Alexios said stiffly.

He did not look at Alexios once through the remainder of the meal, and Auro could not even be sure how he managed to make it through the rest of it. The conversation burbled around him as if coming from underwater, barely registering as his cheeks burned and he ignored Alexios's attempts to catch his eye.

At last, he found an opportunity to excuse himself and fled the room. He could tell Alexios was hot on his heels, but Auro did not stop until he was outside, striding hurriedly down the brick-laid garden path.

"Auro!" Alexios hissed, hurrying after him. "*Auro,* wait!"

He turned around, staring Alexios full in the face at last. "What?"

"I'm so sorry," Alexios said earnestly. "I didn't know how to tell you."

"Ah well, much better that I heard it from your mother, then." Auro glared at him. "You're engaged."

"Yeah, well..." said Alexios, his gaze hardening. "You're cursed!"

They stared at each other for a few beats, and suddenly, without warning, the tension broke and they both burst out laughing. Auro hadn't laughed like this in...well. His sides ached, and he gasped for breath. "Ridiculous, isn't it?" he said at last, wiping a tear from his eye.

"Doomed," Alexios agreed. His smile fell away, mirth melting as quickly as it had arrived. "I didn't mean to hurt you."

"I know," said Auro heavily. "I think it highly unlikely either of us will emerge from this spring unscathed."

Alexios nodded. He cast a look over his shoulder, ensuring they were alone before he reached out and cupped Auro's cheek. "I understand if you don't..." he fumbled with his words and looked away.

A brief burst of boldness took hold of Auro, then. He raised his hands and closed his fingers around Alexios's hand, holding it tight to his own cheek. "I do."

"We could...have something. For a little while, at least."

"We could," Auro allowed.

"Is that—are you alright with that?"

"Yes," Auro lied. "Are you?"

"Yes," Alexios lied. At least, Auro was pretty certain it was a lie. Apparently, though, it was a lie they both needed to believe. The silence in the wake of that was a loaded one, and eventually Alexios released Auro's cheek to instead gather up Auro's hands in his own.

Nine

The following morning, Alexios had to prepare himself for court, and Auro spent the morning in the royal gardens, at the Queen's insistence. With his hair disguised, it was easy enough for him to fade into the background of the bustling staff, the courtiers, the King and Queen's companions, and the guards. As he strolled, he could not help but listen to the needs of the marvelous plants growing all around him. Some had plainly been brought here from distant regions and did not grow as well in the Papian soil, so they did not quite look their best. Auro used his grace to help them along a bit and to take in their specific needs. By noon, he had spoken with one of the royal garden staff, who showed him where the supplies and tools were kept, and by the time Alexios found him after court, Auro had his hands in the dirt, communing with the gardens. A sheen of sweat broke on his forehead as he pushed his grace to feel the roots in the ground and the clouds in the pale blue sky. It had been quite warm, for so early in the season. He thought perhaps an additional spring rain, or a cooler evening to bring the droplets down to dampen the earth would balance out the rays of the sun beating down today.

Alexios sat on a bench, waiting for Auro to finish up so they could share a midday meal together. As Auro returned his awareness to his own body, he became cognizant of waves of displeasure flowing off Alexios, and when he looked up, he saw his face was clouded. "What is wrong?" he asked at last.

"Oh," said Alexios, opening the book he'd been ignoring. "Nothing."

Auro smiled. "It is not nothing," he said. He longed to press the pad of his pointer finger to the crease between Alexios's brows, to smooth the tension from his lovely face. His eyes flicked to where Leofric stood, too close. He kept his voice low when he said, "Just tell me."

Alexios stared at him for a long time, as if he were weighing the cost of every word. Auro could see several emotions flicker across his face, until he finally said, "I envy you."

Auro was so startled he laughed. "Pardon?"

"You, and your work," Alexios clarified. "You always seem so at peace when you perform your...spells."

"My 'spells'?"

"Spells, rituals—whatever you would call them," said Alexios, his cheeks reddening as he pretended to study a page in his book.

"Sorry, yes. Go on."

"You enjoy your work," said Alexios. "I see it in your face, the peace you feel when you maneuver the soil or speak to the trees."

"And you do not feel peace, Alexios?"

"No," he said, and the way he said it, a frightened whisper, gave Auro the distinct impression that Alexios had never admitted anything like that out loud before. "I am to be king, one day, and yet I feel like a boy, still. A child, with no direction and no purpose."

"We all feel as children from time to time."

"This is different. There is so much expected of me, and yet, I feel so adrift."

"Adrift how?"

"My mother is a brilliant scholar, and my father a former imperator, covered in laurels. I am neither. All I do is plan social events, give speeches. I have been telling them I wish to make my own decisions, but should they allow it...I have no idea what those decisions would even be."

Auro took a deep breath and rested a hand on Alexios's shoulder. It wasn't so untoward, a friendly touch. Nothing more. The warmth of Alexios's skin seemed to scorch Auro's palm, even through the fabric of the toga he wore to court. Alexios startled but did not shake Auro's hand away. "Perhaps you should find out."

"What?"

"If you wish to be your own sort of king one day, Alexios, perhaps you should begin by actually doing so."

"How?"

"How indeed?" asked Auro, withdrawing his hand. "I am certain I have no idea what your people require of their king. That is the place for you to start, I would think."

With the arrival of foreign queen and her delegation fast approaching, not to mention the equinox festival, the royal villa was an anthill of activity.

In his official capacity as the glorified royal party planner, Alexios spent the next week chasing down delicacies to please the Neossan Queen, hiring musicians, and visiting Papia City to make certain his family's domus in the city was being properly prepared for the arrival of Queen Petillia and her entourage.

After his discussion with Auro, the tasks grated on him even more than usual. Auro was right. If he wanted things to change, he would have to change them. As he rehersed what he planned to ask his parents, he took care to dress himself formally and don the crown he usually couldn't be bothered to wear.

At present, the King and Queen were ensconced with the Tribune of the Papian treasury in their audience chamber, so Alexios waited just outside so that he could catch them before they retreated to their chambers for midday meal.

"Alexios," said Queen Clio warmly when they emerged. "What are you doing here? I thought you would be taken with tasks for the festival."

"I was," admitted Alexios. "And I have more to accomplish, but I wished to speak with you both as soon as possible."

"This sounds fairly serious," said the King, narrowing his eyes in suspicion.

"It is," said Alexios. "I wanted to ask if you'd given any thought to what we discussed the other day. About my taking on more responsibilities in the kingdom."

The King and Queen's skepticism could not have been plainer, and Alexios's embarrassment mingled with anger. Certainly, he had not shown much initiative in more stately matters before, but his parents had also never truly taught him anything about them. He could recite the most influential works of Papian epic poetry going back two centuries, but perish the fucking thought of knowing how taxes in the capital city were collected.

"It has been a long time since we have made an inspection of the roads in the city," said the Queen at last. "The roads are vitally important to the flow of trade—perhaps you could start there."

Alexios swallowed his disappointment with as much composure as he could muster. *Roads*? He could not think of anything as dull or lifeless as the city's roads. Brick and cement laid upon the ground, most of the time it went entirely beneath anyone's notice. Literally. He accepted the task graciously, however. This may well be a test, and if he scoffed at the assignment, his future great-grandson would have real power over the governance of the realm before he got another chance.

Alexios returned to his rooms following the audience with his parents, shedding his crown and toga in favor of simpler garb. Alexios sat heavily on the edge of his bed, staring at the stone head of Princess Dafina, wondering if his parents would have awarded him a higher honor had he shown more enthusiasm for his impending marriage.

He turned away from the head, gazing instead at the strange cup of dirt Auro had given him, and with a jolt of surprise saw that something was growing out of it. The smile breaking across his face was an unthinking one as he crossed the room to examine the tiny plant. He'd never seen something like this before, a plant brought indoors to grow. The glass gardens were the closest in concept, but those were more like a room built *around* growing things.

This was different. The plant was so small, a tiny barb of green pushing through the surface of the dirt. Like the songbirds Alexios now fed every morning, it was like a little piece of Auro, right here, in his chambers. Alexios reached a hand toward the plant, letting his fingertips whisper over the leaf that had only just begun to emerge from the soil.

The afternoon sun was warm and Alexios found Auro where he knew he would, in the glass-walled gardens. Despite the lovely surprise of his gift from Auro, Alexios still felt a heaviness on his shoulders, thinking of his future and the way that his parents plainly had no faith in him. He sat on a low stone wall and watched Auro work for a while, and Leofric stood by the door, face impassive as Alexios sulked and waited for Auro to notice him.

At last, Auro sauntered over to stand before Alexios. "Alright, my Prince, what happened?"

Alexios scowled. He could tell Auro was teasing him, albeit lightly. Briefly, Alexios explained what happened with his parents. When he finished, he could tell that Auro was not nearly as insulted on his behalf as Alexios would have wished. "...what?" he finished.

"Alexios," said Auro sternly, "What did you expect? That your parents would immediately set you to leading Papia's armies?"

"No," said Alexios. "I don't know."

"Perhaps the maintenance of the roads is not the office affording the loftiest of laurels, but I can scarce think of a better way to know your kingdom."

Auro had the right of it, Alexios realized. "You may have a point."

With an indulgent smile, Auro patted Alexios's arm. It softened Auro's scolding and reminded Alexios of how comfortable Auro had become around him, so he couldn't keep the smile off his face.

"You should have seen my parents' faces when I insisted upon a new task," said Alexios. "It was as if I had sprouted a second head."

"All the more reason for you to prove yourself," said Auro. "Make them regret overlooking your ability to help, thus far."

Alexios set his jaw. "You are absolutely right."

"I usually am."

Alexios laughed and gave Auro a playful shove. They sat in silence for a while, and when Auro rested his hand on the stone wall, tipping his head up to the sunlight streaming in through the glass, Alexios nudged Auro's fingertips with his own. Auro was not slow to take the cue. He wrapped his pinky around Alexios's, tangling them together. Alexios's stomach swooped as if he'd missed a step going down the stairs.

Alexios glanced at Leofric, who looked out into the middle distance, but he didn't want to push his luck, so he gave Auro's fingers a squeeze before withdrawing his hand. "I had a thought," he said.

"Oh?"

"Now that my parents have given me charge of the roads, I better get to inspecting them, don't you think?"

"Certainly," said Auro cautiously.

"I was thinking that perhaps you might like to accompany me and have a tour of Papia City."

What little color there was in Auro's face left it, and Alexios knew it was a daunting request.

"I think it would be good for you," he said quietly.

A muscle in Auro's jaw twitched, but with wide eyes, he nodded. "I'd like that," he said, his voice shrinking as it tended to do whenever he was anxious.

"Excellent," said Alexios, beaming.

Ten

It had been decades, nay, *centuries* since Auro had mounted up to ride upon horseback. He was not overly concerned, though. Auro had always had an affinity with beasts, and he was confident he could win over the spare steed Alexios promised him.

The morning of their planned trip into the city, Auro approached the royal stables. He'd gotten a bit more used to conversing with the staff and the guards, but it still made him anxious. "Good morrow," he hailed the stablemaster. "I am here to meet His Royal Highness."

The man jumped to his feet, but before he could so much as shout, Alexios himself came round the side of the building, already ahorse. He led another mount along beside him, and Leofric came just behind them with a third. Alexios dismounted to greet Auro. "This is Segovax," he said, introducing Auro to his mount.

"He is quite handsome," said Auro, stroking the side of the animal's neck.

"And you know Leofric, of course," said Alexios.

Auro didn't know him, not truly, but they'd been introduced, so he said, "Yes, good morning, Captain."

"Good morning," said Leofric solemnly.

Auro turned his attentions back to Segovax, producing a plum from within the folds of his tunic. He offered it with an open palm, and Segovax mouthed rough lips over his hand to taste the fruit, huffing and whickering happily. Though it was not necessary, Auro found himself quite flattered when Alexios stooped to boost Auro up into the saddle, and he allowed Alexios to assist him and fuss over his riding tack, ensuring the straps and buckles were just so. Alexios let his pinky finger whisper down the side of Auro's calf, looking up at him with a small, private smile.

Mounted up, the three of them set off down the road leading from the gates of the royal villa, due south. Alexios wanted to begin surveying the kingdom's roads, starting with the ones that led to Papia City, the central hub of the kingdom.

Auro felt the eyes of Alexios's guard, Leofric, as they rode. Leofric stared hard at Auro from where his horse walked a few paces behind the Prince, maintaining a respectful distance as was proper for a guardsman. Long years had passed since Auro had last found himself under such careful scrutiny, and he had a difficult time ignoring Leofric and untangling his tongue to engage Alexios in conversation.

"Are you unwell?" Alexios asked Auro at last, after his distracted state stopped the flow of conversation once again. "You flinch and twist in the saddle as if someone were after you."

"Apologies," said Auro in a low voice.

"There's no need to apologize," said Alexios, a frown forming on his face. "I was just wondering what has your head so clouded."

Auro could not help the way his eyes flickered back, over his shoulder, and Alexios seemed to understand.

With his voice scarce above the whisper, he said, "I know his presence makes things awkward—"

"It's not just that," said Auro. "You must understand. Before we met, it had been decades since I'd last spoken to anyone besides the dryadae—and longer still since I'd left the forest."

"Oh."

"Yes," said Auro. "I just feel very...exposed."

"In that case, I should be apologizing," said Alexios earnestly. "We can forget this whole thing and return to the villa. It was never my aim to make you uncomfortable."

Auro smiled at him. "I know," he said. "I wish to do this. It is time I made some returns to the world."

"Well," said Alexios, "I will remain at your side." He brought his horse closer to Auro's, allowing their knees to bump together.

Auro felt a bit lighter after that, clearing the air between himself and Alexios allowed him to relax as they continued on their way. The harbor city was indeed quite different than Auro had remembered it—the buildings had grown larger and grader, the streets wider, and the markets more crowded. Alexios, Auro, and Leofric deposited their horses with the captain of the city watch, such that they could explore the markets on foot. The noise and press of so many people threatened to overwhelm Auro, but Alexios's sturdy, warm hand on the small of his back kept him steady. Leofric walked half a step behind them, his eyes alert as he scanned the crowd for any threats. Some things remained the same, however—and Auro suspected they would remain as such until the world ceased to spin. Whores plied their trade upon the docks, sailors cursed and joked as they unloaded their ships, and gulls screamed overhead.

"Come," said Alexios, leading Auro down a set of stone steps that descended into the basin of the harbor.

Auro couldn't help but gasp; the market was a staggering sight. The capital city of Papia abutted a sheltered bay, the land sloping down in a valley as if the bay were the remnants of soup in the bottom of a vast bowl. In the intervening centuries, Papia's citizens had carved into the valley's slope and built their structures, and a magnificent three-tiered market that descended to the edge of the bay itself. Auro had never seen a market so large, and Alexios explained the different levels to him as they descended.

The High Market held the finest, most expensive shops and elite guild masters of various crafts. The entire structure of this level had been built from the finest white marble, from the cobblestone walkways to the buildings themselves, and it glittered in the afternoon sun.

Down a wide, gently inclined set of marble steps, one could find the Wide Market, or what the common folk called the Red Market, because of the color of the stones that made up its stairs and pathways. The Red Market was the biggest, and the busiest, holding the vast majority of the city's permanent shops, inns, and taverns. Below *that*, closest to the water was the Dock Market, lovingly referred to as the Salt Market, due to its proximity to the seaside. The Salt Market was a mix of rough trade sailors, whores, fishmongers, and all manner of enterprises. It was a place where you were as likely to find the best bargain of your life as you were to find the worst beating, according to Alexios.

They descended to the level of the Red Market, walking past the tabernae and the temporary stalls. Auro twisted his head around in every direction, taking in the thriving, heaving press of shoppers. It had been so long since he'd seen so many people in one place, and the sight made his heart swell. He had forgotten, the joy of life among other people. They were the true reason behind his work, not the punishment inflicted upon him and his brothers. The people, the trees, the beasts—it was to them Auro owed his duties, his efforts, not the ghost of an absent father. He had forgotten that, too.

Alexios immediately sought out a stonemason, who hauled his wares from Neossós to sell in the thriving port, and spoke with the man at length about materials best suited for roads. The man seemed thrilled to have an attentive listener, and a crown prince no less. As they spoke, Auro turned on his heel to observe the tableau of commerce playing out beside the storefront.

A thousand tiny dramas unfolded all around him, and Auro lost himself watching them for a while, until a child's voice rose above the others, shrill and frightened. Auro's eyes fell upon a small girl, who could not have been older than five, spinning on her heel, plainly lost, plainly alone. Auro crossed the crowd without thinking and fell to one knee before her. "Hello," he said. "I'm called Auro."

She hiccoughed, looking at Auro as if she was trying to decide if she could trust him. He took advantage of her distraction and pressed his fingers to the ground, coaxing a stalk of foxglove blooms to grow between the cracks in the paving stones. He plucked it, handed it to her, and a tiny smile stopped her lips from trembling. He dried her eyes with a corner of his tunic.

"I'm Bina," she said. "And I've lost sight of my father."

"Well," said Auro, "where did you last see him? Did you know where he was headed next?"

Bina chewed her lip and shook her head. "I wasn't paying attention," she confessed.

Auro smiled at her. "That's alright. I find the sights distracting, too."

Bina clutched the foxglove in her tiny fist, searching the crowd for her father. From this vantage point, the market was a sea of knees and sandals, and one man's knees looked much like any other's. Auro stood and offered his hand. "Come," he said. "Let's find the harbormaster. I'm certain once he realizes you're gone, your father will rush to him as well."

Knowing Alexios would be able to find him eventually, Auro led the young girl toward a man in a fine toga of deep purple wool who stood talking to a ship's captain. The man had an official look about him, and when Auro introduced himself, and Bina, sure enough, he turned out to be the harbormaster. They asked if he had knowledge of Bina's father, and while he didn't, he suggested they wait by a fountain in the central terrace of the Red Market, a common place for folk to meet up. "I will tell your father the same, should he approach me," the harbormaster told Bina kindly.

While they waited beside the fountain, Auro surreptitiously summoned more flowers to distract and delight Bina, weaving a chain of narcissus and peonies into a crown to lay across her brow.

"Now you!" she said and instructed Auro to sit on the ground before her.

He did as he was told, passing her stem after stem, which she knotted clumsily into Auro's curls.

"Auro!"

He looked up to see Alexios and Leofric approaching through the crowd. Alexios took in the sight of the little girl weaving flowers into Auro's hair and gave him a surprised, fond smile.

"Hello," said Auro, beaming up at Alexios. "I am keeping Lady Bina company while we await her father."

Soon enough, all four of them wore flowers in their hair, even Leofric, who stooped forward solemnly and allowed Bina to stuff blooms into his braid. With his vining tattoos, it looked as if the flowers were growing out of the side of his head, something Bina was thrilled to point out. Auro even caught him smiling, once. For a moment.

"*Bina!*" A haggard-looking man fought his way through the ring of people surrounding the fountain. He dropped to his knees beside his daughter and pulled her into a frantic embrace. "Thank goodness! Are you—" his eyes fell upon Auro, who sat cross-legged on the cobbles beside his child. "Who are you?"

"His name is Auro," said Bina, clutching tight to her father's shoulders. "He gave me some flowers."

"Well," said Alexios. "It seems your work here is done." He hauled Auro to his feet. Bina's father turned from Auro to Alexios, seeing the golden crown on his brow, and Leofric at his back, imposing in his uniform and armor—despite the flowers in his hair.

"Fuck," the man said, paling. "I mean—apologies, Your Highness."

But Alexios only laughed and stopped the man attempting to bow while still maintaining a hold upon his daughter. "None required."

The man lowered his daughter to the ground but seemed reluctant to part from her. He rested a big hand on her skull. "Bina," he said. "We must return to the cartwright's stall swiftly, before he closes up for the day."

"Cartwright?" inquired Auro.

"Aye," he said, a strained look on his face. "We were making for the city, the family and I. My wife is with child, but it has been..." He trailed away. "Anyway, we were coming to see a midwife, here in the city. Our cart ran afoul of a rather nasty rut in the road. My wife and son are back with the cart and the ox, but Bina and I came on ahead to fetch a new wheel and return."

Alexios frowned. "You left your pregnant wife and son by the side of the road?"

The man met Alexios's eye with a hard glare. "Beg pardon, Your Highness, but I didn't see any other choice. She could hardly walk all this way."

Alexios frowned even deeper still. "This is unacceptable," he said, his tone so forceful it startled Auro. "Take me to this cartwright."

Alexios, Auro, Leofric, and their new companions wound their way back through the market to the cartwright, who was irritated that he had to stay open, waiting for Bina's father—who introduced himself as Calvinus.

Alexios paid the cartwright generously for his time and paid for Calvinus's new wheel besides. "Tell me more about what happened on the road," Alexios said, and Calvinus relayed the events of his morning.

They were just about to bid them farewell when Alexios ferreted out that the man and girl were planning on *walking* all the way back to the place where Calvinus's wife and son waited for them—lugging the enormous cart wheel along with them.

"They've been on the side of the road since *yesterday?*" said Alexios, aghast. "This won't do. Come."

Leofric's warhorse was best suited to carrying the extra weight of the wheel, so they lashed it carefully up behind him in the saddle. Bina rode pillion with Auro upon Segovax, clinging tight to Auro's waist. The captain of the guard at the barracks had several extra mounts for his men and was happy to lend one to his prince.

"Do you ride?" Alexios asked Calvinus.

"Some, Your Highness," the man admitted. "Not into battle, perhaps, but I can follow the road."

"Excellent."

Their party set out, Calvinus instructing them where his cart had broken down. The way was a winding one, not like the direct path that led from the royal villa to the city. Auro couldn't help but notice that it was riddled with ruts from carts, broken paving stones, and debris from winter storms. Auro was just wondering how far they were from their destination when a woman's sudden wail cut the silence, sending a flock of birds squawking and flapping from the shrubbery beside them.

"Your Highness!" came Leofric's voice in warning, but Alexios had already nudged his horse forward to round the bend toward the source of the anguished cries. Calvinus's cart had plainly run afoul of a particularly nasty rut. The wheel had become entirely dislodged and the cart tilted dangerously on its straining axle. Calvinus's wife braced herself against the low walls in the bed of the cart, her face covered in sweat, and indeed massively pregnant.

"The baby wasn't due to arrive for another fortnight," said Calvinus faintly. He dismounted clumsily and rushed to his wife's side.

"They tend to arrive when they will," said Auro, helping Bina from the saddle.

A particularly loud scream cut him off, and Calvinus wrung his hands. "I've no idea what to do."

Auro looked quickly from face to face. "Come," he snapped, surprising even himself. "We must first get this cart stable and ease her labor."

Together, the four of them hastened to lift the corner of the cart, remove the broken wheel, and roll a log from the forest's edge to brace below the axel. They could fix the wheel later. With the cart leveled, Auro hopped up beside the woman and brushed the sweaty strands of hair back from her forehead. "My name is Auro," he told her. "I can help."

She looked at him, wide-eyed, panting, as the contractions eased for the moment. But Auro knew they would return with a vengeance soon enough. Some of Auro's duties involved monitoring the many, *many* young of the forest creatures as they came forth into the world, whether they came from the eggs of birds or the wombs of bears, so he had some degree of expertise in this area. He had, of course, never assisted with a *human* birth—but perhaps Calvinus's wife didn't need to know that.

As another wave of contractions took hold of her, she gritted her teeth and nodded, accepting Auro's help.

"What is your name?"

"Sylva," she said, though it ended on a groan of pain.

"Alright, Sylva," said Auro in a clear, but gentle voice. "This is all going to be fine but you must bear down as hard as you can on my count, yes?"

"I can't!" she wailed.

Auro hiked her skirts up above her thighs and hooked his arms in the crooks of her knees. "You can," he said. "And you must. Now, on my count, three—two—one—"

Sylva screamed as she pushed, and Calvinus looked as though he might faint. Alexios took his arm and drew him and his other children away to give Sylva and Auro some room.

"Alright," said Auro, his focus on the woman before him once more. "Take a few deep breaths—you must push again, alright? You will feel the urge coming."

"But—"

"Your body knows how to do this," Auro told her. "Trust it."

She closed her eyes and nodded, and within the span of a few deep, agonizing breaths she pushed again. They repeated this process, over and over, until Auro could at last see the child's head as it crowned. "He is coming!" said Auro encouragingly. "You must help him the rest of the way, Sylva."

Tears and sweat streamed down her cheeks, her face growing redder and redder, but Sylva summoned her strength and courage and pushed once again.

The cries of the little one shook the air, and Calvinus rushed to his wife's side.

"Your son," said Auro, awe in his voice. He'd never held a baby before, but this one, brought into the world by his hand, lay squirming and wailing in his arms. Calvinus clambered gracelessly into the cart to stroke his wife's hair and kiss her brow. Dazed, Auro laid the child at her breast, and with murmured praise he hopped down to give them a bit of privacy.

Alexios turned to stare at Auro. "You're trembling," he said.

Auro hadn't realized, the adrenaline coursing through his system as he'd assisted with the birth was rushing out of him. "It's nothing," he said, a giddy smile breaking over his lips—the sort of smile that only comes after a crisis successfully averted.

Alexios stared into Auro's eyes with an intensity that made Auro shiver and cupped his cheeks with both hands. "You were amazing," said Alexios. "Truly."

"It was nothing," said Auro again, his voice scant more than a whisper. "My duty is to care for all the young of springtime."

Alexios swallowed, his eyes dropping briefly to Auro's lips. "Your Highness!"

Alexios jerked away from Auro at the shout, and Auro staggered slightly—he hadn't realized he'd been leaning into Alexios's touch.

Leofric approached them cautiously, but sidestepped the awkward moment and said, "We should help them get back to the city. It will be dark soon."

As Alexios helped Calvinus and Leofric mount the new wheel to the cart, Auro clambered up into the back where Sylva and the baby rested, as comfortably as could be expected.

"How are you feeling?"

"Tired," said Sylva. "Just...tired." She gave him a searching look. "Not many men know the ways of the birthing bed."

Auro shrugged. "It is a skill of mine," he said. "Though I will admit this is the first time I assisted with the birth of a *person*."

Sylva released an exhausted laugh. "Well, I think you'll find the process much the same, unless you deal with hens and chickens."

Auro smiled. She was correct, after all.

As Alexios, Leofric, and Auro mounted up once more to return to the villa, Sylva called to Auro. "If you don't mind," she said, "I would have your blessing to call my son Aurus, to honor the help you gave us."

Auro was speechless, then stammering and blustering, until Alexios elbowed him gently. "Yes, of course—" he blurted. "You do me a great honor."

Sylva smiled, looking down at her child. "It is truly nothing when compared to the gift you have given."

But to Auro, it was everything.

Eleven

T he sky was bruise-purple by the time Alexios, Auro, and Leofric set off back toward the royal villa. "This should never have happened."

"What do you mean?" asked Auro.

"The road is under the protection of the kingdom—now *my* protection. It should never have been allowed to fall into such disrepair."

"These things happen, Your Highness," said Leofric. "The roads by the country villas and farms are too far flung to receive the same care as those in the city itself."

"Well," said Alexios hotly, "that is unacceptable."

He spurred Xanthos toward home, eager to discuss the matter with his parents. This incident with Calvinus had filled him with new purpose. He could not ignore such a problem, and since his parents had put the kingdom's roads in his charge, then he swore he would see them all to perfect repair and efficiency, if he had to beggar the royal treasury to do so. He bade Auro farewell at the palace gates. Auro hopped down from his borrowed horse, absent his usual floaty gracefulness, limping as he walked, bowlegged, from the stables. Alexios felt a stab of guilt. "Auro!" he called.

Auro turned to him with a pronounced wince.

"Come," said Alexios. "We can arrange for a muscle rub, after I've spoken with my parents regarding the roads."

Auro smiled grimly. "Thank you. It has been...some time since I spent so long on horseback."

Alexios gave one of the porters instructions to see Auro to his chambers and then went off in search of the King and Queen. He found them finishing their evening meal.

"Alexios! Where have you been? You were summoned."

"Apologies," he said, with a slight bow. "I had intended—"

"Queen Petillia and the Lord Praetor arrived today, and your absence was noted."

That brought Alexios up short. He had known the Queen was arriving early for the equinox festival, but he had no idea how early. "Petillia? What is she doing here so soon?"

"Her Grace, *Queen* Petillia," admonished Queen Clio gently, "expected you to be present to greet her. She is to be your future mother-in-law, Alexios."

"I can't believe you would shame us this way," said Nelios.

Alexios frowned. "I should have been made aware she was coming this early," he said. "Is the Princess here as well?"

"No, thank goodness," said the Queen. "She remained in Neossós to manage the kingdom a bit longer in her mother's absence. She is expected the morning of the feast."

"Mercifully, Her Grace was tired from the journey. We made excuses for you, and you will rectify the situation when we go riding with Her Grace and the Praetor tomorrow. We can discuss the matter then."

Alexios held his tongue, with difficulty. He wanted very much to tell his father and mother not to hold their royal breath awaiting Alexios in the morning, but then he recalled the issue he wished to discuss with them. If they all went riding tomorrow, he could show his father what he had seen and broach the subject then. Perhaps if he played the gallant prince, his parents would be more likely to listen. He remained furious, however, that these arrangements were being made without him, so he turned on his heel and strode from the room without waiting to be dismissed.

He walked back to his chambers, Leofric behind him. It was only once he had left his parents behind that Alexios recalled he had invited Auro to his chambers. Originally, Alexios had a notion to summon the physio and her assistants, men and women trained in the art of caring for the body, to massage Auro's aching muscles and set his stiff legs to rights. Now though...Alexios realized he hated the idea of another person laying their hands on Auro. Auro was *his,* he thought savagely. He knew their time was limited, in many respects. Not only would Auro return to sleep at the end of spring, but by the time he awoke the following year, Alexios would be wed—or at the very least, formally betrothed. The thought left him sad and hollow, so he pushed it away.

Though Alexios hardly held the expertise of the physio, he thought he'd be able to work Auro's muscles to a state of relaxation well enough.

Auro, who now lay snoozing in a beam of sunlight streaming in through the window, as if he were a spoiled housecat. It made Alexios smile. One sandaled foot dangled off the edge of the sleeping couch, and Alexios knelt to undo the straps.

Auro stirred as Alexios eased his leg back up onto the feather-stuffed mattress, and untied the leather straps from his other ankle. "*Shhh,*" said Alexios, difficulties with his parents forgotten as he watched Auro's pink lashes flutter open to reveal his startling green eyes.

"I must have dozed off," he said.

"You've had quite a day," said Alexios with a smirk.

"Mmm," agreed Auro, stretching. "And, I had forgotten the pains of returning to the saddle after many, *many* years absent."

"I had forgotten as well," said Alexios. "I spend much of my time riding, and have grown used to the ache." He sat beside Auro, pulling his feet onto his lap. With his thumbs, he worked the arches, and Auro groaned.

"That is bloody *divine,*" he said.

Alexios smiled crookedly. He instructed Auro to undress and lie upon his front. Then, he went to his bathing chamber to retrieve a bottle of fine scented oil. He selected one distilled and pressed with the petals of lilacs. It was a scent he felt suited Auro.

When Alexios returned, he saw that Auro had followed his instructions and now lay on his belly, his cheek pillowed on his folded arms. Alexios sucked in a breath, dizzy at the sight of Auro laid out naked in his bed, and hastily seized a white linen sheet to drape over Auro's buttocks, lest he completely forget himself. For someone so jumpy, Auro was remarkably casual with his own nakedness.

Auro smiled, burying his face in his arms, peeking out with eyes that shone with just a shade too much innocence, the cheeky shit. Alexios began by warming the oil between his palms, filling the quiet air around them with its delicate scent.

Alexios found himself suddenly full of nerves at the prospect of actually touching Auro, of running his palms over the miles of exposed, pale skin. It was too late to balk now, however, and it was the potential embarrassment of creating some excuse for Auro to redress himself that spurred him on. He began with gentle probing at the sides of Auro's neck, exploring the soft skin behind his ears, massaging circles with his thumbs, following the knobby bones of his spine toward his shoulders. While the pain of riding upon horseback focused mostly in the legs, it would not do to ignore the upper body. Alexios worked the oil into Auro's skin till he shone with it, smelling like flowers, glistening in the light from the sconces on the wall.

Alexios cursed under his breath, his cock straining where it was mercifully concealed behind the fabric of his tunic, and the loincloth he customarily wore while riding. He hoped that Auro would not notice, and it appeared his wish was mostly granted, as Alexios realized his hands had hypnotized Auro into a melted state of purest relaxation. In fact—yes. Auro was now snoring into the crook of his elbow.

Alexios grinned to himself, happy to be able to stare at Auro, to touch him like this, and so happy Auro trusted him enough to fall asleep without a thought. Alexios knew he had his palms on something truly divine, blessed to be granted permission to touch, the realization coursing through him that he had a god in his bed. Alexios did his best to refocus on the task at hand, and by the time he massaged the knots from Auro's calves, his hands and arms were stiff with the effort.

He padded quietly to his bath, to wash the travel from his body and the oil from his fingers. Alexios stripped, and as he sank into the bath, he wrapped a hand at last around his aching cock beneath the cool water. In his mind, he imagined what would have happened had Auro perhaps been a bit more awake, in a bit less pain—and, perhaps, if Alexios were just a touch more bold. He could have slipped his hands below the sheet, filled his palms with the round globes of Auro's ass. He could have squeezed, kneaded the flesh. How smooth it must be, Alexios thought to himself. How warm. How—

"Alexios?"

Alexios opened his eyes with a sharp gasp, only to find his vivid fantasy made flesh. Auro stood naked in the doorway, brazen as the sun—and about as blinding. "I woke and you had gone," he said with a pout. He had a crisp white sheet clutched to his chest, which still allowed Alexios an unobstructed view of his leg, his hip, the skin below his ribs. A teasing glimpse of curly pink hair below his navel, disappearing behind the fabric.

Alexios immediately released his cock, hoping Auro would not see beneath the water, and rested his arms innocently on the edge of the bathing pool. "You slept so soundly," he said, struggling to keep his voice steady.

Auro cocked his head to the side. "You are flushed," he said. "Are you quite well?"

"The heat of the day," Alexios lied. "The water will set me right." It was upon his tongue to ask Auro to join him, but something stilled the words, stopped them from escaping past his lips.

"I must return to the forest," said Auro. "There are a few things I must attend. But I had a proposition for you."

Alexios felt lightheaded at the thought of what proposition Auro might pose, and all he could manage was a nod.

"In the glass gardens, there is a truly remarkable flower," said Auro. "Well, more than one. Dozens actually—"

"Auro? The proposition?"

"Yes," he said. "Right. Well, one of the flowers is night blooming—and it only blooms once every nine years."

"Oh," said Alexios. "And you think it's going to bloom soon?"

Auro flashed him a smile, eyes glowing. "I *know* it is going to bloom tomorrow night."

"And?"

"And," said Auro eagerly, "it's the largest flower in the world. I was wondering if—if perhaps you'd like to meet me tomorrow evening and watch it bloom."

Alexios's mouth went dry. The idea of a nighttime liaison with Auro, amongst the flowers, watching a spectacular rarity unfold before them, beneath the stars—and, Auro had asked *him*, which seemed even more important than the rest of it, to be frank. "Yes," said Alexios breathlessly. "I would be delighted."

Beaming, Auro turned on his heel to gather his discarded clothes, and Alexios averted his eyes. Once alone again, he emerged from the tub and wrapped a fresh loincloth quickly about his hips. As he returned to the adjacent chamber, it was to the sight of Auro pulling his tunic down over his tousled curls, allowing Alexios the briefest of glimpse of his flesh as he covered it up. Auro winked at him over his shoulder, and was gone.

Auro spent the next morning preparing for a romantic evening with Alexios.

Even before he had been cursed, Auro had never taken much interest in courting. He now berated himself daily for not asking his brothers for instruction when he'd had the opportunity. Auro sat in his temple and reflected upon this, looking at each brother's face, in turn. Cedras had never taken his nose from his endless studying to take an interest in courting, either—and Cosmo had perhaps taken too much interest, shameless in relaying tales of his conquests with details that bordered on frightening, and Kryos had kept his own tales as well-guarded as he kept everything. And then there was Ozias, who'd had an endless line of suitors without any sort of visible effort or strategy on his own part. So, perhaps asking his brothers would have availed him nothing, even if he'd thought to do so.

Auro wasn't certain about Alexios, but to him, the gardens were one of the most inherently romantic places he'd ever been. Since he'd been staying near the villa and visiting every day, the plants had taken notice of him and responded to his grace. They flourished, even the ones that did not grow naturally in Papia. The air in what Alexios had called the greenhouse—the glass-walled gardens—was moist and fragrant, heavy with the perfumes of exotic flowers that opened as the spring warmed and as Auro spent more time there.

While he waited for Alexios, he made the rounds, coaxing a leaf to open here, convincing a snail to find another place to live, or roots to untangle themselves to reach the choicest nutrients. The steamy greenhouse had dozens of small alcoves, as the Queen had expanded it over the years. The alcove in which the rare corpse flower grew was tucked away, almost overgrown with thick green leaves. Auro gently nudged them toward the walls, clearing a space from which Auro could view the giant, remarkable flower.

It was interesting; Auro's grace touched every growing thing in the world, but there were dozens—hundreds, perhaps even thousands, that he did not see. Either they grew later in the year, or too far from his forest home. Some of them were as rare as the corpse flower before him, and others as common as a ripe tomato.

He longed to see them all, to see the literal fruits of his labors. Apples and pumpkins in fall, holly in winter. Fragrant lilies in summertime. Every growing thing upon the earth was something he and his brothers made together—and he wished he could bear witness to them all.

But he couldn't.

The thought made him sad, so instead of focusing upon that, he focused on tonight. He tried to catch some rest, curled up snug in a hidden tangle of vines in the glass gardens, staying close to make certain they didn't miss any signs the corpse flower would bloom early. When Auro woke, everything was as it should be, and the sun was just beginning to set.

Auro made his way to the kitchens, where by now he was known enough by the staff to come and go as he liked. The cooks had clearly been told to honor any of his requests, as he was now a known companion to the Crown Prince. He requested a few things, some wine, some of the brown bread well known to be Alexios's favorite, butter sweetened with honey. Auro tucked them safely into a basket with some grapes and cheese to make a light supper. As he assembled his basket, Auro overheard a few of the cooks talking. He found that with his newly dyed hair, he could slip as if invisible amongst other people, and he overheard quite a bit. The cooks were talking about the extensive menu for the spring equinox feast, which would be held at the palace soon. Talk turned to Alexios, and Auro couldn't help but listen, smiling to himself just at the sound of Alexios's name.

"He's going to wed a princess," one of the cooks told another, and Auro's smile quickly faded.

"Aye, and be absent from her bed as often as he is from his own," said the other.

The first cook smacked the other with a spoon, but both of them laughed.

Auro frowned. He'd been hearing all manner of similar, troubling things about Alexios since he'd started spending time around the villa, and had been doing his best not to take it to heart. The sick, hot, squirming sensation of jealousy was a new one to him, and he did *not* care for it.

It only worsened as he left the kitchens and returned to the gardens to wait, especially when the sun had set, the stars had come out. Auro laid out their supper and a blanket, right before the corpse flower's alcove, and waited.

And waited.

Where on earth was Alexios? The moon was high, now, and the flower had begun to open.

Had he found some other bed to fall to? It was an unworthy thought, one that shamed him. Alexios would surely tell him if he were courting another, would he not?

Ah, said a snide voice in Auro's head, one that often sounded like it came from one of his brothers. *He already is courting another.*

The voice was right, of course.

Alexios was a prince, the only heir to his family's line, and he had to wed. He'd told Auro as much when they'd first met, albeit unhappily. They had both known what was coming—an end to whatever this was between them. Alexios's betrothal approached them as inexorably as the end of spring when Auro would turn to stone.

There was nothing he could do except wait, and hope Alexios would come.

Alexios woke at dawn, sitting up and looking out the windows at the rising sun. On his balcony, spilling into his chambers, in any patch of available sunlight, were stacked clay pots, full of soil and bursting with green things. Auro had now taken to bringing Alexios small potted plants whenever he came to call, such that Alexios's chambers were slowly transforming into a miniature jungle. It soothed him, gave him courage, made him feel like his world and Auro's world weren't so different.

He made his way down to the royal stables with Leofric in tow. After angering and embarrassing his parents yesterday, he knew he should make every effort not to be late today. He brushed down and saddled Xanthos, who seemed a bit irritated to be awoken so early, but quieted soon enough when Alexios offered him a carrot. Alexios stood patiently, holding his reins and waiting for his father.

The King and Queen arrived shortly after the sun. The stable hands had their preferred mounts all ready for them, and a squadron of guardsmen met the royal party as they made their way from the stables to the villa's southern gates.

Alexios's family maintained a well-appointed domus in the city, usually reserved for visiting family or other guests who had to travel far for matters of state, or social engagements. In this instance, it had been prepared for Queen Petillia and her entourage to stay in advance of the equinox festival. The night of the feast, they would stay in the guest apartments on the second floor of the royal villa, with Alexios's intended. He winced at the thought.

They met Queen Petillia and the Lord Praetor in the dining hall of the domus. Alexios bowed deeply before the Queen, and Alexios's mother offered her a kiss on both cheeks, as if they were long-lost sisters.

Alexios's father gave a curt nod to Janus, the Praetor, and Queen Petillia's consort. Thanks to Gaius, Alexios had collected a fair amount of gossip about him. His father hated the man, called him grasping and greedy. Gaius had told Alexios he was half-mad, too, but Alexios wasn't certain he believed that. Gaius based this claim on Janus's interest in the arcane arts, but Alexios's mother had books on the same subject, and she was as sane as anyone. Janus seemed alright to Alexios, all told, if a bit obsequious. Alexios knew for a fact he was low born, and was vying desperately for Queen Petillia's hand in marriage. It was rumored that she told him she would not accept any suitors until her daughter was wed.

Queen Petillia was younger than Alexios's mother by at least a decade. She had wed the late King of Neossós at a tender age, and Alexios knew she still hoped to bear more children by a new husband. She had appointed Janus, an unknown commoner, to the position of Praetor, and apparently he had helped her a great deal in ruling the kingdom by her side. "It is Janus you must impress," Alexios's mother told him on the ride into the city. "Her Grace will not approve any match unless it has the Lord Praetor's seal of approval."

First, they took Her Grace and the Lord Praetor on a tour

of the city, and Alexios took the chance to observe them. Though Alexios knew his parents felt deeply for one another, this Neossan Queen and her consort behaved as newlyweds, near giddy in their shows of affection to one another. Queen Petillia showered Janus with gifts, and after stopping in the fourth tabernae in the High Market, Alexios's mother told him it would be a show of gallantry to purchase a courting gift for the Princess. He ignored the advice until one jeweler's display caught his eye—but it was not the Princess's throat he pictured when looking at the necklace. In a fit of boldness, Alexios bought the necklace, wrapping it in silk and imagining Auro's face when he gave it to him later. He did not bother to be secretive about the purchase—if they assumed it was for his betrothed, well. That was their mistake, wasn't it?

The true purpose of today's social outing was to begin negotiations for the betrothal contract. Technically, Alexios did not even have to be present. Customarily, the king and queen of a nation would do all of the negotiating on their heir's behalf, and then the treaties would be brought before the treasury, the leaders of the army, and the consuls to be approved before a marriage pact could be sealed. In fact, his parents had tried to convince him he could leave once the extravagant luncheon had been cleared away, but he was determined to remain.

The meal went on forever, or at least, that's how it seemed to Alexios, until at last, Janus pulled out some stacks of parchment and legers. Queen Petillia seemed more interested in the selection of wines available, and to be frank, Alexios was tempted to join her at the sideboard, because for the most part, the next two hours were his mother and Janus discussing the territory lines between their adjoining kingdoms down to the square inch, and the possibility of marrying a few of Neossós's lesser nobles to unwed Papian consuls to form new houses.

Alexios could not help the way his mind began to wander when he heard Janus mention the substantial new vein of marble they had unearthed in Neossós. He perked up, leaning forward onto his elbows to listen.

"We are landlocked," said Janus. "Moving vast quantities of stone over land is expensive, slow, and difficult."

"Indeed, it is," said Nelios carefully.

Janus spread a map over the table. "If we could ship marble from the port in Papia City, it would be more advantageous."

"When foreign kingdoms move commerce into our port, they pay a tariff," said Queen Clio at once.

"Yes," said Janus, "and that's what I wish to discuss. The tariff is thirty percent—with our houses joined, I think perhaps the kingdom of Neossós should be able to use your port without paying the tariff."

King Nelios narrowed his eyes. "It is not your house yet, my Lord."

Janus sighed. "No, not yet." He took Queen Petillia's hand. "But Her Grace has authorized me to make all negotiations on behalf of Neossós. So for all intents and purposes..."

"We need stone for our roads," Alexios blurted.

The four of them turned to look at him.

Alexios felt his cheeks heat, but he didn't back down. "I believe we could negotiate use of the port, so long as a portion of the marble harvested from the quarries can be used to better the roads in the kingdom."

Janus stroked his neat beard. "Both kingdoms."

"That sounds fair," said Alexios. Before his parents could seize the reins of the negotiation, he continued. "I think for the first five years following the union, fifty percent of the stone should go to rebuilding roads. Half of that quantity for us, and half for Neossós."

"Forty-to-sixty," Janus countered. "And for three years."

"And then forty percent of the total stone for the next two."

Janus sighed. "Deal. You drive a hard bargain, Prince Alexios."

Alexios flushed with pride, and he caught his parents' eyes across the table. They looked surprised, but pleased with his involvement in the negotiations. Queen Clio called for a toast to celebrate the successful negotiations. Next, the official treaties would be reviewed by both royal families, signed and ratified by the other officials of both governments.

Pleased, Alexios was about to excuse himself so he could return home in time for his liaison with Auro, when the hammer fell.

"We propose a betrothal period of six months," said Queen Petillia.

Alexios blanched and took a hasty gulp from his wineglass to cover his displeasure. Six months? He had hoped for at least a year before...his thoughts went to Auro, and it was already on his tongue to find a way to push off the date, when Janus spoke up once again.

"To celebrate the union, we would grant Papia one hundred percent of the marble from our new quarry for the duration of the betrothal period, so that Prince Alexios can begin his work on the roads immediately."

"That is very generous," said Queen Clio, with a hard, pointed look at Alexios.

"Yes," Alexios said, clearing his throat around the lump that had formed there. "Generous."

They all stared expectantly at him, and Alexios realized it was for him to agree or disagree. He felt suddenly as though he was falling, the bottom dropping out of his stomach.

"Alexios?" prodded his mother.

Perhaps he hit the bottom of wherever he had been falling

—because a hollow feeling took root in his chest. "Yes," he said blandly. "A six-month betrothal will be perfect."

"Excellent!" said Queen Petillia, and Alexios's mother beamed at him. "Dafina will be overjoyed when she arrives. She has been so excited to meet you, Your Highness."

Alexios's smile felt so brittle he was afraid his entire face would shatter. "I cannot wait to make her acquaintance, as well."

The rest of the evening transformed into a celebration of sorts, and Alexios passed through it as if in a fog. *Six months?* Of course, Auro would already have returned to slumber by then...Auro! The moon was well high up in the sky and Alexios realized he was beyond late for their date. He stared helplessly out between the columns of the portico onto the moonlit street. There was no way he'd be able to get back to the villa in time to watch the night flower blooming. He'd probably already missed it.

He would much rather be back at the villa with Auro than here with his future in-laws, or better yet, back in the forest with no one but the trees and their spirits around them. The warm glow of the fire inside the dining hall illuminated the ground at his feet, and he heard his father calling his name.

It was just dawn when they returned to the villa. Alexios lingered with Xanthos in the stables, his parents entrusting their mounts to the staff as they headed inside to bed. Once they were gone, Alexios walked slowly up to the stairs, and then hesitated, looking out into the darkness toward the gardens.

"Your Highness?" said Leofric gently.

"A moment," said Alexios. "I need to..." he trailed away, but Leofric didn't raise further question as Alexios walked down the gravel path toward the greenhouse. He simply followed silently behind.

Alexios unlatched the door and entered.

"I'll be just here, Your Highness."

Alexios smiled briefly and went inside. He walked through the chambers, and under the moonlight, the green leaves and vines shone black and sinister. When he reached the alcove of the enormous corpse flower, he was greeted with a bloom as tall as a man that had already begun to wither. The mantle of the flower wilted and drooped, and its massive central spike wrinkled like a raisin. The air in the greenhouse, though warm and moist, suddenly felt dank and uninviting. Alexios spun on his heel, searching the strange, overgrown shadows.

Auro was nowhere to be seen.

Twelve

Auro knew that Alexios was to be wed. He knew it.

He understood the way things worked. Auro had been a prince, too, centuries ago. Had he and his brothers not fallen to ruin, toppling their entire bloodline with them, he might have one day shared Alexios's fate—a marriage, children. A throne.

As such, Auro knew that anything he and Alexios might share would always be of the shadows. Knowing that did not make the realities sting any less, however. Sleep came only with difficulty, that night.

In the morning, Auro returned to the villa, his thoughts running darkly through his mind. He was furious with himself, humiliated at being left alone all night, waiting with the romantic supper he'd gathered completely untouched. His head was a tangle of jealousy, of anger, of a few things he didn't even have a name for—all unpleasant. As such, he didn't hear the approach of quick, hard footsteps until they were almost upon him. "You!"

He startled, turning, to face the villa's chief of staff, a woman named Melia. "Yes, my Lady?"

"Come," she snapped. "Less chirping, more working."

"But I don't—"

"Follow me."

Auro did not work for Melia, but her tone was one that allowed for no argument. Warily, Auro followed her inside. The royal villa was bustling with activity, with more people scuttling about than Auro had yet seen. Alexios had told Auro that the spring equinox fast approached and Auro had assumed that meant a feast. But it seemed the royal family of Papia was attempting to outdo any other celebration that had preceded this one.

"We are understaffed in here," said Melia. "All hands are needed. Do you sew?"

"Do I—what?"

"Do you *sew*?"

"I—"

"Oh, for fuck's sake," she said, rolling her eyes, and Auro had never felt so entirely useless in all the long centuries of his life. "Fine. Never mind. Here." She spun him toward the throne room, shoved a horsehair brush into his hands, and pointed him to a bucket of water. "Scrub."

He looked around, clutching the brush to his chest. "Scrub what?"

She stared at him as if he were a fool. "*Everything!*"

He was still standing there gaping as she stalked off.

It wasn't as though Auro had never worked before. In fact, for the last four centuries, all he'd *done* was work. It was just that his work was very different from this particular type of labor. Hours passed with Auro on his hands and knees, scrubbing the floor with everything he had. He rocked back to sit upon his heels, wiping his brow with the back of one hand. His shoulders ached, and his hands stung. He looked at his palms, surprised to see them cracked and blistered.

"Auro?"

He looked up at the sound of his name, and unlike the sharp snarl of Melia's voice, Prince Alexios's greeting was almost musical. The rest of the servants stopped their work, each dropping to one knee as Alexios strode into the room. "As you were," he said. Then he paused. "Or rather, go eat. It is past time for midday meal. Eat, and rest," he commanded. "Auro, remain."

The staff scurried out, murmuring thanks. Alexios stooped to help Auro to his feet. "What are you doing in here?" He asked.

Auro winced, knowing his knees would stand bruised from his morning spent scouring the floor. "My expertise was required in here this morning, apparently."

"Oh?"

"Apparently, when a certain prince organizes a feast, the entire villa must sparkle."

Alexios groaned. "This ridiculous feast will be my undoing," he said darkly.

"And mine," said Auro, bemoaning the pain in his palms.

"Your hands are far too soft for such work."

Auro cocked his head. "I cannot tell if that is insult or flattery."

The grin upon Alexios's sun-kissed face was a crooked one. His smiles usually brought Auro nothing but warmth, but today, it only served to rekindle the anger in Auro's chest. "Perhaps a bit of both. Come."

Auro followed Alexios through the villa, up to his apartments, trying to find the words to tell Alexios how he was feeling. To his annoyance, basking in the warmth of Alexios's presence had the anger siphoning away, like water swirling down a drain. Auro waited, perched on the edge of Alexios's bed while he gathered some soft linen strips from his bathing chambers. He knelt before Auro and gently cleaned the blisters on his palms and wrapped them. "There," said Alexios.

"Someone should have forewarned me about the dangers of scrubbing."

"Yes," said Alexios. "The pages of history are full of harrowing tales of bristles and soap."

Auro laughed, but the sound felt brittle and forced.

This was not lost on Alexios, who turned sharply to face Auro. "Auro…" he started.

Auro shrugged one shoulder, pulling his hands free of Alexios's grasp.

"I am truly sorry about yesterday," Alexios said earnestly. "I would have rather spent the evening with you, but my parents—"

"It doesn't matter," Auro said, sharper than he'd meant to.

"It matters a great deal," said Alexios. "I didn't mean to leave you waiting. I feel truly awful."

"It's alright," said Auro.

"It's not alright," said Alexios fiercely. "I know we can't watch the flower blooming again but…"

"But what?"

Alexios blushed. "I got you a gift," he said. Alexios pulled something from the satchel at his hip, wrapped in a scrap of crimson silk. "Here."

With trembling fingers, Auro untied the ribbon of the parcel and unfolded the wrappings. Resting inside was a shining, dainty chain of rose gold, with tiny matching flowers set with pearls. "*Oh,*" Auro breathed. He lifted the necklace, holding it up to catch the light of the afternoon sun.

"Do you like it?"

"It's beautiful," said Auro.

"Here," said Alexios, gesturing.

Auro turned his back and Alexios wrapped the chain around his neck, sweeping the curls from his nape to do up the clasp. Alexios's fingers were so warm against his skin, in stark contrast to the cool metal of the chain.

"I thought of you immediately, when I saw it," Alexios said. He leaned forward and whispered in Auro's ear. "And *only* of you."

Auro smiled, relenting. "Alright," he said, fingering the chain about his neck. He caught Alexios staring at him out of the corner of his eye. "Is something else on your mind?"

"Well," said Alexios, looking a bit nervous. He took Auro's hand. "As you know, the festival for the equinox fast approaches."

"Indeed," Auro replied, gesturing with his bandaged hands. "What of it?"

"I would have you there," Alexios said in a rush.

"Pardon?" Auro was certain he must have misheard.

"I know it would be difficult..."

"More like impossible," said Auro, yanking his hand back. "How would I attend? Only the nobles and foreign royals have gained invitation."

"You are far nobler than any of them," said Alexios earnestly.

Auro sighed. "It is kind of you to say so, but be serious, Alexios. I doubt my name is on the guest list, nor any other royals who should be four centuries in the grave."

"Perhaps you could..." he trailed away. "Serve? Pour drinks? Based upon what happened today I am certain Melia would take your help in a heartbeat."

Auro took a deep, steadying breath. "No."

"What?"

"Alexios...there are to be *hundreds* at this feast." Auro's voice had dropped to a whisper. He wasn't even *in* the crowd and the feeling of panic already clawed its way up the back of his throat.

"You came to the city with me," Alexios pleaded.

"I know, but the market was under the open air, not packed into the throne room."

It broke Auro's heart to see Alexios so crestfallen, but the terror in him ran deep as bones, and the last thing he wished was to humiliate Alexios by breaking down in such a crowd.

"It is important to me, Auro," said Alexios.

"We would not be able to attend the party together, or be seen together, either."

"I know, but—"

Auro sighed. "Alexios, what are we doing?"

"What do you mean?"

Auro scrutinized his bandages, refusing to look Alexios in the eye, and shrugged one shoulder. He struggled to find the words, so out of his depth with the feeling in his chest. Auro had been alive for four hundred and nineteen years and he could honestly say he had never felt like this. "Never mind."

Alexios put his fingers beneath Auro's chin, forcing him to meet his gaze. "No," said Alexios. "Speak."

"I just..." Auro sighed. "I don't think I'm meant to be doing this."

"Doing what?"

"Having..." Auro's throat closed, and any more words refused to leave it, but Alexios seemed to understand.

"Auro, I don't think you're meant to be unhappy forever." He cupped Auro's jaw with his off hand. "That's just too cruel."

"The world is a fairly cruel place, I've found," said Auro quietly.

Alexios's gaze hardened, but he did not release his hold on Auro's face. "You were willing to wait all night alone in a greenhouse for a glimpse of a flower that only blooms for one night," he said tentatively.

"So?"

"So..." Alexios brushed his thumb over Auro's cheek, and his eyes fell to his lips. "Perhaps a thing can still be of worth, can still be worth celebrating, even if it's temporary."

"But—"

Alexios leaned in and brushed his lips to Auro's, heat sparking between them like a struck flint. It lasted for only the span of a startled heartbeat before Alexios drew away. "I would rather have you for a season than not at all," Alexios said.

Auro was so startled he couldn't form a reply. He had never been kissed before. Ever.

"I would love for you to attend the feast," said Alexios. "But if you don't want to, I understand."

~

Alexios considered pretending to be ill.

The idea of this feast turned his stomach, anyway, so it wouldn't truly be a lie. Add to that his quarrel with Auro, well. Alexios stood in his father's dressing chamber, being fussed over by the King's personal valet. The King, already freshly shaved, garbed, and powdered, stood with his arms crossed, looking on. The accepted dress for the equinox festival was far more lavish than an average formal gathering, and elaborate costumes were expected. The King stood in robes of midnight blue, heavily embroidered with silver, and a sheer silvery fringed toga wrapped up and over his shoulder, draped in the crook of his elbow like he had an armful of starlight.

"Alexios, please."

"Please what?"

"This is a celebration," said the King, "not a trip to the gallows."

"I know that," said Alexios, lifting one arm, allowing his father's valet to wrap the fabric of his toga up and over his own shoulder. It was a heavy, cumbersome thing, and garish, woven of cloth-of-gold, to match the golden powder dusting his chest, arms, and cheeks. The theme of the feast was to celebrate the arrival spring—with flamboyant dress, masks, and all manner of things. Alexios found it rather gaudy. Dressing himself as if he were glorious sun was *not* subtle, but his mother had insisted.

"Then why are you making that face?"

"What face?"

"The face like I've just informed you that you've been sentenced to death."

Alexios forced a smile, though perhaps it was more of a grimace. "How's this?" he gritted out through clenched jaw and bared fang.

A cough drew both their attention, and Alexios thought he just might have caught the ever-stoic Leofric struggling to conceal a laugh. The King let it pass, however, his frustration focused entirely on his son. "Honestly, Alexios. I had thought you were coming around to the idea of marriage. This will be your first chance to debut Princess Dafina to our people as your intended bride."

With what he hoped was a ball-shriveling stare at his father, Alexios said, "Debut her? As if she were a horse, or a painting?"

King Nelios sighed, and Alexios felt a twinge of guilt—a small one, but still. It was hardly his father's fault personally that the world worked the way it did. However, he wasn't about to make it easy for him. Alexios had only just begun to explore his relationship with Auro, and he was determined to enjoy what little time they had left before Auro returned to his cursed slumber—and apparently, Auro needed plenty of convincing. Memories of their brief kiss had kept him awake at night, along with the dazed, shocked look on Auro's face in the wake of it. He desperately wished Auro would be brave enough to attend the feast, but his hopes were not high.

"Alexios, you are so dramatic."

"Your Grace." A serving man entered the room with a

deep bow. "Apologies, but Her Majesty the Queen desires a word."

King Nelios spared a final glance toward Alexios. "I will see you at the party," he said. "And please, try not to look so grim."

Alexios watched his father go, a leaden feeling deep in his gut. He hadn't spoken to Auro since their quarrel a few days ago. In fact, Auro had not returned to the villa since then. Alexios had been far too busy with final arrangements for the party to go chasing after him—even if he could convince Leofric it was a good idea to go traipsing alone through the forest.

The feast sprawled through the entire floor of the royal villa, an overwhelming assault on the senses. Alexios had to admit, he had truly outdone himself, and grudgingly, he thought that had he been attending such an event under different circumstances, he may have found the effect rather enchanting.

Flowers, some real, others cunningly wrought from paper and cloth, covered near every surface, and the walls hung with silken banners, translucent curtains that billowed lazily in the breeze that flowed in from the doors, flung wide open to the night. The shallow pools in the atrium had been filled with fresh, clean water and flickering votives floated on tiny wooden boats, the light reflecting off the water, glittering. Incense burned, and a heady, fragrant smoke filled the room with just enough fog for it to seem otherworldly, and more candles than Alexios could count shone from the wall sconces and winking at him from every surface. Costumed dancers stepped carefully through the pools, wearing lacquer masks and sheer white robes that clung suggestively to their bodies as the water splashed around them.

Musicians played in every corner, and as Alexios walked through the crowd, the melodies blended and faded into one another, echoing strangely off the marble walls. Alexios selected a flute of chilled plum wine from a silver tray, and it was not his first.

Alexios had a weakness for sweet things, and the party was well-stocked with such. Since he'd planned the menu himself, all of his favorite sweet sugary delicacies were on offer. Many more had plainly been brought by guests along with their lavish gifts to glean his favor. Though Alexios would normally have happily gorged himself on all his favorite treats, the notion irritated him. To Alexios, they were not a show of thought or of care, but posturing. Who knew the young Crown Prince best? Who most deserved his favor? An absolute farce—like the display of honeyed dates, five different flavors and mixes of spices, to please the Princess, upon whom Alexios still had not even laid eyes.

Speaking of sweet things, Alexios thought of Auro. He felt guilty and disappointed in equal measure after their conversation just a few days previous, and he couldn't help but hope to see Auro amongst the staff offering trays of food and drink, squinting at their eyes behind their masks, hoping for a flash of jewel-green, but he had thus far been disappointed.

The royal herald's voice boomed above the din, announcing every new prominent arrival. As the host, Alexios had been here from the start, greeting guests and speaking with Papian nobles. He was already exhausted.

Alexios reclined against a pillar, sipping his wine, listening to one of the nearby musicians play. Hadrian, he was called, a singer of some renown. Alexios's mother had a soft spot for the man's dulcet crooning. However, the song he now sang was a sad one. The man plucked his lyre with clever fingers, his deep voice singing of things lost, a lover cold, indifferent, ice and stone. The lyrics provoked an eerie sort of melancholy, at great odds with the revelry all around, as if his words and notes held power to chill the very room. The song's grief hung heavily on Alexios—though perhaps that was merely his own projection. He wished to leave the hall, the man's mournful voice, the entire party far behind. Since he was certain his parents would have his hide if he did, he at least moved away from the place where Hadrian played.

"May I present, the esteemed consul, Festus Ursus, and his son, Gaius!"

Alexios perked up, thinking at last there would be someone pleasant to talk to, and moved through the crowd to greet Gaius and his father.

"Your Royal Highness," said Festus formally, with a bow to Alexios.

"Welcome, Consul," said Alexios. "You honor us with your presence."

"The honor is ours, Your Highness," said Festus. "Now, where might I find your royal father?"

"I believe His Grace is over by the buffet," said Alexios, who had been tracking his parents' movements carefully, so that he could avoid them as much as possible. "He's discussing the upcoming games with the Aedile."

"Ah, excellent," said Festus. "If you'll excuse me, Your Highness."

With his father gone, Gaius visibly relaxed. "You've truly outdone yourself with this party, Alexios."

Alexios rolled his eyes. "Yes, I think I shall go down in Papia's history as its most prestigious event planner."

"A coveted laurel," said Gaius seriously, but his eyes twinkled with mischief. Gaius had dressed in a costume made almost entirely of fur, complete with the head of a bear serving as the hood of his cloak. He was big and broad, and the outfit made him seem as if he truly *were* a bear. Alexios peered around behind him. "Where is your sister?"

It was Gaius's turn to roll his eyes. His twin, Gaia, and he did not get along. "The official reason for her absence is a migraine," he said. "The real reason is that she has a nasty pimple on her forehead and was too embarrassed to leave the domus. But you did not hear that from me."

Alexios laughed, in spite of himself. He was glad Gaius was here, at any rate. Gaius surveyed the crowd with an appraising eye. "There are a lot of women here," Gaius remarked.

Alexios looked around and realized he was right. "Huh," he said, trying to sound as if the number of female guests interested him, and not quite managing it.

"I think many of my peers are hoping to sway your royal parents away from marrying you off to a foreign princess."

"Well, they are likely to be disappointed," he said before he could stop himself. "My parents are quite set on this match."

"Your parents," Gaius echoed. "But not you?"

Alexios tripped over his response, but luckily, the herald's voice rang out, calling the guests' attention to the entrance to the throne room. "Her Grace, Queen Petillia Hostus Neox, of Neossós," the herald called, "And her daughter, Her Royal Highness, Princess Dafina Hostus Neox, of Neossós."

Alexios looked up and laid eyes on his intended bride for the very first time.

Gaius cursed under his breath. "Some princes have all the luck."

Dafina swept elegantly into the throne room, her costume bloodred, drawing every eye. She was tall and willowy, with shining dark hair pulled back into a severe braid that accentuated the fine features of her face, the small pointed nose, pronounced cheekbones, the slender neck. Alexios mentally compared her living flesh to the stone head just upstairs in his apartments. Yes, it was plainly the same woman, and the stone had not exaggerated her beauty. "Yes," said Alexios thinly. "What luck."

Gaius cast Alexios a peculiar look, but before he could

open his mouth, Alexios spun on his heel and turned away. He needed to collect himself, to prepare to charm this girl he had no desire to charm, to convince her and his parents and everyone here that he was the proper sort of prince. All at once, Alexios couldn't face it.

Alexios knew he couldn't hide forever, but if he didn't get at least a few moments to himself he would surely lose his mind. He fled to the library, of all places, knowing his mother would have her precious books carefully guarded with so many strangers present for the feast. As he expected, there were men flanking the door, but they knew Alexios and let him inside immediately.

Alexios had just prepared to let out an enormous sigh when he realized he was not alone. "Your Royal Highness," said a voice, startled.

Alexios turned to the sound to see Praetor Janus standing beside the worktable, a stack of books spread out before him. "My Lord?"

"Apologies," he said, smiling. "I have been desperate to get a look at your mother's collection." Janus wore a tunic dyed black, and a draping toga of shining black raven's feathers. Completing the ensemble was a black neckpiece, cunningly wrought in the shape of a beak. It partially obscured the lower half of his face.

"Ah," said Alexios. "A peculiar time to do so, if you don't mind my saying."

Janus laughed lightly. "I know, but I would never have forgiven myself if I missed my chance. I am something of a collector, myself."

"I had heard that," said Alexios.

"Yes," said Janus. "I'm making a list of titles your mother has, and I hope to send scribes along to make copies for my own collection, if Her Grace would be so obliged as to allow it."

"I'm certain she would," said Alexios, who could not shake the feeling that Janus was using this thin pretext to avoid the feast—though, Alexios could hardly fault him for that, since he was doing the same thing.

Janus closed the book he'd been perusing and gave Alexios a long, searching look. "Is everything alright, Your Highness?"

"Oh yes," said Alexios airily. "I just needed a quiet moment to gather my thoughts."

"Ah," said Janus.

Alexios frowned. "What?"

"You are nervous, meeting my stepdaughter." It was not a question.

Alexios could have pointed out that Dafina was not his stepdaughter yet, but he didn't. He pretended to adjust the drape of his heavy toga, to buy himself a moment to form a reply. "A bit," he said. It wasn't truly a lie. He *was* nervous.

"Am I to understand the prospect of marriage does not thrill you, Your Highness?"

Panicked, Alexios opened his mouth to spew any number of excuses, but Janus cut him off before he could.

"I understand," he said. "But a political marriage *can* be a joyous one."

"Perhaps," said Alexios, thinking of his parents. Before he could stop himself, he added, "With the right partner."

"Yes," said Janus, frowning a bit. "With the right partner."

They stared at each other, and Alexios had the distinct feeling Janus was seeing him for the first time, and he did not like it. "I best get back to the party," said Alexios. "Her Highness will be wondering where I've gotten to, I'm certain."

Alexios wasn't entirely sure how to feel about his peculiar interaction with Janus, so he decided to file it away in his mind for later examination. Instead, he decided to face the problem at hand, the Princess waiting for him in the throne room below.

Steeling himself, Alexios rejoined the throngs of guests, meandering his way as slowly through the crowd as he dared, but still making his way toward the small cluster of people that included Princess Dafina, her mother, and Alexios's parents. Apparently, he wasn't moving fast enough. "Alexios!"

He hastened over. "Father," said Alexios, with a respectful bow. "Mother."

"Joyous equinox, Prince Alexios," said Queen Petillia. "This celebration is truly a feast for the senses."

Alexios bowed and kissed her hand. "Gratitude," he said politely.

"May I have the honor of presenting my daughter," said Queen Petillia. "Dafina?"

Dafina, who had been standing off to the side, frowning down into her wineglass, allowed herself to be summoned to her mother's side. "Honored to meet you, Princess," said Alexios. He bowed and kissed her hand as well.

Dafina was even lovelier up close, with severe dark brows, icy blue eyes. Her skin was pale, paler even than Auro's. To Alexios, her eyes appeared to have a shadow behind them, but they were clear and intelligent, and utterly disinterested in him, he knew at a glance.

"And may I have the...pleasure of introducing King Cletus of Órnio," said Alexios's father, as though he had a foul taste in his mouth.

Alexios's immediate impression of King Cletus was that of a wolf, battle-hardened and wary. He reminded Alexios of his father, though in actuality the two looked nothing alike—it was more in their bearing, the way they carried themselves. Both were soldier-kings.

"Aye," said Cletus, with far less formality. "Blessings."

"Gratitude, Your Grace," said Alexios with a deep bow. He knew the man had only been invited for the sake of appearances. He could see his mother's hand in this—she had been working hard to convince his father to open trading negotiations with Órnio, but it was a tough sell, even for her. Though Alexios's father now ruled as King of Papia, he had commanded the Sokolian army for many years as imperator, and the border skirmishes between Sokol and King Cletus's kingdom of Órnio went back generations, festering bad blood and claiming thousands of lives.

Alexios stood by Dafina, scanning the crowd and pretending to listen as the kings and queens made polite-sounding, passive-aggressive chatter with one another.

"Come," said Dafina suddenly, looping her arm through the crook of Alexios's elbow. He startled, surprised by her bold touch. "Escort me to the refreshments."

Alexios allowed himself to be steered toward the sprawling, elaborate buffet. With the noise in the cavernous room, they were well out of earshot of their parents. Dafina dropped his arm suddenly, as if she could not bear to touch him one second longer than she had to. "There," she said, under her breath. "Now, you select one of these and offer it to me."

"Pardon?"

"Come, they're still watching," Dafina hissed, adjusting the bangles on her slender wrists. For the event, she had dressed from head to toe in a deep, bloodred stola with matching jewels on her fingers, at her throat, and dangling from her ears. The palla wrapped around her shoulder and over her hair seemed to be made entirely of crimson roses. It set off her dark hair and pale skin magnificently, Alexios had to admit.

Utterly confused, Alexios did as she said, offering her a bite of a tiny cake, one of his favorites. Dafina took a dainty bite, chewing behind her hand, before laughing merrily and touching Alexios's arm as if he'd just said something hilarious. "Alright," she said through her teeth before turning aside to spit the bite of cake into a napkin. "They've turned away."

Alexios's eye followed her hand, curled to conceal the scrap of sweet.

"Close your mouth," she said, before shooting him a calculating look. "Based upon your reputation, I would have thought you would be better at this."

Alexios was lost. "At...?"

Her eyes darted meaningfully to where her mother and Alexios's father stood, still deep in conversation. It was obvious they were still trying to watch what transpired between himself and the Princess.

"I hear you have purchased a gift for me," she said.

Alexios blushed, regretting his impulse to flaunt his purchase for Auro. "Um," he started.

Dafina simply waved him off. "No matter," she said. "Men have horrid taste in jewels."

But Alexios barely heard her; a flash of pink had caught his eye from across the room.

Auro had arrived.

When Alexios had begged Auro to attend the feast, he'd assumed he would have kept his hair dark, maintaining a low profile, trying not to be noticed in the crowds of nobles.

Auro had not done this.

He stood at the entrance to the throne room, his head held high and regal as any noble in the room, his hair washed clear of dye, shining pink with a crown of matching peonies resting on his head. Alexios had consumed enough wine that his first impression was that Auro wore a cloud of mist. In actuality, it appeared to be a tunic made of dozens of layers of the floatiest, sheerest fabric Alexios had ever seen, stirred by every errant breeze in the airy throne room, but layered so many wisps on top of one another that one couldn't *truly* see through it. At least, not at the distance Alexios found himself. He was *quite* curious how opaque it would be up close. The toga Auro had draped over the tunic was covered with peonies, to match his crown, and he shimmered as he walked past every candle and torch, glowing with a pale, silvery light.

"...Prince Alexios?"

"Hmm?"

"I said, 'lean in toward my ear,' and we can walk outside in the garden."

Alexios did as he was bid, pretending like he was whispering to the Princess while still trying to watch Auro as he floated through the groups of guests. He made no move to find Alexios in the crowd but seemed to glide as he approached and greeted other partygoers, serene and smiling as if he belonged among them. Alexios had no idea what he was saying to them, what story he may have concocted, but whatever he said to them appeared to be working. "Ouch!"

"Will you move?" Dafina had actually elbowed him in the ribs.

"What?"

"*Move,*" she said. "Outside."

Alexios tore his eyes away from Auro, but not before Dafina saw where he was looking.

"That's certainly a bold color," said Dafina. "I have a palla dyed a pink like that, but it's so pale it makes me look like a corpse. Come."

She led Alexios past a trio of flutists, through the wide doors into the blessedly cool night air. He was happy to be outside, at any rate, despite the strange behavior of the woman beside him.

Outside, the air was fresh and crisp. The party spilled out onto the wide flagstone terrace that abutted the gardens, but to a far less strangling degree. Alexios had seen it decorated and lit with torches, and the servers still strayed out here with trays of refreshments. He selected another glass of wine and offered one to Dafina. She declined, politely, albeit with a wrinkle of her tiny nose.

Alexios decided she was fussy, too picky.

"This is not the first time my mother has attempted to foist a match upon me," she said, drawing Alexios away under the pretext of examining a topiary. "I have posed for more betrothal busts than I can count. Unfortunately for us both, I feel my mother will not be deterred this time. Her consort, Janus, knows he has no chance of wedding her if I remain unwed, so he is eager to force the issue as well."

"Have they told you they wish us to wed in six months?" Alexios asked her.

"They had that timeline in mind before they'd even left Neossós."

Alexios could not hold in a groan. He should have known. "I had hoped for some time, to breathe," he said ruefully.

"Then you're a fool," said Dafina flatly. "You can never let your guard down where such things are concerned." Her hand fell to her stomach and she grimaced. "This wretched rich food, and the travel, upsets my digestion. I think if we speak for a while more my mother will allow me to retire." After a pause, wherein she looked Alexios over from head to toe. *Fussy, picky, and a snob,* he decided, comfortable now in disliking her.

She stared out over the darkened gardens, Alexios close beside her, so it might seem that they were huddled in private conversation, when in actuality, they were huddled in strained silence.

"I think that will suffice, for now," said Dafina abruptly. "Place lips to cheek, and I shall retire before I vomit this heavy fare all over the flagstones."

Alexios watched her curiously as she threaded her way back through the crowd and disappeared.

Thirteen

Auro could not recall the last time he had been so taken with nerves.

His life had much the same for so long, every change in routine seemed monumental, and since he'd first seen Alexios unconscious on the forest floor, there'd been nothing *but* changes. Auro tried to calm his mounting anxieties. This feast should be no different than the ones Auro had attended for years. In fact, it should be no different to the ones he spied on immediately after he had been cursed. In the years directly following Ozias's death, Auro had been so desperately lonely he would have done anything to taste the world from which he had been banished. He'd spied on spring bacchanals each year upon waking, until the life he had left behind became far too painful to gaze upon, and he gave up the practice.

Alexios had practically begged Auro to attend this gathering, and the look on his face when Auro had refused...

They hadn't spoken in days.

Auro simply *had* to be there. He only had two cycles of the moon with Alexios, and he couldn't let this tarnish their remaining weeks. How could he let his fear spoil the only thing he'd allowed himself to want in four hundred years? Perhaps Auro could never truly have Alexios, but he would be damned if he wasted any more precious time.

Before the feast began, Auro retreated to the woods to prepare himself. Normally, he balked at the idea of the tree spirits attending him as servants. Auro did not often feel like royalty, but tonight he needed the courage. His forest friends were *thrilled* to help him. They bathed Auro, washed and brushed his hair, cleaned his nails, perfumed his skin. The costume of confident nobleman was as important tonight as the clothes he wore.

As they helped him dress, the dryadae teased Auro about the shining golden boy who'd captured his interest so completely. He gently chastised them, but if he added a bit of spider silk to his tunic to give his clothing an iridescent sheen, well. That was his business. He debated adding more of the walnut dye to his hair but decided against it.

The opulent feast was ostensibly to celebrate the spring equinox.

Auro's time.

Long ago, this feast would have been thrown in his honor. How could he let the fear of mortals keep him from celebrating? From being celebrated? Why should he hide his hair when he knew Alexios loved the color? Anytime his courage threatened to falter, Auro brushed his fingers to his lips, recalling the way Alexios's had felt pressed eagerly against them.

However, once Auro approached the front doors to the villa, thrown wide to mingle the sounds of spring evenings with the sounds of human revelry, the heavy air pressed upon him, suffocating, and there were people staring, staring at him, he was certain. He was hardly the most opulently dressed— nor even the only one with hair of an inhuman hue, but he still felt out of place. The decorations and music and smells from the kitchens bombarded Auro. The very walls vibrated with sound as he walked through the interior atrium of the royal villa where the feast was in full swing.

Auro froze in the arched doorway that led to the throne room, the centerpiece of the celebration. Musicians played, their songs echoing discordantly with the sounds of gossiping nobles, and Auro found himself tempted to turn heel and flee back out into the night, where it was cool and dark and quiet.

But no. He could not allow this chance to slip from his grasp, especially after how disappointed Alexios had been, and after the lovely gift Alexios had given him—and all it represented. After their sweet, hesitant kiss had left an unanswered question in its wake. It was a question Auro was determined to answer tonight, so he steeled himself and stepped cautiously into the crowd.

His eyes found Alexios immediately, as if they couldn't help it, every time he turned around. Alexios was festooned in gold, from head to toe, and Auro did not think even the sun could possibly hope to outshine him. A crown of gilded leaves nestled in the waves of his thick hair, but his face was pinched, his smile strained and false. Auro watched sullenly as a beautiful young woman drew him apart from the crowd, laughing as she touched his arm. His stomach dropped, and his hands shook so badly he almost dropped his drink. Auro edged behind a massive urn, watching as Alexios fed the girl a morsel of something from the table, his guts twisting like burning hot snakes.

The next time Alexios disappeared from his line of sight, Auro was determined not to find him straight away, afraid of what he might see. Auro retreated inside himself, allowed his years of social grooming to take over, instincts he'd forgotten he had about how to stand, how to smile. The right words to say to flatter those around him. People engaged him in polite conversation, and he supposed he answered them. He allowed himself to be carried in a drifting eddy of conversation, music, wine, and laughter, until he found himself washed up on the fringes of the party.

His feet had brought him outside, and he stood by an ornamental tree whose branches overhung the terrace: a flowering dogwood Auro had helped by amending its soil and coaxing the branches of nearby trees to grow in a different direction. He had to prune some of the neighboring trees back, too, to allow the dogwood to get enough sun to bloom. Auro touched one of the buds now, thinking how pleased he was to have helped it.

"You know," said a voice behind him. "I've had that tree for four years, and it has never once flowered."

Auro jumped and turned to find himself face to face with Queen Clio, Alexios's mother. He bowed deeply. "Your Grace," he said.

"Auro," she said. She stepped up beside him and examined the tree herself. "You have quite a way with plants."

"You are kind to say so," he said carefully.

"You're far too modest," she said. "Some people have a gift, a true gift, for helping things to grow and flourish." She paused. "My son is different since he met you."

"Oh?" He wasn't sure he understood the connection.

"He's never been so determined to be a part of matters of state. I didn't think he was mature enough to negotiate the tricky waters of a betrothal treaty, but he did well. I was very proud."

"You should be," said Auro, before he could stop himself.

The Queen gave him a knowing look.

"He just wants to be the sort of prince his people need," said Auro. "The sort of prince you and His Grace would be proud of."

"Well, he's certainly becoming one since meeting you."

"You give me far too much credit," Auro stammered. "Perhaps it was the head injury."

The Queen laughed, and Auro couldn't help but smile sheepishly, too. She looped her arm through Auro's, and he startled but did not pull away. Her touch was comforting, nurturing. "Someday soon," she said, "You must tell me all your secrets."

"My—my what?"

"Your gardening secrets," said Clio. "Alexios tells me you leave for the next leg of your journey at the end of spring."

Auro's heart sank. "Yes, that's right."

"Well," said the Queen. "Alexios will be sorry to see you go."

"Yes," said Auro faintly. "I'll be quite sorry to leave."

Alexios was drunk.

Not so drunk as to humiliate himself, or fall down in the wading pools, but certainly drunk enough. He'd watched Auro in the crowd, tracking his movements. Now, Auro stood well to the side of the party, talking to his mother as they both examined a tree in the garden. Since Auro's arrival, he'd spoken not one word to Alexios. It left him feeling surly. But he'd come. That had meaning, did it not?

Although, his neck stood bare of Alexios's gift. Had it been too forward? This thing between them had only just begun to blossom, and perhaps Auro had balked at being claimed in such a brazen way. Or, perhaps, Dafina had been right, and he simply had horrible taste in jewelry.

"Alexios!"

He grimaced. For the second time, his father summoned him, and Alexios made certain to seize a fresh glass of wine before taking his place at his father's elbow. Janus had finally left the library to join the party at Queen Petillia's side.

"I was just telling your father, my daughter, Dafina, is such a lovely girl," said Janus. "Don't you agree, Your Highness?"

Alexios's own frustration seemed matched only by that of King Cletus of Órnio, who openly scoffed at Janus. "She is not your daughter yet, *Praetor.*" Cletus spat out the honorific, dripping with venomous sarcasm.

Janus's eyes flashed cold, narrowed dangerously above the beak of his costume, but his Queen laid a hand on his arm to steady him, giving a tiny shake of her head. "No," said Janus smoothly. "Not yet. But I love her as my own flesh and blood."

After his brief, but illuminating talk with Dafina herself, the claim seemed a bit less sincere.

"And where is your daughter?" King Cletus asked. "I don't see her."

"Travel upsets her constitution," said Queen Petillia primly.

King Cletus scoffed again. He turned to Alexios's father, sizing him up. "You don't want some frail thing for a daughter-in-law, Nelios."

Alexios had to hide his grin. He had no need to stir things up, just get three kings—or would-be kings—together and stand back. Their peacocking would provide enough of an upset. He caught the eye of King Cletus's daughter, Princess Eleni, who looked mortified at her father's behavior.

"My daughter is not *frail,*" said Queen Petillia shrilly. "Though perhaps she is not as...robust as some. She loves to paint and play the harp, and she rides horses just as well as you, Alexios, if you'll forgive a mother's boasting."

"How delightful for her," Alexios snapped. The wine had loosened his tongue and dulled his sense of decorum.

King Nelios's eyes flashed, but Janus and Queen Petillia laughed good-naturedly. "Your son is as blunt of word as you,

Nelios! I am certain that will only endear him to Dafina, who values honesty above all else..."

King Cletus rolled his eyes, a muscle going in his jaw. Alexios knew how he felt.

"They will make a *splendid* match," said King Nelios firmly, with a glare at Alexios.

"Agreed," said Janus, while Queen Petillia nodded earnestly.

"If this is the sort of affair Prince Alexios plans, I do believe I will surrender all preparations for the royal wedding to his discerning eye," said Queen Petillia.

Alexios put on his most gracious smile. "You are too kind, Your Grace. I would be delighted to do so."

That should satisfy them for the moment. Queen Petillia, at least, seemed mollified, and Alexios's father gave a reluctant nod to show he'd done well enough. King Cletus, however, looked livid. It was clear he had no idea how far along the betrothal process had already progressed, dashing his hopes of throwing his own daughter's hat in the ring, so to speak. He turned rudely and strode from the conversation absent any words, Princess Eleni trailing behind him. Alexios caught her eye and saw she looked a bit relieved, unlike her father. A wake of heated whispers followed them as they left the hall.

With King Cletus's rudeness to occupy his father's thoughts, Alexios managed to slip away. He made straight for the corner of the terrace where Auro and his mother stood. "Good evening, Mother," said Alexios.

Auro jumped, but even as he startled, a smile broke over his face, as if he couldn't help it. He dipped his head quickly, putting his face into shadow, but his eyes sparkled.

In fact, all of Auro seemed to sparkle—but that could very well have been the wine.

Alexios knew people watched them, a thing Auro must know as well. "Your Royal Highness," he said, bowing deeply.

His title in Auro's mouth did something to Alexios. It made him hot and squirmy, and he could not tell for sure if he liked it. "Pardon," said Alexios. "I must borrow him for a moment."

"A garden matter to discuss?" asked Queen Clio archly, looking between them.

If Alexios were more sober and less frayed that might worry him, but as such, it didn't. "Yes," he said bluntly. He was out of patience with this party, and everything that came with it. He wished to abscond with Auro and escape the strangling press.

The Queen left them, with a lingering look at her son. Auro accompanied Alexios a bit farther into the garden, outside the ring of candlelight and floating banners. They approached a low marble bench. "What is it?" Auro asked, as soon as they were out of earshot of the Queen.

Alexios shrugged, wrong-footed. "This party. My impending marriage. All of it. You."

"Me?"

"I didn't think you were coming."

"I wasn't—but it was important to you."

"It was. Is." Alexios noticed something hard in Auro's eyes, something he had never seen there before. "What?"

"Was that her?"

Alexios did not need to ask who 'her' was. "Yes."

Auro seemed to chew on that a bit. "She's lovely," he said after a while, taking a step away from Alexios.

"I suppose," Alexios admitted.

They stood in silence for a while, until Alexios said, "We're to marry in six months."

Auro examined his fingernails. "Oh."

"Yes."

"I will be asleep then."

Alexios felt his heart compress in his chest, squeezing, crushing. "You will."

Auro turned to look at him, lips in a hard line, eyes blazing. "I am not asleep now."

"No," Alexios agreed, looking Auro over from head to toe. "You are not."

Auro did not look away this time, as he often did, dipping his head to hide, demurely. He stared at Alexios, waiting.

"I had hoped to spend the whole season with you, Auro," said Alexios.

"Can't you, still?"

Alexios cast a nervous look over his shoulder, toward where his parents stood, slouching as if by doing so he could disappear entirely.

Finally, Auro tutted impatiently. He placed a hand on Alexios's chin, tilting it up into the light cast from the party. "Alexios," he said sternly. "You are the Crown Prince. The heir to this kingdom. Perhaps you must remind them of that."

"What?"

"You told me before that you feel like a child, unable to make your own choices. That will never change if you do not start."

"Start what?"

Auro gave him a fierce look. "Making your own choices. Forging your own path. What can they do? You are the *prince*."

Alexios blinked stupidly, opening and closing his mouth like a fish.

"Do not think overmuch," said Auro. "Just clear your mind and think about what *you want*. What do you want, Alexios?"

Alexios's pulse hammered in his ears. Despite the fact that he had grown up having every whim catered to, no one had ever, *ever* asked him that question. He'd always felt like he "wanted" for nothing, but absent any wants of his own—who was he? Auro's green eyes shone out of his face as he stared at Alexios, piercing. Alexios opened his mouth to blurt that what he wanted most of all was Auro, any way he could get him, but he was momentarily distracted by his mother's high, clear laugh.

He turned toward the sound and saw her standing close with his father. He, Queen Petillia and Janus had joined her on the terrace. King Nelios now stood gazing at Queen Clio fondly, wearing the soft smile he donned for his wife alone. He was a tall man, and he stooped to press a sweet, tender kiss to Queen Clio's cheek.

Alexios realized, watching his parents, *that* was what he wanted—the bold display of casual affection, the love between them obvious to anyone present. He wanted Auro, surely, but he did not want him in secret, in shadows. He wanted him here, twirling to the musicians' songs, eating tiny delicacies from Alexios's hand while they shared a private joke. He wanted to kiss his knuckles where their fingers intertwined, and not care who saw.

Alexios stood, stepping into Auro's space. With trembling fingers, he cupped Auro's cheek. Auro's eyelids fluttered closed, and Alexios leaned in, pausing when he could feel Auro's breath skitter across his cheeks, allowing him the chance to pull away if he desired.

Auro did not pull away. The sounds of the party melted into the background like the hum of insects, and their lips were only a whisper apart when the noise of shattering glass and hissed curses brought reality screaming back. Alexios jerked his head back, heart pounding. He wanted Auro here, or anywhere really—but he couldn't. Not with half the kingdom and his parents looking on—not to mention his future mother-in-law. Auro's brows knit together, and he made a small, disappointed sound, but when his eyes fluttered open, they were full of understanding.

And, unless Alexios was mistaken, heat.

Alexios's mind filled immediately with a deluge of lustful thoughts and images, passing through him as if he stood below a waterfall. He swayed on his feet, struck by the promise in Auro's eyes as they gazed up at him.

"What I want," Alexios whispered, "is to leave this party. With you."

Auro smiled. "As you wish, Your Highness."

Alexios and Auro walked several paces apart, but he still felt as though every eye was upon them as they threaded through the fringes of the crowd at the edges of the throne room. He could feel the stare of his father on the back of his head, but he forced himself not to acknowledge it.

When they reached Alexios's door, he half expected Leofric to follow them inside, but he simply bowed and said, "Your Highness," before taking his place to stand guard outside the doors.

In the dark, quiet air of Alexios's bed chambers, the silence descended upon them like cold water. Alexios froze, twisting his hands over each other, suddenly at a loss of what to do now that he had Auro alone. Without the lavish backdrop of the rest of the feast, its costumed guests, Auro shone like a beacon. His costume suited him, making him look so otherworldly, so divine. Auro deserved to be taken care of, worshipped, and Alexios wished desperately to burn away the thought of everything they could not have—and he had no notion of how to do that.

Luckily for Alexios, the same paralysis had not struck Auro, who crossed the room to collide with Alexios, full force. At the first taste of Auro's mouth, Alexios's nerves vanished— especially when Auro stretched his neck, allowing Alexios's lips to claim the column of his throat. "*Oh,*" he said softly.

"Yes." Alexios encircled Auro in his arms, pressing them together, his cock stiffening beneath his tunic as they clung to one another. "Stay with me tonight," he whispered, resting his forehead against Auro's.

Auro's grin was wicked, his lips kiss-plumped and delightfully slick. "How could I refuse a prince?"

"You couldn't."

Auro fell upon Alexios, ravenous for his touch, tangling his fingers in the wool of Alexios's toga as if he couldn't bear to let him go. Neither of them paid much heed to where they were going, and Alexios felt the small of his back collide with his desk. The wood shuddered as Auro shoved him against it, knocking something heavy off the edge to shatter upon the floor.

Alexios gasped, looking down at the broken pieces of Dafina's face strewn around their feet.

"Oops," said Auro innocently, and Alexios grinned.

He pushed back against Auro, guiding him toward his bed in the center of the room, eager to see Auro garbed in moonlight and nothing else. Auro, it appeared, was of a similar mind. "I would undress you, Your Highness."

"You have to stop calling me that," said Alexios, the title crawling hot and squirmy under his skin.

Auro grabbed two fistfuls of fabric and repeated, "I would undress you...*Alexios.*"

He groaned, his name on Auro's tongue the most erotic thing he'd ever heard. Alexios spread his arms and allowed Auro to unwrap the vast swaths of fabric and undo his belt before kneeling to take off his sandals.

When Auro busied himself with the leather straps, his curls parted, exposing the bare nape of his neck. The wine, the kissing, all of it made him bold. "You do not wear your gift," he said.

Auro did not look up, so focused on his task. His palm on

Alexios's calf scorched as he lifted his foot to remove one sandal, and then the other. "Yes, I do."

Alexios had to windmill his arms a bit to keep from toppling over as he stepped out of his shoes to stand barefoot on the floor. "You—hang on," he said.

When Auro regained his feet, Alexios placed his palms on either side of his delicate neck, feeling for the chain.

"It is not around my neck," Auro said absently.

Alexios had the distinct impression of his mind wiping utterly blank, as if it were a new universe being born. "What."

Auro toed off his own sandals, and Alexios could wait no longer to seize the bottom hem of Auro's tunic and yank it up over his head. When Auro stood naked in the room, Alexios could only gape. The tiny, dainty links of rose gold wrapped about Auro's hips, nestled against the soft flesh of his waist, the flowers and pearls joining together where one end of the chain dangled down into the pink hair around Auro's cock.

"*Fuck*," Alexios swore and tumbled Auro back onto the sleeping couch. He blanketed Auro's body with his own, ignited by the feel of their skin pressed so close together, the heat of Auro's flesh and the softness of him, with one notable exception, pushing hot and insistent against his thigh.

The cold metal of the chain tingled against Alexios's lower abdomen, sending a shiver down his spine as he rained kisses upon Auro's brow, his cheeks, and finally his lips.

"I cannot recall the last time I spent the night in a bed," said Auro suddenly when Alexios drew back for breath.

Alexios stopped in his tracks, shocked. "Pardon?"

"Well," said Auro, "During the spring, I always find myself in the forest. When I sleep, I make my bed in the boughs of a friendly tree, or on the floor of my temple."

Now he thought about it, Alexios wasn't certain what he pictured when he imagined Auro spending his lonely nights every spring. Watching him now, seeing the lovely picture he made here, in Alexios's bed, he felt a pang for how Auro had been living for centuries.

Auro arched his back a bit, blinking up at him, wriggling about on the luxurious cushions beneath his body. The moonlight streaming in illuminated his pale skin, bounced off the chain around his waist, the shine of it drawing Alexios's eye to Auro's groin. "No longer," Alexios vowed. And he meant it. "You deserve only the finest things." He lowered his lips, offering Auro a soft kiss. "You should be laid out in silks and worshipped," he declared.

Perhaps the wine had not entirely left him yet.

Alexios's face reddened, but he was determined not to look away. He might have kept such declarations to himself—but that did not make them untrue—and Auro gazed up at him, eyes hazy, like he quite liked that idea being worshipped a bit. As if absent thought, Auro let his thighs fall open, making a safe cradle for Alexios between them.

The weight of that trust was sobering. For a while, Alexios just *looked.* He loved having permission to feast his eyes, and he intended to gorge himself on the sight of Auro's body. Auro reclined on the cushions, one arm crooked behind his head, the other resting by his side, hand splayed across his belly. Alexios began at the top of Auro's head, examining the shine of his curls, so happy to see them washed of the dull, ugly dye. He wished Auro did not have to hide it, but part of him loved that he was the only one who knew the truth of Auro. His eyes raked over Auro's face, his brow, his flushed cheeks, the hollow below the apple of his throat. Alexios was determined that he should commit every detail of this vision to memory.

Auro's expression was quizzical; perhaps he did not expect Alexios to have this level of restraint once they were abed together. It wasn't restraint, Alexios would have told him, had he asked. He needed this time. When Alexios was certain he would not forget a single eyelash, a single candlelit shadow playing across Auro's skin, he carded a hand through Auro's hair and leaned down for another soft kiss that quickly turned hungry. Alexios let his eyes fall closed and slid his tongue between Auro's lips. A muffled sound escaped where their mouths met.

"Wait," gasped Auro, sitting up. He laid a palm on Alexios's bare chest.

Alexios was pleased to see Auro flushed from navel to hairline, the pupils of his eyes blown wide, his chest heaving.

"I..." Auro gazed down, breaking eye contact. "When I told you it had been a long time since I had been touched...it wasn't the whole truth."

Alexios drew away, puzzled. "Oh?"

"In fact...I have never been touched, like this. I've never done any of this before," he confessed in a whisper.

Alexios blinked. How was that possible? Auro was sweet and beautiful, and a *god*...was it truly possible no one had taken him to bed before?

"Apologies," said Auro, plainly embarrassed. "I never considered taking a lover before I met you."

Alexios surged forward, capturing Auro's mouth in a kiss. When they broke apart for breath, Alexios said, "You have nothing to apologize for."

Auro cupped his cheek. "Are you certain? I assume you expected someone with more...experience."

Alexios turned his head, kissing Auro's palm. "I have never been with anyone, either," he admitted.

"Truly?"

"Truly. In fact, I was nervous about failing to please you."

When Auro kissed him again, he tasted a fresh fire. "Well," said Auro, his voice husky. "Then, why don't we learn together?"

Their next kiss was mostly a clack of teeth through bashful, excited smiles, before Alexios began, timidly at first, to touch Auro. It seemed almost as though it shouldn't be allowed, his laying hands on Auro. It felt brutish in a way. Alexios had never been ashamed of his looks—but compared with Auro's delicate body, the softness of his curves and the creamy smoothness of his skin, Alexios felt big and ungainly, rough, like some sort of clumsy, elbowy oaf.

But the look on Auro's face...

Alexios smiled, his doubts melting like the frost Auro chased away each spring. He retraced the path he'd made with his eyes, teasing his hands through Auro's hair, touching his curls, and Auro preened, closing his eyes with a happy sigh. Alexios explored the dainty features of Auro's face with his fingertips—the bridge of his nose, his eyelids, his round pink cheeks, each touch featherlight, reverent.

Alexios's mouth ran dry, his body taut as bowstring as he moved his hands down Auro's throat to stroke his collarbones. He found so many delights as he touched and explored, like the pale birthmark in the triangular divot between Auro's neck and shoulder, shaped like a cloud.

Auro's hands were small and soft. Alexios brought each of Auro's fingers to his lips and kissed them, and then the tiny bones of his wrists. Auro's chest was mostly hairless, his nipples like two flower petals, until Alexios thumbed over them. Then, they darkened, tightening into buds instead. Auro sucked in a breath, closing his eyes as he arched into Alexios's touch. Smirking, Alexios gave each one a parting pinch, loving the way Auro responded to every pass of his fingertips, his plump lips parted, his breath coming in short pants.

They were both hard, but Alexios made no move to touch Auro where he plainly wanted most to be touched, favoring instead this slow exploration as if he weren't seconds from bursting himself. Auro's middle was pillowy, thickly fleshed with curves Alexios wanted to sink his teeth into. The chain belted his hips, framing Auro's groin like a masterpiece of berries and cream, his cock and balls cradled in a thick thatch of rosy curls.

Later, when he relived this night—which Alexios would do many, *many* times—he would not be able to quite identify the moment he stopped using his fingers and began using his lips, but it seemed all at once that Alexios was bathing Auro in kisses. He couldn't stop himself from sucking bruises into Auro's thighs, biting the skin of his hips, using his teeth to tug on the chain around his waist. The desperate, pleased sounds falling from Auro's lips were his guide, as were the fingers tugging frantically on his hair.

"*Alexios,*" Auro breathed. "*Please—*"

Unable to form words of his own, Alexios merely nodded, blanketing Auro once again with his weight so he could smash their mouths together. Auro clutched tight to Alexios's shoulders, his fingers digging in hard enough to bruise, but Alexios did not care. He gasped as his cock slid along Auro's, igniting him tailbone to scalp as he rutted desperately against Auro's groin. Auro canted his hips, pressing every inch of their flesh close so they could thrust against one another. The friction was dry but scorching hot. Alexios had a notion to ease their way with oil, but that would mean disentangling from Auro and leaving the bed, which he did not think he had strength to do. Auro bent his knee to hook his calf over Alexios's hip, digging his heel into the meat of his ass, as if he could not get close enough. Alexios knew the feeling. The pleasure licked up his spine as they moved faster and harder, and then all at once, Auro released a startled mewl, the heat of his release pooling between them.

The idea of their seed mixing hot and sticky on Auro's perfect, smooth skin, tipped Alexios over the edge, too, his climax punching the breath from his lungs, sudden as a storm.

Auro and Alexios clung to one another, panting. Auro's head fell back, his throat upturned as he gasped for air, and Alexios pressed weak, open-mouthed kisses to the side of Auro's neck. A feeling of embarrassment kept him hiding there, and a strange sort of mourning that he had quaked so quickly—but then, so had Auro, who now released a weak, giddy chuckle.

Alexios kissed Auro's temple and stood, padding across the room to fetch a small cloth and douse it with cool water from the wash basin on his sideboard. When he turned back, his heart stuttered at the sight of Auro so debauched, a stream of pearly cum pooling in his navel, his chest and cheeks red, his lips slick and parted. Alexios offered the washcloth first to Auro, to wash the seed and sweat from his body, and then cleaned himself up. He unclasped the chain from Auro's waist and let it pool on the table at his bedside. Fresh, floaty, and naked, Alexios slid beneath the blankets. He found he quite liked the way Auro fit against him, his smaller body curled on one side with Alexios wrapped around him like a shield.

He kissed Auro's shoulder blade one last time before drifting off to sleep, a smile upon his lips.

In Alexios's dream, he was on his knees before Auro, who sat naked upon a golden throne. He used his mouth to pleasure him, loving the taste of dream-Auro on his tongue. As in life, Auro's hands tightened in his curls, tugging against them. All at once, Auro pulled harder. Alexios hissed, dropping Auro's cock from between his lips He felt the yanking again—hard. Harder. Cruel. Something deep in his sleeping brain said, *Not Auro.* Alexios opened his eyes, disoriented, and a large rough hand clamped over his mouth and nose.

Then, he was hauled from Auro's embrace. He flailed, but this man was far larger, far stronger than Alexios, and held him fast. Alexios made attempt to open his mouth, but the man stuffed a rag between his teeth to cut off the shout forming on his tongue. He pulled Alexios through the darkened bedroom by the hair, and into the bathing chamber. Before Alexios could free himself, or divest himself of the gag, the man pushed him toward the bath and used his grip on Alexios's hair to shove his head below the surface of the water.

All Alexios could do was hope his splashing would awaken Auro, who could fetch help. Leofric stood outside his door, but that may as well have been a thousand leagues away. He managed to claw the gag from his mouth and when Alexios's head broke the surface of the water, he took a hasty gulp of air before the hands twisted in his hair and forced him under once again. His heart fought like a caged beast in his chest, his pulse pounding in his ears as his vision blurred at the edges. He thrashed and fought, and heard the sounds of his own struggling as if from far away. He needed to *breathe.* His world narrowed to two things: the searing pain in his scalp as his hair was yanked out by the roots, and the burn in his lungs. Desperate, Alexios shot his hands skyward, clawing at anything he could reach, and with his nails raking against what he imagined to be the arm of his captor, he was able to get his feet beneath himself. The pool was not so deep that Alexios could not stand upon the bottom of it, and with his feet planted he managed to shove upward and back, breaking the surface and slamming his back into the sharp edge of the pool, pushing what little breath remained from his lungs, even as he found his head at last above water.

The man with his claws in Alexios's hair cursed, and Alexios thrashed wildly until he was able to flop up onto the edge of the pool. Thankfully, he was still naked, and now slick as an eel with his skin sopping wet. Alexios squirmed and twisted, hysterical strength surging through him, but when he tried to call out, his lungs remained empty, and a wet cough was all he could manage. At last, he was able to strike a blow; his elbow flew back and connected with a meaty, well-muscled chest. The assailant grunted, cursing again, and he yanked

Alexios's head back before dashing his head upon the tiles of the chamber floor. Lights popped in front of Alexios's eyes, and he held on to consciousness like a man clinging to a cliff with merely his fingertips, knowing that to slide from such would mean his death.

His lungs burned as he tried again to call for help, but no sound passed his lips.

uro woke to the sounds of splashing with a smile half-formed on his lips. As he left the world of dreams behind, he thought perhaps the sound was Alexios, and how lovely it would be to join him in the bath. As his sluggish brain churned to life, however, he realized something was very, *very* wrong.

The splashes coming from the adjacent room were not the easy, gentle movements of someone reclining and resting, nor even washing. They were the unmistakable sounds of a struggle. Auro's eyes snapped open. He flung back the blankets and leapt to his feet. A hunched shadow was crouching over Alexios, who writhed on the ground, coughing up water, face twisted in pain.

His Alexios.

Before Auro could even begin to reconcile the fury rising in his chest, it burst from him in an explosion of raw power that sent him staggering sideways. He flung out his hand and yelled, "*Stop!*"

The man attacking Alexios paid Auro no mind. He had his hand fisted in Alexios's hair, the strands wrapped around his fist so tight he'd torn some of it out. A bloody, coin-sized wound wept above Alexios's ear. The assailant didn't listen to Auro—but the small, ornamental tree he'd given Alexios did. The plant burst from the soil, shattering its clay pot into shards that clattered across the tiles, and the tree shot thick, ropey vines across the room. One seized the assailant's ankle and pulled, upending him. He maintained his grip on Alexios's hair, though—and Alexios cried out, flailing back to scrabble against the massive hand and its iron grip. Behind Auro, the door to Alexios's bedchamber exploded inward, and Auro turned to see Leofric framed by the torchlight streaming in from the corridor beyond. To the man's credit, he seemed flummoxed by the violent tableau in front of him for less than a breath before he reacted to it.

Leofric charged into the bathing chamber, drawing his sword. Without hesitation he brought one foot down, hard, stomping on the assassin's wrist. He released Alexios's hair at last, and Auro rushed to his side, dropping to the floor to encircle Alexios in his arms. Leofric made quick work of the assassin, striking a sharp blow with the pommel of his sword to render the man unconscious. He pried the knife from his grasp, and watched as the tendrils from Auro's tree retreated meekly to their broken pot on the other side of the room.

Leofric turned slowly and fixed his eyes on Auro, a look that said, quite clearly, *I see you.*

Auro broke eye contact first, his attention refocused upon Alexios. He cupped Alexios's cheeks, looking into his dazed eyes, noting the bruises already forming on his pretty face. Alexios seized Auro's wrists and jerked from his touch, and Auro recoiled as if struck, rocking back onto his heels as Alexios surged to his feet.

Alexios seized a towel and wrapped it about his waist, a muscle twitching in his jaw as he watched Leofric bind the man lying on the floor. His knuckles were white where they clutched the knot in his towel.

"Alexios—"

"Dress."

"What?"

"*Dress*," Alexios repeated. He turned his head toward the broken doorway, and it seemed the sounds of their struggle had awoken others within the villa. Auro heard frantic shouts echoing from elsewhere in the darkened villa. "And go."

"Alexios, please, I would not be from—"

"Auro, I said, *go*." Alexios refused to look at him, and it was Leofric's steady hand that reached out to Auro.

"He is right," Leofric urged him. "It would not do for you to be found here in the wake of such things. Go."

Everything in Auro thrashed against the thought of leaving Alexios's side, but he did see the wisdom of Leofric's words, and Alexios's brusque dismissal. He could not will his feet to move. He parted his lips, but Alexios merely threw a tunic at him and said, "Go."

Auro went.

Alexios shook from head to toe. His head ached, and the surge of adrenaline that had allowed him to stay conscious bled out of him as he stared at the assassin on the floor. He was an ordinary man, in truth, only made larger by shadows and Alexios's own terror.

He kept his knees from buckling by sheer force of will, and already guilt churned his stomach at his harsh words to Auro, but there was sense in sending him away. A newcomer to the villa, found in Alexios's company so close to an attempt on his life would seem suspect to any outsider looking upon the facts.

It seemed a bit suspect to Alexios, too.

He did his best to squash those insidious doubts. It shamed him, that not only could he ever suspect Auro of such villainy, but that he'd sent him away when he wanted nothing more than to burrow back into the warmth of Auro's arms. Instead, a squadron of the royal guards was arriving on the scene. At Leofric's command, they remanded the villain's unconscious form to one of the holding cells in the bowels of the royal villa, to be transferred to the royal dungeons in Papia City at first light. Alexios watched numbly as the soldiers rushed by him in a bronze blur, listening to Leofric bark commands as if from very far away. He remained upright, though his legs threatened to dissolve into water beneath him, his head throbbing with every beat of his pulse. Perhaps it should have been Alexios commanding the men, but he couldn't summon the strength to be concerned about that now. Once the assassin had been removed, Leofric stood as a shadow at Alexios's back, and the tension vibrating off him did nothing to soothe the frayed edges of Alexios's nerves.

A guardsman approached them and sank to one knee. "Your Highness."

"Rise," said Alexios, relieved to find his voice steady—if perhaps a bit higher pitched than normal. It was as if a stranger spoke through his own mouth. "Give report."

"We have secured Their Majesties, your royal parents, in their own apartments. The King commanded you be brought to them at once, while our men secure the villa."

"Very well."

Alexios allowed the guards to flank him, and their presence did not ease his worry either. Something about their scrutiny and care made him feel more exposed. He wished he had been given time to see himself to proper dress—even a bed robe, to make him feel less vulnerable. He felt naked with just the towel around his hips.

He felt naked without Auro at his side, but he shook that thought away.

When they reached the wing that held his parents' apartments, Alexios and Leofric went inside while the remainder of the guards remained on the other side of the door.

"Alexios!" King Nelios strode across the room at once. He seized his son's face in his large, callused hands, inspecting what Alexios imagined to be some truly horrific bruising, if the throbbing in his entire skull were any measure. King Nelios scrutinized his face, and when his father's fingers caught in Alexios's hair, he winced. Nelios's face softened, and it was that—his father's pity, that snapped Alexios's brittle composure. He shook off his father's concerned hands and turned away to collect himself. "It is nothing."

"Does the villain yet draw breath?" asked Queen Clio. She clutched her bed robes around herself like armor.

"Your Grace," said Leofric, bowing. "He does. The guards brought him to the holding cell below."

"I want him hanged!" shouted Nelios. "No one lays hands on my blood and lives."

Clio touched her husband's arm. "We must give him a chance to break words, first. Confess who moved him to this purpose." She took a deep, steadying breath and turned her eyes upon Leofric. She did not raise her voice, but quiet anger threatened every syllable, more intimidating than the King's bluster. "Explain to me how this happened."

Leofric did not flinch from her accusation, but he dropped to one knee and bowed respectfully to answer her. "Apologies, Your Majesty. It should never have been so."

"It certainly should not—" began King Nelios.

"Hush," said the Queen. "Continue."

"I stood at my usual place outside His Highness's bed chambers, and all seemed quiet. I heard a disturbance from within. When I entered, the attacker was making attempt to drown His Highness. He shook the man off, and I seized the chance to intervene."

Leofric hesitated, clearly wondering if he should mention Auro. He exchanged a brief, sidelong look with Alexios, and held his tongue. Alexios felt a surge of gratitude, unrelated to Leofric saving his life.

"Explain to me how this man got past you at your post," said the Queen.

Leofric met her eye, a look on his face like defiance, despite the fact he remained on his knees. "He did not get past me at my post, and no man ever could. The villain must have secreted himself in Prince Alexios's chambers while all were down at the feast."

Alexios fretted, noting that perhaps Leofric would have done a more thorough sweep of Alexios's chambers had he not been attempting to grant him and Auro some privacy. He feared Leofric would be punished or relieved from his post for something that was not his fault. The King opened his mouth in anger, clearly bursting with the need to vent his rage somewhere, but the Queen held up her hand to silence him once more.

"Leofric, this will *not* happen again."

"Yes, Your Grace," he said. "I mean, no. Your Grace."

Alexios's mother shot him a look, like she was trying to read his thoughts, and Alexios was far too raw to hide anything. He was certain she knew exactly why Leofric had not secured Alexios's chambers, with so many strangers in the villa, though she said nothing out loud.

A sharp rap upon the door drew their attention, and Alexios hated himself for the way the sound had him cringing in fear.

"Your Majesties, it is I, Paulus."

"Enter," snapped King Nelios.

Paulus was the commander of the King and Queen's

personal guard. He entered the room with another man, his uniform unfamiliar to Alexios. They both knelt before the King and Queen.

"Rise," said the Queen impatiently. "What have you learned?"

"This is Kato," said Paulus, indicating the man beside him.

"I have the honor of captaining the personal guard of Her Grace, Queen Petillia of Neossós."

"And why have you left your queen's side?"

"Begging your pardons," he said, wiping his forehead—which bled freely upon the carpet from a rather ghastly slice—with the corner of his cloak. "There was an attempt on Princess Dafina's life, as well."

Nelios cursed and Alexios ran cold all over. How many assassins had made it into the palace this night?

"Is the man in custody?"

Kato bowed his head. "Apologies, Your Majesties, but in the struggle, I dispatched the fiend to the afterlife."

"And the Princess?"

"Quite shaken, but unharmed. Queen Petillia and the Praetor are likewise safe."

"Good," said Queen Clio. She turned to one of the other guards. "Fetch the medicus, and have him see to my son and Captain Kato. Paulus, you must sweep every crevice of the villa and the grounds. Report back before dawn breaks."

Paulus nodded and turned to gather some of his men.

"Leofric," said the Queen. "Is there a man you trust to relieve you?"

"Your Majesty, I would prefer—"

"I do not care what you would prefer. You must rest. It has been a trying evening and I require you at your best. You may sleep in the servants' quarters in my son's apartments, if you wish."

"Of course, Your Grace," he said. "I will fetch one of the men."

"Good," said Queen Clio. Then, once again, to herself. "Good."

Alexios staggered over to a sofa in his parents' parlor, submitting to the fussing of the royal medicus, who peered into his eyes, examined the bruising on his cheek, probing with his fingers to make certain there wasn't a break to the bone. He also mixed Alexios a sleeping draught, but he did not drink it, afraid what might happen if he closed his eyes. He sat, staring into the goblet, wishing Auro was there.

Fifteen

Auro paced around his plinth in the ruined temple. He stared at the faces of his brothers and found himself wondering what they thought when they looked upon *his* marble likeness when it was each of their turns to walk the earth.

The attempt on Alexios's life had shaken Auro to his bones. They had only just begun to explore this thing between them, and some vile fiend had ripped Alexios from his arms and nearly from this world entirely, all in the span of a few frantic moments. It had been quite a while since Auro had thought about how fragile mortal life could be.

How fleeting.

The curse upon Auro and his brothers had been his only reality for so long, he barely remembered a life without it. He had never before attempted to find a way to lift the curse, to change his fate. In fact, he was fairly certain it was not even possible to do so.

Did his brothers ever wonder? Had they ever fallen in love? He couldn't believe he'd never asked them, before. And now...

The first few years, after they had been cursed, when things were so raw and fresh, he had tried leaving them messages, each in turn. For five years he had tried, and never awoke to an answer, come spring, from any of them. He had not tried again after that.

He did miss them though, his brothers, when he allowed himself to think of them, in his weaker moments. As now. It had been a long time since he had truly felt the ache of their loss, but he felt it now. It was as if spending time with Alexios had worn away the protective, thorny briar that Auro had grown around his heart, allowing not only Alexios to take root there, but longing for his brothers to sprout fresh, as well. He looked at each of their statues in turn, thinking of Cedras and his calm, gentle demeanor, Cosmos's wild laughter. Even Kryos's stern face swam before him, the pain in Auro's breast so sharp he gasped. He thought of Ozias, trying to heal the wounds between them all, and dying for it. Shame and fear and grief all muddled in Auro's stomach, until he could no longer tell which was which.

When Auro had first begun his courtship of Alexios, he tried to convince himself he'd be content spending what time he could with him during the spring, returning to rest when the days grew long. Theirs could be a casual affair, and when Alexios eventually took a bride, they would deal with that then. And yet, now—though Alexios had sent him away, Auro felt it would be easier to rip his own heart from his chest than remain this far from Alexios's side.

As if in reflection of his mood, the sky darkened above Auro, the clouds he'd woven for an overdue rain ripening earlier than intended. Irritated, Auro turned his face skyward, waiting for the first fat drops to break and fall. When they did, he closed his eyes, remembering a time before he had the power to command the spring rains. The gentle but pervasive *hush* of the falling water transported him back to the wild spring evenings of his youth.

He had been young, so young. All of them were, Auro and his brothers. Four young princes, and Ozias, all living at court as children. It was before their father had begun to siphon off his own grace and feed it to them, before he had blessed each of them with powers of their own. Auro had always been afraid of thunderstorms, especially since Ozias had told him the thunder was the sound of invisible giants pounding on the walls, and that one day they would rip the villa from its foundation and devour everyone inside. In the present, Auro smiled to think of it—the resounding crashes were like a lullaby to him now. He thought with a pang of the way Ozias had always woven such fantastical tales.

Back then, the crashing thunder had been a terrible and unknowable song. One night, a storm shook their villa so hard Auro was certain it was the night the giants would feast upon them all. Trembling, he had found his way through the airy corridors to his elder brother's bed chambers. Cedras sat on the floor, curled in the corner by the window that led to his balcony, reading by the flashes of lightning. He was always reading, Cedras. Auro had been sure his eyeballs would fall out from reading so much. Cedras didn't look up from his page, but patted a spot on his pile of cushions, right beside him. Auro had sat beside his brother, who lifted an arm to wrap protectively around Auro's shoulders. When he felt Auro still shivering, Cedras had said, in that sedate, calm he had—even as a boy—"Thunder is nothing but the friend of lightning, always chasing after. The sound is her footsteps. Count the spaces between the flash and the sound, and you'll know how close she is to catching him."

Auro closed his eyes and counted.

"See?" said Cedras. "It's nothing to fear."

The door had creaked, then, and Auro had opened one

eye, peeking across the vast chamber to see Cosmo poking his head in. Auro beckoned, and Cosmo scurried across the room to join them. "You weren't in your bed," he told Auro.

"So?" said Auro.

Cosmo twisted his fingers in his lap. "I know you get afraid, so I came to check on you."

"I'm alright," Auro said, and he explained the game of counting the moments between lightning's flash and thunder's answering sound. It was only years later that Auro realized perhaps Cosmo had been afraid, too, and perhaps that was why he had come searching for Auro.

At the time, Cosmo had transformed the game into something else entirely, and soon enough, he and Auro laughed themselves stupid trying to tell each other an entire story in the space between lightning and thunder, talking as fast as they could. Cedras simply huffed, slid his spectacles up his nose, and ignored them—but he never told them to quiet down, or behave, or leave him to his books.

It was long after Cedras and Cosmo had drifted off to sleep, curled up in the pile of cushions on the floor, and Auro lay on his side, still counting each time lightning streaked across the cloud-laden sky, that Kryos came in. He was the oldest, not given over to childish fears, but plainly something had called him from bed. Afraid of getting into trouble, Auro had quickly closed his eyes, playing at being asleep. He watched through his lashes, watched his stern brother's face soften when he saw them all piled up on the floor. Kryos had simply tutted fondly, brought the thick coverlet from Cedras's bed to tuck around Auro, and sat on the stone tiles beside them.

That was the only time Auro had ever heard Kryos sing, a quiet lullaby their mother had sung to them all. His voice was low and warm, like the blanket he'd tucked around Auro. Eventually, Auro felt his eyelids growing heavy, lulled by his brother's gentle song. In the morning, Auro woke in much the same position he'd fallen asleep, but Kryos was gone.

He had always wondered if Kryos knew Auro was awake that night to hear him sing. Perhaps he wouldn't have done it, had he known—but then, to whom had he been singing? Himself, perhaps. Auro never found out.

Here, now, Auro opened his eyes, pulled from memory, watching the water pooling on the marble floor around his feet. Dawn was near, Auro realized. He looked up at the statues of his brothers and sighed, his grief, fear, and loneliness heavy upon him.

The swiftness with which danger had struck Alexios terrified him, beyond any fear he'd ever felt. Before Ozias had been caught in the crossfire of Cosmo and Kryos's last duel, Auro had never pictured a day when someone he loved so dearly would be ripped from his grasp. Now, he should know better. What if he went to rest, at the twilight of spring, and woke next year to find Alexios's flame had been snuffed out while Auro had slept?

No.

The pain of losing his bright, shining prince to marriage paled in comparison to knowing Alexios had been struck from this world, and Auro had stood by, had not realized the danger present until it was too late. It had happened before, with Ozias. Auro would not be such a fool as to allow someone else he cared for to be unwritten from the pages of history, not again.

He had not one single idea how to break his curse, or if he even could.

But he had to try.

Auro was lost in thought as he walked on the submerged stone path from his island to the lakeshore, so distracted that he didn't realize he was not alone until a twig snapped underfoot a few feet from his right.

Auro froze. "Hello?"

Leofric stepped out from behind a tree, and Auro would have been less surprised had one of the giants from Ozias's story appeared in front of him. "Hello."

Auro's eyes darted around him, wondering if it would be possible to fully conceal himself—as if Leofric hadn't already seen him. "Is…" he faltered. "Is His Royal Highness with you?"

Leofric shook his head. He stared at Auro like he was trying to peer inside his skull. "He's with a squadron of other guardsmen, in the villa."

"Oh." Auro wanted desperately to ask why Leofric had journeyed all this way into the forest, but part of him already knew.

Leofric clasped his hands at the small of his back. "Who are you?"

"I'm just…Auro."

Leofric's brows contracted severely, giving him a hawkish appearance. "I have a hard time believing you are 'just' anything, Auro."

They stared at one another, and Auro wondered if he could simply outlast Leofric. Chances didn't seem good, even though Auro had the immortal edge—Leofric was just as immovable as the statues of Auro's brothers.

"It's difficult to explain," said Auro.

"Try."

Auro's brain shuffled through dozens of possible excuses, dozens of reasons he could command plants to do his bidding, or have pink hair. Dozens. After mentally sifting through them all, he finally settled on blurting, "I'm the God of Spring."

Leofric's eyes widened in shock, his mouth opening slightly as he turned this over in his mind. Auro watched as

Leofric blinked rapidly, then looked around his own feet like perhaps he'd dropped something.

"Um—"

"I actually need to sit down," said Leofric faintly.

"Oh!" said Auro. "I can help you with that."

He guided Leofric over to a mossy log that sat on the sandy mud only a few spaces away. Leofric sank down upon it. "Thank you."

Auro stood before him, waiting.

At last, Leofric looked up at him, a world-weary expression on his face. "You'd better just...start at the beginning, I suppose."

A few days passed, and Auro had not yet returned. It set Alexios's teeth on edge. Auro had left the villa at Alexios's word, but he hadn't anticipated this prolonged absence. Since the attack, he rarely left his chambers but spent a great deal of time on his balcony. That morning, he thought at last he'd caught a glimpse of Auro down in the gardens, and could not hold in the gasp that slipped out—but it was just a pink blossom on a tree.

"Your Highness?" Leofric emerged behind him. "Are you well?"

The man had been hovering, of late. More than before, even. "I am *fine*," said Alexios through gritted teeth.

"Of course, Your Highness." Leofric hesitated, like there was more on his mind. His eyes followed Alexios's down into the yard below, and Alexios felt his cheeks heat. "He has not returned?"

Alexios set his jaw and shook his head.

"He might—"

"That will be all," said Alexios loudly.

Leofric hesitated once again, before saying, "Are you hungry, Your Highness? I could fetch you something from the kitchens."

The thought of food turned Alexios's stomach. He'd managed a few sips of honey wine and bites of bread...when? Last night? Yesterday morning. He frowned, trying to recall, but something else snagged in his mind. "I thought it was not your duty to fetch and carry," said Alexios wryly, recalling Leofric's terse words when he'd first taken his position.

Leofric looked at his feet, and if Alexios wasn't mistaken, the man was utterly ashamed. "This should never have happened."

Alexios tried to keep his expression neutral but could not stop his fingers from flitting to his temple, like he could still feel the pain in his scalp, the water burning in his lungs. "If I recall correctly, the man would have introduced my brains to the tiles had you not intervened."

"Perhaps," said Leofric. "But I should have swept the room before I allowed you to enter."

"Well," said Alexios, around the sudden lump in his throat. *What was wrong with him?* "Next time."

"Indeed."

Alexios turned his back to the balcony. Before Leofric could say anything else, a sharp bang on Alexios's newly repaired door had him flinching like a coward and a fool. "Enter," he said, and his voice cracked like a boy's.

It was Paulus, the captain of his parents' guard. "Your Highness," he said, falling to one knee. "Their Majesties the King and Queen request your presence in their private audience chamber."

Alexios nodded vaguely.

When he left his chambers, a squadron of guards fell in step around him, as they did the few times he'd felt moved to leave his private apartments. They did not make him feel less afraid. He'd only just begun to get used to Leofric's constant, grating presence, and these other men were worse. He didn't know them well. He didn't trust them. However, Leofric had been awake all night, and with Alexios in the custody of an entire squadron of guards, he requested leave to take a few hours' rest.

Alexios's immediate, childish thought was to beg Leofric to attend him so he could dismiss these other guards. But he didn't.

Alexios dug his fingers down into the neck of his tunic, tangling them around the chain he'd given Auro. In his haste to banish Auro from his side, the necklace had been forgotten on Alexios's bedside table. He'd taken to wearing it himself, pressing the tiny links into his skin as if he could feel Auro's touch with it.

"Alexios," said Queen Clio as a steward bid him enter. "It is good to see you up and well."

Alexios knew immediately that his hibernation had been a mistake. "Yes," he said, forcing his shoulders back and his spine straight. "I am feeling much better."

"Good," she said. "Alexios, sit."

He did as he was bid, doing his best not to let his apprehension show on his face. "Have Paulus and his men learned anything new about the...?" he trailed off.

"He has turned over every brick of the villa," said Queen Clio. "And found no evidence of the villain's motives, or employer."

"Have you questioned everyone who was at the feast?" Alexios asked.

"Most of the royal guests have already departed," said King Nelios. "And we found no cause to suspect any of the Papian nobles."

"What? You just let them all leave?"

"We could not detain them," said Queen Clio. "Not

without any proof against them, and not without causing an incident."

"I think we lost our chance to avoid an incident when someone tried to slit my throat," said Alexios. He'd aimed for a flippant tone, but his words squeaked out high and hysterical.

"I told you," said Nelios. "The boy is not ready to shoulder delicate matters of state."

"*Excuse me?*"

"You are irrational and prone to dramatic turns," said Nelios.

Which was rich, Alexios thought, coming from a man who bellowed and blustered as much as his father. "I—"

"*Enough,*" said Queen Clio. "Both of you. It matters not if Alexios is ready. He must become ready."

"What aren't you saying?" he asked his parents.

"The night of the feast, though most of the royal guests were not due to depart for several days, King Cletus and his entourage departed in all haste, riding hard for Órnio. *Before* the attempt was made on your life."

Alexios frowned. "Why would he...?" This made no sense, and his head hurt.

"It was as good as a confession, as far as I am concerned," said Nelios. "Why leave as a thief in the night if not to escape in advance of his own dark deeds?"

"What did he have to gain?" Alexios wondered aloud. "And why would he not remain, to at least ensure success?"

Alexios knew his father mistrusted King Cletus, his history with the Sokolian army written with blood from both sides.

"We do not *know,*" said Queen Clio, "which is why we had to give leave for the others to depart. We have no proof, my love," she said to her husband.

Nelios pointed at Alexios, his face still covered in bruises. "There is your proof, writ on my son's face. Our line, nearly snuffed out in an instant."

Alexios wished to hide, but he forced himself to stand, straight backed, as if he were the sort of man for whom an assassination attempt was nothing more than an intriguing anecdote. By the expression on his parents' faces, Alexios was fooling no one.

"Alexios, please sit," said the Queen.

He sat.

"I believe it's time we discuss what happened the night of the feast."

Somehow, Alexios knew she did not mean the attempt on his life, but he said nothing.

"Paulus and his men have questioned the guests who remain in Papia," said Queen Clio. "*All* of the guests. And we have found no connection with any of them and the events of the night—nor any of our staff."

Alexios dared let a tiny sigh of relief escape.

"However," the Queen continued, eyes narrowed. "Everyone at the feast saw you leave with your...companion, Auro."

Alexios forced himself not to flinch, not to even blink. "What of it?"

"What of it? Be serious, Alexios."

Alexios let his hand float to the chain around his neck, for strength. He could not claim Auro as his own, nor could he bring himself to deny him entirely, so instead, he said, "People only saw us talking. There was nothing to see."

"Alexios—"

He recalled what Dafina had said to him. "Everyone at the feast knew my reputation. Even Her Grace and the Princess."

King Nelios scowled. "And?"

Alexios shrugged. "They came anyway." When the words left his mouth, Alexios could scarce believe he'd said them. But they were the truth. He stared defiantly at his parents. "They know how the game is played."

"It is not a game," snapped Nelios. "You will do as—"

"Commanded?" said Alexios. "Of course, I will. I will wed, and I will do my duty to our people—as I always have. As I always knew I would have to. But I will also do what I wish." *At least, in private.*

"Alright," said the Queen, sounding as though the word aged her beyond her years.

Alexios strode from the room, his heart hammering in his chest, blood pounding in his ears. His head ached, he was lonely and afraid, and his small triumph over his parents was short-lived as his squadron of guards fell in around him on the walk back to his chambers. Something tugged in his hair, and he flinched, a vicious crick in his neck accompanying the motion for what felt like the hundredth time that morning. It was the final straw, the tugging on his scalp reminding him of how easily he'd been overpowered, dragged across the floor by his ridiculous hair, and almost...

It happened every time he felt any pressure on his scalp. Even an errant tangle on a comb, a catch on his crown as he removed the wretched thing, or the clasp of a cloak snagging in his curls had him wincing and twitching like a madman, fighting down fear that rose like bile in his throat.

He could not take one more fucking second of it.

Alexios stormed into his apartments, slamming his chamber door in the face of the guards. Leofric had taken up in one of the small servants' quarters adjacent to Alexios's own, where he now rested. If the slamming door had woken him, he must have immediately fallen back to slumber, because he did not emerge. Alexios grabbed the dagger from his bedside table, with which he now slept clutched tight in his sweaty palm. He'd woken to bloody sheets the past few mornings, and scratches on his arms, after he'd rolled over it in his fitful sleep. No matter. The blood would wash away, and he felt marginally better having it close to hand. Now, he hefted the hilt, examining the blade. It was a fine thing, the handle carved from bone and inlaid with gold, a gift from his father on a birthday years past. Alexios gripped it, white-knuckled, and strode to the polished silver shaving mirror beside his wash basin.

He seized a handful of his own hair, and before he could second guess himself, he sawed brutally with the blade of his dagger, taking savage pleasure in the sight of his honeyed curls falling in a pile at his feet. He dragged the blade back and forth, thinking that to rid himself of the messy, troublesome mop would rid him of the accompanying fears and twitches. Perhaps then, he could get some fucking sleep. One such twitch seized him now, even as he watched *himself* in the mirror, and the blade slid across the thin skin above his brow.

"*Fuck!*" Alexios swore, and the papery flesh parted like silk, blood flowing down his forehead and into his eye.

"Your—*Alexios!*" Leofric had stirred at last, and he ran across the room to seize Alexios's wrist. "Drop it," he said.

"No." Alexios grappled, pathetically, with Leofric, who aside from being older, taller, and stronger, was also a trained fighter. A clever twist of Alexios's wrist had the dagger falling from limp fingers.

"What the *fuck* were you trying to do? Put your eye out?"

He had never heard Leofric swear before, never seen his professional, stoic demeanor slip. Alexios laughed, an unhinged, hysterical giggle that was half a sob. He was truly coming unglued. "Trying to rid myself of this fucking hair," he said.

Leofric released a tut and grabbed a washcloth for Alexios to hold against the slice. He marched Alexios into the bathing chamber and deposited him upon a marble bench. Then, Leofric left him holding the cloth to his eye, though he made sure to take the dagger with him.

When Leofric returned, he took the cloth from Alexios's

trembling hands to examine the wound. "It is not deep," he said. "It will heal just fine. Forehead wounds bleed overmuch, even when not serious."

"Gratitude," mumbled Alexios, already humiliated at his ridiculous outburst. He looked sullenly down at his feet, refusing to make eye contact as Leofric cleaned the slice, and pressed a small square of cotton bandage to it. His parents were right—he *was* being such a child.

"Keep pressure," said Leofric.

Alexios did as he was bid, sitting mutely as Leofric got to his feet.

"Now," he said, leveling a careful, calculating gaze at Alexios, who felt more helpless and foolish with every passing second. "What's all this then?"

"I have let my hair grow over long," said Alexios evasively. "It is the style of a boy, not a man."

Leofric shot him a crooked smile. His hair was longer than Alexios's by several inches, and somehow Alexios couldn't imagine anyone accusing him of being less than a man. "I don't think rending yourself bald is the answer, Alexios," he said gently.

Dimly, Alexios registered the use of his given name. "Well, I didn't know what else to do." He paused, and then groaned, his fingers touching the jagged tufts now sprouting above his ear—just below the scab from where part of his hair had been ripped out the night of the attack. "And now, I have a bald spot. Another bald spot."

Leofric turned his head to the side, displaying his neatly maintained, partially shaved head. "I may not be a barber, but I can tidy up the attempt. Perhaps you will spark a new fashion trend among the other lordlings."

In spite of everything, Alexios laughed, relieved to hear it sounded more normal this time. "Why not?"

While he held the square of cloth to the wound on his

forehead, contemplating what a mess his face must be, Leofric retreated once again to his small chambers and returned with a bowl of soap and a wicked razor. He cleaned up the side of Alexios's head with sure, deft strokes, and upon gazing in the mirror, Alexios found himself not disliking his new, rakish appearance.

"Now," said Leofric. "Let us get to the root of this matter, for I know it's not hair."

Alexios scowled. He felt he had already revealed far too much. His parents had distilled in him from an early age the need to maintain a mask, at all times. To be royal was to be vulnerable, and to show that vulnerability was to invite challenge, mistrust, and death. Alexios could never admit he was reduced to blind panic and shame at every errant tug on his hair.

However, Leofric seemed to sense something of this in what Alexios did not say. "I can teach you to defend yourself, Your Highness," he said. "And please recall it is my duty to keep your secrets and your confidence."

Alexios considered the offer. "I would appreciate that."

"Also..." Leofric hesitated.

"What is it?"

"It may be out of turn for me to say, Your Highness."

"Speak," said Alexios.

"You have been hiding," said Leofric bluntly. "I know you have put off your audience with the consuls regarding the roads in the kingdom, and you have not left the villa in days."

Alexios wrapped his arms around himself, unsure of what to say. "It is difficult to put a name to my specific fear," he admitted.

"Let me just say this, then," said Leofric. "Sometimes, a thing grows larger when we allow it to conceal itself in shadows."

"You think I should confront the killer?" Alexios asked him, startled.

"I do," said Leofric. "And remember—you live, Your Highness. This man is *not* a killer, because here you stand. He is nothing but a failure, who now rots condemned in a dungeon. You overestimate him, and allow fear to fester."

Alexios nodded. "Well said. I will think on this."

Leofric bowed his head. "Of course, Your Highness." He hesitated once more.

"What is it?"

"Nothing. Only, I am glad to have saved the majority of your hair—it is my understanding it's much beloved of your... Auro."

Alexios smiled, pleased, and nodded once again. As Leofric turned to go, Alexios called to him. "Leofric?"

"Yes, Your Highness?"

"Thank you."

e had been working tirelessly all day, and yet, Auro had a hard time sleeping. He missed Alexios desperately, and it had been almost a week since the attempt on his life. Auro was totally in the dark, with no news and no word from Alexios since Leofric had come to visit him days ago.

Auro had left the temple behind to make his bed at the very edge of the forest, where the trees would instantly alert him if Alexios approached. He hunkered down at the base of an enormous, old oak tree and tried to sleep. He drifted in and out of dreams, each more disturbing than the last. In some, he was back at the scene where he'd found Ozias's bones, in the wake of Kryos and Cosmo's duel. In the dream, Auro knew what he'd find when he approached the valley where they had fought—but instead of a skeleton, covered in glittering ice crystals, it was Alexios's body staring sightlessly up at a black, starless sky.

In others, he walked through the royal villa that had been his home, footsteps echoing off the marble halls, and then he woke exhausted, as if he truly had spent the whole night walking. In yet another, he sat in the temple on the lake, but instead of statues of his brothers, the temple was full of statues of the princess Alexios was supposed to marry, staring at him with cold, judgmental eyes that followed him when he moved.

And finally, he ran through a forest, branches tearing at his clothes and skin—the trees didn't recognize him any longer, they scraped and clawed at him. Then the trees were ravens, shrieking and grasping at his hair, and Auro's footsteps slowed, the mud of the forest floor sucking at his sandals and pulling him down, down, down, beneath the pressing wet blackness of the earth. His only hope was to reach, reach, desperately reach toward the sun, the blinding golden light in the sky that would be his salvation. With his arms, his hopes, his heart, his very lungs Auro reached until suddenly, he was on the floor of Alexios's bedroom.

He tried to stand, to call out, to cross the room to Alexios who slept restlessly nearby, glowing faintly with an aura of golden light, but he could not move or speak. Then, Auro blinked, and he was back in his own skin, awake, in the forest. Panting, Auro sat up and knuckled his eyes. All of the dreams had felt real when he was in them, but something told Auro the last one *had* been real, at least in part.

It reminded him of the time he so eagerly awaited Alexios's visit to the forest—when he yearned so badly for Alexios's arrival it seemed that he *felt* it, through the trees and other growing things, before Alexios had arrived. The strange awareness felt inhuman, the golden light—and now it had happened again. Auro had missed Alexios so desperately that his grace had reached out to him, sending Auro's awareness somehow into one of the many plants he'd left in Alexios's bedroom.

Auro got shakily to his feet, stumbling, like his body wasn't used to having legs, and the freedom to move. Lingering effects of the plant he'd visited, he supposed. He'd never known he could do something like that—didn't know until he wanted something so badly he couldn't stop reaching for it, even in his sleep.

He'd intended to wait until summoned, but Auro could not bear to stay away from Alexios any longer, and besides, he knew he'd never get back to sleep. Dawn was just breaking, and under cover of lingering darkness, it still took all of Auro's skills to creep into Alexios's chambers absent notice. The patrols of guards prowling the villa had doubled in number since the attempt upon the Crown Prince's life.

Auro also could not shirk his duties as warden of the spring. People across the continent would be reading the land, waiting for the signs it was time to lay in their crops. Auro had to prepare the earth, make certain it was warm enough to cradle the seeds until they sprouted, and if he neglected his tasks, the people would starve.

As Auro begged the ivy to grow once again outside the window to Alexios's private apartments, he worried Alexios would think he had been abandoned, when in actuality he had not been for one second from Auro's thoughts.

When at last he swung a leg up and over the railing of the balcony, Auro found Alexios's chambers empty, his bed dressed and cold. Unsure how welcome he'd be wandering the villa before break of day, Auro decided to stay put. He poured himself a cup of water and paced around the room, awaiting Alexios's return.

It was long hours, threatening to seem an eternity before he did. At the sound of the door opening, Auro looked up, but he was unable to help how his face fell when he saw it was Leofric entering, not Alexios. The man sighed, in a long-suffering manner, and said, "Your Highness, there is someone hiding in your chambers. I suspect an ambush."

"Oh?" came Alexios's voice, and to Auro's ear he sounded winded. "I know I am a quick study, Leofric, but perhaps it is still best if you—*Auro!*"

And to Auro's delight, Alexios galloped across the room and wrapped Auro in his arms. The Prince was soaked in sweat, a dizzying and intoxicating smell clinging to his skin, and Auro nuzzled eagerly into his chest to inhale more of it. Alexios squeezed him tightly, pressing his cheek to the crown of Auro's head.

As they embraced, Leofric examined every inch of Alexios's apartments. "I'll be just outside, Your Highness," he said, and at the soft click of the door behind him, Alexios immediately seized Auro's face in his hands and pulled him close for a kiss.

It was only when they broke apart a few moments later, breathless, that Auro truly took in the state Alexios was in. Bare-chested, sweaty, bruised. And his hair! A large patch above one small, perfect ear had been shorn away.

"What on earth has happened to you?" asked Auro, laying a palm on Alexios's cheek. Despite the bravado and eagerness he displayed, he seemed gaunt, eyes never still, and sunken into his face in a way that belied several sleepless nights. The bruising around his eye had faded to a greenish yellow, but the ones upon his chest, knees, and arms appeared fresh and blue —and there was an angry slice upon his brow.

Alexios tossed his sweat-dampened curls and turned his head to display the shaved patch. "I decided to try a new style."

"Aye," said Auro with a small smile. He stood back, raking his eyes over Alexios from head to toe. He wore nothing but a subligaria. "I imagine you have become quite popular."

"Oh, that. I have been sparring with Leofric," he said. "I would not be caught helpless, ever again."

Auro did not fail to notice the way his fingers twitched, the way his hand flew to his temple, to the patch of hair he had shaved. "An excellent notion," he said carefully, but used his own fingers to trace the bruises that bloomed across Alexios's chest. "Though perhaps you should be more cautious."

"Each bruise is a lesson well learned," said Alexios harshly, shrugging off Auro's concerned hands. "Not to be repeated."

Auro frowned. This did not sound like the same Alexios he had left days ago. "Alexios?"

He was already turning away, striding toward the bath. "Yes?" he asked over his shoulder, one hand resting on the knot of his loincloth.

"Are you...well?"

With his back to Auro, Alexios shrugged one shoulder. Auro approached him timidly. This Alexios seemed to him like a wild animal, likely to bolt or snap teeth if provoked. The air between them was tense, and Auro ached to break that tension. He knew then he should not have left Alexios's side in the aftermath of the attack, consequences be damned. He chewed his lip, uncertain, before crossing the rest of the way to slide his hands around Alexios's middle, moving close to press kisses in the valley between his shoulders.

Alexios heaved a deep, shuddering breath. "I have been so afraid," he confessed quietly.

"I know."

"I have missed you."

"I know that, too," said Auro. "And I missed you fiercely, as well."

Alexios spun in Auro's hold, using his own arms to wrap Auro up, enveloping him in the musky smell of his body. "I would have you join me for a bath, if it would please you."

"Nothing would please me more."

In the adjacent chamber, Alexios stepped down into the water, and Auro peeled off his own tunic and followed him, collecting a sponge from the lip of the pool. Auro dunked the sponge and used it to gently cleanse the sweat from Alexios's body. As he washed Alexios, Auro realized that the proximity of him, the touch of Alexios's fingers carding through his hair, no longer frightened him. In fact, it soothed him, erasing the raw edges of the last few days. He liked caring for Alexios. And it seemed Alexios enjoyed it, too. He hummed contentedly as the sponge skated across his back, his chest, his long, lean thighs. Auro scrubbed his hands and toes, the shells of his perfect ears, the ones he'd been so taken with when they'd met.

They stayed in the water a long time, and Alexios finally relaxed, melting into Auro where he leaned his back to Auro's chest against the side of the bathing pool. Auro pressed kisses to the top of Alexios's head, letting his hands roam beneath the water, mapping the planes of Alexios's chest and stomach, the muscles of his arms. A strange, possessive creature had been waking up inside of Auro. Alexios was *his.* "Alexios," he said quietly, after a while.

"Mmm?" said Alexios.

"Will you help me try to break my curse?"

It had been too long since Alexios had ventured outside, felt the wind in his hair and a horse between his legs. Leofric had been right. He had remained far too long in the confines of his private apartments.

Alexios woke that morning determined to regain some semblance of control over his life. The night before, he and Auro had shared an indulgent supper, brought to Alexios's chambers, and eaten it curled up naked in bed. He felt braver, stronger—as if a fever had broken at last. After a few days training with Leofric, he felt...well, if not *strong* then at least *stronger.* More prepared. He fell asleep with his nose buried in Auro's curls, determined to return to the world upon the morrow.

So it went that he found himself mounted up beside Leofric and Auro, headed toward the city. Alexios hoped that by facing the man who'd made attempt upon his life, he could lay the matter to rest, and progress with something far more rewarding. He had the project with the roads to consider, an impending betrothal to navigate, and Auro had decided at last he should make attempt to shed the bonds of his curse. Alexios was determined to do everything he could to see Auro freed. He knew he could not keep Auro, not truly, but he aimed to keep him—and be kept *by* him—for as long as he possibly could—and, regardless. Auro deserved his freedom.

Unfortunately, the task would prove even harder than Alexios anticipated. "How can you not recall?" he asked Auro, annoyed.

Auro wrinkled his brow. "It was four centuries ago, Alexios."

"Yes," Alexios allowed, "and yet, it was of no little importance!"

"I never dreamed breaking the curse would even be possible," said Auro, frowning more deeply still. "And...I remain unsure."

"Well, certainly, with that outlook, it will remain insurmountable," Alexios snapped.

"Apologies," said Auro. "You must understand, this has been my only reality for so long."

"I do understand," said Alexios earnestly. "But I can't sit by and watch you turn to stone. In fact, I refuse to."

He could tell Auro was trying very hard not to smile at his bold words, trying very hard not to get his hopes up. No matter. He did not need Auro to believe. He could believe enough for the both of them. Alexios would tear down Auro's temple brick by brick if he must, searching for clues, until he discovered something of worth.

"We approach the city gates, Your Highness," said Leofric.

His stomach gave an uncomfortable lurch. As long as they had been discussing Auro's problems, Alexios could more easily ignore his own.

But now, they faced the vast, well-guarded walls of Papia's harbor city. The prison fortress lay just outside them, its own walls abutting the water's edge. It was close enough for the guard to be enforced by the city watch, and far enough from the thriving city not to disturb its inhabitants.

Leofric had sent a messenger ahead so the jailers would be aware of their coming, but even so, Alexios recognized their surprise at seeing the Crown Prince arrive at their door. He ignored the stunned, nervous looks on their faces and demanded to see the prisoner.

The head jailer exchanged worried glances with a few of his men and begged His Highness's pardon to speak with Leofric privately. Perhaps, as a show of his own authority, Alexios should have refused to be brushed aside, but he was surprised enough to allow it.

"What on earth do you think that's about?" Auro asked him. He seemed determined to ignore the stares of the guards, who plainly found his pink hair alarming. Alexios had told him not to redye it, and their official story was that Auro had dyed it for the equinox party, and the color had proved more permanent than anticipated. It was a thin lie, but then again, Auro's hair plainly stood pink as the sunset, so how could anyone argue? Alexios liked it, and he decided he didn't much care what anyone else thought.

Alexios shrugged, clenching his jaw. Waiting. The hairs on the back of his neck prickled with the awareness that something was not right. The longer the others remained on the other side of the door, the more certain of it he became. The man had not escaped, had he?

At last, Leofric reemerged, looking angrier than Alexios had ever seen him. "The man is dying, Your Highness," he said bluntly.

"*What?*" gasped Auro. "How?"

Alexios let it wash over him. Something *had* been wrong.

The second he had set foot in the fortress he'd known, somehow. Leofric was saying something, but it sounded as though his words came from underwater. He shook his head to clear it. "Pardon?"

"We can still see him, Your Highness," Leofric said. "But the man is not long for this world."

Alexios nodded numbly. As much as he wanted Auro not to be one second from his side, Alexios knew he must not show his true feelings, nor any perceivable weakness, in front of the soldiers who guarded the prison, so with a sharp look he wordlessly bid Auro wait in the vestibule before following Leofric inside. Alexios noticed a change had come over Auro since he'd returned to Alexios after the attack. He was still soft spoken, sweet as ever, but somewhere he'd found a confidence that allowed him to stand with his head high, not caring if anyone would question his strange hair or his presence by Alexios's side. It made Alexios smile and gave him the courage to face the assailant, knowing Auro would be right there waiting for him.

The key keeper led them down a dank, torchlit corridor, past the airier cells that boasted small windows and clean rushes on the floor, for higher-born prisoners who may have committed more civilized crimes, and into the small infirmary in the jail, which was surprisingly well-kept for such a dismal place.

Under Papian law, prisoners were allowed to gamble with their lives in the arena within the city walls in exchange for reduced sentences, and were condemned to do so if convicted of a violent crime. The victors must be healed up before they resumed their captivity, and this was where it happened. A narrow, hard bed in the corner of the room was the only one occupied at present. The medicus hovered over the man upon it, sponging off his sweaty brow with a cloth.

Alexios and Leofric approached and the man's feverish

eyes fell upon Alexios. It took everything within Alexios not to physically recoil. While Alexios's fear had swollen the man in the moment, the direct aftermath of the attack had proven him more averagely built, though strong. And yet, the man lying before him now was little more than a skeleton. Only a week or so had passed in the wake of the attempt on Alexios's life—this level of wasting should not have been possible. When the man in the bed recognized Alexios, he laughed, a mirthless, high-pitched wheeze that sprayed a mist of blood past his broken lips.

"Ah, Your Highness," he mumbled. "Forgive me for not rising."

Alexios ignored the jibe. "Who sent you?"

The man cackled again. "No idea," he said. He coughed and a bubble of blood burst at the corner of his mouth. "Plainly, I should have asked, but the purse he offered was fat."

Indeed, Alexios thought. It would have to be, to make attempt on a prince. "Tell me what you know."

"Little enough," he admitted. "Seemed I was destined to be double-crossed, at any rate."

Alexios waited, schooling his face into as blank a mask as he could muster.

"He said I should sneak in, try to kill you. Escape."

Alexios frowned. "Try?"

"Aye," he said, sputtering through another cough. "I thought it might have been a test of sorts, for your man here." He gestured weakly at Leofric, whose scowl sharpened.

"And what of Queen Petillia and her daughter? Did you know the man hired to make attempt upon the Princess?"

He laughed again, a terrible sound as he gurgled on the fluid in his lungs. The stink of blood and death was like to choke Alexios, but he forced down the bile rising in his throat. When the assassin calmed, he said, "What man?"

"The man who was slain in attempt on Princess Dafina's life," said Alexios. "Did you know him?"

"Did you ever lay eyes upon his corpse, *Your Highness?*"

Alexios, hadn't, of course, but he did not say so. He wouldn't give this raving, dying man the satisfaction.

"I would have made attempt at escape that night," he said thickly. "But no one warned me about your little pink witch."

He ignored the slight on Auro, desperate for any usable information. "Tell me who hired you—tell me *anything* of him!"

But they could get no coherent words from him after that, and it was within minutes that he breathed his last, and stilled, eyes open to the ceiling. Alexios stared at the ruin of his body, unable to look away.

"Tell me of his sickness," said Leofric to the medicus.

He pulled a rough spun sheet over the dead man's face. "There is not much to tell. He was hale and hearty one day, wasting away the next."

"Who else came to see him?"

The medicus looked at Leofric as though trying to read his thoughts. "Is this some trick?"

Alexios stood. "No trick," he said, a feeling of dread pooling in his gut.

"It was you, Captain," said the medicus to Leofric. "You came not two days past."

Both Leofric and Alexios were black of mood when they returned from questioning the would-be assassin. Auro looked from one stony face to the other, but neither of them spoke until they were mounted up and well on their way back to the royal villa.

From horseback, Alexios turned to Leofric. "What make you of this?"

Leofric hesitated, and it unnerved Alexios to see him so visibly shaken. "It is not my place."

"It is if I command it," said Alexios.

"Well, first, you know I have not left the villa," said Leofric. "I have not been from Your Highness's side, save to sleep."

"You have not," agreed Alexios. "To my great annoyance at times."

Leofric nodded, considering. "The person who hired him must have found someone who shared my look. To be frank, I find it quite suspect."

"Perhaps, a uniform…if they used makeup to imitate your tattoo…" said Auro.

"Or the jailer and the medicus were lying," said Alexios.

"It is not them I find suspect," said Leofric.

"Untangle your tongue," said Alexios, irritated by his hedging. "I would have you speak your mind."

"It is not merely the man's death I find suspect," Leofric amended. "It is the whole affair."

Alexios frowned. "Go on."

"Apologies," said Leofric. "I don't mean to minimize what happened that night, but it makes me wonder why he would choose such an uncertain method to bring you harm."

Alexios frowned deeper still. It did not take much to call the image to mind. Death had seemed a certain thing to him, at the time. "He shoved my head beneath the water…"

"He had a dagger on his person," said Leofric. "Forgive me, for saying so, Your Highness, but had it been me, entering your chambers of a night with dark intent, I would have simply put blade to throat. Yours and Auro's both, for he slumbered in your embrace, and could have awoken—did, in fact. I would have given neither of you the chance to raise cry, had it been me."

Alexios's hand flew to his neck, cupping his own throat as if he could protect himself from Leofric's words. What he said had a ring of truth to it. Why had the assailant risked all, risked waking Auro? "What of the Princess?"

"I will admit," Leofric said, "It is as the man said—I did not have cause to lay eyes upon his corpse...we had Kato's word, and then I was fixated on protecting your royal person."

Alexios considered this. "It is almost as if..."

"Almost as if whoever orchestrated this did not wish you dead at all."

"Then what was his goal?"

"What, indeed, Your Highness?"

Seventeen

"Again."

Auro stood looking on as Alexios lay on his back, chest heaving, the point of a blunted dagger at his throat. By way of answer, Alexios could only groan.

Leofric stepped back and regained his feet, tossing the practice knife from hand to hand as he watched Alexios on the ground. When he offered a hand to help Alexios up, he pushed it away. It was difficult to watch, but Auro knew that to show his concern would make Alexios furious, and when his temper flared, Leofric's lessons did not land as well.

When Alexios heaved himself to his feet, he doubled over, hands braced upon his thighs in attempt to catch his breath. Leofric prowled before him. "Do you know where you erred?"

Alexios shot him an irritated look. "I'm certain you are about to tell me."

Leofric used the hilt of the practice blade to tap on the back of his own left hand. "You ignored my free hand," he said. "You focused too intently upon the hand that held the blade."

"I can't imagine why *that* would be," said Alexios sarcastically.

The words were barely out of his mouth when Leofric cuffed him on the side of the head with his empty hand.

"*Hey!*" said Alexios.

"Your eyes must miss nothing," said Leofric, unapologetically. "Again."

Auro had watched this play out similarly for the last two hours. He knew Alexios was determined he should not be caught again unawares, but he pursued his training in a feverish, manic sort of way that led to him on his back more often than not. It worried him.

After a few more bouts, Leofric called a halt. Alexios begged another round, or two, but Leofric insisted he needed a chance to rest and eat and prepare for the evening watch. Auro suspected it was for Alexios's sake that Leofric stopped their training, more so than his own.

Auro approached Alexios, wordlessly offering him a towel to dab the sweat from his brow and a cup of fresh water, which Alexios gulped greedily, tiny trickles spilling from the corner of his lips as he drank. In the wake of their visit to the prison fortress, Alexios stood changed. He was no longer the timid, unsure boy Auro had first met—nor the anxious creature he'd encountered directly following the attempt on his life. His fire blazed now, and like fire, he was never still. It worried Auro, as much as it entranced him, to watch Alexios so possessed.

A porter hovered near the edge of the practice yard, and Auro crossed to greet him. Alexios had claimed Auro to his personal staff in the days following their visit to the city. If his parents held issue with the appointment, Alexios kept such things from Auro, who now held title of Alexios's personal valet. He approached the porter and accepted a message on Alexios's behalf. The seal upon the parchment appeared to be that of Gaius Ursus, the son of one of Papia's landed consuls.

Alexios had written to all of Papia's consuls, explaining his need for each consul to appoint someone to oversee the inspection of the roadways in their territory, to discover the extent of repairs needed. The fact that the seal on this response belonged to the son, and not the father, was not lost on Auro as he handed the letter to Alexios. He need only read the look upon Alexios's face as his brown eyes scanned the contents of the missive to know it was nothing good. Alexios crumpled the parchment in his fist, mouth twisting into an angry frown. Before Auro could question its contents, Alexios turned to him and said, "Leofric is absent, but I would have another chance for practice. Care to see what you have learned through observation of our bouts?"

"I would not know where to begin," said Auro, surprised. He had never trained in such arts.

"Begin by undressing," Alexios said. "I would not have your uniform soiled or torn."

Auro looked carefully over his shoulder to ensure they were alone before replying. "Is that the game, Your Highness?"

"No game."

Auro weighed Alexios's suggestion, his expression, the tension in his shoulders, wondering what desire lurked behind his eyes. Perhaps Alexios merely wished for an easier foe than Leofric. Perhaps the frustration at whatever was in the letter from Gaius needed to be vented somewhere. And here Auro stood.

He did not think Alexios would, or truly could, hurt him.

Even before Auro's father had bestowed upon him the powers to sway the seasons, he had grown from the seed of a god. His skin stood strong, impervious to injury—at least, before his father had drained away the lion's share of his grace. He had not cared to test it, after, keeping that particular door to freedom from his cursed life firmly closed and barred. But, maybe it was high past time he found out what strength truly remained to him.

Auro peeled his tunic off over his head and toed off his sandals, leaving him in just a subligaria tied about his hips.

Alexios, garbed the same, faced him, balancing upon the balls of his feet. "Alright," he said. "I will make attack, and you attempt to defend yourself."

"How?" asked Auro.

"However you can," said Alexios, and he lunged.

The breath punched from Auro's lungs as Alexios's shoulder collided with his chest, upending him upon his ass before he could so much as spit. Auro's head collided with the packed earth beneath him and he winced. Alexios followed him to the ground, and they grappled in the dirt. Auro had nothing but his instincts, which he swiftly learned were quite lacking in the ways of combat. Soon enough, he was flat on his back, Alexios kneeling on his chest, his hands pinned to the ground beside his head.

Alexios's grin was triumphant—if a bit feral. "Apparently, I have learned much at my tutor's hands."

"Perhaps," Auro gasped. "But there is a key lesson that appears to have escaped you."

"Oh? And what's that?" Alexios's eyes fell to Auro's hand, which twisted against the packed earth beneath them, a few seconds too late.

A tree root shook itself loose of the dirt and wrapped itself around Alexios's wrist, yanking him off Auro and tethering him to the ground.

"You celebrate victory far too early," said Auro.

After that, they moved their sparring sessions to the privacy of Alexios's apartments, the receiving area cleared of furnishings to create space to train. Leofric was keen to see more of Auro's powers, and the use they could be put to in combat.

A few days later, while Alexios was in court, Auro sat cross-legged on his plinth, eyes closed, recalling the day his father had cursed him. He had finished his work early that morning, and he found himself wondering what had put Kryos in such a mild mood this year. Winter had not been aggressive, had not truly culled as much life as it often did, had not been as cruel. Auro stared at Kryos's statue and shivered, as if his brother were awake, turning that hard glare on Auro and blowing his winter winds through the temple.

The aftermath of Ozias's death had been a fog of misery for Auro, mourning and grief and shame clouding the days following his demise. His father had draped all the lands in darkness for forty days and forty nights, so that all might share in his mourning. Add that to a distance of four hundred years of solitude, well. His recollections were...shoddy, at best.

Their father had condemned them, damned them beyond any hope of redemption. Auro recalled suddenly that it was autumn when Ozias had died. He only remembered because he had woven Ozias a shroud of tulips and they had been very difficult to conjure. But Ozias had loved tulips.

Auro recalled being bled of his grace by a father who would not look him in the eye. Four centuries later and he could still feel the cruel bite of the crystal dagger in the crook of his elbow, the pulse of his blood flowing away, being siphoned off...he frowned. Siphoned off, where? He kneaded his eye sockets with the heels of his hands, as if the pressure could force his memories to fight through the fog of hundreds of years, but it was like trying to hold cupped water in his palms. Temporary, fruitless.

He slid from the pedestal, his toes wriggling in the young spring grass that pushed its way through the cracks in the temple's ruined floor, more and more each year. Auro took comfort from that. If the tiny, soft blades of grass could overcome the heavy press of cold stone, so could he.

Alexios was of a mood. The letter from Gaius had proved the first of several tepid responses to his proposals regarding the roads, and the most illuminating. He wrote to Alexios directly, though Alexios had made attempt to contact his father. Festus Ursus was premier among the landed consuls of Papia, his lands covering the largest territory, his villages the most populous. Alexios had hoped to gain his support, but the response from his son explained why his father hesitated.

Neither the King nor Queen put seal to summons, Gaius wrote. *My father wonders if they are in support of this notion of yours.* Alexios had fumed when he'd read the words, though he did his best to conceal his anger from Auro. He didn't wish to cloud Auro's mind with such pedestrian concerns, wishing for him only to focus upon his memories so they could find *anything* to point them toward breaking the curse. It was becoming harder and harder for Alexios to maintain his optimism in this regard, but he did his best, for Auro's sake.

When he arrived at court that afternoon, he'd hoped to speak with Gaius and gauge his ability to sway his father. Instead, he found Festus absent his son's company, and instead, he had brought with him his daughter, Gaius's twin. The implication was plain—perhaps His Highness would consider Gaia as a potential bride? Rumors of the disaster following the equinox celebration had the local nobles doubling down on their own bids to see their houses elevated. They had quickly decided a foreign princess would bring with her only trouble for Papia—strange customs, unknown dangers, and assassins. Why not shore up their defenses at home, wed the young prince to a daughter of Papia? It had been endless. And then, when Alexios had demurred, they had stonewalled his attempt to discuss the roads.

His parents had proved little help in the matter.

"You would have our infrastructure held hostage by squabbling children?"

"Alexios, these are your people," said the Queen. "You must guide them, and help them. This is diplomacy, something you claimed you were beyond ready to face."

"I know that, but—"

"If you cannot bend them to your will through negotiation, perhaps this task would be better accomplished by someone else." His father's bluntness was like a slap to the face.

"I will figure it out," he snapped.

His parents were furious with him regarding his willful disobedience regarding Auro, and they sought to punish him for going against their wishes. It was a small, petty way for them to remind him that he did not stand king, yet, and he must bend to their wishes regarding marriage, and outward displays of propriety. They'd suggested he take Gaius Ursus as a valet, and Alexios suspected his refusal to do so had something to do with their reticence to aid him in the matter of Papia's roads. Alexios refused to give them the satisfaction of being defeated by tangled webs of bureaucracy. At least, he hoped not to give them the satisfaction. However, the fact remained he had not made nearly as much progress on inspecting the roads as he would have liked.

He felt as though he had taken one step forward in his role as crown prince only to be knocked back several more. Returning from court, Alexios wished nothing more than to crawl into bed. Unfortunately, he had no time to rest. His own projects aside, they had Auro's curse to consider, and the matter of the damned assassin and whoever had hired him.

Leofric had been tasked with making attempt to unravel

what he could in that regard, but at present, all three of these tasks seemed little more than wheels spinning errantly on a broken cart. The days grew longer, which allowed more hours to work, but it troubled Alexios. For Auro, time was running out. He would return to stone in less than two months' time. Alexios promised over and over that they would find something, but he could not help but see doubt in Auro's eyes—deepening every day.

The fact that the consuls and their posturing kept him from spending more time with Auro only served to further his ire. He had not thought the roads would be a simple matter to repair, far from it. However, he may have been...well. Auro would smile kindly and use the word "optimistic." Alexios would curse himself for a fool and use the word "naïve." He had been naïve to think the consuls would move an inch to better the lives of their constituents without the promise of further riches and glories for themselves.

What he wanted now, more than anything, was wine, perhaps a bath, and to have Auro rub the knots from his shoulders, perhaps even to use the taste of Auro's lips to wash the taste of this wretched day from his mouth. As he stepped into his apartments, Leofric did his customary sweep of the rooms, then bowed—albeit a bit more stiffly than usual. "See yourself to some wine, and a chair for fuck's sake," snapped Alexios. "You must have been as miserable as I was in that endless meeting."

A heartbeat lasted longer than Leofric's smile did, but Alexios took it as a win. Leofric ever so slowly crept toward friendly. In fact, before he had begun his work on the roads, Alexios would have said wresting a smile from his stone-faced guard to be the more impossible of the two tasks. Not so, now.

Within his chambers, Alexios breathed a sigh of relief. The sigh and the relief itself deepened when he caught the scent of lilacs. "Auro?"

The man himself hurried in, a smile breaking over his face at the sight of Alexios, who, in turn, felt the stain of his day cleansed by Auro's grin. Auro approached, standing on tiptoe to offer Alexios a sweet, chaste kiss.

There were servants' quarters in his private apartments, a vestige of a previous prince who must have been more high maintenance than Alexios. They'd remained empty for most of his life. Leofric now occupied one of the two modest bed chambers, and there was another adjoining one, and a small, shared privy. Leofric had the place to himself, of course, as Auro spent almost no time in the room marked for his use.

Alexios now stood in the center of his bed chamber, arms spread, and allowed Auro to help him undress. Despite Auro's new official capacity as valet, Alexios had balked at first to Auro actually attending him like a servant, but for some reason, it pleased Auro. The heavy wool of the toga Alexios donned for court was stifling, even in the springtime. Perhaps it was just the weight of station that it carried. Up and under and over and around and finally he stood free of the ridiculous thing. Auro draped the fabric over the back of a chair to be laundered later, leaving Alexios in his belted tunic and sandals. Auro knelt to undo the leather straps around his calves and ankles, and Alexios could not resist stooping to card a hand through his soft pink hair.

Auro looked up at him and smiled before regaining his feet. He wore a thin, unbelted tunic of muslin, which Alexios did not appreciate, for it obscured the lovely shape of Auro's body. He placed his hands on Auro's hips, scrunching up the fabric with his fingers, feeling the curve of Auro's waist, his soft belly, his thighs. With a laugh, Auro peeled off the offending garment. It always shocked Alexios that Auro treated his own nakedness with such casual nonchalance, but blushed a shade to match his hair when presented with a gentle kiss.

Alexios did so now, sucking softly on Auro's plump bottom lip, hoping to inspire that beautiful flush. Since meeting Auro, pink had become Alexios's favorite color. Eager to soak all traces of this day from his skin, Alexios steered a naked Auro into the adjacent bathing chamber.

Auro reached around Alexios's back, taking the opportunity to rub his bare skin against Alexios, teasing him through the fabric of his tunic. With nimble fingers, Auro untied the belt from Alexios's waist and dropped it to the floor, allowing Alexios to yank the tunic over his head and toss it aside. Alexios descended into the water, letting the fragrance of lilacs soothe his frayed nerves, and he settled in his favorite submerged seat near the corner of the bath, resting his arms on the edges of the pool. Auro sat between his spread thighs, and Alexios found his peace complete. When Auro leaned forward a bit, Alexios seized a sponge and began to soap his back, scrubbing Auro's skin until it was slick and clean, glowing. He laid gentle kisses along the nape of his neck, sweeping Auro's dampened curls aside to map the sloping bow of his shoulder with kisses.

Auro sighed and stretched, tilting his head up and back, allowing Alexios access to the side of his throat. Alexios nibbled on the cords of Auro's neck, the meat of his shoulder, relishing the pressure Auro's resultant wiggles put upon his hardening cock. Soon enough, Auro turned in his arms, eyes alight with mischief, to straddle Alexios's lap. Alexios's entire body thrummed with arousal as Auro ground against his groin, and he slid his palms down Auro's soapy back to grab two fistfuls of his ass. Alexios squeezed and kneaded the round, lush cheeks, unable to keep the eager, pleased sounds from escaping his mouth at the feel of Auro's plump flesh filling his hands. Auro smiled into the kiss before biting Alexios's lip.

Alexios surged to his feet, and with a startled *"Hmmph!"*

muffled against Alexios's lips, Auro locked his ankles about his waist to keep from tipping back into the water. Alexios carried Auro across the bath, the water just below his hips cleaved into a wake as he made his way to the opposite edge. He set Auro down upon the lip of the pool without disentangling from his embrace. When he first had Auro in his bed, Alexios had vowed to worship him, and he planned to make good on that promise every chance he got.

If a soft kiss to the lips could summon blush to cheek, Alexios was determined to paint Auro's whole body in reds and pinks. He gently pried Auro's locked ankles from his waist, taking a step back so he could feast upon the sight of Auro seated on bath's edge—and what a sight it was.

Auro sat with his head tipped back, his thighs spread, his skin blotchy and red from the heat between them. Alexios nearly drooled at the sight of his tight, rosy balls and straining cock nestled in their thicket of sunset curls, dripping with crystalline beads of water. It was a lovely vision, as lovely as the flowers Auro called forth each spring. Lovelier even, in Alexios's opinion. Auro's hand fluttered nervously, settling on his thigh, then again on the bath's edge—back to his thigh, and Alexios remained still, tracking the movement, waiting, until it seemed Auro could wait no longer to reach for his cock, seeking some sort of relief. Even as he gave in to the urge, Auro turned his head to the side with a soft whine, and Alexios smiled, seizing Auro's chin in his hands so he could capture his lips in a hungry kiss, swallowing every needy sound Auro served him. A low stone bench fit into the bath, and Alexios knelt between Auro's legs, and he dug his fingers into his thighs to keep them spread, so Auro could not hide.

He kissed Auro breathless, kissed him stupid, kissed him until his lips were swollen and slick and bruised. When Alexios finally drew back for breath, Auro's eyes were heavy-lidded, pupils blown big and black, his chest heaving.

Alexios had never counted himself pious, until Auro. With a grin, he bowed his head to leave a trail of kisses on the interior of Auro's creamy thigh. If this was prayer, Alexios would happily spend the rest of his life on his knees. The dreariness of the morning seemed far away as he licked droplets of water from Auro's skin. Auro's hand still encircled his shaft, and Alexios peeled his fingers away, encouraging Auro to brace his hands beside him on the tiles. "Allow me," Alexios said, resting his chin on Auro's thigh, peering up at him. "Allow me to see to your pleasure."

Auro's eyes widened.

"You are a god, Auro," Alexios reminded him, placing a kiss on his knee. "When was the last time you were treated as such?"

He did not wait for an answer, instead nosing the crease where Auro's thigh met his groin, huffing big lungfuls of the scent of him, clean and bright. He had been wanting to give this try since—well, he'd been about to think 'since the night of the equinox feast,' but if he were being honest with himself, he'd wanted to do this since he'd first laid eyes on Auro. With the tip of his tongue, he traced the groove of Auro's hip, smiling once again at the hitch in Auro's breath.

Alexios mapped the cradle of Auro's pelvis with his lips, and when Auro wound his fingers through Alexios's hair—timid, gentle—and cupped the back of his scalp, Alexios did not flinch. With one hand wrapped tentatively around Auro's shaft, he guided the head of his cock toward his lips. The tip of his tongue poked out, eager for the first taste of Auro to land upon it. He pumped Auro's shaft, watching Auro's foreskin glide up and down, to hide and reveal his cockhead, slick and pink and leaking. Auro gasped, and Alexios glanced up at him through his fringe to see Auro staring at him in slack-mouthed awe. The sight gave him courage, and he dipped his head to swipe his tongue gingerly across the dew beading in Auro's slit.

Auro gasped again, and Alexios groaned—at one taste he was hopelessly lost. Auro's cock tasted of fresh grass and rain, bitter and salty-sweet, the slickness of it divine on Alexios's tongue. He bobbed his head, and Auro moaned brokenly from somewhere above him. Fuck, the warmth of him, the smell, the taste, the noises—all of it was bordering on too much for Alexios, who thought perhaps the act of pleasing Auro alone might see him to his own climax, his cock aching between his thighs as he rocked his hips uselessly in the water. He could take himself in hand, to be sure, but he didn't wish to lose his grip on Auro's legs, so he surrendered himself entirely to pleasuring Auro.

That was enough. That was *plenty.*

Alexios sucked heartily on Auro's cock, hollowing his cheeks, drawing him deeper and curling his tongue around Auro's shaft. Auro thrust into Alexios's mouth, deep into his throat. His cock wasn't overlarge, and it seemed perfectly at home between Alexios's lips, filling his mouth so well. The muscles of Auro's thighs twitched beneath Alexios's hands, and Alexios backed off, not wanting this to end yet, not when there was so much of Auro still to taste. Alexios released Auro's cock with a wet slurp, and Auro turned his head to the side once again with a needy, embarrassed whine. The sound shot through Alexios like a lightning strike. He buried his face in the wiry pink hair between Auro's legs, kissing, nipping, sucking the skin of his thighs, maneuvering him to drape his legs over Alexios's shoulders.

Auro tipped back, unbalanced, and Alexios mouthed over his balls, sucking them gently into his mouth, teasing them with his tongue before moving lower, further, deeper. Alexios found his target, just there concealed between Auro's cheeks. His hole was tiny, furled, and like so much of Auro, it was pink. He could not say entirely what possessed him in that moment, only the strange and primal thoughts that swirled in his head distilled down to one, singular desire—and before his mind could weigh in, Alexios flattened his tongue and laved it over Auro's pucker.

Auro gasped, sitting upright and making attempt to close his legs. "*Alexios!*"

Alexios peered up. "Yes?"

"What are you doing?" Auro's eyes had gone big and round, the flush on his cheeks going from pink to deep red. He squirmed in Alexios's grasp, but Alexios held fast to his legs, keeping them spread wide.

"I just..." Alexios trailed away. "Thought you might like it."

Auro's mouth dropped open, and they stared at each other for several beats. "I do," Auro blurted, before covering his face with his hands. He allowed himself to fall back on the title, and Alexios took that for a surrender, so he grinned and returned to his task.

Alexios kissed, lapped, and teased the delicate skin around Auro's opening. They'd just bathed, so the taste of him was fresh and clean, but something dark and musky lurked there, too—something just nearly...*wrong*, something debauched and dirty. Alexios loved it. Auro's shuddering moans and breathy sighs didn't hurt either, and soon enough Alexios felt Auro's hips twitching as he ground himself against Alexios's mouth, seeking, needing, wanting.

For some time now, Alexios had been wondering what Auro felt like, inside. No, not wondering. He had been burning to know. Without stopping the movement of his tongue, Alexios reached blindly, groping for the small bottle of oil Auro had used to scent the bathwater.

Alexios had dexterous fingers, he was not ashamed to boast. He had wrung climax after climax out of himself over the course of his life, and while the angle was surely different, he imagined the general idea to be much the same.

Auro hissed, arching his back as Alexios worked his finger in beside his tongue, probing, pressing, until Auro bore down enough to accept the intrusion. "Are you alright?" Alexios murmured, kissing Auro's trembling thigh.

"*Y—yes.*"

Alexios made to withdraw at the strain he heard in Auro's voice, but Auro dug his own fingers into the meat of Alexios's upper arms.

"More," he breathed, throwing his head back.

Alexios heaved himself out of the water, lying on his hip beside Auro to kiss his brow, his cheeks, to whisper endearments. And, to nip and suck the shell of his ear as he did. He couldn't resist latching his lips to Auro's exposed throat, sucking hard, scraping with his teeth. Shifting awkwardly, Alexios added more oil to his fingers so he could work a second one into Auro's tight hole.

The change in Auro did not come all at once, but Alexios felt it all the same. Slowly, Auro's weak pleas transformed, becoming desperate commands. Timid at first, then growing in confidence. "Slower, *deeper*, more—there, there, *there!*"

Alexios more than enjoyed obeying Auro, enjoyed coaxing out this forceful, demanding side of him with every crook of his fingers.

Auro's brows knit together, his eyes screwed shut, the frantic clenching of his channel told Alexios he was close. Before he could spill, Alexios hunched over and took Auro's throbbing cock in his mouth once again. He wrapped his lips around the head of Auro's cock just in time to receive his seed, sharp and salty. It felt sacred, and Alexios did not waste one drop. He drank Auro down, eager and ravenous, licking his flushed crown clean until Auro softened between his lips. Alexios kissed his way back up Auro's trunk, the two of them now flopped ungracefully on the marble like a pair of hauled-out seals.

Alexios was still hard, every beat of his heart pulsing with need, his cock bobbing obscenely to slap against his lower belly. Auro walked his fingertips up the shaft, making it jump. "Touch yourself," he commanded. His voice was but a whisper, but it echoed with the authority of the divine.

Alexios froze, his breath catching in his chest. "P—pardon?"

"I would watch," said Auro imperiously, rolling onto his side, propping himself up on one elbow. "I want to see how you give yourself pleasure."

Alexios heaved a shaking, shuddering breath, his skin positively burning. He could not imagine why on earth Auro would want to watch such a thing; he'd caught a glimpse of himself once, in the mirror beside his bed, and found the sight not at *all* arousing. But Auro smiled and Alexios knew he'd do anything Auro commanded him to.

With fingers trembling at the notion of being so exposed, Alexios wrapped a hand around his dick and began to stroke it. Auro sighed dreamily, with the air of one gazing at a truly exquisite work of art, and Alexios squeezed his eyes closed, unable to face the power in that look. As such, when he felt a brush of an errant fingertip trail over his abdomen, Alexios gasped, hips bucking as he fucked his fist. Auro's touch was lighter than a mothwing, but it arrested him utterly all the same.

"*Yes,*" said Auro. "So beautiful."

Alexios moaned, a small whine of embarrassment, of arousal, of *need,* his muscles so tense he felt his entire body might snap as he jerked himself even faster. The catch of his palm on the skin of his shaft only added to the heady awareness of what he was doing, touching himself as if he couldn't control himself, couldn't bear *not* to—and he couldn't. Not really, not with Auro's burning gaze and gentle fingertips exploring every heated inch of him.

Something cool dribbled on his fingers, startling him, but it was just more of the bath oil, filling the air with the scent of lilacs and easing the passage of his hand, allowing him to pump himself more quickly. He was close. Alexios shut his eyes once more, thinking that if he locked eyes with Auro he would fracture entirely.

Then, a white-hot lance of pleasure-pain shot through him and he yelped, eyes flying open. Auro sat beside him, still grinning wickedly, twisting one of Alexios's nipples between his forefinger and thumb. Alexios watched, hand flying over his cock, mouth agape, as Auro sucked his own lip between his teeth and walked his fingertips across Alexios's chest. He pinched his other nipple, hard enough to startle and sting, but not so hard as to eclipse the pleasure, and certainly not so hard as to stop Alexios coming, explosively, with a few final, jerky thrusts of his hips.

Auro continued to torment him as he shot thick, ropey spurts of cum up his belly, a look in his eyes like nothing Alexios had ever seen there before. He finally took pity on Alexios's over-sensitive skin and stopped teasing. He searched around them for a towel so Alexios could clean himself up. Alexios floated in the afterglow, skin humming, choosing to ignore the cool tile digging into his back in favor of pulling Auro close, losing himself in the feel of their damp skin plastered head to toe against each other.

"I know we said we'd do some research this evening," said Alexios after their breathing had slowed to normal. "But this was far more fun."

Auro laughed, nuzzling closer to Alexios's side. They stayed like that until the chill of the tile floor became too much and the call of Alexios's featherbed too enticing.

Eighteen

Alexios adored waking up with Auro beside him. He did his best to shut out the snide voice in his head that reminded him that the number of such mornings dwindled rapidly. Some mornings, like this one, when Auro looked so...otherworldly, the voice was harder to chase away. How could he be lying here, with a god in his arms? It truly confounded.

The light from the rising sun filtered in through the gauzy orange curtains of Alexios's bed chambers, bathing them both in a serene golden glow. It was just after sunrise and the light bounced off Auro's brow, illuminating his soft features, adorning him almost like a...

Alexios gasped. "*Auro.*"

"Nuhh," said Auro, squeezing his eyes shut tight and rolling away.

"Auro!" Alexios flung the covers off them both. "Auro—I think I've got it, I think—"

Auro groaned again, groping for the blanket. When he came up empty-handed, he stretched, rolled onto his front, and propped his head up on one hand. "What are you doing?"

Alexios grabbed yesterday's tunic from where he'd left it on the floor, and after a cursory sniff he pulled it over his head. When his face poked out through the neck, he saw Auro, naked and draped in sunlight, and it was almost enough to dislodge the fresh idea from the front of his mind. Almost. He knelt beside the bed and pressed a kiss to Auro's sleep-slack lips. "Dress," he said eagerly.

Auro trotted after Alexios, a pair of royal guardsmen trailing after them both. Alexios decided against waking Leofric, letting him rest a while longer. He anticipated an earful when he returned to his chambers, but no matter. This revelation was far too important.

"Where are we going?"

"My mother's library," said Alexios. When they reached the door, the guardsmen stayed outside, flanking the door. Plainly they did not have the same suspicious nature as Leofric, but it was irrelevant today. Alexios had no designs on slipping from villa grounds. At least, not yet. It took some searching before Alexios found the book he was after. It was old and enormous, one he hadn't read or even thought about since he was a boy.

"*The Sun Queen's Compendium of Tales,*" Auro read over Alexios's shoulder as he set the book on the desk.

"I haven't looked at these since I was a child," Alexios admitted. "But when you first told me your story...it felt familiar. I just realized where I have heard its like before."

Auro frowned. "You didn't mention that."

"There wasn't anything to mention, truly—but I just realized..." he flipped through the ancient pages to a particular story.

The Dawn Prince

. . .

The story was a simple one, a fable meant to illustrate to children the importance of family. As an only child, and a pampered one besides, Alexios could honestly say it had not been one of his favorites. In fact, when reading the story, he mostly just imagined how lucky he was not to have been cursed with brothers.

At any rate, the story was about the children of the Sun Queen: The Dawn Prince, the Day Prince, the Dusk Prince, and the Night Prince. They were always quarrelling, each thinking they belonged on the throne of the sky kingdom. It was a fanciful tale, and the youngest brother, the Dawn Prince, pulled gold from the rising sun to wear upon his brow as a crown—which is what had struck Alexios so forcefully that morning.

"See?" said Alexios, pointing. "It's *you.*"

Auro frowned down at the page, reading with his finger sliding upon each of the words. "But—"

"No, listen—"

"Alexios, this is just a story."

"This book is old, Auro," said Alexios. "These stories are from before the fall of your empire."

With a skeptical *tut,* Auro flipped back to the front of the book, touching the worn, thick leather of the cover. "The Sun Queen..."

"The Sun Queen was just a name given to an imaginary woman who told all of these stories," said Alexios. "Perhaps a traveling bard from the old empire...or a character spun to give a form to such tales. Or—"

"Or my mother."

Alexios blinked, certain he had misheard. "Pardon?"

"There," said Auro, pointing. His finger, and his voice, shook. "This sigil."

Alexios looked, finding a faint etching in the corner of the book's cover. It was a small bird with a flower clutched in its beak. It was the only decoration on the leather that had not been richly embossed—almost as if someone scratched it there with a knife or a pin. "Are you certain?"

Auro nodded, and Alexios could see the strain in the corners of his mouth. "She must have left this for us—my brothers and me. But why?"

The weight of the book seemed to double, triple, as Alexios held it, watching Auro touch the leather of the cover, again and again and again. "Why?" Alexios echoed, incredulous. "To help you, of course!"

Auro allowed the book to fall closed again. "Alexios," he said. "This changes nothing. Perhaps my mother left this as... as a gift, or—I don't know. But she had no magic of her own. She could not have taken on a god's curse herself."

"She was his wife," Alexios said. "She might have held more knowledge than you knew."

"Like what?"

Alexios flipped through the pages of the story. "It says something here about each brother and his counterpart—the way they have to help each other to save themselves."

"*Please*," said Auro, attempting to close the book on Alexios's hand.

"You really do not believe it possible, do you?" said Alexios.

Auro opened his mouth, utter misery on his face, but no words came out.

"Why did you agree, then? To try?"

"I don't know," said Auro. "I've long ago divested myself of the false hope that things would ever change."

"Or, you're too afraid to *try* to change them," said Alexios. "You might fail. Or worse—you might succeed. And you'd have to face your brothers, and what you all have done."

"I face what I have done every day," said Auro.

"For three months of the year, maybe," scoffed Alexios, "knowing if things get too difficult to bear you will soon return to slumber—safe from past and future both."

Auro took a step away, and Alexios immediately regretted his words. Before he could make any attempt to temper or recall them, Auro turned heel and fled.

Auro had never felt so alone—which, when one thought about it, was really saying something. Alone, and also ashamed. He'd spoken the truth, if perhaps a bit harshly, but the look on Alexios's face had been difficult to stomach.

Auro had allowed himself to be swept up in Alexios's optimism, but faced with something actually touched by his mother's hands...was Alexios right? Was he as much of a coward as Alexios suggested?

Yes, said a voice inside his head.

There was never a doubt. Had Auro been less of a coward four hundred years ago, he could have stopped Ozias, or gone with him—protected him. Ozias hadn't been granted the same power of Auro and the others. How could he have hoped to stand alone against the fury of dueling gods? But Ozias had been brave enough, desperate enough, foolish enough to try.

And Auro had let him go, let him go alone.

Auro's feet took him back to his temple, wishing Alexios had never recalled the storybook, wishing Auro hadn't seen the etching on its cover. It was like hearing a dying gasp from his mother, like losing her all over again. She had been gone from the world by the time Auro had awoken, the first spring following their curse. He had awoken to a world emptied of everyone he'd ever loved—for those first terrible years, Auro had felt like a ghost. He felt like that again now, as he haunted the place where his brothers rested.

Looking at his brothers, Auro tried to pull to mind the few details he'd allowed Alexios to share from the storybook before he'd run off. The word counterpart stuck itself like a thorn in Auro's brain. Which brother was his true opposite? Auro's first reaction was to think, *all of them*. They were all strong, brave. Smart. Powerful. And he was a weakling, a coward, and a ghost. All the same, he forced himself to examine the idea, and when he looked directly across the temple from his own plinth, his eyes fell upon Cedras.

Spring, and fall. Waking, sleeping. Dawn, and dusk—if Alexios's storybook were to be believed. Cedras stood opposite to Auro in so many things, but one could not exist without the other. He crossed the temple to more closely examine the statue. Cedras stood, back straight, eyes tilted down. His was the only statue that turned its face toward the earth, as opposed to the sky. As in life, Cedras the statue wore spectacles upon his face that gave him a serious, owlish appearance, echoed by the stone bird perched upon his shoulder. His pet and companion, Nicodemus. An enchanted bird given to Cedras by their father. Clasped in one of Cedras's long-fingered hands was a scythe, and in the other, an abacus. Autumn was a time for planning, a time for care. A time to harvest one's crops and shore one's defenses for the cold winter months to come. Spring was a time of hope and endless possibility. Autumn was a time for careful reflection and planning. Auro looked forward, while Cedras looked back. Auro hopped up onto the stone pedestal beside his brother, touching his stone curls and searching for something of the cautious, calm young man he had once known. He sighed, letting his fingers explore the statue, studying it in ways he honestly never had before, in all his years being bound to this place. It had caused far too much pain to look too closely upon the visages of his brothers.

It caused pain now, too.

Alexios was right, he was a coward, unable to face anything.

It was that, more than anything, that urged him on.

The stone was so lifelike, Auro had to stop himself from attempting to brush an errant curl from in front of Cedras's eyes. He let his hands wander over the stone, searching for a clue, for anything that might point him in the right direction. Cedras was the only one who had been awake in the months immediately following their curse; it had been autumn after all. Auro had never considered before what that must have been like.

When his slow inspection reached the abacus, he found the only blemish on the entire statue. Frowning, Auro squinted at it, a series of etchings carved into what, in life, would have been the wood frame of the abacus. The lines were faint, and he could not make out their meaning. On an ordinary statue, Auro might have considered this simply a symptom of four hundred years exposed to the elements—but there was nary a scratch on the entirety of the rest of Cedras's statue. Just to be sure, he searched Cosmo's statue, and Kryos's. Both were flawless. The etchings on the abacus had to be meant for Auro, and Auro alone.

He returned to his own plinth, drawing up his knees to rest his chin upon them, so he could sit and stare across the temple at Cedras, like he could will the statue to come to life and answer his questions. A whisper on the spring wind warned Auro that he was no longer alone seconds before a timid voice broke the silence.

"Auro?" Alexios approached him timidly, his face contrite. "Hi."

"I left Leofric on the edge of the lake," said Alexios. "I didn't want to bring anyone else here without...asking."

Auro smiled. "Thank you."

Alexios approached Auro where he sat and wrapped his hands around Auro's ankles. "I'm sorry," he whispered.

Auro leaned forward, resting his forehead against Alexios's. "You have nothing to apologize for."

"I do, though," he said, squeezing Auro's ankles. "I do. I think it's alright, really, if you don't want things to change."

Auro frowned. "It is?"

"I just wanted to help you," said Alexios. "But if you're happy—"

Auro lunged forward, smothering Alexios's words with a kiss. "I have not been happy for four hundred years," he said when he pulled back.

Alexios blinked at him, startled—and the words surprised Auro too. It wasn't something he'd ever admitted, even to himself.

"You were right," said Auro. "I am afraid. Terribly so. But I'd rather be afraid than live like a ghost any longer."

"Are you certain?"

"Yes." Auro leaned in for another kiss, but Alexios leapt backward, vibrating in his eagerness.

"Excellent, because I spent some time reading the Dawn Prince story, and I had some ideas!"

Auro could not help but smile. "Tell me."

"Well, I think, when the story is talking about your counterpart, it means—"

"Cedras?"

"Yes," said Alexios, with a small frown. "How did you—"

"I *may* have been overhasty in my dismissal of the story," Auro admitted. "I began looking at Cedras's statue for clues."

"Did you find anything?" Alexios asked, disappointment forgotten as quickly as it arrived.

Auro led him by the hand to inspect the etchings on Cedras's statue. Luckily, Alexios had brought with him a few sheafs of parchment and a hunk of charcoal. Auro pressed the parchment against the etchings to take an impression by rubbing over it with the coal. The grey-black smudge upon the parchment revealed a phrase:

TRUE FREEDOM

"True freedom?" Alexios said, squinting down at the words.

"Freedom...from the curse? Freedom from the statue, perhaps?"

"What good is that?" asked Alexios, annoyed. "We already knew we had to do that!"

"I am not certain yet," said Auro. "Perhaps this is not the entire clue."

They remained at the temple until sunset, going over every square inch of Cedras's statue, but found nothing else.

"It matters not," said Alexios, as they rode back through the forest. "We will start fresh tomorrow. Perhaps there is something in my mother's study to aid the search. And you can read the storybook more carefully."

Auro tightened his grip on Alexios's waist. They rode double, and Auro pressed his cheek against the valley between Alexios's shoulders. He smiled against the fabric of Alexios's tunic, where he now rested his cheek. It was impossible not to get swept up in Alexios's confident optimism. It seemed with each passing day, Alexios's fire burned brighter and hotter.

In a way, the change in Alexios reminded him of his brother, Cosmo, whose temper always ran so hot. In Alexios, it was as troubling as it was enticing. Cosmo's temperament had gotten him in trouble more times than Auro could count, and in the end, it had engulfed them all in flames.

Nineteen

Auro sat cross-legged on Alexios's bed, *The Sun Queen's Compendium Of Tales* spread open in front of him. Alexios had gone with Leofric on some sort of vague errand, but Auro knew he was trying to be respectful, to give Auro the space to look this storybook over in private, first.

Auro spent a few moments just examining the book. He caressed every inch of its leather binding, touching the etching left by his mother. He wondered if she had been the one to carve the clue on Cedras's statue, too. Unless *Auro's* statue held a clue, Cedras's was the only one that had any blemish, any hint at a way to break the curse. And if his theory about counterparts was correct, it meant that the clue had been left for Auro. It was painful, frustrating—like his mother was speaking to him from beyond the grave, and only him, in a language he did not understand.

Auro opened the book, skipping directly to the story of *The Dawn Prince.* On the surface level, it was, as Alexios said, a simple fable to illustrate to children the importance of family. The brothers in the story had been transformed into cursed paintings, and it was only by working together that they could free themselves and break the curse. The story wasn't long, and he read it a few times, before flipping back to the beginning of the book and beginning to read the other stories. Alexios arrived back in his apartments, bearing a tray of cheese and grapes. Auro hadn't realized the entire morning had passed. Alexios sat opposite Auro and set the tray on the bed between them.

"You are staring," said Auro mildly, turning one of the heavy, yellowed pages.

"Sorry," said Alexios. "Did you find anything?"

"I'm not certain," said Auro. "The story isn't precisely the same as what happened."

"No," Alexios agreed.

The story of the Dawn Prince and his brothers differed from what happened to Auro, Cosmo, Cedras, and Kryos, but the similarities were too blatant to discount, especially with the seal of Auro's mother on the cover of the book. "I think the key part here is about the counterparts," said Auro. "Myself and Cedras, and then Kryos and Cosmo."

"I agree," said Alexios.

The moral of the story involved each brother being unable to restore *himself* to power. To be frank, that seemed like something only a mother of eternally quarrelling sons could come up with. Auro smiled, thinking of it. As a boy, Auro had spent a lot of time in his mother's company. He was the youngest, the most likely to run to her with his troubles. After Ozias had come to court, and with him a constant reminder that her husband had strayed from their marital bed, she had withdrawn significantly. As the five boys grew to manhood, their mother had focused almost all of her time on the empire she ruled, leaving her sons to their own devices and to the whims of their father.

It was as if Alexios read Auro's thoughts when he said, "This story makes no mention of Ozias—even in allegory."

"Nor does it discuss my father," Auro agreed. "But perhaps they weren't relevant to breaking the curse."

"She wanted you all to help each other," said Alexios. "She must have held faith that you would be able to mend things between you."

"Well," said Auro, "Then she would be quite disappointed to see us now."

Alexios didn't answer. He merely rested a comforting hand on Auro's shoulder and gave it a squeeze. "You will figure it out," he said. "And I know she'd be proud that you are trying."

Auro wasn't so certain, but he let it lie for now. "One thing I had been trying to recall," said Auro instead, "was what our father did with our grace when he took it back."

"What are you talking about?"

"That was how he had given us our power," Auro explained. "When he deemed us ready, he would use a crystal dagger to draw his own blood, and we would drink it."

"You drank his blood?" Alexios looked a little queasy at the thought.

"We did," said Auro. "And when we failed him, he turned the blade on us."

"That's...horrifying," said Alexios.

Auro had never really thought of it that way. In fact, he spent most of his time trying not to think of it at all. "My point," said Auro hoping to divert their attentions back to the matter at hand, "is that I don't know what became of the blood he took back from us."

"And your...power. It was in the blood?"

"In a sense, yes. When he drained our blood, what he really took was our grace."

"And you are certain you recall nothing of what he might have done with it?"

Auro shook his head. The memories were murky, almost

to the point of feeling as though they may have been deliber-ately obscured.

"What if he just...took it back? It was his to start with, after all."

"I don't believe he would have," said Auro. "My father desired less responsibility, not more. It was why he had us in the first place. And besides—if my mother's storybook is to be believed, we are somehow able to reclaim it. That would not be the case if my father had taken it with him to the Godsrealm. And..."

"And what?"

"I can...feel it." Auro put a hand on his chest. "It's like an...awareness. My father took most of my grace, and I can feel it—somewhere."

"Could you just follow that feeling?" Asked Alexios.

Auro shook his head. It was difficult to put into words, but he just knew. "And besides," he said, "The whole point of the thing is for us to help each other."

"True."

They sat in silence for a moment, considering.

"So where is it? Your grace?" Alexios asked. "Where would he have put it? Doesn't seem the kind of thing one forgets about it a cabinet."

"No, it does not." Auro dragged his fingers over the words of the Dawn Prince again. "This must tell us. My mother must have hidden it, somehow. And it's not my grace we must find—"

"—it's Cedras's. Yes."

"The place must have meaning," Auro decided. "As you said, the power of a god isn't something one sets carelessly aside. And it must have meaning to Cedras."

Alexios rubbed his eyes with the heels of his hands. "I swear, my eyes are going to tumble from my skull if I read this story one more time."

"Shows what you know, my sweet Prince," said Auro. "As my brother used to..."

"Used to what?" asked Alexios, lowering his hands, but Auro was barely listening. His hands vibrated where they clutched the book. "Auro?"

"Cedras used to say, only in the world of stories are we ever truly free."

Alexios gasped, now fully alert. "'True Freedom'! That has to be it—doesn't it?"

"Yes but where..." Auro frowned, remembering. "There was a library, a massive one. One of the biggest structures in the entire empire. It stood nearly the size of the royal villa I grew up in."

"Where?"

"Here," said Auro excitedly. "Here, in Papia."

The kingdom of Papia was the former seat of the Mykellian Empire, the region central to the harbor and the rest of the continent. "And you think that's where your mother might have put Cedras's grace?"

"I can think of no place on this world that meant more to Cedras," said Auro. "He told me once he would have lived there, if he could."

"Auro," said Alexios, "I don't know if you're remembering correctly. The biggest library in Papia is here, in the royal villa—it was built *after* your empire fell, by my ancestors."

"Do you have a map?"

Alexios stood and crossed the room to where he had a series of documents on his worktable. He spread a large map of the area, weighing down its curled corners with a dagger and a few clay cups. "Papia is in the center, here," said Alexios, pointing.

"If I recall correctly, the library was somewhere in this region..." he slid his finger west, "but this seems to be outside of Papian territory. This area was part of Papia when I was growing up. Now—"

"Now, it's part of the kingdom of Neossós," said Alexios unhappily.

"That's the seat of—"

"Queen Petillia," said Alexios. He grimaced. "Mother of my future bride."

~

"Absolutely not."

Alexios sighed, doing his best to remain calm. Of his parents, Alexios had always found his mother to be the cooler head, which was precisely why he sought her for a private audience, so that he could suggest his plan before broaching the subject with his father. Apparently, he had underestimated the fear a mother might have about her son's life. Under other circumstances, he would have been touched.

Following their revelation about the probable location of Cedras's grace, Alexios and Auro had spent a few days combing through histories to confirm it. The royal family of Neossós had made their seat in the former grand library of the Mykellian Empire. The building had been elegant and large enough to be a sizeable villa, and in the dissolution of the empire, the lion's share of the collections of texts had been picked over, plundered, and dispersed—but the structure itself remained.

"But, Mother—"

"No."

"Father and Queen Petillia had already begun arrangements for a visit between myself and Princess Dafina," said Alexios.

"That was before," said the Queen hotly. "I cannot send my only heir out into the world, vulnerable and unprotected, when we have no idea whose hand moved the assassin to purpose."

"Well," said Alexios, "the same hand moved against Neossós. We would do well to shore up our alliance with them."

The Queen eyed him suspiciously. "You have been talking to your father."

He hadn't, but if she thought he had been privy to his father's diplomatic councils, all the better. "I can read a map," Alexios hedged. "And I know father has dispatched agents to Órnio."

Leofric had ferreted out that bit of intrigue. While he spent much of his time in Alexios's company, he also trained and dined with the other guards. He'd reported back to Alexios that in the wake of the assassination attempt, several of the most seasoned men had begun keeping strange hours—and then not returning to the barracks at all. He had questioned the other men and found out they had been sent on a mission for the King. Alexios had borrowed some of Auro's winged spies, and put the rest of it together, based upon his father's mistrust of King Cletus.

"If those men are discovered, it could mean open war with Órnio. In that case, the more powerful allies we have, the better placed we are. To win—or, perhaps, avoid conflict altogether."

"Regardless," said the Queen after a long hesitation, looking at Alexios as if she had never truly seen him before. Alexios had to admit he was pleased to have thrown her off her footing—perhaps even earning her respect in the process. "It is far too dangerous."

"It is dangerous," Alexios allowed. "But that is all the more reason to secure a marriage. I will remain vulnerable, and our line as well, until I have secured a bride and an heir of my own.

I am certain Queen Petillia feels the same, after what nearly happened to her daughter."

Alexios willed himself not to blink as his mother stared at him, plainly attempting to unearth the truth of his newfound interest in a possible betrothal. Everything he said was true, and in fact, an argument he anticipated his parents would make *to* him—and Alexios could see her wondering why Alexios was making it first. Why would he be so eager after so much resistance?

What would she believe?

The truth, of course. Or—part of it, at least. "Mother," said Alexios carefully. "After what happened I...I have never known such fear. I do not wish to be that vulnerable again."

The Queen sighed. "I will think on this, Alexios."

He nodded, accepting the dismissal, though his instinct was to stay and press the issue until the Queen agreed. Auro was running out of time, and that alone had Alexios wanting to charge off to Neossós that very night. The only way to sway his parents, however, was with a clear head and patience.

Later that night, Alexios and Auro lay abed, each on his side facing the other. Auro explored Alexios's brow with his fingertips, then touched his nose, his cheeks, his jaw. He touched with purpose, he touched with ownership, and Alexios was happy to let him. "It is true, what you told the Queen," said Auro. It was not a question.

"Yes," said Alexios. "In a sense. I still have no wish to wed another, but I know I will have to. And when I spoke of the fear...that much was true. I would do much to never feel that way again."

He seized Auro's hands and drew his fingers to his lips, pressing dainty kisses to each, hoping to take the sting from his admission. Something told him he hadn't succeeded, if the look of hurt on Auro's face was anything to judge by. They had known from the start their time together was limited, but that did not make it hurt any less.

"My mother remains unconvinced," said Alexios. "It may not even matter."

"You will convince her," said Auro loyally, cupping his cheek with his free hand.

Alexios nipped the pad of Auro's thumb, then soothed it with a kiss. "I am not so certain."

They spent a few moments in silence, and Alexios turned the problem over in his mind. He needed to get Auro to Neossós, and he needed to get Auro *inside* the royal villa. Alexios had been mulling over any remaining cards he might yet have to play, and after his conversation with his mother, he was fairly certain he'd be forced to play them. "I think, to get her to agree, I'll need to sweeten the pot, as it were."

"Sweeten it how?"

Alexios sighed. "I don't think the interest in continuing my betrothal will be enough," said Alexios. "Perhaps I can offer to move up the timeline."

"Alexios, no!"

"Auro—"

"I don't want you to sacrifice your freedom for mine," said Auro flatly. "Your parents granted you half a year, why would you seek to sacrifice that?"

Alexios smiled sadly. "My freedom was an illusion," he said. "What is the difference between a wedding now, and a wedding in a few months? My freedom was always temporary. But yours...Auro, I would get married tomorrow if it meant seeing you freed from this curse, seeing you put your family back together."

Twenty

Alexios waited a few days before approaching his mother again.

When he was summoned to the second audience with the Queen, he found her in the garden, sipping tea and reading from a book of poetry. She slid a scrap of fabric between its pages before closing the book and inviting him to sit.

"Alexios—" she began.

"I will foreshorten my betrothal period," Alexios said, though saying the words proved difficult. Alexios had to force them out. "If the Princess and Queen Petillia are agreeable, we can move the date of our wedding up."

Alexios's mother was plainly surprised by that, which was all to the good. "I see," she said.

"We can both agree it is imperative that I wed," said Alexios. "I believe that if I were to visit Neossós, I could negotiate a shorter betrothal with the Princess."

Queen Clio startled.

Good, Alexios thought.

"Well, Alexios," she said, "I am happy you seem to be taking the situation seriously. But these things cannot be rushed."

"I would argue that these things *must* be rushed. The attempt on both my and Dafina's lives has rattled us, and it has rattled Queen Petillia as well. If we wait, we might be asking the Queen to take sides in a conflict with Órnio. If the Princess and I are wed, they will have already chosen their side. Ours."

It took another two days for Alexios to convince the Queen, and another week for her to convince Alexios's father. They dispatched a messenger in all haste to Queen Petillia, and as soon as they received word back, signed not only by Her Grace but by Janus as well, Alexios launched into preparations for the trip.

His initial plan was for him, Auro, and Leofric to make the journey alone. Alexios now realized how foolhardy that notion was, because his father wanted to send him to Neossós with a full century of guardsmen. They haggled over it, ad nauseum, until finally an agreement was reached that they would select a squadron of twenty men.

"How are we supposed to carry out our mission with soldiers following us about?" Alexios fumed, after returning that evening to his chambers.

"I agree with your parents on this," said Auro. "It would be improper, first off, for you to go without an escort. It would also be unwise given what...what happened."

Alexios clenched his fists, and his jaw.

"We can still enact our plan. I can sneak about absent notice, while you play gallant suitor and gracious guest."

Alexios cut him a look. "The day you sneak about absent notice is the day I sprout wings and *fly* to Neossós."

"What other choice do we have?"

"We can adapt as we go, Your Grace," put in Leofric. "The best plans are flexible."

Alexios wasn't so certain about that, but Auro was right. What choice did they have?

Twenty-One

Auro watched as Alexios gathered his things into a bag that would be easy to bring on horseback. For a pampered prince, Alexios showed little reticence to life upon the road. One thing he, his royal parents, and Leofric all agreed upon was the necessity of traveling absent notice as much as possible. At first, the Queen had been certain the royals of Neossós would take it as a grave insult if Alexios arrived as if a vagabond, but eventually she agreed that after what nearly happened to the Princess, the Queen would be far more open to unconventional practices. Besides, Alexios could still manage to stuff all manner of princely trappings in the variety of saddle bags poor Xanthos would be made to carry.

The party was to leave at first light, and Auro begged his leave from Alexios's chambers for the night. It wasn't that he didn't want to spend the night curled in Alexios's arms, as he had spent every night the past few weeks, it was that he wanted an evening alone to gather himself, to prepare for the journey, and to try to feel something of his brothers in their lifeless statues that told him the errand he embarked upon was not a fool's quest.

To the King and Queen's thinly veiled chagrin, Alexios had demanded Auro travel with the party as his personal valet, dismissing several of the palace's far more qualified staff. Auro assumed that by now, Queen Clio and King Nelios understood what sort of relationship Auro enjoyed with their son, but perhaps were so relieved Alexios no longer resisted the marriage match that they didn't mind if he kept a pink-haired bed warmer at his beck and call. Or rather, they didn't mind enough to derail Alexios's present determination to journey to Neossós.

Auro sat upon the floor of the temple, facing the statues of his brothers and his own empty plinth. He allowed himself to stare at each of them in turn, silently asking whatever gods might remain to hear to watch out for them all and to grant them the strength to forgive each other. Alexios had been right. Ozias's death was a tragic accident, one Auro now knew none of them would ever truly leave behind, but they did not deserve to suffer for an eternity of seasons because of it. He suspected that wasn't what Ozias would have wanted, anyway. As if in answer, a wind ruffled the leaf litter on the floor of the temple, scattering them to the corners. Auro crouched beside the mosaic that had been made to mark Ozias's place and recalled the last conversation they had shared.

Auro had been in his bed chambers, dressing himself for the day. He'd woken with worry souring his gut, as he often had those final few months before all had fallen to ruin. If only he had acted sooner, been braver, like Kryos, or smarter, like Cedras...

"I have a plan," Ozias had told him, his dark eyes sparkling.

"I am not certain even you could talk sense into them," said Auro.

Ozias had laughed. "Trust me," he'd said.

And Auro had.

Looking at the faces of his brothers now, Auro sighed,

cursing them all for how foolhardy they'd been. Ozias, too. What would be different now, really? What if he broke the curse, and with their power restored, they resumed their endless feuding? Surely, he should put the welfare of the earth before the desires of his own heart.

He hoped that when they woke, they would be different. Surely four hundred years was enough time for them all to realize the error of their ways.

Auro hoped *he* was different now, as well. Surely, they missed each other, as much as Auro did. They would see.

And if not? He would have to make them.

Alexios, Auro, and Leofric mounted up at dawn, with a company of twenty hand-picked, seasoned guardsmen for the journey to Neossós. Energy buzzed over their small party, and Alexios was not immune. He tried to recall the last time he had left his own kingdom and thought perhaps it had been ten or fifteen years—a trip to Sokol, with his father, as a young boy. He had been nervous then, as well—but it was nothing compared to now.

Alexios turned Xanthos in a small circle, scanning the trees that surrounded them. The King and Queen and a few of their personal guard rode out with them through the rear gate of the royal villa, and as he bade his parents farewell, Alexios felt a stab of guilt. They both expressed their pride in him, now that he'd fully accepted his responsibilities, but he hadn't, not truly. They knew nothing of Alexios's true purpose in making this journey, and he hoped they'd never learn. He planned to do his best *not* to speed up the timeline of his betrothal—he simply could not bear the thought of being unfaithful to Auro, at least until he returned to rest. They both knew that their affair would come to an end on the last day of spring, and they both knew Alexios would be married by the time he woke the following year. Alexios could only do his best to make certain they had the rest of this spring together, and make certain Auro awoke next year to a world where his family was whole.

If he could do that, perhaps he would not feel so guilty wedding someone else. Alexios could never give Auro his hand, but perhaps he could give him his freedom, give him a reunion with his brothers. Healing centuries of bad blood had to weigh more than a few months of stolen kisses, didn't it? The notion still left a hollow feeling in Alexios's chest. He felt wrong accepting his parents' praise and this princess's hope for a favorable match, just as he felt wrong accepting Auro's love. It seemed no matter what, he was betraying someone.

He hoped he would be able to make it up to his parents someday, by being the sort of king they could truly be proud of. The way his parents had immediately placed their seals of approval to Alexios's plan to form a committee to inspect the roads had eased his guilt somewhat. They'd plainly been withholding it as some sort of manipulation. Well, in Alexios's absence, Gaius Ursus would take point as magister of roads, and things would at last begin to move forward. Hopefully they would not kill his project the second they realized he had no plans on committing to a marriage until the last possible second—but he could not worry about that now. One thing at a time, and right now, that one thing was helping Auro find his brother's grace.

One day, Alexios told himself, he would be a king the people loved, who served them and made their lives better. When Auro returned to rest, he would throw himself into serving them and when Auro awoke next spring, the curse would be broken and the kingdom of Papia would be thriving. But for now, he had to maintain his focus on helping Auro. Focusing on Auro was hardly a challenge when he mounted up beside Alexios, shining in the spring sunshine, his green eyes wide and a smile upon his lips. Leofric, too, stayed at Alexios's side, close enough to protect him, as they set out deeper into the trees. Over the past few weeks, his trust in Leofric had done nothing but grow. They sparred daily, and Leofric did his best to advise Alexios and Auro both on tactics that would avail them in a scrap, inexperienced though they were. Alexios had done his best to internalize all the lessons Leofric could offer. He might have lived a soft and pampered life, but he was young and fit and strong, and he excelled under the regimen of drills Leofric pressed upon him.

The journey to Neossós would not be overlong as the crow flew, but for the sake of safety, they took a more circuitous route, through the richly wooded forest separating the two kingdoms. Leofric kept them at a brisk pace, and under his command the men scouted around the royal party in a wide net, each reporting back to Leofric regularly that nothing out of the ordinary had been sighted by the time they made camp for the night.

Auro's face had grown a bit pinched over the last couple hours of riding, and Alexios was eager to get him into his tent so he could rub the aches from his tired legs. While Alexios had exercised and sparred with Leofric, Auro had spent time riding to strengthen his body, but the distance they traveled now was far more than he'd had cause to practice. Even Alexios found himself stiff from hours in the saddle; poor Auro must be in agony. Alexios took Leofric's counsel when selecting the safest place to set his tent, and he took pride in erecting it himself. He didn't want the guards to think him soft, or that he considered himself above them.

His legs were stiff from the day spent in the saddle, but he stretched them a bit, jogging in a circle, waiting for Leofric to finish setting the watches for the evening.

"Your Highness?" Leofric approached him as he paced in front of his tent.

"Yes?"

Leofric glanced over his shoulder to ensure they were not in earshot of the other men. "If you could forgive my frankness—"

"Leofric, are we not past this?" asked Alexios tiredly. "You should speak your mind."

"Yes, Your Highness, well—" he looked desperately uncomfortable.

"What is it?"

"It would not do for you to invite Auro to share your tent."

Alexios felt as though Leofric had doused him with a bucket of icy water. "Pardon?"

Leofric sighed. "Most of the villa staff are aware of your relationship with him," he said. "And I know you value his company beyond all others."

"So why bother pretending?" Alexios asked. He peered around Leofric in order to catch a glimpse of Auro. He stood beside his borrowed horse, Segovax, talking softly to him and petting his mane. Alexios could not help his smile.

"When we arrive in Neossós," Leofric said, "My men will mingle with Queen Petillia's staff. Her guards, her porters. Servants talk."

Alexios returned his gaze to Leofric with a slight frown, waiting for him to continue.

"While kings and queens have been known to keep paramours, even when wed, they are *discreet*. It will not serve for you to flaunt your relationship. If the men tell tales you could not remain from Auro's bed for even the span of a short journey..."

"It would reflect poorly on my intent to form a marriage pact, yes."

"Yes," agreed Leofric. "It would be an insult to your intended, Your Grace. They might even question your ability to…"

"To what?"

"To even get the Princess with child," said Leofric, clearly mortified.

Alexios bristled at the insult to his manhood, but he tamped it down. Leofric of course had a point.

"And…I know you do not feel passionately about her, but it is not…*kingly* for you to humiliate your future bride with such blatant disregard for the charms of women."

He was right. Alexios knew it. This possible betrothal was not only *his* decision—Dafina was as royal as Alexios, and if she sensed the match would be an unhappy one, or that Alexios would be unable to perform his marital duties to produce them both an heir, she might take her…*charms,* as Leofric put it, elsewhere. Alexios was hardly the only prince on the continent. Part of him, a large part—perhaps even all of him, wished her to find another prince. Alexios would never strive to make their marriage an unhappy one, but did this princess not deserve someone who would love and adore her?

That would never be Alexios, but it seemed they might be stuck with one another anyway.

The least he could do in advance of his arrival was show the lady the respect she deserved.

He sighed. Alexios had been looking forward to cuddling with Auro beneath the fur blankets in his tent that night. He simply slept better with Auro at his side, to say nothing of the other comforts and pleasures they had both hoped to enjoy once the day's traveling was done. Alexios patted Leofric's shoulder, to show he did not resent him for his frank counsel, and went to tell Auro they'd be sleeping apart for the journey, at least. Auro's face fell immediately, but he recovered himself and smiled, though to Alexios's eye, the smile seemed a little sad. The urge to pull Auro into his arms, to tuck him under his chin and breathe in the scent of spring from the top of his head was overwhelming, so Alexios took a step back and politely inquired if Auro required assistance with his own tent.

He declined.

In attempt to distract himself, Alexios approached Leofric once again. "I thought perhaps we could spar," said Alexios.

Leofric gave him a calculating look. "It's been a long day of riding, Your Highness."

"And?"

Leofric sighed. "And nothing. Let us find a likely spot."

Half an hour later, Leofric had put Alexios on his back three times. He wheezed, the breath punched from his lungs after a sharp blow to the chest.

"Get up."

Alexios rolled onto his hands and knees, coughing. "You seem upset."

"I'm not."

"You strike with purpose, then," said Alexios.

Leofric pointed at him. "And *you* do not."

"So that's why you're upset?"

"I am not upset," Leofric bit off.

"Alright," said Alexios, regaining his feet. "Again."

A twig snapped in the distance, and Alexios whipped his head eagerly toward the noise. He realized his mistake a split second later when Leofric kicked his legs out from under him and sent him sprawling. "That's enough," said Leofric.

Alexios spat out a mouthful of dirt. "What?"

"Your Highness," said Leofric. "I am yours to command, but I do not appreciate having my time wasted. Your head is in the trees, with Auro, not here, training. The day has been long. I am tired. I would ask *permission* to rest, so I can better serve you tomorrow."

"I didn't think you got tired," snapped Alexios, picking a dead leaf out of a fresh scrape on his knee. "I thought you'd just go into your tent and sharpen your sword until morning. Lift weights or something."

Leofric turned and left him there in the dirt—and Alexios couldn't blame him, really.

Once he retired for the evening, Alexios tossed and turned all night. He kept falling asleep, only to jerk awake, lingering anxiety from a forgotten dream preventing rest for another hour or two, only for the circle to repeat again and again. By the time dawn broke over their camp, and Leofric called the men to mount up, Alexios was more exhausted than before they'd stopped for the night. He swung himself gracelessly into the saddle, feeling like a sack of turnips.

Auro trotted up beside him, looking fresh as a dewdrop. Alexios tried not to take it personally that Auro had plainly no trouble at all finding rest without him. This was made far easier by Auro bumping his knee into Alexios's and saying quietly, "I have slept alone for centuries, but after weeks in your embrace, I find I no longer wish to."

Alexios blushed happily. "I missed you, as well."

Their gazes lingered upon each other across the short distance between their horses, before Alexios broke the look and turned his eyes forward. "Come," he said. "The day will be long."

"The faster we make the journey," said Auro, "the sooner we can return to...to the villa."

Alexios furrowed his brow. He heard the unspoken *home* that Auro had almost said. Looking at Auro's profile as they rode, Alexios found himself wishing with all his heart that such a place existed—a home, *their* home. It could never be so. But returning to Papia with Auro at his side would be almost as good, would it not?

Twenty-Two

It was all Auro could do not to simply roll off the back of his mount to land in a heap upon the grass. After four days of travel, his abdominal muscles shook, his legs ached, and his head pounded behind his eyes. When he stopped for the day, Auro still had his duties to attend. Suffice it to say, he was exhausted, drained. Spending the nights alone did not help, either. He'd become accustomed to Alexios's soothing warmth, his long limbs tangled around Auro as they slept.

As he rode that day, Auro had felt the earth begging for rain. He knew his brother, Cosmo, rarely ever graced the lands with rain over the summer months, so it was for Auro to prepare the living things for the time of drought. It was a careful balance to maintain—if he simply unleashed a deluge whenever the earth thirsted, the land would drown. He must dole the water from the clouds with care, so the seeds and sprouts and mosses could drink it down in safety, leaving everything fat and moist and prepared for Cosmo and his unyielding sunshine.

Auro dug his fingers into the ground, feeling the dirt,

feeling the vibrations of everything that lived. The hairs on his arms, the back of his neck, rose as the clouds grew heavy, ready to birth a storm. For the sake of Alexios and his men, Auro hoped their party would reach Neossós before the storm broke. Regardless, they would be riding in a drizzle tomorrow, of that much he was certain. The needs of the natural world outweighed the comfort of their convoy, and Auro's priority was ensuring the season progressed as it should. The dirt on his fingers felt soft and familiar, welcoming him, and with every movement, he dislodged the smell of freshly turned earth. The scent never failed to comfort him, and with the electric energy that always came before a storm, Auro's skin prickled, as if he could feel the static sparking across his skin.

"I suppose I could not convince you to keep this storm at bay."

Auro jumped. Alexios now stood beside him, staring up at the sky. So lost in his own thoughts, Auro had not even heard him approach.

Alexios tore his gaze from the clouds and sat on the grass beside Auro.

"Apologies," said Auro, resting his head on Alexios's warm shoulder. "The earth needs the rain."

Alexios turned to kiss Auro's forehead. "I surmised as much."

Auro felt a good deal of tension leeching out of him at the simple presence of Alexios's body beside his own. They sat in the quiet for a moment, the rustling leaves, the insects, and the few birds awake at this late hour filling the air between them with the soft music of spring evenings. Auro shifted closer to Alexios, as close as he possibly could, pressing hip to shoulder where they sat side by side upon the ground. Auro always marveled at the warmth of Alexios's golden skin, as if he were a brazier meant to keep Auro bathed in sultry heat.

Alexios turned his head, nuzzling into Auro's hair. The

vibrations of his breath rolled down Auro's spine in such a way that he couldn't tell which came from Alexios and which came from his own resulting shiver. Alexios twirled one of the pink strands around his finger. His next quiet words were muffled into the column of Auro's throat, though there were naught but the trees to hear them. "I have missed you."

"And I you," Auro said, tilting his chin up, allowing Alexios's lips more room to roam.

"We arrive in Neossós tomorrow night," Alexios said, drawing back, his breath still gusting over Auro's skin.

"Yes," said Auro. He turned his head, tossing his curls to catch the glow of the moon, hoping to entice the return of Alexios's sweet lips on his neck.

Instead, Alexios brought his fingertips up to trace the same path he'd made with his kisses. When the pads of his fingers reached the shoulder strap of Auro's tunic, Alexios teased them below the fabric, dragging them along Auro's skin. Asking. Auro twitched his shoulder, encouraging the strap to slide down and bare his skin.

Alexios released a low groan, from deep in the back of his throat, so quiet Auro was certain it was not meant to be heard. He kissed Auro's shoulder, allowing his lips to trail over the exposed slope of Auro's neck, up to his ear. After giving the shell of Auro's ear a sharp nip, Alexios once again stuffed his nose into Auro's hair, inhaling deep.

"What will happen," Auro asked hesitantly, "when we arrive in Neossós?"

Alexios withdrew with a sigh, drawing his legs beneath him to sit curled upon the grass. "I am not certain. I don't think we'll be able to share a bed there, either."

Auro must have made a face, because despite everything, Alexios laughed. To retaliate, Auro pulled a chunk of grass out of the ground and threw it at him. But he was smiling too. He had to—it was either that, or really examine what came next for them both. The clod of dirt left a smudge on Alexios's cheek before falling back to the ground. With a twirl of Auro's fingers, the clump of grass rooted itself back into the soil, and Alexios's eyes tracked the movement of Auro's hand, lips parted hungrily. He looked so lovely in the moonlight. In any light, really. Auro could see the stars reflected in Alexios's big brown eyes. He cupped Alexios's cheek, using his thumb to brush the dirt from his skin, and pulled him in for a kiss.

Kissing Alexios was like nothing Auro had ever experienced in all of his centuries upon the earth. It had changed him irretrievably from the very first brush of their lips. Alexios was eager and hungry, but content to let Auro lead the dance tonight. His mouth was warm and inviting, his lips pillowy. He tasted of wine and the evening meal they'd shared around the campfire. The smell of woodsmoke clung to his skin. Beneath that was a flavor all his own, fresh and full of life. *Alexios.*

Auro leaned back and spread his legs, a clear invitation for Alexios to slot himself between them. Alexios answered this summons, shuffling forward on his knees. He noticed Alexios had something concealed in his palm, but he was immediately distracted by Alexios reaching below the hem of his riding tunic and pulling it off over his head. Auro gulped, drinking in every inch of Alexios's bare body as he cast his tunic aside and reached back to slip off his sandals. With trembling fingers, Auro reached forward to the knot of fabric below Alexios's navel, removing his subligaria like unwrapping a gift. The dew of sweat on Alexios's chest shone in the moonlight, leaving Alexios glowing where he towered over Auro, up tall on his knees. *This was where Alexios was meant to be*, thought Auro. Here, naked in the grass with the moonlight glowing off his skin.

Alexios leaned down, bracing his weight on his arms to claim Auro's lips once more. Stoking the fire between them,

Auro spread his thighs, hitching one leg up and over Alexios's narrow waist to keep him close. They ground against each other, and Auro would not have been surprised if his own clothing took fire then and there. When Alexios slid his palms up Auro's legs, pushing his tunic up over his hips, he let his head drop back, panting to the stars above them both. Soon, Alexios had worked the fabric up even further, and peeled away Auro's loincloth, leaving him bare from the chest down. There was something so debauched about the pose—he still wore his sandals, and the fabric of his tunic was bunched up near his chin, tangled under his armpits. Alexios latched his lips around one of Auro's nipples, suckling on it until the bud was hard, shiny, and wet, a pinprick of pleasure. He moved to the other side of Auro's chest, and Auro gasped and whined, bucking his hips to grind his cock against Alexios's thigh.

"I want you naked," Alexios murmured against the fine trail of pink hair on Auro's belly.

Words failed Auro, who nodded, though Alexios couldn't really see him from this angle. He worked his rumpled tunic up over his head as Alexios yanked the leather straps from his calves to remove his sandals. When Alexios resumed his place on top of Auro's body, he carded a hand through Auro's hair, his gaze tender.

"When you asked what would happen when we arrived in Neossós, what did you mean?"

Heat flooded Auro's cheeks, and he turned away.

Alexios caught his chin, forcing Auro to meet his eyes. "Tell me."

"I was curious if we'd be able to share a bed once more," Auro hedged.

"*Hmm*," said Alexios, dragging his thumb across Auro's bottom lip. "To what end?"

"*Yours*," said Auro, nipping playfully at Alexios's thumb. "And mine, hopefully."

"I don't think that would be on form," he said, as his eyes darkened. "But I also don't think I can wait until we next share a bed to have you."

Their next kiss was heated and Auro melted into it, thinking he might liquefy entirely and the earth would absorb his body like rain. That would be an alright end, Auro thought. Alexios pushed one of Auro's knees up toward his chest, and with his other hand, fumbled with the small bottle he'd had concealed in his hand. When he removed the stopper, the rich, tart scent of olive oil filled the heated air in between them.

"You were certainly confident when you came into the trees tonight," said Auro with a cheeky grin, watching as Alexios slicked up his fingers.

"I like to be prepared," said Alexios. "One never knows when an opportunity might arise."

"An opportunity for what?"

Alexios let his eyes rake over Auro's naked body. "Worship."

Auro groaned, dragging Alexios down on top of him once again, and joined their hands in a slippery, messy tangle. Auro lined up their cocks, encircling them with both his hand and Alexios's. Alexios allowed Auro to guide their hands, setting the pace and the pressure with which he stroked them both.

They both thrust eagerly into the slick space created between their palms, and Alexios lowered his lips to Auro's neck, sucking and biting the skin there. "Harder," gasped Auro, his body arching off the ground.

Alexios sank his teeth into Auro's throat, scraping against the tendons of his neck until he reached his ear. "You have the softest hands," he whispered, like a secret.

Auro hummed, heat rushing to his face. He'd often felt perhaps he was too delicate—for his father's liking, to fit in with his brothers, for the power he bore. But Alexios liked him that way, relished in Auro's softness.

Well, he relished in Auro's hardness, too.

Alexios disentangled their fingers, trailing his pinky down the crease between Auro's thigh and his groin, pressing their foreheads together as his eyes tracked the progress of his own hand. When he palmed Auro's balls, Auro did his best to keep stroking them both, but maintaining the grip was a challenge with his hand alone—it was smaller than Alexios's, with its broad palm and long, elegant fingers. Auro loved Alexios's fingers, the way they tangled with his own or cupped his cheek or tugged on his curls. The way they moved inside him.

When Alexios had finished toying with Auro's balls, those fingers found their way to his hole and Auro bloomed, opening for Alexios and yielding eagerly to his fingertips as they trespassed within him. He opened his mouth, too, surrendering to Alexios and his demanding kisses. Auro had never felt anything like Alexios's hands, so dexterous, so exacting—but tonight, it was just shy of enough.

Alexios traveled toward his future, his future with a wife, and children, the people of his kingdom. Auro only had him now, for one season. The span of one season was little more than the blink of an eye to someone like Auro, who'd lived four hundred years. How could he put all of what he felt for Alexios into one season's worth of days—or even a hundred season's worth of days?

He couldn't.

"Auro?" Alexios's fingers stilled. He tilted his head to the side, stroking Auro's cheek with his off hand. "Where did you go?"

"Nowhere," said Auro, and he kissed Alexios again, something aching and hungry waking up in his chest. "Fuck me," he blurted.

Alexios stilled immediately, breathing hard like a startled animal at bay. "I have never heard you curse before."

"You make me forget myself," said Auro. This was a lie, though. Alexios, in truth, made Auro remember.

Alexios made a sound, a feral animal sound that was somehow both submissive *and* possessive. It was as if he wished to submit to anything Auro wanted, wished for Auro to do whatever he wanted, but *only* to him. Auro had never heard Alexios make that sound before. "Auro," Alexios said, and his voice rumbled low in his throat, low enough that Auro felt it in the bones of his own skeleton. "I have never wanted anything as badly as I want you."

"Take me, then," said Auro, breathless. Alexios drew back, his fingers sliding out and Auro gasped at the feeling of emptiness they left in their wake. He lay on his back, flayed open and untethered as Alexios pulled away to retrieve his oil. Auro did not like that moment, not at all. "*Alexios*," he said, his voice cracking around an absurd lump in his throat.

"I'm here," Alexios murmured sweetly, returning at once, one hand busy between them as he slicked up his shaft. "I'm here."

The blunt head of Alexios's cock nudged his hole, and Auro closed his eyes, exhilarated and afraid at once. Auro's own cock stood hard as a spear shaft, curved against his lower belly, weeping drops of precum to form a sticky puddle on his skin. He swiped his fingers through it, embarrassed by his own eagerness, but Alexios seized his wrist, brought Auro's fingers to his lips and sucked them clean. Auro's mouth dropped open in awe as a shockwave of lust fired through him—and in that moment, Alexios sank inside. Auro released a long, low groan. The burning stretch, the ache, the fullness of Alexios inside him immediately overwhelmed, and the look on Alexios's handsome face was one of rapture. Auro canted his hips at once, welcoming Alexios as far inside as he could go, until his hips lay flush against Auro's ass.

"*Oh,*" he said softly, his head falling back in the grass.

They stayed still for a moment, each of them adjusting to the feel of the other—searching each other's eyes for traces of fear or reticence, and finding none. And then, Alexios began to move. Sweat beaded on his forehead, his beautiful eyes screwed closed as he drew out and thrust home once more. Each slow, exploratory thrust was a sweet and exquisite torture as Alexios found his sea legs, leveraging his weight onto his knees so he could sink into Auro again and again. Alexios was far from heavy, but Auro welcomed what bulk he possessed, holding him close to the ground, sandwiching him between the earth he loved so well and the heat of Alexios's body.

As he relaxed into the reassuring pressure, things began to change. From his back, up over his shoulders, from his scalp to his toes, burning through the muscles of his thighs, Auro tingled. His grace thrummed in every pore of his skin as Alexios twisted his fingers into Auro's hair to kiss him once more, fucking his tongue into Auro's mouth in time with the thrusts of his hips, and to Auro it was like...being *fed*.

"*Auro,*" said Alexios, his voice raw as he pulled back. "Auro, I—do you smell honey?"

A sweet, fresh scent stirred on the breeze around them, and Auro opened his eyes to see that where merely grass had been before, a bed of sweet alyssum had sprung up beneath him, the dainty little blooms peeking out around his body where Alexios had laid him down.

"Woah," said Alexios. "I didn't know you could—*oof!*"

Auro cut off Alexios's startled observation by upending him, swapping their positions, leaving Alexios flat on his back. Auro climbed atop him, power buzzing in his veins, so intense he could hardly see. He straddled Alexios's narrow hips, one hand braced over the heart on which he now staked his claim, and the other holding his shaft to slide down upon it. If possible, Auro felt even more full as he sank down to rest on Alexios's hips. More complete.

Whole.

Auro curled his spine, squeezing Alexios inside him, hard enough for Alexios to release a startled gasp. His hands flew to Auro's waist, digging those beautiful fingers into the thick flesh of Auro's hips. Perhaps hard enough to bruise. Auro hoped so.

He circled his hips, used his thighs to post up and down, to grind against Alexios's lap. Auro had never done this before, and he wished to find what he liked best, and what movements would make Alexios come apart for him.

Auro leaned forward, bracing his hands on either side of Alexios's face. More sweet alyssum sprang up between his fingers, its scent curling around them, the smell of honey and sweat and sex and earth and grass and *Alexios. Alexios. Alexios.* He rode hard, faster, chasing...something.

A secret part of Auro, dark and twisted and covetous, wanted to destroy Alexios, to ruin him. He wanted to bring him a pleasure so intense that only Auro could put him back together again. It was an ugly impulse, but it hooked its fingers into Auro's chest and wouldn't let go—the hope Alexios would recall this night. For years to come, as he lay abed with his future bride—forever unsatisfied without Auro's tight heat clutching him, ensnaring him, holding him, loving him.

Alexios was his, and whether Auro was flesh or stone, he would never release that hold. Ever. Alexios cursed and moaned, tried to match Auro thrust for thrust from his position upon his back, but he could not. *No one could,* thought Auro, flush with savage elation as he rode. Auro was no mere man. He was a god, and Alexios was his. This moment was his. This pleasure, all of it, was his alone.

"Yours," agreed Alexios on a ragged gasp.

Auro had not realized he'd made his claim out loud, but he had no thought to recant it. Why bother? What could it possibly matter—Alexios *was* his, and he'd sealed that covenant with his own agreement.

Pleasure unlike anything Auro could have ever conceived mounted deep within him.

How had he gone four hundred years without the joy of fucking?

How had he gone four hundred years without Alexios?

Alexios slid his hands around to cup Auro's ass, to squeeze and knead his cheeks, to pull them apart so he could fuck him even deeper, harder. Auro rocked back, bracing his hands on Alexios's thighs, arching his spine like a bowstring, his cock jutting out hard and proud in the air between them. Alexios followed him, sitting up to wrap his arms around Auro, to clutch desperately at the blades of his shoulders, and stroke his back, to bury his face against Auro's throat and bite him, hard. It changed the angle of his thrusting, and suddenly Alexios was hitting a place inside Auro that made his eyes roll and his toes curl. They moved faster, bumpier, but it hardly mattered, hurtling them both toward release as if they plummeted together off a cliff, only instead of hurtling to shatter upon the ground...

They burst into the sky.

Alexios muffled a cry into the skin of Auro's neck, but Auro made no such attempt to quiet himself, his climax punching the air from his lungs and any thoughts from his head as he painted Alexios's golden skin with creamy white streaks of cum. Auro's last conscious notion was the desire to lick Alexios clean before Alexios went rigid in his arms, his cock swelling even further as it twitched and pulsed inside him. For a few heartbeats they were locked in a strange sort of rictus, before Alexios's hips stuttered, tiny aborted movements like he simply couldn't help rutting into Auro as he spilled.

Auro did not wish to part, ever. He clung to Alexios as the aftershocks of his release settled into a pleasant, floaty feeling. Eventually, and Auro wasn't certain how, he found himself sprawled on his back in the cool grass, the scent of sweet alyssum washing over him as he rode the pleasurable afterglow. Alexios lay on his side next to Auro, he'd propped up on one hand, eyes hooded and lazy. He dragged his fingertips over Auro's flesh, which still sang under every touch. He could feel his grace sparking in the wake of each feathery touch, like Alexios summoned the power from deep in Auro to swirl on the surface of his skin.

Auro sighed and allowed his eyes to flutter closed.

"Hey," said Alexios.

Auro may have grunted in response.

"Hey," said Alexios again, giving the flesh below Auro's ribs a poke.

"*Unh*," said Auro, opening one eye.

"You can't fall asleep here."

"Why not?" The breeze ruffled his hair, cool on his sweaty skin. This was how Auro had slept each night for nearly four hundred years, comfortable and free beneath the stars, and the grass was far more welcoming with Alexios beside him.

Auro rolled over, mirroring Alexios's position, resting one hand on the sharp jut of Alexios's hip. If anyone should have been immortalized in marble, it should have been Alexios, Auro thought. He imagined a temple full of statues of Alexios, thinking he would like to have one to capture each of his moods, each of his varied smiles. They would all fall short, he knew—unable to truly capture his warmth, his fire.

"Alexios," he said. "I—*mmf*."

Alexios surged forward, cutting off his words with a kiss. When he drew back. Auro was surprised to find Alexios had a broken, haunted look on his face. Their knees just brushed together, and Auro used his thumb to stroke the delicate skin of Alexios's waist, staring into his golden-brown eyes, asking.

Alexios didn't answer, except to close his eyes, like he was pulling shut the curtains to keep Auro from looking into his thoughts. "I know," he murmured, almost to himself.

Those two words shattered the sphere around them, and Auro felt as if he'd crashed to earth. He was no longer a god.

He was simply a man, powerless as any other mortal foolish enough to fall in love.

Auro clung desperately to Alexios, trying to anchor himself in the swirling tide of what passed between them, afraid that if he didn't, he would be swept away.

Twenty-Three

Alexios woke at dawn to the sound of Leofric calling the men to form up. He'd become used to it over the past few days. The storm brewing in the sky, Auro's storm, would be upon them soon, and Leofric wished to get as much distance out of the day as he could before it broke. He knew Leofric still hoped to reach Neossós by nightfall, to get Alexios off the road and into the safety of the royal villa.

Alexios, however, wished they would never reach the place, rain be damned. He wished instead to return to the glade where he and Auro had made love under the stars the night before, and possibly remain there forever. But that was a foolish dream, for many reasons.

Not least of which was that Auro would return to stone in a month's time.

Perhaps Alexios should have allowed Auro to confess his feelings last night, and shared his own in return. It would have been easier, whispers of love in the dark, than telling Auro how he really felt—which was as if he was being ripped to shreds.

He did love Auro, of that much he was certain.

But Alexios refused to be the sort of man who made beautiful promises, empty of any deeds to make them true. That had been his reputation, the lies he'd hid behind—and he refused to make it true now. How could he profess to love Auro, and then marry another? How could he love Auro, and then condemn him to a lifetime of sneaking and hiding? Even if they succeeded in breaking the curse, that was no way for one such as Auro to be loved.

Auro deserved to be loved and worshipped in glorious sunlight, claimed for all the world to see by someone who could make that claim with honesty and pride. That could never be Alexios, as much as it broke his heart to admit it, as much as it nearly killed him to think of Auro finding someone else one day.

The beginning of their day's journey took them through the small clearing where he and Auro had spent the night, and Alexios found himself flushing. In the grey light of the cloudy morning, he could see a near-perfect silhouette of a human body sprawled across the grass, formed by the tiny, delicate blooms of sweet alyssum. It was as if Alexios could track the rolling of his and Auro's bodies—a patch of flowers shaped like a hand, his toes, the spread of Auro's thighs. Small clusters representing Auro's knees where they'd pushed into the ground. Heat pooled in his groin as he stared at the formation of the flowers.

Auro's face grew drawn and pinched as they rode on, however. Each flinch sent guilt stabbing through Alexios, and under that, something he could not quite name. Auro had declared Alexios his own, last night, and a twisted part of Alexios was happy to know the claiming went both ways. He rode up beside Auro, reining in Xanthos to keep pace with Auro's borrowed horse, Segovax.

"Apologies," said Alexios quietly. "I should have thought..."

Auro huffed. "Each hurt is a lesson," he said, echoing what Alexios told him after sparring with Leofric. Auro cast a cheeky, if not a bit grim, smile Alexios's way. "Don't ride an amorous prince the night before you have to ride a horse all day."

Alexios let out a sharp bark of surprised laughter, but he noted that Auro's jesting smile did not reach his eyes.

The rain began a few hours into the day's journey and did not let up. The entire party was bedraggled and sodden by the time Leofric's advanced scouts rejoined them a few miles from the gates of Neossós. With them was a man Alexios recognized from the night of the equinox feast, the captain of Queen Petillia's guard, Kato. He was tall, broad, and stern enough to give even Leofric's stony countenance a run for its money. He dismounted and sank to one knee in the mud, bowing his head. "Your Royal Highness," he said respectfully, ignoring the rain that *plink-plinked* on the hammered silver of his breastplate.

"Rise," said Alexios. "Well met, Kato. It is an honor to be welcome in Neossós."

"Aye," said Kato. "We still have a few leagues to cross. Let us continue on before we all drown."

Alexios could not agree more. He was wet, cold, and in dire need of a bath and a hot meal, but it was more than that. Auro had been strangely silent, and Alexios could possibly chalk it up to the pain of a day's ride in the saddle after the night they'd shared, but something told him it was more than that. He had come to know Auro's moods, and he didn't like the pained cast to his usually cheerful face, the dimness in his usually bright eyes. Alexios knew Leofric would encourage him to let Auro bed down in the servants' quarters at Neossós's royal villa, and before things had soured in the wake of their loving, Alexios would have agreed. But he refused to cast Auro so far from his side while things stood so unsettled between them.

Leofric also appeared out of sorts. Though Alexios hardly claimed to *know* Leofric, he had come to understand him over their few months together. He could read the tension in his cheek, the cant of his frown, the furrow of his brow. Alexios could tell when something truly weighed on his mind, and when he was simply being his grumpy self. Leofric did not offer to share his current thoughts with Alexios however, which left him on edge, wondering.

They approached the capital city of Neossós from the north, directly into the royal grounds. It was a roundabout way to go in the rain, if Alexios recalled his maps correctly. Before he could raise a question, Kato said, "After what nearly happened the night of your feast, Your Highness, both to your royal person and the Princess, we have tightened security a great deal. Begging your pardons, we thought it best for you to arrive in secret, absent the fanfare of a traditional royal welcome."

That sounded prudent to Alexios, who wouldn't have cared much for an extravagant royal welcome anyhow—especially given the state of his party. He assumed he was not alone in wanting a rest and a cup of something hot. Leofric narrowed his eyes, squinting suspiciously at Kato, but he too let it pass.

They reached the royal stables just as the sun began to set, and Alexios was startled to see it was nearly empty. "Increased border patrols," said Kato, when Leofric finally pried open his jaw to pose inquiry.

They hadn't seen any border patrols, nor were they hailed by scouts as they crossed from Papian territory into Neossós, but then again, Leofric had taken pains to screen their movements, so perhaps it wasn't so peculiar. Alexios swung down from his horse, landing unsteadily on the straw-strewn floor. After so many days in the saddle, he felt a bit like he'd forgotten how to walk. "My men will take quarters in your barracks, if there is room for them," said Alexios. "Leofric will remain with me, and my personal valet, Auro."

Both Leofric and Auro covered their surprise well, and Kato seemed not to notice. "Of course, Your Highness. We have prepared quarters for your men, and there are guest apartments in the western wing of the villa. I can show you there personally. Queen Petillia has requested the honor of your presence at evening meal, if you would be so obliged."

Alexios would much rather eat alone in his rooms with Auro and Leofric, but of course he knew how he was meant to respond. "The honor would be mine," said Alexios politely. "If you could inform Her Grace I require some time to bathe and freshen up, I would appreciate it."

"Of course."

Kato escorted them inside the villa, and as he looked around, Alexios thought he could see the remnants of the villa's original life—shelves built into the walls that once held thousands of books and scrolls stuck out like ribs, now dressed with sconces, busts, and vases. Alexios noted that many of the statues and fixtures had a layer of dust, and here and there a few cobwebs. It was like the Neossan nobles had wanted to fill the shelves so they did not appear empty, but did not actually care for the pieces placed there.

When they arrived at the guest apartments, Alexios found them to be lush and comfortable, if a little cold from disuse. It had the feel of a place no one had set foot in for a long time. No matter. It would serve for Alexios, and there was a heavy door and a small private bathing chamber. A servants' alcove with its own wash basin and window stood on the opposite side, with enough sleeping couches for four, had Alexios traveled with a larger household staff.

Kato bowed his way out of the room, and as soon as the door clicked shut, Leofric started on him. "Your Highness—"

"I know," said Alexios. "I am fine with the risk of keeping Auro with me. But your concern is noted."

Alexios tried to convey through his tone that he would not hear another word on the matter, but Leofric plainly had more on his mind. "Your Highness," he said again, stepping closer to Alexios and Auro, lowering his voice as if he feared being overheard. "I am glad to have Auro with us, in actuality. There is something not right here, and I prefer to have people around us I trust."

Auro blinked in surprise. "You trust me?"

"Of course, I do," said Leofric. "Your love for His Highness is plain to anyone with eyes to see."

Auro and Alexios shared a glance, and Auro cut his eyes away almost immediately.

Leofric frowned. "Alright, what was that about?"

The man was too clever, too observant. "Nothing," said Alexios brusquely. "Now, tell me what has you in a state."

Leofric huffed. "My scouts should have been the ones to greet us, with Kato's men."

The thought had not occurred to Alexios. "Perhaps Kato simply did not wish to send them immediately back out through the rain."

"It is possible," Leofric admitted. "I shall feel much better after I talk to them personally. The royal stable was very empty, which was odd. And, finally, Kato brought us to our rooms himself."

"So?"

Leofric raised an eyebrow. "When was the last time you dispatched me from your side to play porter to a guest?"

Alexios furrowed his brow. That was peculiar, now that he thought about it. If Queen Petillia and her consort were so concerned about security, why had Kato been from the

Queen's side at all? Alexios's head ached, and he had not expected to be unraveling puzzles with foreign royals while he helped Auro search for fall's grace. He recalled the dying words of his would-be assassin, who implied there had been no attempt on Princess Dafina's life the night he'd come for Alexios. If that were true, Kato would have been privy to that elaborate deception, and perhaps he was still aiding the Queen in such things. But why?

If she didn't want Alexios to marry her daughter, she hardly had to resort to skullduggery and attempted murder. She could simply have refused the invitation to Papia, or refused to accept Alexios's offer to travel here to court the Princess. It defied logic. He had been hoping the most complicated part of this visit would be the unraveling of a four-hundred-year mystery—but perhaps that had been foolish of him.

For now, he needed a moment to think, a moment alone with Auro to try to repair the damage between them. To Leofric, he said, "Go, see to your scouts, and make certain the rest of the men are settling in to the barracks. I will see you at evening meal, and then, we'll talk."

Leofric cast a long look between Auro and Alexios before he nodded. "Your Highness," he said, bowing from the room.

The silence in his wake was deafening, and Alexios did not seek to break it immediately. Instead, he hauled Auro into his arms, embracing him with a soft *squelch* from their sodden clothing. He kissed the top of Auro's head, burying his nose in his damp curls for a moment before stepping back. "Come," he said. "Let us have a bath."

The bath water was warm, and Alexios washed Auro's hair, scrubbed his back, his legs, scrubbed him everywhere. When Auro's creamy skin shone burnished and clean, rubbed pink and fresh with soap, Alexios drew him to sit on his lap. They soaked in the quiet for a while, until Alexios said, "I'm glad for you to remain by my side while we are here."

Auro sighed and leaned back into Alexios's embrace, tilting his head to kiss along his jaw. "Leofric was right."

"Hmm?"

"He was right," Auro insisted. "Something is odd about this place."

While Alexios thought perhaps Auro was allowing personal feelings to cloud his judgment, Leofric certainly wasn't. Besides, he had learned the evening of the equinox feast that he should take nothing for granted. "Share your thoughts."

"It's hard to place my finger on," said Auro, moving from Alexios's lap. "But my shoulders feel as though they wish to climb up to my ears."

"Then come back here, and I will rub them for you," said Alexios, but his heart wasn't in it. Auro was right. And besides, they had things to accomplish, and their time was not unlimited.

Auro ignored him anyway and climbed from the bathing pool to fetch a soft towel. When Alexios joined him, they dried quickly, and Auro helped Alexios dress for dinner.

A knock sounded at the door. "Enter."

Leofric stepped inside, and Alexios was relieved to see some of the tension had gone from his face. "Your Highness."

Alexios turned to Auro. "I will see you after evening meal."

"The servants eat in the kitchens," Leofric told Auro, who nodded and set off down the corridor.

Leofric had bathed and prepared himself for the welcome feast, and Alexios realized he'd never seen him dressed formally before. His hair was freshly washed and braided, and he wore a knee-length tunic dyed a rich forest green that accented the tattoos around his ear.

"You clean up well," said Alexios as they walked toward the feasting hall.

Leofric frowned, plainly flustered. He adjusted his tunic. "I am armed beneath the finery, Your Highness. You needn't worry."

Alexios laughed. "I meant only to speak a kindness, Leofric. You can relax."

He huffed, to show what he thought of that, and said, "I did not know I would be invited to guest," he said. "I borrowed this from one of Kato's men."

"The color suits you, at any rate." Alexios found himself wondering if Leofric was married. He didn't speak of anyone, or his past, or his family. He didn't speak much at all, of course, but Alexios had come to trust the man striding purposely beside him and thought of him now as a friend. He hoped Leofric felt the same, but he knew better than to pry.

"You are kind to say so," he replied stiffly.

The feasting hall was massive and lavishly decorated. Upon the dais sat Queen Petillia, Janus, and the Princess Dafina. The seat of honor to the Queen's right was empty, and Alexios grimaced, knowing that was where he would be meant to sit.

Alexios wore a crown, the metal cold on his forehead. Since he wasn't known here, he felt he must do his part to display his station with more formality than he might have done at home in Papia.

"His Highness, the Crown Prince Alexios Velius Papinus, of Papia," called the herald, bowing them into the hall. "And his royal guard, Leofric, of Sokol."

They walked up toward the high table, but Leofric veered off toward a table just below the dais—still a place of honor but below the royals and nobles. The rest of Leofric's men were there as well, mingled with Kato and the rest of Queen Petillia's guardsmen.

"Your Majesty," said Alexios, bowing deeply before the

Queen. "Praetor," he added, addressing Janus respectfully. "I am honored to be welcome at your table."

"Rise," said Queen Petillia. "Come, sit, and let the feast begin."

Alexios took his place beside the Queen. The Princess sat on his other side and barely looked at him as he sat down and called for wine

"Your Highness," she said vaguely, her voice so quiet he barely heard it. She spent the next several minutes staring off into the middle distance, as if the entire dining hall stood empty as a tomb. He relaxed a bit, thinking that at least he would not have to endure forced flirtation for the entire meal.

Auro knew from growing up in a palace, and from his time in Papia, that the kitchens were the best place to start when trying to get the feel of a place. He did not like what he'd seen of Neossós so far, and it seemed to him that neither Leofric nor Alexios stood pleased by their reception, either. He didn't wish to spend any longer here than he absolutely had to.

He found his way to the kitchens, though not without getting himself turned around a few times. Auro had visited this place once before, with Cedras, when it had been a library —but it had been so long ago. He wondered where all of the books had gone.

The entire place was like a carcass, picked clean, and House Hostas now resided in its bones. What struck Auro was that as he wandered, he encountered not one single other soul. Neither a servant nor a guard.

The palace at Papia, on the other hand, had so much staff Auro wondered how they didn't trip over each other. By the time he found the kitchens, he was relieved to see signs of life. Despite the stillness that seeped from every crevice in the corridors above, he found the kitchens lively and bustling. Perhaps all the staff not required to serve at the banquet simply took their meals at the same time.

The head cook was a friendly woman named Della who served him a plate piled high enough to feed three Auros. The food was delicious, fresh, and warm, and Auro's troubles felt far away as he sat by the immense ovens. He tried to remain inconspicuous, but of course, it was impossible. House Hostas kept a small staff, apparently, and any new face was immediately noticed, especially one beneath a head of pink curls.

A skinny youth sat down beside Auro and introduced himself as a stable hand. "Though, I haven't had much to do, recently," he said, shoving cheese into his mouth with the air of a man starving. "I'm Titus. Your hair is crazy."

"Auro," said Auro, smiling in spite of everything. He looked to shake the lad's hand but feared to lose a finger as Titus inhaled his food. "I had a mishap dying my hair for a party," Auro explained. "And the color stuck. Why does the royal stable stand so empty?"

Titus pulled a face, opening his mouth to answer, when his head snapped forward. "Ouch!"

"Mind that mouth of yours," snapped Della, seeming to appear out of nowhere. "If you're lacking for chores, I have plenty for you."

Titus reddened, rubbing the back of his head, where Della had smacked it with a wooden spoon.

"Scram," she said. "And stop bothering everyone."

Titus snagged a final roll from a basket on the table and dodged another blow from Della's wooden spoon before vanishing into the corridor. "Apologies," said Della. "The boy doesn't know when to hold his tongue."

Auro had watched this whole interaction, perplexed. "He wasn't bothering me," said Auro hastily, but Della had already returned to her ovens, her friendly demeanor evaporated.

No one attempted to engage Auro in conversation again. In fact, no one so much as looked at him, at least, not when he could catch their eyes. He felt the stares, however, whenever he looked down at his food. The kitchen that had seemed so warm and inviting only minutes ago now seemed as unwelcoming as the rest of the villa. Auro finished his meal quickly and escaped back out into the halls.

Once back in the corridor, with a strange feeling creeping up his spine and no intelligence to show for it, Auro wondered if he should give up and start with a fresh plan tomorrow. However, his conversation with Titus had put him off his footing and he did not want to return to Alexios's guest apartments having learned absolutely nothing. Besides, with just about everyone up in the feasting hall, the empty corridors provided him ample opportunity to explore, to see if he could find a further clue as to the location of Cedras's grace.

Unfortunately, Auro had no idea where to begin. He'd hoped to glean something from his conversations in the kitchen but that obviously had not gone to plan. All of his brother's precious books were long gone, even the shelves had been moved elsewhere, or perhaps broken down and destroyed when they were no longer needed. The villa was a warren, twisting and turning with only study alcoves and built-in shelving remaining. Auro wondered if the clues to the location of Cedras's grace had been eradicated.

Auro silently cursed his parents. He'd always accepted the fate foisted upon him, both before *and* after being cursed. He never questioned that he and his brothers had deserved their punishment for killing Ozias. But now, faced with the chance to break the curse and redeem himself, he couldn't help but feel, once again, as if the obstacles were insurmountable. Clearly, his mother had left clues, done something—and trying to conceal it from a wrathful god, perhaps that's all she dared.

But still.

How were they supposed to work together the way she plainly had wanted? How could they ever come to terms, to peace with one another, if they could never speak face to face?

Auro wandered aimlessly for a while, feeling ashamed and lonely and stupid all at once. Beneath it all simmered a sense of deepening unease. The royal villa of Neossós was as different as could be from the one in Papia, different, too, from the one Auro had grown up in. The entire place had an air of neglect and coldness. It set his teeth on edge, the hairs on his arms standing at attention.

He found himself facing a door.

He'd been so lost in thought that he hadn't even taken care to remember where he placed his feet.

The door called to Auro. Something beyond that door was meant for him, he could feel it. Trembling, he reached for the thick handle, but before his fingers could connect, a sharp voice said, "You there! Boy!"

It took Auro a second to realize 'boy' meant him. He turned and stumbled, light-headed as a sensation like vertigo swooped through him. "Yes?"

Kato hurried toward him. "What are you doing here?"

Auro could not for the life of him remember. He had been searching for something, but his thoughts were muddled. Tangled up, blurred, somehow. "Apologies," he said. "I left the kitchens after evening meal and got turned around."

Kato nodded, as if this made perfect sense. He wrapped a hand around Auro's upper arm, his fingers like a vice, digging into his skin. "I'll escort you to His Highness's rooms," he said.

Auro twisted from his grip, his skin crawling where the man's fingertips had been. "Alright."

His expression did not falter, as if he was accustomed to looks of revulsion from people he touched. Kato escorted

Auro back to the door of Alexios's guest apartments and nearly shoved him inside. Auro stumbled across the threshold, still out of sorts and deeply shaken. He wondered if he'd had too much wine with his evening meal, before remembering he'd only had one small cup of cider. The door snapped shut behind him and Auro felt he heard the distinct *clunk* of a lock.

His blood ran cold and his mind cleared, and he immediately tried the handle. Sure enough, it was locked.

He considered a mad escape out the window, but he feared he wouldn't be able to regain entry to the royal grounds if he fled that way. Auro had only spent about three minutes mulling when the door swung open to reveal Alexios and Leofric, looking completely fine—or at least, no more or less tense than when Auro had last seen them.

The look on Alexios's face morphed into one of deep concern. "Are you alright?"

"They just locked me in here," he told them.

With a frown, Alexios said, "No, they didn't."

"Of course they did," said Auro, irritated. Why was he struggling so badly to recall what he had been doing before Kato had interrupted him? "I heard it, and also, I tried the door!"

"There isn't even a lock on the outside," said Leofric. "The room only locks from within."

Auro's heart fluttered madly, like a bird trying to escape the cage of his own ribs. He felt scattered and frayed, like he'd been fleeing some...*threat.* Alexios cupped his cheeks and stared into his eyes, like he was searching for some evidence of illness that could cause a demigod to lose his mind, but Leofric frowned, deep in thought. "Who locked you in?"

"It was Kato."

Alexios and Leofric exchanged a look. "Kato was at the feast all evening," said Alexios at once.

Concerned, Leofric prowled the rooms, searching every

crack in the mortar before using a device from his travel pack to wedge the door shut from within, even though they'd done up the lock. He also hung a small bell from the doorhandle, and several from the draperies on the windows overlooking the adjacent forest. "If anyone attempts entry, we will hear them at once," he explained.

"It has been a trying day," said Alexios, one hand cupping Auro's elbow. Auro knew he was including last night—had it only been last night?—in the statement.

Auro nodded, stepping one timid half-step closer. Things still felt strange between them,

but he couldn't deny the comfort he felt when stepping into Alexios's orbit.

"Let us fall to bed, and we can talk more in the morning. I have had a strange evening, as well."

When Leofric at last retired, bidding Auro and Alexios goodnight, Alexios blew out the candle on the bedside table and pulled Auro close beneath the blankets. Watching Alexios sleep soothed Auro, but it still took a long time for him to fall to slumber, and even when he did, his dreams were strange, filled with pages of books falling like autumn leaves, locked doors shrouded in darkness, and a prevailing sense of dread.

Alexios woke to find Leofric already up, standing on the balcony. Auro stirred in his sleep, face crinkled and his lips twitching. He looked haunted by some nightmare, so Alexios swooped in to kiss him awake. Auro's sleep-soaked gaze brightened immediately upon seeing Alexios.

"Bad dreams?" Alexios asked him.

Auro peeked at Alexios through his lashes. "Yes." He screwed up his face in concentration. "Though I can't recall them."

Alexios kissed the crease between Auro's brows. "Come," he said. "Let us have something to eat, and then I would see more of this place."

Their arrival in Neossós had been marked by several things that seemed off. Dafina's behavior at the banquet last night had been disconcerting, to say the least. At first, Alexios had been relieved that the Princess had made no attempt to draw him into conversation. After a while, though, he found it strange. Had he been in her place, and she in his, Alexios's father would have been spitting mad if he'd behaved that way —not just to a potential bride but to any noble guest. Alexios could not imagine the customs in Neossós were *so* different than those of Papia. And besides, the Queen and Janus had both spoken to him amicably enough. After a while, Alexios had made attempt to engage *her* in conversation, if only because he found himself so unnerved by her silence.

Her replies had been stiff, and she'd pushed her food away after only a few bites. Studying her profile as she stared resolutely over the sea of guests, he thought there was an air of weighty melancholy all around her.

Beneath all of the things on Alexios's mind, he could not help being a bit offended. He was clever and polite and handsome enough—at least, Auro certainly thought so—and would be a very fine match. Dafina had behaved last night as if she were being wed to an ogre. Of course, there was plenty chance she found the whole notion as unappealing as Alexios did, but there was no cause to treat him personally with such disdain. The ruse of his visit depended on both of them, he knew. If Dafina rejected him so openly, his thin pretext for remaining in Neossós would become thinner still. He needed time for Auro to locate and retrieve his brother's grace—especially when he seemed so off. He could only hope the Queen wouldn't send him away when she realized the depth of her daughter's disinterest.

When Alexios had met Dafina at the equinox feast, she had seemed weary but very...confident. Sure of herself and determined to master the situation her mother and Alexios's parents were foisting upon them. Last night she had seemed like a woman who had entirely given up. Her face was pale, as it had been on the night of the equinox, but last night it had seemed sickly—her cheeks hollow, her eyes red and distant. There was a mark upon her cheek that she had plainly tried to conceal with powder. Alexios had spent much of the evening trying to find a way to inquire after her health without drawing undue attention, and failing.

And that was hardly the only thing off about the feast. Janus had talked to Alexios almost nonstop, as if he wished to keep attention solely on himself, and nothing else, *including* his future stepdaughter. But Alexios was no fool. He noticed that there were scarcely any nobles present at the meal, and though of course, as a person Alexios knew Leofric deserved a place of honor, his title didn't necessitate it. In fact, it was odd to allow him to guest at all. The tables below the dais had been filled out with men and women who, like Leofric, were plainly guards and soldiers—despite how they were dressed. Alexios had spent enough time around his father, not to mention evading his own guards, that he knew a soldier's look.

Only a few tables were filled with men and women of station, at least, by appearance. He could be mistaken, but he did not think he was. Alexios cursed himself, because if he had been truly invested in a courtship between himself and the Princess, he would have taken pains to memorize the nobility of Neossós, the extended entourage of the royal family, and Queen Petillia's court. As it stood, he had barely passing knowledge of the key players in this kingdom.

"Have you any notion where your mother might have hidden Cedras's grace?"

Auro shook his head. "Not the faintest. I found myself

wondering if they may have been swept from the villa when the library was dismantled."

"Could Cedras's grace be gone, as well?"

"I do not believe so," said Auro. "According to the story, our mother made such that only I could retrieve it, and it would most likely be carefully warded against mortals stumbling across it and misplacing it."

"In that case," said Alexios, "You will have to overturn every stone of this place."

"I did a small amount of searching last night..." he trailed away. "Before Kato stumbled across me."

"I am still not certain how Kato managed to be in two places at once," said Alexios.

"Or how I did, following the attempt on your life," put in Leofric.

"You think these two things are related?"

"It would be a staggering coincidence if they were not," said Leofric.

"None of this makes sense," said Alexios. "If we *were* truly here to negotiate a betrothal, I would suggest packing up and going home at the earliest opportunity."

"That is what I recommend we do, Your Grace," said Leofric. "I have a bad feeling about this place."

Alexios looked at Auro, so sweet in the dawn sunlight, his hair sleep-rumpled and the blankets tangled around his waist. "No," said Alexios firmly. "We are not leaving without what we came here for." He cupped Auro's cheek and brought him in for a reassuring kiss.

"Are you sure?" said Auro. "I do not wish to put you or Leofric in danger."

"Yes," said Alexios. "In truth, when I return home, I will have to confer with my parents about whatever is going on here—and as of now, we have nothing concrete to bring them."

"Your Highness—" said Leofric, but Alexios didn't let him finish.

"Regardless of my desire to help Auro, I have a duty to my kingdom," said Alexios. "Neossós is close enough to pose a threat to us, and I will not have my people blind to enemies right outside our gates."

Twenty-Four

Alexios left their chambers to meet Queen Petillia, Janus, and his intended for breakfast—*and* to provide Auro some cover to do some more snooping. Auro felt so peculiar after last night, so wrong-footed, pieces of his memories missing like the empty socket that had once held a tooth. And, just like with a missing tooth, Auro could not help but probe the area with his tongue, some part of his brain called to the thing that was absent.

So, he decided to retrace his steps. He returned to the kitchens, where the servants broke bread at long, low bench tables by the warmth of the ovens. Immediately, Auro spotted Titus, the boy who'd spoken to him the night before. Auro collected a small bowl of porridge and approached him. "Hello," said Auro, keeping his tone even and friendly, as if nothing amiss had happened the night before.

"Good morning," said Titus, casting a furtive look at Auro from under the unruly curtain of his brown hair.

"Apologies, if I caused you any trouble," said Auro lightly, spooning up a big bite of porridge. "I was not offended by your attempt to make conversation."

Titus glanced at him again, but did not say anything.

Auro knew that this would be a more difficult nut to crack than he'd originally thought. So, instead of asking Titus immediately for information, he began to speak casually of their journey from Papia. "I am no master horseman," Auro confessed honestly. "I fear Segovax, my horse, was ready to dump me into the mud by the end of the trip."

Titus frowned. "And why is that?"

"Well," said Auro. "I believe he didn't care for the travel rations, first of all. They did not agree with his constitution."

This much was true. Segovax, Xanthos, and all the other royal horses were outrageously spoiled. His pronouncement had the desired effect, and Titus launched into a long-winded explanation of proper feeding for horses of various breeds, and their different dietary needs, how to keep them happy and healthy. "Have you any duties this morning?" Titus asked Auro when he'd finished.

"None whatsoever," said Auro. "His Highness is dining with the Princess, and he will have no need of me till after midday meal."

Auro followed Titus out through the servants' exit in the kitchen, which led through a low-ceilinged tunnel out into a small stone staircase. When they emerged from beneath the earth, Auro found they were right beside the royal stables.

He made a mental note of the tunnels and planned to inform Leofric of its existence as soon as they had a chance to speak that evening. With Alexios's party, the stalls looked to be about half full. "Such a large stable," said Auro carefully. Looking at the building, he could tell it was newer than the palace. Plainly it had been built when the first kings of Neossós had transformed the library into their family's seat of power.

Titus's face darkened. He approached one of the stalls, containing a dun-colored filly. Stroking her nose, he said, "Aye.

We used to have a much larger force of mounted guards." He hesitated like he wanted to say more, but Auro didn't press. Not yet. He wanted information, but he also didn't want the lad to get into any trouble.

"This is Segovax," said Auro, introducing Titus to his horse.

Segovax whickered, and Auro prayed he would be on his most charming behavior. Titus plainly loved the animals in his charge, and Auro thought perhaps his tongue would loosen even further when relaxed around the beasts he cared for. Titus led Segovax confidently from his stall and offered him a carrot from within the folds of his tunic.

While Segovax munched on his treat, Titus inspected every inch of his coat, his mane, his tail. He found several small burrs in his hooves which he removed and treated, clucking good-naturedly at Auro for being such a disastrous horseman, told him of the proper food and best treats for this breed, and advised Auro on grooming practices. By the time he had finished, Segovax nosed into Titus's tunic in search of more carrots, flicking his tail as Titus stroked the side of his face absently. Auro had been an attentive student, asking questions and internalizing all the advice. Aside from his ulterior motives in the conversation, Auro could use all the advice he could get.

During a lull, he finally asked, "What happened to the other royal mounts?" in as light a tone as he could manage.

Titus frowned. "We lost a fair amount of guards over the last two years," he admitted. "This winter was especially hard for us—before that, a...a sickness tore through the kingdom."

"The sickness was in the horses?" asked Auro, confused.

"No," said Titus. "We lost a lot of men, and Her Majesty arranged to sell their mounts in other kingdoms." He paused. "Some deserted as well. The Praetor had sealed the borders—

saying none must leave the kingdom until the illness blew itself out. But some escaped."

Auro cocked his head, looking at Titus, who now refused to meet his eye. The boy stared resolutely at the side of Segovax's head. "You lost someone," said Auro. It was not a question.

"Most people did," said Titus, hiding his face behind the horse's neck. After a beat, he added. "My brother."

"Oh," said Auro. "I'm so—"

"My sister. My father. A few cousins."

Auro was speechless. So much grief and loss in one family...and someone who had high position here at the royal villa. What must have happened in the villages to those too poor to afford the treatment of a trained medicus? "When?"

"The blight claimed its last victim perhaps...last summer."

"Have you any notion what the sickness was?"

Titus shrugged. "No one does. People in the towns began to fall ill. Most didn't recover. We lost our medicus, a lot of the staff. Autumn saw crops dying on the vine, with not enough hands to work the harvest."

"That's awful," said Auro. "Why on earth didn't Her Majesty seek aid?"

"It might be hard to believe," said Titus sarcastically, "but she didn't actually talk to me much about it."

"Fair point," said Auro.

"You mustn't tell anyone what I told you."

"What?"

"Please," he said, "I forgot myself—I shouldn't have—"

"It's alright," Auro soothed him. He settled his hands on Titus's shoulders. "I will not get you into trouble. I swear it."

After bidding an uneasy farewell to Titus, Auro returned to the royal villa through the same servants' entrance and found his way back to the guest apartments to contemplate his next move. He observed the interior of the villa in this new light. Where before, the neglected halls had seemed dreary, they now seemed sinister. It was as if ghosts stalked the corridors beside him. No wonder the place had collected dust—there were not hands enough to maintain the many shelves and twisting corridors.

The thought gave Auro an idea. The royal villa of Queen Petillia was enormous. Far larger than the library had been. Her ancestors had plainly added to the grandeur of the original structure, transforming it into an ornate labyrinth of rooms and halls. Surely Cedras's grace would not be in any of these newer wings but concealed within the original structure. To narrow his search, he must first discern which parts of the building were original, and which had been added in the many centuries since fall's grace had been laid to rest here.

As a mere servant, Auro could hardly request documents from the royal study, but he could tell Alexios of his idea, and *he* could make polite inquiry. Or, perhaps he could find his own way in and read tonight when all were asleep. Pacing around the guest apartments, Auro was restless. The storm still battered the villa, nourishing the earth and all its inhabitants, even while those inhabitants hid from the driving rains.

Auro would touch the earth tomorrow and see what its needs were, coax the storm through its natural span, and see what was next needed. He flopped backward onto the large bed in the center of the room. As he ran his fingers over the blankets, Auro listened to the rain outside, letting the constant hush soothe his frayed nerves. Perhaps he would even venture outside tonight, in the rains, to clear his head. He could slip through that very same door in the kitchens and be outside, where he was meant to be.

Where he was meant to be.

Auro sat bolt upright. Memories of the night before came ripping into the forefront of his mind with the violence of a sword thrust. The door. The door he had found upon leaving the kitchens, after exploring the darkening corridors.

There had been something of vital importance beyond that door—how could he have forgotten? He had the distinct impression that the memories had been fighting to get out, throwing themselves against a barrier in his mind since last night, and they'd finally burst through. Something had thrown up the barrier in his brain.

Something powerful, something dark.

"Enter," called Queen Petillia through the door to her private dining chamber.

Alexios had dressed himself that morning, donned his crown, and allowed Leofric and Kato to escort him through the halls of the villa. At the Queen's bidding, Alexios entered the chamber. The table inside was far smaller than the one in the feasting hall below, though no less extravagant. It was laden with expensive delicacies, platters heaped with fruits and sweet cakes, wooden boards with bread that's aroma was warm and sweet.

"Your Grace," said Alexios with a bow. "Praetor."

Janus sat beside the Queen, and to his right, an empty chair. To the right of that chair sat a young man who was perhaps around Alexios's own age. Princess Dafina was notice-ably absent. Janus followed Alexios's eyes and said, "Apologies, Prince Alexios, for my stepdaughter's absence. She is taken with a woman's complaint."

"Ah," said Alexios. He wondered how Dafina would feel about her soon-to-be stepfather calmly discussing her private matters at the table. "Perhaps if she is feeling well later, we could take a walk through the city."

"If the rain lets up," said the Queen, dribbling a healthy

amount of honey onto a slice of bread, so warm it steamed in her hand.

It would not, Alexios knew, but never mind. As he took his seat, his eyes fell upon the young man beside him. He had fine, noble features and round doe's eyes, a crop of thick, chocolate dark hair that fell in his face. He greatly resembled Lord Janus, but something about his appearance nagged at Alexios, in a way he couldn't quite place.

"This is my natural son," Janus said, "Petar."

"Good morning, Your Highness," he said, but he kept his eyes cast down toward his plate. He kept peeking demurely at Alexios through his fringe.

Alexios had not known that Janus had a natural son, much less that he lived at court. The rumors surrounding Janus were mostly of his *own* low birth, and the mistrust of his dark studies—not to mention the way Queen Petillia had fallen so fast for him. Not even Alexios's friend Gaius had mentioned a bastard son.

"I had been hoping to tour your city," said Alexios. What he actually hoped was to draw Janus, Kato, and the royal guards far from the villa, providing Auro the time to explore unencumbered.

"Impossible," said Janus.

Alexios startled at his brusque tone.

"Forgive me, what I meant to say, is that the rains would make such a tour a dreary affair."

"We could travel by litter—"

"Another time," snapped the Queen. "The city would be a waste with the sky so grey."

Alexios frowned. What on earth was going on here? "Your Grace—"

"Your Highness," said Janus, after dabbing his lips with a napkin. "I must beg your pardons, I have things to which I must attend." Without even waiting for a courtesy by-your-leave, from either Alexios or the Queen, he departed.

Alexios made pleasant chatter with the Queen for the remainder of the meal and even attempted to engage Petar in conversation, simply in the interest of staving off long, pregnant pauses. When at last he felt he could leave the room without appearing rude, Alexios excused himself.

Leofric fell in step with him. "I did not know Janus had a natural son," said Leofric as soon as they were alone.

"Nor I," said Alexios, but something else had snagged his attention. "Why do they wish me not to see their city?"

"I do not know, Your Highness, but it is peculiar. I will be happy when we are quit of this place."

"Agreed." He sighed, hoping Auro had more success with his morning. Alexios kept telling himself the strangeness of this place was nothing of his concern. Despite his wish to avoid *any* royal marriage, he had a feeling this match with Princess Dafina would not be as advantageous as his parents had originally thought. The sooner he could return to Papia and explain, the more he could relax. Perhaps it would even purchase him some more time—if he played up how disappointing his welcome in Neossós had been.

Alexios hesitated. Putting Auro from mind, he considered how he would respond if he had earnestly wished for this betrothal—how a *king* would react if a neighboring kingdom harbored such secrets and strange ways.

So, instead of returning to his guest chambers to pace, Alexios decided to go straight to the heart of the matter. It took him a while to locate a porter, who directed him to the Lord Praetor's study. Technically, Alexios thought this would more rightly be the King or Queen's study, but plainly Queen Petillia had given it over to her consort. He dispatched Leofric to the barracks to check on the other guardsmen and make certain they would be ready to depart at a moment's notice, should the need arise.

Alexios knocked softly and entered when Janus bid him to do so. "Your Highness," said Janus politely.

"Praetor," said Alexios. Surrounding him was plainly what remained of the Mykellian Empire's library—and of course, whatever house Neox had added to the collection over the years since the kingdom's founding.

"Marvelous, isn't it?" said Janus.

"Indeed," said Alexios.

Janus followed Alexios's gaze. "Is there something specific I can help you with, Your Highness?"

"I had read your villa was once entirely given over to books," he said cautiously.

"Yes," said Janus. "The old Mykellian library was a wonder. Or so I have read," he added with a smile. "There is great power in these old walls."

That seemed a peculiar thing to say. While he thought of a response, he let his eyes roam over the tables and shelves. Startled, he realized he recognized a specific book cover on the table. It was one of his mother's, Alexios was certain.

Before he could question it, Janus said, "Her Grace was kind enough to lend me a few of her rarest volumes—to have them copied and illuminated for our collection here."

Alexios narrowed his eyes. This was by far the most suspicious thing anyone in Neossós had said to him, and it solidified his opinion that he should get Auro, Leofric, and the rest of them well away from this place as soon as possible. Janus had plainly stolen this book, and possibly others, from his mother's private study the night of the equinox feast. The question, of course, was why?

The books were valuable, surely, but something told Alexios it was far more than that.

"Much of the original structure of the building has

remained unchanged," said Janus, turning and striding off down the rows upon rows of shelves.

Alexios hurried to follow him. "I know my mother would never forgive me if I didn't learn everything possible about the ancient library," he said, concealing his growing suspicions.

"Well, I would hate for us to disappoint her," said Janus with a light laugh. "Here."

He handed Alexios several enormous scrolls.

"These are some of the original floor plans," said Janus. "They've been copied over so many times, so as not to be lost as the paper ages and the ink fades. It's fascinating—you can see how each person who copied the piece had their own little flourishes. I think the oldest one we have dates just after the fall of the Mykellian Empire.

"Fascinating," Alexios echoed. "May I bring these back to my chambers?"

Janus hesitated, clearly nervous about allowing his precious scrolls to leave the library walls—but one did not deny a crown prince. Alexios didn't often flex his influence, but he flexed it now, keeping a bland, expectant look on his face that said he was accustomed to getting his way and anticipated no difficulties in doing so now. "Of course, Your Highness."

"I will treat them with the utmost care," Alexios assured him. "They'll be returned tomorrow."

Janus nodded. "Apologies, Your Highness," said Janus. "One can never be too careful when preserving history."

"I am in total agreement," said Alexios, but as he watched Janus, it seemed the man had something else on his mind. "Is everything alright, my Lord?"

"Yes, Your Highness," he said at once, almost too quickly. Alexios's skepticism must have shown on his face because Janus hesitated only briefly before asking, "Would you perhaps do me the honor of sharing a cup of tea before you return to your chambers?"

"Of course," said Alexios politely.

In the center of the study was a pair of matching dining couches and a small table. Janus summoned a servant, who brought them a silver tray of tea, grapes, and flat bread crusted with nuts. Alexios nibbled nervously on a corner of flatbread, wondering what was on Janus's mind.

"Your Highness," he began. "I believe it will be to both of our advantages if we speak plainly to one another."

Alexios set down his bread. "Alright," he said carefully.

"I saw you leaving the equinox celebration with a man," said Janus. It was not a question.

It took all of Alexios's faculties to keep his face an expressionless mask. He took a sip from his tea. "Oh?" he asked. Janus had seen him leaving with Auro with his own two eyes, but Alexios was no fool. He'd learned diplomacy from his father—he wanted Janus to tip his hand before Alexios showed his.

"It's alright," said Janus. "It doesn't matter to me where your...tastes lie."

"It shouldn't," said Alexios before he could stop himself. What he wanted was to tell Janus to shut his mouth and mind his own business.

"Do you know much about kings, Alexios?"

He bristled a bit at being patronized, at being spoken to as a peer—at Janus not using his title. "I know enough."

"Well," said Janus. "It seems you could study their history a bit more. Kings often keep lovers. Queens as well."

This took Alexios aback. He knew this, of course. Royals had kept paramours since the advent of monarchy. One of his grandmothers had kept a string of lovers, and it had never truly affected her rule, nor her marriage to his grandfather. It was impolite to discuss such matters, however. "They do," Alexios allowed.

"A marriage to my daughter would not preclude you from slaking your appetites, Your Highness. So long as you were able to produce an heir, no one would need to know what you do in the privacy of your own chambers."

There was a hint of something there, behind his words. Alexios spoke carefully, ensuring he did not admit to anything. "True enough."

"I wish to marry Her Grace, the Queen," said Janus. "She does not wish to marry until her daughter is...taken care of."

"Taken care of?"

Janus shrugged. "If I marry Her Grace, and we have another child, Dafina's place in the line of succession would be questioned."

"Would it? Her Highness is the eldest child," said Alexios.

"She is," Janus agreed. "But some would say that a child of both the Queen and the reigning king consort would be a surer bet for the preservation of our lineage."

"You mean, your lineage," said Alexios, catching on.

Janus smiled, and Alexios was struck by the coldness in that smile. "At any rate, we were discussing *your* lineage, weren't we?"

Alexios didn't speak; he wasn't one hundred percent certain *what* they were discussing any longer.

"Let us say you decide to break your betrothal with Princess Dafina," said Janus.

Alexios began to protest, but Janus held up a hand.

"I told Her Grace we should never allow you to visit us here," he said. "A plague hit Neossós, just before I came to court. I promised the Queen I could help her kingdom survive and prosper if only she agreed to do what I said."

Alexios wondered why Janus was telling him this.

"I got us through the plague," said Janus. "My stewardship

allowed Neossós to limp along and survive. My reward for that service was Her Grace's hand in marriage—once her daughter had been wed, as well.

"At any rate," Janus continued. "I know how things must look, through your eyes, Alexios—and I'm certain you have sent your man, Leofric, to prepare his men to leave in all haste, if necessary."

Alexios stayed mute, annoyed that his plan had been unearthed so quickly.

"To be frank, Your Highness, you would be well within your rights to call off this betrothal. There are other women you could marry, or you could forestall a marriage to anyone, as you so clearly wish to do. But that would invite questions. Others will wonder why. Matters of state are too delicate to trust to gossiping nobles, I am certain you'd agree. Some vague notion of incompatibility would be put forth. But they would wonder. Dafina is young, well-bred, intelligent...as of now, sole heir to the Neossan throne."

"She is," Alexios allowed.

"There would be questions—questions as to *why* you would choose to break such a betrothal. If the answers to those questions should become public knowledge, it could make it...more difficult for you to find a bride. I don't believe His and Her Grace, your royal parents, would appreciate that difficulty, would they?"

Alexios frowned, setting down his tea with an aggressive *thunk*. "Are you threatening me?"

"Of course not," said Janus, his smile stretching even wider. "I'm merely pointing out some key facts regarding our situation. I know this visit has not been what you expected, and perhaps you were wishing to forestall further commitment to my stepdaughter, to reconvene with your parents, tell them that things in Neossós are not quite as settled as they had thought."

Alexios swallowed. Of course, this was precisely what he intended.

"If that were the case, perhaps my stepdaughter would find another to marry—"

"—and the questions," said Alexios tiredly. "Yes."

Janus gave him a few moments of silence, to collect his thoughts.

"What is it that you *want,* my Lord?"

"Why, isn't it obvious?"

Alexios shook his head.

"All I want is for everything to hum along as designed. This plan has been in motion for far longer than you realize, and I think you'll find I'm quite invested in its outcome."

Alexios frowned, thinking there had to be more to this than assuring a marriage between himself and the Princess.

"Think on it," said Janus. "Now, if you'll excuse me, there really are matters to which I must attend."

Though he technically outranked Janus, Alexios felt himself well and truly dismissed. He left the study as quickly as he could, wondering what on earth he was going to do next.

Twenty-Five

Auro spent the few days examining every possible route from the kitchens, trying to recreate his path from their first night in Neossós.

Alexios returned to their shared chambers every evening, tense and irritated. His intended had finally begun to show an interest in him, but it seemed to him that he was only shown the parts of Neossós that the royal family wanted him to see. The rain had ended days ago, and Alexios's request to tour the city had still been rebuffed at every turn. Alexios had told Auro the troubling things the Lord Praetor had said to him, too. The threats to Alexios made Auro queasy, and Leofric furious, but they had only solidified Alexios's determination to help Auro find autumn's grace. "We can discuss this issue later, but we *must* find Cedras's power here, while we can."

Auro used Alexios's fervor to fuel his own search, and after a week of combing the structure, consulting crumbling building plans that Alexios was able to fetch him from the hall of records, he finally had something.

When Alexios returned to their chambers that night, Auro bounded up to him. "I have found it," he breathed. He leapt into Alexios's arms and kissed his nose, his cheeks, his lips. "I found the door."

"Excellent," said Alexios, spinning Auro around a few times before setting him back on his feet. "Will you be able to enter it?"

"Yes," said Auro, with certainty, "but it will take time."

"Why?"

"The door is meant for me," he said. "I am certain of it. I can unlock it, but I need to use my own grace and the lock is enchanted and very complex."

Alexios frowned. "Your mother certainly did not wish to make any of this easy on you and your brothers, did she?"

"No," said Auro sadly. "But perhaps she did not have a choice."

"Did you know she had the power to do this?"

Auro shook his head. "I had no idea she had dabbled in the arcane at all."

"How did the door cause you to forget?" Alexios asked him. "If it was meant for you, why would it try so hard to turn you away?"

"I'm not certain," said Auro. "I have only...a feeling."

"A feeling?"

"I think there might be two forces at play here," said Auro. "Opposing ones."

"What do you mean?"

"It's difficult to explain, but the enchantment on the door itself is meant for me. The one that made me forget...I think it was meant for everyone."

Alexios frowned.

"It was like...someone found the door, sensed what was beyond it, but when they couldn't open it, or access it...they wished to keep anyone else from doing so."

"It's Janus," said Alexios at once.

"You think?"

"I know," said Alexios with certainty. "There is something...off about that man. And the other day, he mentioned that there was a power in this place that called to him."

"He must be the one who put the enchantment on the door," said Auro.

But Alexios seemed to find this only more troubling. "How powerful he must be," he said. "To make a god forget."

"Half a god," said Auro, but he wondered. "Regardless of the Lord Praetor's power, our course of action must be the same. I must get through the door. As soon as possible, so we can leave this place."

Alexios kissed Auro again. "What do you need from me?"

"I need time," said Auro simply.

"I think I can accomplish that," said Alexios. "When do you wish to make attempt to get beyond the door?"

"Tonight," said Auro firmly.

"Agreed," said Alexios. "Once we have the matter of your brother's grace settled, I will bring what I have learned here to my parents. They will wish to know something is amiss in Neossós, and perhaps it will dampen their eagerness to marry me off to the Princess."

Auro fought to keep his face neutral. Alexios still valiantly kept his outlook about his impending marriage positive—or not, depending upon one's point of view—but despite the way Auro felt for Alexios, he knew in his heart it was futile. If not this princess, there would be another, Mykellos had no shortage of daughters of would-be queens. Unless Alexios were to abdicate his position on the throne, he must wed. And Alexios would never do that. He cared far too much for his family and his responsibilities to the people of Papia. A true prince, a true king, lived for his people—not for his own pleasures.

Auro could not bring himself to take the confident smile from Alexios's face, so he smiled back and kissed him again.

While Alexios dined with the royal family, Auro climbed out over the balcony of their rooms and down the side of the villa. He had spent days stealthily growing a sturdy trellis of ivy up the wall, to allow for just such a thing. The ivy was thicker and sturdier than he would normally have required because he wished it to have the strength to allow Alexios and Leofric to clamber down as well, should the need arise.

The rain had let up at last, and the earth sang with life. Auro could feel every pulse of it as if the very grass had heartbeats of its own. It filled him with confidence and purpose. The dewy cushion of lush green beneath his feet helped steady Auro as he crept in shadow around the perimeter of the castle. The guards and staff of the villa were spread thin in the wake of their struggles with the plague, which served to aid Auro in sneaking about.

He had carefully mapped the villa and knew of a storage room long neglected that led into a wine cellar. The wall of the storage room had a weakened foundation, helped along by Auro's meddling. Roots pushed their way through the cracks in the stone bricks, allowing Auro to wriggle a few loose and slip inside. A strange hush took hold of him when he landed on the earthen floor of the cellar. Everything seemed to echo in the muted dark, and Auro's own heartbeat was deafening. He paused, waiting as long as he dared. Auro did not wish to dally, but he also did not wish to be caught, of course. So, he crouched behind an oak barrel and strained his ears.

No sound greeted him but for the steady drip of water in the corner of the room, where rain bled through the well-soaked earth and seeped down the stone walls. When he was certain no one had heard his entrance to the cellar, Auro replaced the bricks behind him and placed his hand upon the damp wall to feel his way through the dark.

The storage room led to the wine cellar, and the wine cellar to an underground tunnel. The tunnel led to a set of steps that wound upward into a corridor adjacent to the door Auro sought. He stood before it, the gravity of his situation slapping him as he regarded it.

The door was carved from darkened wood, dense, and Auro could still feel a tiny kernel of life within it, even after all these years. Perhaps it had been shielded with other magic, kept alive through some sort of power. Graven into the door, which Auro had not noticed the first time, was a scythe. The scythe was one of Cedras's personal emblems. Auro sat upon the floor and stilled every part of himself. Before he began, he listened, straining his ears once again. When he was as certain as he could be that no one knew he was down here, Auro placed his palms against the wood of the door.

It took a long time for him to coax the tiny ember of life to a flame. The door was thick as a tree itself and had its own roots that plunged deep into the walls and floor and ceiling, locking it into place. One might think fire or the blade of an axe to be the most direct route of passage, but Auro had been one with the earth for a long time. As such, there were plenty of things he knew, just by feeling them. And he knew that destroying the door would not work. So, he remained upon the floor, cross-legged, and rested his forehead against the wood.

Auro did not know how long he sat, breathing into the living wood, but eventually felt the creak and stretch of it waking up, like a giant who'd long been sleeping. With Auro's gentle, but firm, coaxing, the roots and tangled branches, the tendrils anchoring the door in place, shook off their centuries of slumber and came alive under Auro's fingers. Auro directed them, cajoled them, coaxed them, until each one had been painstakingly redirected, growing into the room beyond as opposed to the doorframe.

Sweat broke on Auro's forehead as he clenched his jaw, straining his muscles against the stubborn magic of the door.

When at last it opened for him, he was exhausted, jelly-legged when he tried to stand. But a branch from the door caught him before he could fall. Auro gave the living gate, now open before him, a loving pat and entered the chamber beyond.

After the intense struggle of opening the door, the interior of the chamber beyond was somewhat of an anticlimax. It was a simple stone room, about ten-foot square, empty save for a stone well at the center. Auro felt a tug in his chest, looking at the well, which was also covered with a circle of wood. Carved into the wood was an abacus—another icon that called Cedras's bespectacled face to mind.

Auro sighed heavily, shaking the exhaustion from his limbs. He laid his palms upon the vast wooden disk, about a yard in diameter, and pushed with his grace. Calling out to his brother, whose presence he could feel faintly, as if Cedras were speaking to him from across a vast chasm. The cover to the well yielded more easily to Auro than the door had, and for that he was grateful. Auro's body trembled as he peered down into the well, squinting at the darkness. He was weakened by these two barriers, greatly weakened. Nothing had tested his power like this in centuries—and Auro now felt as though he had fought off a serious fever. Perhaps that was the point. He wondered what else he might face. Auro felt around the inside of the well, and where his fingers touched, tiny phosphorescent flowers bloomed against the stone, illuminating a ladder of wrist-thick vines that descended into the dark below.

The climb was a dizzying one, and weakened as he was, Auro was nervous about his ability to make the return journey. Perhaps he would spend the night at the bottom of the well, to regain his strength. By the time he hit the floor, his hands and calves ached with the exertion. He staggered against the interior wall of the well to catch his breath. The hairs on the back of Auro's neck rose and he shivered. A trickle of sweat fell down the nape of his neck, between his shoulder blades, despite the chill at the bottom of the well. As his eyes adjusted to the dark, Auro saw a small door opposite him. Mercifully, this door appeared to be a normal one, or as normal as one could expect in this situation, and it opened with the simple turn of a handle.

It clicked open, and there came an expectant rush as Auro's entry disturbed the still air beyond it. He could see a soft golden light ahead, through a short tunnel. The tunnel was small enough that even Auro had to stoop to traverse it. The feeling of stone and dirt pressing all around him should have made him anxious, but everywhere he stepped, the small, glowing flowers opened and lit his path, like little friends helping him on his quest.

When he reached the end of the tunnel, Auro stood, his spine cracking as he straightened up and found himself in a massive underground cavern.

His breath caught, and a lump rose in Auro's throat, hard and hot as he felt the presence of his absent brother all around him, as if Cedras himself stood at his side, arm thrown over Auro's shoulders in a protective embrace. At the center of the chamber stood an enormous tree, larger than any Auro had ever seen, though perhaps that was a trick of the eye as the tree's boughs threatened to engulf the entire cavern. The tree glowed faintly, giving off a warm, welcoming light that pulsed through the air, drawing Auro on. Some instinct told Auro to stoop and unlace his sandals, and he toed them off to leave them in the shadow of the doorway.

Beneath his now bare feet were centuries of fallen leaves, orange and red and brown, rich with the colors of fall. The tree shed its leaves before Auro's very eyes, the dry, translucent things dropping like golden snowflakes, thick and fast, though the leaves on the branches seemed never to thin. As Auro watched, he realized that with each leaf that fell, a bud formed and unfurled to take its place, and over the course of a few minutes would complete its cycle, turning green, then yellow or red, and fall to the earth.

It struck Auro then that it had been four hundred years since he had seen the beauty of autumn, of winter, or summer. Even the comparison of leaves to snowflakes in his mind fell flat—how long had it been since he'd last laid eyes on snow? His eyes stung as he watched, enchanted, and his breath caught in his throat. Auro had lived four hundred years in perpetual spring—a lovely time to be awake, to walk the earth. He'd told himself that a thousand times until he'd believed it. He hadn't missed the other seasons.

Just like he'd told himself for so long that he didn't miss his brothers.

Perhaps it should have been sad, a tree in a perpetual purgatory of fall, but Auro felt a prevailing sense of comfort, standing here in the chamber. He approached the tree with caution, but nothing acted to stall his progress. At the very center of the tree's trunk, a knot had been carved to resemble the face of an owl. As Auro drew near, its wooden eyes blinked open, and Auro nearly slipped and fell backward in surprise, but the tree merely blinked dolefully at him. Auro could sense the owl-tree meant him no harm, and he again stepped cautiously over the roots toward the trunk.

The eyes were the only part of the carved face that did not appear to be hewn from the wood of the tree. They shone with a golden light, as if each contained a tiny sun. Auro raised a trembling hand and traced the outline of the owl's face, caressed the wood that felt warm and alive beneath his fingers. As he reached the beak, the owl yawned, its maw stretching wide, the space within shining with the same golden light as the sockets of its eyes. Part of Auro knew it was foolish to reach inside, but at the same time, he knew in his heart to trust the tree. It contained no small part of his brother's grace. It would not harm him.

Auro reached into the owl's mouth, extending his hand deep, almost up to his armpit, and his hand closed around something so warm it felt as if it had been under the rays of the sun for hours. He pulled it out, and it was clear it was the source of the tree's light.

Wrapped in Auro's hand was a bottle wrought of some sort of crystal, full of a sparking amber liquid, shining so brightly Auro could almost not bear to look directly upon it. The liquid sloshed merrily inside, warming Auro's palm through the crystal.

Fall's grace.

Cedras's grace. Auro could not help it, he laughed. Laughed at the joy that he was able to find this, and retrieve it, that his mother had not abandoned him and his brothers to their curse. Whatever else happened, he would at least be able to free one of his brothers. Even if all else failed, Auro would awaken next spring and embrace his brother for the first time in four hundred years.

Alexios returned from dinner, and Auro still had not made it back after his search. He knew it was something Auro must undertake alone, and this thing with his brothers was, in many ways, more fragile than his own relationship with Auro. There was nigh on half a millennium of bad blood between them, and reconciling that would be no small feat—magic doors and godsblood aside. He wished with all his heart that he could walk beside Auro in this, even if just to offer what comfort he could.

But he knew it was not possible.

So, he waited.

Leofric had bid Alexios remain in his chambers at any rate. He was visiting the barracks, to discuss any observations his men might have made in their time here. Leofric was an exceptional guard, but he did have to sleep and eat and rest like any man, and even then, he was just *one* man. The twenty other guards and scouts that had traveled with them and mingled among Queen Petillia's men would have thoughts and observations of their own. Leofric wished to hear them all. He assured Alexios he would be back by the time the moon had fully risen.

When a soft knock shattered the quiet, Alexios was surprised. It was barely after sunset, and neither Leofric nor Auro was expected back for some hours yet. "Who goes there?" he called.

A feminine voice answered. "Princess Dafina."

Curious as to what would bring the Princess to his door, Alexios hurried across the chamber to let her in. When Alexios opened the door, he saw the Princess indeed stood upon his threshold, holding a flagon of wine. And she was not alone.

Dafina swept into the room with Petar, Janus's natural son, on her heels. He turned and locked the door behind them. "Where is your man, Leofric?" asked Dafina.

Alexios was so startled by her direct question that he answered. "He is visiting his scouts, down in the guardhouse."

She nodded, striding about the room as if she owned the place—which, Alexios supposed she did. Petar drifted over to the bed and sat right upon it, also looking far more confident than Alexios had yet seen him. Dafina drew the gauzy curtains, though the probability of anyone seeing into the chamber from beyond the balcony was remote.

"My Lady," said Alexios awkwardly. "My Lord. To what do I owe the honor of this visit?"

Dafina turned from the window and cut him a harsh look, and Alexios took a step back. The morose, weary girl from the welcome feast was long gone, leaving a blazing woman of harsh beauty in her stead. "Sit," she said, indicating the spot on the sleeping couch beside Petar.

Alexios sat, utterly bemused.

Dafina crossed the room, unstopped her flagon of wine, and poured Alexios a cup. He cradled it in his hands, feeling very out of sorts. Dafina poured a cup of her own, and one for Petar, before she, at last, sat on the other side of Alexios.

This was highly inappropriate, not to mention surprising. Alexios shifted, making to move to one of the chairs on the other side of the chamber, but Dafina and Petar each set a hand on one of his thighs, keeping him in place. "Alexios," she said. "I believe we have gotten off upon the wrong foot, so to speak."

"Oh?"

She nodded, and did not remove her hand from his thigh. Neither of them did. "I apologize, sincerely, for treating you so poorly when you first arrived."

"It's—"

"It was childish," she said, giving his leg a squeeze. "I had heard rumor, carried back from my mother's servants, passed then to my own, after the equinox feast."

Alexios's mouth ran dry, after his conversation with Janus, he could only imagine what people were saying of him. "Rumors?"

With another long-suffering sigh, Dafina ran a finger down Alexios's cheek. "I attempted to draw you in, to see if the rumors were true but..."

Alexios tried to think on any action that could be construed as 'drawing him in' but he came up short. "But what?"

With a sharp twist of her wrist, Dafina dug her fingers into Alexios's chin and turned his head to face Petar. "Your tastes run more toward cock than cunt, do they not?"

Alexios startled, twisting away from her crude words and brazen accusations both.

Dafina released his chin, and Alexios took a hasty gulp from his wine glass, simply to stop his mouth from gaping open. The sip bought him some time to gather his thoughts. She was right, of course, but he hardly had expected to be confronted in such bald terms, especially by a woman who'd said barely two dozen words to him since they'd met. Perhaps, though, it was better. More honest. Strangely, Alexios felt as though a weight fell away from his shoulders. There was no cause to hide from this princess any longer. "Yes," he said, resigned. "I am truly sorry for leading you on, my Lady."

"I thought so," she said. After a pause, in which she took a sip of wine, she added, "Your valet is very pretty."

The mention of Auro had Alexios's hackles up. He did not answer, but Petar's hand crawled higher up his thigh. "He is," said Petar. "Though, I imagine, not of royal blood."

Something in Alexios's gut boiled. Auro *was* of royal blood, the blood of the old Mykellian empire, but that was hardly the point. "You are correct," he said, his tone icy. "No more royal than you, my Lord."

Petar only laughed, high pitched and strange, like that was the funniest thing anyone had ever said—but only he was privy to the joke. Instead of explaining himself, Petar gave the meat of Alexios's leg a flirtatious squeeze.

"Tragically, though, your pretty valet does not come equipped to bear heirs," said Dafina, stroking Alexios's face once more. She tucked an errant curl behind his ear. "And he will be gone when spring ends."

The room was growing very hot, and Alexios did not like the way Dafina and her soon-to-be brother were touching him. How did she know Auro would be gone at spring's end? He opened his mouth to ask them to leave, but Dafina bowled right over him.

"If we wed," said Dafina, "we could be the closest of friends, you and I. Allies. Partners."

Alexios froze. He did not have many friends and fewer allies. Those simple words did far more to tempt Alexios than any of their brazen pawing. His heart squeezed at the thought —of being seen, being known. Living as honestly as he was able. "We could," Alexios allowed. He took another sip of wine, wondering what she was getting at.

"We have discussed it," said Petar. "At length. An... arrangement could be reached, between the three of us, to see all parties happy, and both families elevated."

"What sort of arrangement?" asked Alexios.

Petar trailed his pinkie finger up the inside of Alexios's thigh. "Given your tastes...and mine," he said, "I could keep you *well* satisfied."

Alexios turned to look at Dafina, unable to believe what they were suggesting. "This is—"

Dafina scoffed. "No need to play the innocent, Your Highness," she said. "Petar would be there to...help. As long as we produce at least one heir together, there is no need for us to share a bed. Think of what is best for your people. My stepbrother is very comely, is he not?"

Petar lowered his lips to kiss the bare skin of Alexios's shoulder, and it was that featherlight touch that jolted through him like a lightning strike. He pushed off the bed, shaking them off. "You forget yourselves," he said furiously. He downed the rest of his wine, picked up the flagon from the sideboard, and shoved it at the Princess. "I would be alone, please." Hopefully, Auro was successful in his quest and they could be quit of this place tomorrow.

Neither Dafina nor Petar made any move to leave their seats on the edge of the bed. If anything, they drew closer together, watching him, matching looks of amusement on their faces.

"My Lady, my Lord," said Alexios firmly, though his tongue felt rather thick and clumsy "I bid you goodnight. Please, leave."

Dafina rested her temple against Petar's, and to Alexios, the resemblance between them was suddenly striking—though he knew they were not blood. It was as if they were one creature with four eyes, then three eyes, then four...he blinked, as if something clouded his eyes. "We can't go just yet," said Dafina, smiling serenely.

Alexios pointed to the door, but his arm seemed slow to respond. "Go—" he said, though to his ears his own words were garbled. Confused, he looked down at his hand, which swam before him as if he peered at it through water.

"What is the matter, Your Highness?" asked Petar innocently. "Are you quite well?"

Alexios drew his brows together, and belatedly, looked down into his wine glass. He staggered a few steps to the left, and the stone floor rose up to meet his knees. He barely had time to fling his arms out to break his fall before the room spun to blackness.

Twenty-Six

Auro cradled fall's grace to his chest, basking in the giddy relief of his success. Though he could hardly use Cedras's power for his own, having it close to hand seemed to lend strength to his drained limbs and his own wrung grace as he climbed out of the well and sealed it behind him. He wondered what would happen to the tree and the chamber without the source of magic. The tree had looked dark and empty once Auro had removed the light from within, but not in a bad way. It seemed to Auro like the carved owl's face on the tree's trunk had gone to rest. It was serene and silent, still and peaceful.

When Auro left through the small chamber with the magic door, sealing it behind himself, he retraced his earlier steps down through the wine cellar, into the adjacent store room, and out through the wall of the villa. The moon was high, and Auro frowned, peering up at it. Time had warped around him as he traversed the series of chambers to find his brother's grace. It seemed as though ages had passed, not a few hours. He made his way swiftly to the servants' entrance to the palace kitchens, eager to return to Alexios, to share his triumph. Besides, the sooner he returned, the sooner they could leave Neossós behind them.

When he approached the guest apartments, he, Leofric, and Alexios shared, Auro heard movement and voices within.

"Your Highness, I don't—"

"Leofric, you are the only one I trust with this," came Alexios's voice through the door.

Not wishing to barge in, Auro knocked.

"Enter," Alexios barked.

With a frown, Auro pushed open the door. Alexios sounded harsh, like something had deeply upset him in Auro's absence. Auro tucked the crystal phial in the folds of his tunic, shielding its light from view. "Alexios," said Auro when he entered, relief at seeing his face short-lived when he saw the expression Alexios wore.

Leofric, too, looked unhappy—caught somewhere between confused and irate. He opened his mouth, but Alexios held up a hand, cutting him off. "That is a command, Leofric. You ride at once. You are dismissed."

"Your Highness—"

"I said, 'dismissed.'"

Auro startled. He'd never heard Alexios speak to anyone this way, let alone Leofric, whose counsel he valued so highly. Leofric bowed stiffly and withdrew, and for some reason, he refused to look at Auro.

When they were alone, Auro withdrew the phial from the folds of his tunic.

"You have it?" said Alexios, breathless and eager.

"I do," said Auro, bumpiness of their reunion forgotten momentarily as he unwrapped the glowing, golden bottle.

The light illuminated Alexios's golden-brown eyes, giving them an almost feverish glow. He wore a strange, triumphant expression—hungry, almost—but it was gone the instant Alexios turned his face out of the light. He turned his back on

Auro and laid the phial on the bed, wrapping it in a square of cotton. When Auro's eyes tracked the movement, he realized that Alexios must have laid out all Auro's things while he was gone—his pack, his riding tunic, his sandals.

"Are we to depart?" Auro asked curiously. He was eager to leave as well, but fleeing in the night like thieves would not reflect well upon Alexios.

Alexios did not turn back, or answer.

"Alexios?"

When he turned around, the look on his face was pained, a mask of mourning. "You are."

Auro blinked. "Pardon...I—what?"

"You and Leofric return to Papia tonight. At once."

"I don't understand," said Auro, feeling like he was sinking below a frigid sea. "I thought we determined it would be dangerous to carry on with this betrothal. Dangerous for you, dangerous for Papia!"

"I spoke with Her Grace and the Lord Praetor this evening, and they explained everything. It was all a misunderstanding."

"Misunderstanding?" Auro nearly choked on the words. "The Praetor threatened you, Alexios. He—"

"He showed me how beneficial continuing with his design would be," Alexios said. "For everyone."

Auro frowned. "Everyone...what about us?" *What about me?*

Alexios pressed the bundle containing the phial into Auro's hands. "You as well, Auro. This is far too important to delay," he said. "You must return your brother's grace to Papia, to keep it safe."

"Alexios, there is something you are not saying. What is it?"

"I am to...remain here. To plan my wedding."

"Your—" the air punched from Auro's lungs. He had told

himself over and over again that this was the destination to which he and Alexios had been hurtling since they met, but he'd allowed himself to believe, believe in Alexios's optimism at finding another path, believe in their shared desire to enjoy whatever time remained to them. But now, Alexios was sending him away, weeks early. "How long will you stay?"

"A moon's turn, at least," he said, and the pain in his eyes was a knife thrust to Auro's own breast, so sharp it stole what little remained of his breath. "There are border agreements and trade negotiations that accompany the marriage pact."

"A moon's turn?" Auro asked, unable to keep his voice from breaking. Alexios would not even be there to say goodbye when he returned to stone at spring's end. "But..."

Alexios crossed the room, clutching at Auro's shoulders. "I have to think of what is best for my people, Auro," he said. "I can't avoid my duties any longer."

A hollow, gaping rift opened in Auro's heart. "I understand," he said, though he did not. "But I could remain—"

"No," said Alexios. He hesitated. "My betrothed insists. Our relationship, our...affair is known."

"But—"

"Auro, please," said Alexios, his own voice straining. He handed Auro his small pack, containing the few belongings he'd brought for the journey. "You must go with Leofric, I couldn't bear it if you were unsafe upon the road.

Auro nodded numbly, his heart already shying away from this conversation, this pain. "What changed?"

Alexios cupped his cheeks tenderly. "Nothing changed. You know that."

And he did. He did know that.

Alexios clasped Auro's hands, squeezing them tightly as if he could hardly bear the thought of letting go, either. "Alexios..."

He placed a hand to Auro's lips, much as he had done to

him the night they'd fucked in the grass by the light of the moon. "Know that I love you, with all of my heart."

Auro frowned, his mouth opening in confusion. Alexios kissed him softly on the lips, but Auro was too stunned by his confession to respond.

Twenty-Seven

Alexios's skull felt as if it had been emptied of brains and filled with pebbles and broken glass. What on earth had happened? He groaned, his mouth dry, with a taste like he'd attempted to swallow the wool directly off the back of a sheep. There was a bandage wrapped around his arm, and a sharp ache there, that traveled from the crook of his elbow up to his shoulder.

He coughed and flopped onto his back. The ground was cold, hard, and just damp enough to be uncomfortable.

"Thank goodness you're not dead."

Alexios flung himself to a seated position, squinting in the dark. "Where am I?"

"I believe you are an honored guest of my mother's royal dungeons," came the same voice sardonically. "I had hoped you'd have had the brains to flee Neossós by now."

Alexios's eyes began to adjust to the darkness. The only light in the room came from a small window, high up upon the wall, through which bled an anemic sliver of moonlight. His head still clouded and ached, fit to burst besides, so it took a moment for him to draw the face opposite into focus. "Princess?"

"It is a pleasure to see you again, Your Highness," she said. Despite the wry tone of her words, her eyes were bright with fear. Her face was filthy, her hair lank and unkempt. Her frightened eyes sunk into deep bruises on her face, which had a sickly greyish tinge to skin stretched tight over hollow cheeks.

It was *hardly* a pleasure. Alexios scowled. "What did you give me?"

"What?"

"You and your stepbrother put something in my wine!"

She frowned, too. "Alexios, I have been down here for over a week. Since the night of your welcome feast."

"You've—you've *what*?" Alexios stammered. Another wave of nausea punched through him, and his vision swam. "I need to lie down."

"By all means," said Dafina, but Alexios was already slipping away.

When he next woke, Alexios's head felt somewhat less like he was going to die. He sat up to find Dafina watching him, sipping from a cup of water. "Are you with me, Alexios?"

"Yes," he said, massaging his forehead, and then kneading his eyes with the heels of his hands. "Apologies, for my lack of constitution."

"No matter," she said. "I went through much the same when I awoke here, albeit with a bit more crying and carrying on."

"So, it was not you who poisoned my wine?"

"I assure you, it was not me. And, I don't have a stepbrother."

"Well, then who came into my chambers and poisoned me? And what happened to my arm?"

"I am certain I have no earthly idea," she said. Alexios noticed she wore an identical bandage to his own. "But perhaps we can fill in the gaps in each other's tales, and find out what is going on here."

"I will admit I am far less concerned with *what* is going on and far more concerned with getting out."

"There is no way out," she said morosely. "I think my stepfather hid me down here, and my mother is trying her best to forget all about me. Apparently, they want to forget you, too."

"But why?" This made absolutely no sense whatsoever. "Your mother seemed so intent on a marriage between us."

"Aye," said Dafina. "She was hoping to put the two of us together as quickly as possible."

"Why?"

She tipped her face toward the ceiling, resting the crown of her head against the stone wall. Alexios tracked the movement of one of her hands, around which a thick iron shackle had been locked, as it moved to curve protectively over her stomach. "I am with child," she said simply.

"Oh," said Alexios stupidly. "When we met—"

"I didn't know yet." Her other hand wrapped around her slightly swollen belly. "I found out when we returned from Papia and..." her voice choked off on a dry, broken sob.

"Princess?" asked Alexios gently.

"The Lord Praetor had him killed," she whispered.

"*What?*" asked Alexios.

"I can't prove it but—I don't know," she said. "I have a feeling."

"I believe you," said Alexios. "I am so sorry, Dafina. Was he...?"

"The father, yes. My love. He was one of my mother's guardsmen. Laurus, he was called."

They were silent for a while.

"My mother was desperate. Our kingdom was in shambles, and she had a shamed heir in trouble, and not a lot of options to preserve our line and legacy." She tossed Alexios an apologetic, watery smile. "The noble Prince of Papia was our only hope, or so she thought. When you wrote, begging to come for a visit, she was thrilled. If I could charm my way into your bed, we could claim the child was yours. A royal bastard is far preferable to a common one. And if we were to wed swiftly, no one need know the details of when the child was conceived."

"The night of the welcome feast," Alexios said. "That was you...being charming?"

Dafina cut him a look. "Of course not," she snapped. "I was in no way to be charming anyone. Still am not, in fact. I think it became clear to the Praetor that I would not be as pliant as he had wished, so he stuck me down here. Seems you weren't, either."

"I seem to be disappointing queens and kings left and right these days," grumbled Alexios.

Dafina laughed, but it was an unhinged, hysterical sort of giggle that could have been half a sob. "You have no idea how nice it is to have someone to talk to. I've been talking to the child, of course," she said, rubbing her stomach. "But he doesn't respond much."

"Have you been alone in the dark for a week?"

A shadow crossed her face. "They bring food and water once a day," she said.

"They? Who?" If the guardsmen could be spoken with, bribed, perhaps they could escape.

Her lips clamped shut. "You'll see. You wouldn't believe me if I told you."

Alexios was not sure what to do with that cryptic pronouncement, and silence fell between them. As he sat, Alexios replayed the memories of the evening before, trying to discern some sort of pattern, a piece of information they could exploit to escape. If Janus had wanted Alexios and the Princess dead, he presumed they already would be, by now. Auro,

Leofric, and the rest of Alexios's guard were still in the royal villa—surely, they would arrive to get him out, sooner or later. Perhaps the best course of action was to wait them out.

"So, Prince Alexios," said Dafina after a while. "Tell me your story. You seem awfully underwhelmed by all of this."

"That could be the blow to the head," said Alexios evasively. Magic of any kind was not common in Mykellos. When the gods had left the mortal realm behind, all of the magic had gone with them—or so Alexios had always been told. The only reason Alexios could even describe it as "not common" as opposed to "fodder for crib tales and legends" was because he had witnessed it with his own eyes. He shared a bed with a god, after all. He wondered if he should tell Dafina about Auro, tell her that she shouldn't fear because they had a god on their side. But something nagged at him. If he'd been down here for almost a day, absent Leofric tearing down the villa brick by brick, it could only mean one thing. He too had been replaced by an imposter, just as the Princess had. No one knew Alexios was missing, and no one knew to search for him.

He and Dafina were on their own.

"I mislike this," said Leofric, for what felt like the hundredth time.

Auro had agreed enough times that he didn't think this required a response, so he merely grunted from where he sat, slouched in his saddle.

The moon was still high, the stars twinkling merrily above the dappled ceiling of their path through the trees. Leofric was hardly the most engaging conversationalist at the best of times, and after a few hours of Auro's own black mood bouncing back at him off of Leofric's scowl, he craved comfort like a drowning man craved air. Auro twisted in his seat, fishing in his pack until he felt the residual warmth of Cedras's grace through its wrappings. He pulled out the bundle, cradling it gingerly in his lap. He trusted Segovax's plodding pace more than he trusted his own ability to steer the animal—especially now, with his thoughts so twisted up. How could Alexios send him away like this? Cast him so easily aside—as if what they shared meant nothing. Perhaps it had. Auro didn't want to believe that, didn't want to think of Alexios that way—but the evidence was fairly damning.

With a lump in his throat, Auro unwrapped the cotton and rested his palm on the bottle. The warmth was there, much as it had been since he had retrieved it from the chamber. But...Auro frowned. The warmth felt different. Simple, shallow. More like the actual result of being beside a fire, than the emotional warmth he felt when he'd first laid his hands on the crystal. That warmth—Cedras's warmth—was more akin to a hug, or a kiss, or gentle instruction from someone who knew so much, and loved to share that knowledge. It felt like Cedras.

This felt like a phial full of hot water, and the heat leeched out slowly, such that he had to keep turning it in his hands to feel the warmth on his skin.

Perhaps it had been the triumph of finding Cedras's grace that had warmed him, the feeling that he had at least succeeded in what he could do to help his brothers. And then, Alexios's dismissal had soured it. Perhaps that was all it was. He told himself that, over and over.

Auro squeezed the phial tighter. Something lingered in the back of his throat, a foul taste, a bitter one. The contents of this crystal bottle no longer felt like Cedras, the way they had when he'd first found it.

"Alright," said Leofric abruptly. "Speak."

Auro looked up from the object in his lap and turned to blink at Leofric through the moonlight. "Pardon?"

"I can feel despair rolling off of you in waves," said Leofric. He sighed, as if the next words were difficult to part with. "It might make you—feel better. To talk of it."

Auro turned the bottle over and over again in his hands. "I have a...a feeling."

Leofric didn't respond to that; Auro couldn't blame him. It was hardly a revelation.

"I just..." He clutched the crystal bottle in his hand, looking at the light shining through his fingers. Where it had before seemed to shine with its own light, it now had an unhealthy, anemic glow to it. The more he looked at it, the more wrong it felt. There was a time, perhaps most of his life, even, when Auro would have dismissed his misgivings. He had always been so afraid of causing problems, of facing them. There were always others, better suited to solving things than Auro, who was so naive and foolish. But now, there wasn't anyone else. And this quest, this thing his mother had charged him—and only him—to do... "This does not feel like my brother," he said at last.

Leofric knew of their quest, but he seemed to be skeptical of anything involving the arcane. He was a man who believed in what he saw. "Well," he said, albeit gently, "it isn't your brother."

Auro furrowed his brow, trying to figure out how to phrase the feeling of unrest. "I know it isn't, not truly. But I could feel something of him when I first retrieved it. Now..."

"You mean it's changed?" Leofric's voice turned whip sharp.

"Yes. And..."

"And?" Leofric prompted. He reined up his horse, and Auro did the same.

He turned Segovax to face Leofric. "Alexios."

"What about him?"

Auro sighed, and the heat rose in his cheeks. "When he sent me away, he—he told me he loved me."

Leofric's frown was so harsh his brow appeared carved of stone. "He does love you."

It was not a question, and Auro smiled, a small smile, sad and fleeting. "Perhaps," said Auro. "But—he had never told me so, before. And in fact, took pains to avoid doing so." Auro sighed. He was being ridiculous. "It's nothing," he said. "Forget I said anything."

Leofric reached across the gap between them and seized the reins of Auro's horse. "Auro," he said sharply. "Stop. Listen to me."

Confused, Auro met Leofric's gaze.

"You have been alive for four *hundred* years. Your gut is telling you something. What is it?"

Auro chewed his lip, afraid. The last time he'd felt this way was the day Ozias was killed. His voice was tiny when it came out. "Something is wrong." He swallowed and steadied himself. "Very wrong."

Leofric nodded. "Then what are we waiting for?"

"What?"

Leofric rolled his eyes and put his heels to his horse, leading Auro on a wild gallop back through the trees toward the place they'd just left behind.

Twenty-Eight

Alexios sat beside Dafina on the floor of their dank cell, talking of nothing, but Alexios could almost hear them both thinking hard of a way out of their predicament.

"So, the rumors are true, then," Alexios said abruptly.

"What rumors?" asked Dafina.

"The rumors about your stepfather."

"Ah," she said. "Well, of course, when they first cropped up, I thought—of course not. But now..."

"Yes." Alexios looked around their cell, considered the manner in which he'd been captured. "This evidence is fairly damning."

"This and—" She broke off, stiffening beside him, and he could feel her tremble against his shoulder where they sat pressed together.

Alexios cocked his head, listening. Then he heard it. A slow, plodding *clunk* that echoed strangely in the underground chamber beyond the bars of their cell door. "What is that?"

But Dafina pressed her lips together and shook her head.

The noise grew louder, closer. A brittle, hollow *clank*

followed by a series of scraping sounds, moving inexorably *toward*. Alexios had the wild, childish idea to cover his eyes with his hands, but he didn't. When the source of the sound stepped at last into the circle of the orangey glow from the wall sconce, Alexios wished he had.

It was plainly a guard. At first, Alexios thought, *hoped*, it was a guard in peculiar armor. It appeared their jailor was wearing armor made of clay pots. The sound of it clunking came from great clay shoes. In another situation, the effect may have been comical, but when the light from the torch on the wall shone on its helmed face, Alexios could see that the armor was empty. Within the clay helm and at the joints of the plate was only darkness. The creature's helm had a visor slit, but no eyes that Alexios could see, the effect throwing hollow, sinister shadows as it turned to stare at Alexios and Dafina. It had no eyes, no face, but Alexios could *feel* its gaze.

Alexios realized he was holding his breath, but when he tried to release it, he choked on fear and revulsion. The golem guard clunked its way closer to the door of their cell, and with its clumsy, pottery fingers it withdrew a ring of keys. It took its time opening the door, its movements slow and ponderous. Had their guard been human, even so armed, Alexios would have taken his chances and made attempt to bullrush him as he opened the door. As such, he found himself rooted to the floor of the cell in fear. Clinking ominously, the guard laid a tray before them on the floor and withdrew. Neither Alexios nor Dafina spoke until the echoing footsteps had faded entirely.

"What on earth *was* that?" asked Alexios.

"I have no idea," said Dafina. "But it comes every day with food."

Alexios eyed the tray mistrustfully. "And the food is safe?"

"Well," said Dafina, "at first I didn't think so but...after two days I couldn't resist anymore." Her hand fell to cover her stomach and the child within. "And...I've experienced no ill effects."

They divided up the food between them, and it was plain fare, but filling. The flagon of water was crisp, cold, and fresh. Once he was certain the guard was out of earshot—if it could even hear at all—he said, "What about your mother?"

Dafina snorted. "What about her?"

"Does she know what her consort is doing? Does she know you are down here?"

"My mother is very practiced at shutting her eyes to things she does not wish to see."

"Perhaps she does not know," said Alexios. He meant to be encouraging, but he could tell by her face that would be its own sort of pain. What mother did not recognize her own child had been replaced? Even if the darker mysteries were involved. And yet...Alexios supposed he had no idea how deep this magic went.

"Perhaps," said Dafina, her face closed off. "When Janus arrived at court, he had money, a silver tongue, and an abundance of wits. He was lowborn—or at least, we did not know of his family. My mother was immediately enchanted by his attention and flattery, and at first, I was so happy. She'd been so lonely since my father departed for the afterlife these ten years past.

"Janus asked nothing of her—at first. He offered his counsel at a time when our kingdom was in dire need and expected no reward. My mother showered him with them nonetheless, be that a favored place here at court, lavish gifts, or her affections. Again, I was happy. No one person should have the weight of an entire kingdom on their shoulders—it is far too much.

"The plague finally began to blow itself out, and at Janus's insistence, we had kept all news of it from leaving our borders. We survived..." she trailed away, grief on her face once again.

"For the most part, at least, due to Janus's counsel. When he at last begged my mother's hand in marriage, it seemed a reasonable request, especially given how taken she was with him already.

"My mother said she wanted to see me wed favorably before she agreed," she sighed. "Unfortunately for her, because she didn't know that I was...soiled, so to speak."

Not for the first time, and likely not the last, Alexios reflected that the world was a truly unjust place. "My Lady—"

She shook her head and held up a hand. "It matters not. Soiled or no, I have another man's child within me, a bastard who would have made succession complicated. Janus offered to remove the child from consideration, but I refused."

Alexios had heard of such things and knew the choice was not made lightly.

"This little one is all I have left of Laurus," she said. "And bastard or no, I already love them. I told my mother it was *my* decision, and she respected that. After he took care of Laurus, Janus concocted another plan—and your letter arrived, very timely." She smiled at Alexios. "Janus said if I could charm you fast enough, no one ever need know about..."

"Charm me?"

She raised her eyebrows, and Alexios flushed.

"At any rate," Dafina went on, "You were far more difficult to charm than Janus anticipated."

Alexios sighed. "Sorry about that."

"It's alright," she said. "I'm thankful, in truth."

"Oh?"

She smiled. "I have no interest in marrying you, or anyone, Prince Alexios."

"Well," said Alexios, "thank goodness for that."

They shared a sad little laugh, neither mentioning that it hardly mattered one bit with them both locked in a dungeon.

They approached Neossós from the north, much as they had the night of their arrival. A thick copse of trees masked their position, and Leofric squinted through a lens tube. "It's too bloody dark," he said, annoyed. "But I suppose that will let us slip through unseen."

"What about the rest of Alexios's guardsmen?"

"I think this type of confrontation might be more suited to your approach, than theirs."

"My approach?" Auro's voice went a little high and squeaky. He really did not have *any* approach to confrontation.

Leofric squeezed his shoulder. "I will retrieve the men, but we are outnumbered. I think stealth will suit us better, here. Stealth and...your magics."

Auro blanched. Auro had been using his grace to spar, but the only time he'd ever truly used his "magics," as Leofric called them, in combat was the night Alexios had almost been killed, and he hadn't even used it on purpose. It had simply exploded out of him when he'd realized Alexios was in danger —and Alexios was in danger now. Auro set his jaw and nodded. He could do this. For Alexios. The time for softness was done, as was the time for uncertainty.

He was a god. What mortal could hope to stand before him?

Leofric met his eye, and startled, staring at Auro like he had never seen him before. Auro didn't have time to make sense of that. He had to find Alexios and get to the bottom of what had happened here. They hobbled their mounts in the cover of the trees and crept through the dark toward the walls surrounding the royal villa. They parted ways at the eastern gate, Leofric promising to infiltrate the barracks and rouse the rest of their men. "If we move carefully, we might be able to take the castle. You find Prince Alexios."

Auro retraced the steps he'd taken just the evening before, allowing him to sneak through the weakened stone wall into the storage basement. Once again, he crouched on the earthen floor, listening to make sure he was alone, and that no one had heard his approach. His pulse hammered in his ears, and Auro felt he could feel the pulse of the dirt through the soles of his feet, as well. All at once, he realized something.

The heat from Cedras's grace was entirely gone. Frantic, Auro shoved a hand within his tunic to withdraw the phial and gasped. Where before, it had been a fine, spun crystal bottle, it now stood an average clay flagon with a wooden stopper, sealed with wax. The bulb of the bottle threw no heat whatsoever, and when Auro broke the waxen seal, and sniffed the bottle's contents, he realized it was filled with wine. There was no warmth, no glow, not even a sickly thin trace of his brother in the flagon. Auro had been tricked.

Cursing himself, he set the decoy aside, wondering when it had been replaced. The only thing he had done between retrieving the actual bottle and leaving the villa was speak to Alexios. He replayed their brief, confusing conversation in his mind's eye. Alexios had briefly taken the bottle from him, turned his back...he could easily have replaced it, but why? And how had he disguised it so deeply?

Auro closed his eyes, imagining the parting between himself and Alexios, focusing hard on him—the movements of his shoulders, the twitch in his jaw. His eyes. His voice. The hands that Auro loved so well, the arms that wrapped him up at night. As he focused, something peculiar happened. It became as if Alexios were being scrubbed from the memory. His form became blurred, swollen, and strange, like a clumsy doll made in Alexios's vague likeness. *What sort of dark sorcery is this?* Auro thought.

He shook the mental cobwebs from his mind's eye and leaned his back against the stone wall of his hiding place, realizing he had no idea where to begin. He didn't know where Alexios was, nor where the fake-Alexios had taken Cedras's grace. Auro could hardly just blunder through the bowels of the palace, and he had no—*huh.*

Auro hadn't realized he'd been absently petting the earthen floor, but all at once he felt a tiny pinprick of warmth beneath his palm. Curious, he flattened his hand against the hard-packed dirt and tugged gently with his grace. A small, fibrous root system lay mostly dormant beneath the floor of the cellar, the bead of life within it faint, but thrumming constant all the same. Auro pushed again, and his awareness traveled along the root, and as sweat beaded on Auro's forehead, he realized he was using his grace to travel along the roots, as might water or nutrients from the earth. The room before him swam and blurred as he put more of himself into the ground, into the earth, and left less of himself in his body.

He found his conscious mind could hop from root to root until he ended up in the hyphae of a fungus, growing somewhere damp and cool and dark. It was a happy place to be, for the fungus, but the next adjacent life he felt was tremendously unhappy. A sluggish beat of Auro's faraway heart later he realized the next adjacent life was human. Two humans. And one burned hot and bright and golden, calling out to Auro as strongly as if it stood beside him whispering in his ear.

Auro came back to his body with a thump, with a name on his lips. "Alexios!"

Twenty-Nine

Alexios did not think he would sleep that night, but he must have dozed off, because suddenly Dafina was shaking him awake. "*It's coming back*," she hissed, her voice full of dread.

Alert at once, Alexios sat up, straining his ears. Sure enough, he caught the sound of the thick, clunking steps. "Perhaps it is bringing food once again?"

Dafina chewed her lip. "Thus far, it has not come twice on the same day. Besides, it is the middle of the night!"

Dread coiled in Alexios's chest, and he cast his gaze around the cell in search of anything he could use as a weapon, trying to recall everything Leofric had taught him during their sparring sessions. He scrambled to his feet, moving to shield Dafina with his body. However, when the ceramic guardsman shambled into the light cast by the torches on the wall, something appeared...off.

Even more *off* than one would expect a pile of sentient pots to be.

Where before, the golem moved slowly but confidently, the guard's steps were now clumsy, ungainly, and lacking their steady rhythm. It lurched into the bars with a riotous clangor, its clay hands shooting between them. Alexios and Dafina moved as far as they could toward the rear of the cell, pressing against the wall.

"What...?"

The golem fumbled against what could be described as its belt, until it grabbed for its large keyring. Alexios and Dafina could only watch in confusion as it struggled to shove the correct key into the lock. When it at last got the door unlocked, it windmilled its arms, lurching violently into the cell as the door swung open with the sound like a great, echoing gong. The guard tripped over the straw strewn all over the floor, fell, and shattered its own head.

Dafina let out a small shriek as a piece of pottery skittered across the floor toward her, but Alexios fell to the ground beside it, reaching his hand into the cavern where its neck would have been. "What are you doing?" Dafina asked.

But Alexios didn't answer. He'd seen a flash of green in the golem's helmet, where before there had been only darkness. Sure enough, his fingers connected with what was unmistakably a wriggling vine. It coiled around his wrist like a friendly pet snake, and when he pulled his arm back, he smiled. "We're getting out of here," he told Dafina.

He released the vine and fumbled for the golem's keys, undoing first Dafina's chains and then his own. "What the *hell* is that?" she asked, clutching so tightly to Alexios's arm that her nails left little half-moon indents in his skin.

"It's kind of a long story," he said. "Do you trust me?"

She scoffed. "What's my alternative, here?"

"Fair point."

"It's alright, my Lady," said Alexios. "Or...rather, it's certainly better than staying in this cell for one more second."

Dafina rolled her eyes with a sigh and said, "How low my bar for 'alright' has become."

The vining plant that had seized control of their guard trailed out through the darkened stone corridor, so they followed it to the source. Alexios's heart thudded faster and faster in his chest. Though he knew the vines were sent by Auro, though he *knew* it had to be Auro at the source of them, when he reached a small earthen chamber, and actually *saw* Auro, he still gasped.

Auro sat cross-legged on the ground, his hands pressed flat against the earth. Around him, the remnants of three smashed golems overgrew with green tendrils that clutched so tightly to the clay pieces it seemed to Alexios that the vines themselves were angry. Auro's pink hair blew around his face, though Alexios could not feel the slightest stir of breeze. His eyes were wide, unblinking, his green irises blown so wide they eclipsed the whites entirely, and they *glowed.* In fact, the only light in the small chamber seemed to come from Auro. His skin, the fluttering locks of his hair, his eyes, all of it luminous.

"Who. The fuck. *Is that?*" Dafina hissed in Alexios's ear.

"Uh," said Alexios. "That's my...he's my...Auro. His name is Auro."

At the sound of his name, Auro's head turned sharply toward them, and he blinked over his strangely glittering eyes a few times, and all at once, the other-worldly aura dissipated. "Alexios?" he breathed. His eyes cleared, the vines fell, docile, to the ground, and Alexios could not help the smile.

"Yes," he said. "It's me."

Auro leapt to his feet and flung himself into Alexios's startled embrace. He supposed he should show more restraint but he couldn't help it. He leaned back, lifting Auro off his feet, breathing in the herbal, grassy scent from the top of his head.

"It's really you," Auro mumbled into the front of Alexios's tunic as Alexios set him back on the floor once again.

"Of course, it's me," said Alexios. He took a small, but hasty step back. Alexios still was not sure entirely how he should behave in front of Dafina—though he supposed they did not have many secrets between them now. "Who else would it be?"

"I—you sent me away. Or, I thought it was you."

Alexios cupped Auro's cheeks fiercely. "I would never send you away."

Auro's answering smile was a tremulous one. He wrapped his hands around Alexios's wrists and gave them a squeeze. "I know that, now—but someone did, and he looked an awful lot like you, and they stole Cedras's grace."

"They *what*?"

"*Hello*?" said Dafina. "I feel as though I am a few leagues behind the two of you."

"Apologies, Princess," said Alexios. He turned to Auro. "Dafina was replaced by some sort of enchanted form, as well."

"Your Highness," said Auro respectfully. "It's a pleasure to make your acquaintance."

"Oh yes, it's a bloody enchanting time," she snapped. "Will one of you *please* explain what on earth is going on?"

Auro kept looking sidelong at Alexios, partly expecting him to vanish at any moment, or transform into a grotesque being made of clay. Now that Auro had learned the look of these illusions, he trusted he would not be fooled again—but he could not help being afraid. The copy of Alexios had seemed so real.

Alexios seemed to sense something and took hold of Auro's hand as they made their way through the bowels of the dungeons below the royal villa of Neossós. Princess Dafina, Alexios's intended, kept looking at them, and the place where their hands joined with a look on her face so etched with pain and longing it took Auro's breath away. A few times he made to slip his fingers from Alexios's, but Alexios only tightened his grip, like he refused to part from Auro's touch. The selfish part of Auro was grateful for that, so grateful. The warmth of Alexios's palm was to him like a safe anchor, keeping him grounded to the earth. However, whether or not the Alexios who had sent him away was real, he was still supposed to marry the girl who walked beside them now.

But that was a matter for another time. Auro knew Leofric was making moves to secure the villa, but things could easily turn to bloodshed if it appeared they had ill intent toward the royal family. They had Dafina with them, but if she could be replicated, would the guards believe their Dafina or the imposter?

"It is Janus," said Alexios, interrupting Auro's thoughts. "He was the only one who knew you were trying to get beyond the enchanted door. He wanted what was behind it."

"What of the Queen?" asked Auro nervously, with a glance at Dafina.

Her gaze was hard. "If my mother knew of this, she and I will be having words."

The threat was present despite the mild turn of phrase, and Auro's immediate thought was that this young woman was not someone one wanted as an enemy. Dawn was not far off, and they crept out through the stones Auro had loosened —*had it only been two days ago?*—and onto the villa grounds. It was still dark, but sunrise was coming.

"My mother and Janus usually break their fast in their private dining solar shortly after dawn," said Dafina. "If my mother does not know of Janus's plans, the false me should be there with them, playacting the dutiful daughter."

"We should hide within the stables," said Auro. "Hopefully Janus will not yet know you two escaped the dungeons."

"What if they don't believe us?" Alexios asked. "What if they think the other Dafina is the true Dafina?"

"When I began to suspect that some enchantment had been worked, it was like…I could see the edges of the magic, and then, when I pulled at the threads of it, they fell away," said Auro.

"So, we just have to hope our Dafina can provide enough shadow of doubt to lift the caul from her mother's eyes."

The stables still stood mostly empty. The three of them huddled into one stall, crouching in the hay to avoid being seen. When dawn broke, they crept from the stables and into the villa.

"I mislike how easy this is," said Alexios.

"Agreed," said Dafina. "Our force of guardsmen has been a shadow of itself since the blight, but this…"

The villa was emptier than Auro had yet seen it, which was saying something indeed. They did not see one single soul until they reached the door to the private dining chambers shared by the Queen and her consort. There was not even so much as a steward standing by to announce their approach.

Auro and Alexios heaved the doors open to find Queen Petillia and Janus tucking into a full banquet spread to break their fast, as if nothing was amiss. Sure enough, Dafina sat at the table with them—or rather, a copy of her did. The actual Princess seemed to take this as a great personal affront. Not one of the three people at the table looked up when Auro, Alexios, and Dafina had burst into the room.

"*Mother?*" Dafina asked, taking a step forward.

"Wait—" Auro hissed, grabbing her arm before she could get closer.

"What?"

"Look at them," said Auro, putting an arm out in front of Alexios, too. "*Really* look."

Now that Auro truly knew that glamours and illusions

were at play, it was like he could *see* them. The princess at the table looked like Dafina at first blush, but when he focused upon her face, there were signs. Her eyes were closed, and she gripped her knife by the blade, attempting blithely to cut a loaf of bread with its wooden handle. Her other hand had six fingers.

Alexios let out a sharp gasp. "The Queen!"

The Queen turned her head to say something to Janus, and when she opened her mouth, Auro startled to see she had no teeth, and her tongue was grey and thick, unmoving. At that, the illusion fell away entirely, dissolving before their eyes as if it had been made of sand. Now, the table stood occupied by three enormous clay guards, like the one Auro had repurposed to free Alexios and the Princess from the dungeon.

No sooner had Auro made that realization than the one in the center lurched to its feet, shoving the table away from itself to tip over and send dishes and platters of food tumbling to the floor. "*Run!*" said Alexios, and Auro surely did not need to be told twice. Dafina looked as though she were about faint, but Alexios seized her arm and dragged her back through the doors. They slammed them, leaning their weight against the doors just as the clay golems collided on the other side.

"Can we lock them in?" asked Alexios, throwing his shoulder against the door.

Dafina shook her head. "Not from this side."

Auro glanced frantically around the corridor. "Hold them!" he told the others.

He sprinted to the interior courtyard within the villa's entryway. It had lovely statues, a shallow pool of water, and most importantly a vining crop of ivy. Auro dove to his knees, skidding across the smooth tiles until he could shove his fingers into the dirt. With Alexios in danger, his power hummed right below the surface of his skin, and the ivy seemed ripe and ready to take action. Dafina shrieked as the vines hurtled toward the doors, but Auro urged it on, and soon enough the vines wrapped around the doors' thick bronze handles, binding them tight. Alexios and Dafina scurried away as the vines moved like angry snakes, and soon the door stopped shaking.

"That won't hold forever," said Auro, standing. He bent to brush his knees off and staggered, dizzy.

Alexios caught him with an arm around Auro's waist. "What is it?"

"I'm just not as accustomed to using my grace like that."

"I'm sorry, your 'grace'?" asked Dafina. "Who *are* you?"

"It is something of a complicated story," said Alexios, tightening his arm around Auro.

"Now, where would Janus go, and your mother?"

"His study," said Dafina. "It's in the eastern tower, above the library. My mother had it built for him."

"Show us."

"Wait," said Auro, adjusting his weight to steady himself. "We can't just go bursting in there."

"Well, what do you propose?"

Auro walked over to the courtyard once again, where the ivy was growing in through the cracks, and sat right upon the floor. He worked a few of the stones loose to expose the earth below and searched again for a path of living things that would allow Auro to find Janus and the Queen.

Auro flitted from root to root, hyphae to hyphae, to a blade of grass, a tree, and then he gasped, vertigo swooping through him as he realized he looked down upon the entire royal villa of Neossós through the eyes of a chaffinch. The finch perched on the window of a stone room, and Auro found it far easier to watch through his eyes than to perceive the world through a plant.

"I do not understand," Queen Petillia was saying.

"It doesn't matter," said Janus. He moved feverishly

around the room, stuffing things into a bag. Auro could see Cedras's grace on a worktable, glowing and warm. Even through a finch's eyes, he knew it was the real thing. The bottle was surrounded by books and papers, and it looked as though Janus had been trying to use several tools to get it open.

"We have the Prince," said the Queen. She followed him around the room. "Your plan worked perfectly! Once he and my daughter are married, we can wed—"

Janus turned to face her. "I have no more need to marry you, you foolish woman. I have everything I need."

Queen Petillia looked as if she had been slapped. "What?"

Janus opened his mouth to answer her, but his gaze fell upon the chaffinch. He held a finger to his lips, silencing the Queen. He stared at the bird, and three floors away, Auro felt as though Janus was staring directly into his own eyes. Before he could react, Janus snapped his fingers, and Auro's world was obscured by midnight black feathers. He knew one moment of blinding pain in his shoulder before he returned to his own body with a cry of agony.

"Auro," said Alexios, sinking to the ground beside him, wrapping Auro in his arms. "Are you—"

Auro shook him off. "There is no time," he said, getting unsteadily to his feet. "They are in the study," he confirmed to Dafina. "Janus is packing to leave—I think he means to leave your mother behind."

Dafina led the way through the villa to a small wooden door at the end of a corridor in the eastern wing. It swung ajar, as if someone had just passed through it in a hurry.

Auro clutched Alexios's tunic. "He has Cedras's grace," he said, panicked. "If he gets away—"

"He *won't*," said Alexios fearlessly, and he charged up the narrow staircase. Auro's stomach lurched with guilt, how he'd led a poor, innocent bird to some terrible end, but he could not think about that now.

The three of them were panting by the time they reached the second door at the top of the tower. Alexios lunged for the handle, but Auro flung out a hand. Voices argued on the other side of the door. "*Shh—*"

"My love, *please,* I don't understand—" that was the Queen's voice, thick with emotion.

"Stand aside," snapped the other voice, Janus. "This is the only thing that matters."

"No, there must be some—" The Queen's plea broke off in a scream.

Dafina shoved her way past Auro and flung the door open before he or Alexios could stop her. "Mother!"

The study was chaos—scrolls, books, and scraps of parchment had been thrown about the room, scattered underfoot like leaves. Auro gasped, his hand going to his chest as he felt his brother's presence in the room like a punch to the sternum. There, on the table—a leather satchel that had been hastily packed with items, and a warm golden light spilling from the top. Auro lunged for the bag. At the same time, Janus made a grab for it.

"Mother, let him *go*—" Dafina pleaded, tugging on her mother's arm.

The Queen, in turn, had a grip on Janus's robes. "Just tell them," she begged him. "Tell them it's a misunderstanding."

Auro shoved his hand into the bag and the second his fingers made contact with the crystal bottle, he knew it was the true artifact. Janus lunged for him, grabbing the bag. Auro locked eyes with him as they grappled for the bag, but before he could so much as spit, Queen Petillia punched Janus in the stomach.

It was so peculiar that Auro dropped the leather strap in shock before he realized that when the Queen had punched him, she'd left a dagger buried in his gut. Janus realized it too, looking down at the handle of the knife, the slowly darkening stain on the front of his robes.

The Queen panted, backing away toward the wall to collapse against it, her breathing ragged. Janus wrapped one long-fingered hand around the knife's hilt, and before anyone could stop him, he yanked it out in a gush of blood. He staggered and collapsed face-first to the ground. Auro went chasing after autumn's grace, which had fallen from the bag and skittered across the floor. He clutched it tight with both hands, determined not to let it go.

The silence in the aftermath of the brief struggle was deafening, and when Auro turned, he saw Alexios moving like he was in a trance toward Janus's body. Alexios rolled him over, searching for some way to prolong his life—there were so many questions yet unanswered—but they all watched as Janus breathed his last.

Shakily, Auro moved to the windowsill, where a small, blue-grey shape lay in an untidy heap of feathers. It was the chaffinch, and it still lived. Auro cradled the tiny body in the folds of his tunic, vowing to heal him in thanks for his brave service. He was strangely calm as he brushed his thumb over autumn's grace, until Alexios let out a startled yelp.

All eyes were on Alexios where he held on to Janus's body, his face completely horrified. The body in front of Alexios, in its growing pool of blood, rippled and changed before their very eyes. The hair grew longer, the nose shrank. The cheeks and lips grew rounder, softer...more feminine. All at once, the body on the floor was revealed, not to be that of Janus—but that of Dafina's mother, Queen Petillia.

Auro whipped his head to where the Queen had been slumped against the stone wall beside the Princess, only to be met with Janus's cold stare. He shoved Dafina forward, and she stumbled straight into Auro's arms, allowing Janus to make a dash for the window.

Before Auro could so much as make a sound of protest or warning, Janus dove out the open tower window. Auro raced to the sill, leaning out just in time to see the falling man explode—into a murder of ravens, cawing noisily as Janus's rich robes fluttered and fell to the ground. The ravens went off in a dozen different directions, and faster than Auro would have believed, all of them were black specks against the morning sky.

Thirty

They burned the Queen at dusk, her body draped in lilac silk, for Dafina had said that was her mother's most favorite color. She stood rigid beside Alexios in her mourning clothes, black wool robes and a sheer black lace veil draped over her face. She clutched her mother's crown in pale hands that trembled, and Alexios couldn't help but stare at the way her knuckles shone white as the bones beneath her skin.

The guardsmen stood looking on, Leofric's men and the small staff that remained at the palace gathering to see the Queen on her way. Alexios had tried to shield Dafina from her mother's broken body, but she'd refused, insisting that she must look upon her mother's face to say their final goodbyes.

She hadn't spoken a word since then and did not until the sun was well set and the funeral pyre was the only light burning in the garden. They had sent messengers to the people of Neossós's capital city that any who were able should make the journey to the villa so that Dafina could address the crowd at dawn two days hence.

"I have no idea what I will even say to them," she said, the first thing she'd said out loud in hours. "What am I going to do?"

Alexios frowned. This kingdom was full of people who needed help, who needed hope. No one person could fix all of this, no matter how strong or experienced. "Come home with me," he blurted.

Dafina turned to him, incredulous. "Pardon?"

"Auro, Leofric, and I leave on the morrow," he said. "Come with us, to Papia."

The look she gave him was full of scorn. "I'm not certain what made you think I'm the kind to abandon my people," she said, "but—"

"No," said Alexios hastily. "That is not what I meant, my Lady."

"I think we're past 'my ladies' now, Alexios."

"Yes," he said, clearing his throat. "Dafina, I do not think Neossós is equipped to recover from this tragedy on its own."

She bristled, briefly, but the fight seemed to whoosh out of her even faster than it arrived. "And yet, I am all they have. I'm their queen, now."

Alexios set his jaw. "Once, Neossós was part of Papia. Perhaps it could be so, again. Your people need help to recover from all that has happened."

Dafina stopped, placing a hand on the center of Alexios's chest. "You're serious."

"Aye," said Alexios. "We could rule both kingdoms, together. Your people would follow you, and Papia has the means to help."

Dafina rested a hand upon her stomach, which had only just begun to show signs of her pregnancy. "And this?" she whispered.

Alexios shrugged. "What if we were to say...he's mine?"

Dafina laughed. "Oh sorry, I'm sorry. It's not funny, it's —" but she broke off again in sickly, hysterical giggles.

"What?" said Alexios, affronted. "It could happen. That was the initial plan, anyway, was it not?"

"But—"

"I know there are details to work out," he said. "But think about what's best for your people. I could name your child my heir—and through us, both our kingdoms are secure. Papia can help you, can help Neossós."

"Perhaps it isn't so mad after all," said Dafina. "But what about...Auro?"

Alexios sighed. "I don't know."

"Well, mayhaps you should discuss this with him before you make plans to marry me."

Alexios frowned. "I said nothing of marriage."

"But—"

"Who is to say two cannot be partners in rule without being partners in bed? You do not wish to marry me, do you?"

"No, of course I don't—"

"Well, there you have it then."

"You are mad," she said, something akin to awe in her voice. "This has never been done before."

Alexios looked her in the eye. "So what?"

Thirty-One

I n the end, Dafina decided to remain in Neossós, for the time being. Her people would hardly feel as though she looked out for them if she fled the kingdom immediately after her mother's bones had been laid to rest.

Neossós was in shambles, and it needed Papia's help—needed Alexios's help. But Alexios had someone who needed his help first, and his timeline was far more pressing.

Alexios dispatched Leofric's squad of scouts to Papia, to inform his parents that he was safe, but things had really not gone to plan. He decided to leave the sordid details from the message—after writing three separate letters explaining the events in the last few days and subsequently tossing them into the hearth, Alexios thought it best to explain in person. Even leaving out Auro's role from the tale, and the strange magic of Janus and his golems, the story was absurd when seen in print.

In the immediate wake of her mother's death, Princess—no, *Queen*—Dafina threw herself into unearthing all of Janus's secrets. It was proving even more difficult than one would have thought—the man had been clever when concealing his plots. Using the books and scrolls left behind, she was able to piece together at least some of what he'd been doing. The golems were made from a special clay, and unfortunately, its recipe wasn't among the documents recovered. Perhaps Janus had been making such golems for long enough that he didn't require it. However, she found dusty crystal bottles of blood, which had been used in making the most convincing duplicates. Apparently having the blood lent strength to the enchantment.

Alexios wrapped his fingers around his elbow, where Janus had taken his blood and used it to trick both Auro and Leofric, and shuddered. This man was far too dangerous, too powerful to be ignored. Once he had seen that Auro returned to rest, the plan to help his brothers safeul put in motion, Alexios would have to hunt him down and make him answer for his crimes.

Auro's dream of a swift return to Papia proved a foolish one. After Queen Petillia's funeral, Alexios was loath to leave the people of Neossós entirely rudderless. They had their new queen, Dafina, and Auro felt privately that she would be a monarch to be reckoned with—but she was still deep in mourning. Overwhelmed by the weight of her losses and her new responsibilities, she barely left Janus's tower. Alexios had met with a few of the Neossan consuls in her stead, as neither of them had officially announced a break in their betrothal.

Auro spent much of his time outside, tending to his duties and caring for the injured chaffinch, whom he'd named Pipilo. Apparently, one of the ravens in Janus's thrall had attacked Pipilo when Janus realized Auro was spying through his eyes. Pipilo's wing was badly damaged, but he still sang bright and loud, and with Auro's care he was on the mend.

A few days passed, and Auro barely laid eyes upon Alexios.

He and Princess Dafina were ensconced in talks of trade and treaty more often than not. Auro knew it was necessary, that Alexios wouldn't want to return home to Papia with such a gaping vulnerability on its borders. They made a good team, Alexios and Dafina, Auro realized with a pang.

Auro hated himself for his bitter, churlish thoughts, knowing that Alexios had duties far beyond any commitment he might feel to Auro, but he could not stop the thoughts coming. Eventually, he stopped returning to their chambers at night. Alexios never retired until the wee hours, and lying in bed alone proved worse than sitting outside, beneath the trees and the stars—seeing to the end of spring.

He could feel it coming, as he always did—the tug behind his navel, calling him back toward the temple. It felt different this year, though, than it had in years past. Auro felt like something being reclaimed by the earth. A field, plowed over for crops and then left to be reconsumed by nature, which abhorred a vacuum. Touched and cleared by human hands, but without constant attention, the weeds crept back in, steadily erasing any evidence that it had been touched at all.

One morning, the day before they were set to return to Papia, Auro was startled to see Dafina sitting on the bench in the gardens that he had been occupying alone for days.

"You've been scarce," she said to Auro when he approached.

"Your Grace," he said respectfully, bowing.

"Have you been hiding?"

"It's been hectic," he said carefully.

"And you're avoiding Alexios," she said.

"What?"

"Come, Auro," said Dafina. "I'm not blind."

Auro's face reddened. "I was trying—"

"Alexios told me some of your...situation," she said. "And

if I hadn't seen what you can do with my own eyes, I might have thought him to be absolutely raving."

Auro waited, unsure where she was going with all of this.

"You are leaving him, soon. And you're pulling away from him already."

Auro bristled at that. "I am not *leaving* him," he said.

"No?" Dafina tilted her head to the side. "It seems like you are—and he knows."

"What?"

"He watches you, all day. You are hard to miss in a crowd, Auro. Alexios's eyes and mind are upon you, always."

He couldn't help the tiny twitch of his lips as he fought against a smile. "I'm merely trying to stay out of his way," he said. "There is much to do, much required of him."

"And he requires you," said Dafina. "For as long as he can have you."

"My Lady—"

"I said what I came to say. Only—don't take any time remaining to you for granted. Trust me."

Auro frowned, watching her retreating back as she returned to the villa.

Thirty-Two

The final few days of spring were a whirlwind to Alexios, who could barely keep up with things from one moment to the next. He said goodbye to Queen Dafina, then it seemed all too soon he was returning to Papia with Leofric and Auro—swept into an endless run of discussions with his parents, explaining the situation in Neossós, and negotiating the possibility of merging two kingdoms.

He barely saw Auro, who resumed his post as Alexios's valet, but every night they fell into each other's arms, and Alexios tried his best to ignore that the last few days remaining to them trickled away like raindrops. All too soon, spring was ending.

They began their farewells at dawn.

Well, no. That was not strictly true, Alexios supposed. In actuality, they had begun their farewells the night before. Later, Alexios would reflect that he had been saying farewell to Auro since the day they met.

At dawn, upon the last day of spring, Auro woke Alexios with his lips on his ear, his teeth at his throat. Auro pressed kiss after kiss to Alexios's skin as the glow from sunrise lit his face, his hair, his eyes. It was as if Auro burned with golden fire as he stared at Alexios from his perch astride his thighs. They did not speak; they simply stared at one another, and Alexios felt a lump begin to burn in his throat that he wished to banish with kisses, so he tangled his fingers in Auro's pink curls and pulled him close.

Last night, Alexios had given Leofric specific instructions not to disturb him unless the villa were legitimately on fire, and perhaps not even then. With Auro's mouth upon his, Alexios could almost pretend that spring would last forever. Almost. He could feel the hardness of Auro's cock pressing against his abdomen where he lay draped across him, insistent and hot with the thin sheet between them. With a groan of frustration, Alexios shoved his hand between their bodies and yanked, pulling the offending fabric so hard he dislodged Auro entirely. With a sad, soft little laugh, Auro rolled onto his back, blinking up at Alexios who now kneeled above him, balling up the sheet so he could toss it aside.

Auro's heavy-lidded gaze fell to Alexios's cock, flushed and angry when he wrapped his hand around it. His tongue darted out, licking his plump bottom lip, and Alexios tracked the movement. He had intended to take his time, but with the whole day and Auro's naked body sprawled out before him, he thought perhaps they had time enough to enjoy each other both ways, fast and slow. Hard and soft—and he wanted to enjoy Auro, *now.*

He coated his cock with oil and positioned himself between Auro's legs. When he sank into Auro, it felt like coming home. It felt like it was where he belonged. The pleasure burned through him where they joined, and Auro canted his hips to welcome him deep and deeper, rising to meet him with every thrust. There was much Alexios wished to say, so much—but the words caught in his throat, tangled up and fearful, so he entwined his fingers with Auro's, gave his hand a squeeze, and hoped he understood.

As much as Alexios tried his best to stop it, the day marched on. Auro was insatiable, tireless, and Alexios suspected at more than one point in the day that loving with a god wasn't something a mortal could survive. Nothing Alexios could give him seemed enough, but he was more than happy to give all of himself over to Auro, trying. They came together over, and over, and when Alexios felt he could not have gotten hard again if his very life depended on it, he reclined back on his pillows, and Auro curled beside him with his head resting upon his hip. His body was wrung, and he tried with all he had to stay awake, but his eyes drifted closed, and he gasped in surprise when he woke sometime later with the sultry wet heaven of Auro's mouth around his soft cock. Not moving, not sucking, just holding it there, like Auro could not bear for time to pass without their being joined. Without Alexios inside him. Alexios let his head fall back, blinking against the stinging behind his eyes, blinking against the damning rays of the sun as it threatened to set just outside his windows.

Auro nuzzled the hair between Alexios's legs, tonguing lazily at his soft cock, and Alexios found his next wind, soon enough his thighs flexed, his hips chasing the pleasure of Auro's mouth, and his cock hardened again. Alexios groaned, torn between exhaustion and desire to have Auro one more time, thrusting up as Auro hollowed his cheeks and sucked him down. When he made eyes at Alexios, lips stretched wide around his shaft, Alexios could wait no longer and hauled Auro up toward himself, kissing him thoroughly, tasting his own seed on Auro's tongue. He pushed Auro onto his back and shoved his thighs apart to enter him again.

Auro arched against him, clawing desperately at Alexios's shoulders, using one hand to push against his tailbone, urging him on—but it seemed there was something missing because after a few moments, Auro released a frustrated huff and wilted back against the pillows. Alexios slowed the movement of his hips, settling his weight on top of Auro's chest. "What is it?"

"Nothing," said Auro, but he turned his head away. "It's nothing. Don't stop—"

Alexios seized Auro's chin, forcing Auro to meet his eyes. "Tell me."

"I need—I can't," Auro. He blinked rapidly, lashes fluttering over his eyes, which swam with unshed tears.

Concerned, Alexios cupped Auro's face, brushing his thumb over the apple of his cheek. "Auro, please, talk to me."

Auro pulled Alexios in for a hard, desperate kiss. Alexios let him take what he wanted, and soon enough, Auro's lips found his ear, panting hot breaths against his skin as he gathered the courage to speak his mind. "I want it—more, harder. I want to *feel* it. I need you to take me harder, Alexios, please."

Alexios pulled back, searching Auro's face. "You want me to...hurt you?"

Auro covered his face. "I don't—no, not exactly."

Alexios took a deep breath, shifting his weight to slide out of Auro with a wince. He knelt between Auro's thighs and seized his hands to pull him up so they sat face to face. "Then what is it?"

"I want—I want to still feel you when I go to sleep," Auro whispered in a rush. "I want you to fuck me so hard I still feel the ache of you inside me when I wake up next spring."

Alexios's mouth dropped open. "*Fuck,* Auro," he swore, heat rising in his cheeks.

"Well," said Auro, pulling away, embarrassed. "You asked."

"No, Auro, you mistake me," said Alexios hastily. He clasped Auro's face between his hands. "I can—I can do that." He kissed Auro, shoving his tongue between his lips with a bit less care than he usually would, and Auro moaned in reply. "I want to...to—give you that."

When Auro met his eye, the mischievous gleam was back, despite the tears still threatening to spill over. "Oh? You do, do you?"

"Yes," Alexios whispered, tightening his fingers in Auro's hair. "I want it, too. I want the statue of you to recall the feel of me, so you wake up next spring and need me once more to feel whole."

"I do," said Auro. "I need you. I love you, Alexios."

The muscles below Alexios's navel clenched, hot and tight as he pulled Auro in again for another fierce kiss. He bit savagely at Auro's lip, and when Auro gasped and threw his head back, Alexios knew he was on the right path toward giving Auro what he needed. "I love you," he murmured into the column of his throat. "With all my heart, I love you."

Sucking hard on the soft white skin of Auro's throat, Alexios wondered if the statue of Auro would reflect the bruise he left with a shadow on the marble. He hoped it would. He could visit the temple every day and press his finger to the stain and know that Auro remained his, and his alone. Alexios shuddered, a hungry, possessive beast waking up behind his breast. He wanted that. He wanted to mark Auro as his own, to lay a claim on him that neither a curse nor the passing of seasons nor the will of gods could erase.

Braced on his knees, Alexios seized Auro's hips, turning him to lie on his front. Auro pushed back against Alexios, needy and eager, his ass thrust up in the air like an offering. Alexios dug his fingers into the flesh of Auro's waist and used his other hand to line up the head of his cock with Auro's hole. He pushed inside, slowly at first, and then slid home with one fluid thrust until he was pressed against Auro's thighs.

With one hand still clasped to the bone of Auro's hip,

Alexios slid his other up his ribs, over his shoulder blade, to cup the nape of Auro's neck. He squeezed it, the pressure just enough to warn Auro that Alexios planned to follow through on the promise he'd made before he trailed his fingers up into Auro's hair. Fisting Auro's curls, Alexios pulled, yanking Auro's head back. Auro gasped, his spine bowing as he clenched down hard on Alexios's cock, squeezing it within him as if he was afraid Alexios would pull away.

He did—only briefly, till just the head of his cock remained sheathed in Auro's silky, hot channel, before slamming back in. Auro *wailed,* the sharp, hard shock of Alexios pummeling him like nothing either of them had yet explored together. Their intimate moments had always been tender, exploratory—thorough, as they learned everything they could about each other's bodies.

This was different.

This was Alexios flexing his thighs to hammer Auro as hard as he could, as fast as he could. It was as if Alexios could only fuck Auro hard enough, he might stave off the sunset that meant their time together was at an end. Sweat beaded on Alexios's forehead, his chest, and his muscles burned as he savaged Auro, impaling him again and again, and the slick, harsh slap of their bodies connecting was loud as thunder in the quiet of Alexios's chambers—though not as loud as Auro, who cried out helplessly each time Alexios struck home.

Alexios considered trying to stifle Auro's cries but decided against it. He craved the sounds of Auro's pleasure, needed them, and he added his own noises to the song: groans and animal grunts, growls, sounds Alexios had never made before —had not even known he *could* make, but they came out of him on every stroke, sounds that accompanied the urge to *take,* to make Auro his.

His fingers still in Auro's hair, Alexios twisted his hand, almost cruel as he yanked Auro's head to the side, wanting to get a glimpse of his face, the way it twisted in pleasure-pain, plump lips gaping wide. Those lips were his, too, and Alexios slowed his pace just enough so he could lunge forward and take them. Auro gave as good as he got, tugging Alexios's bottom lip with his teeth, nipping hard at the side of his jaw as they rocked together, mouths locked in a ferocious kiss. Panting, Alexios pulled back, a feral grin on his face as he released his hold on Auro's curls and placed his palm between his shoulders. He shoved, pushing Auro's chest to the mattress. Auro released a startled *oof!* as Alexios started fucking him again, hard, driving into Auro like he meant to fuck him through the bedframe to the floor.

Alexios felt his universe narrow to a deep, *deep* chasm behind his groin—a pull like gravity, like a maelstrom, sucking all of his awareness into this tiny, white-hot point where he plunged in and out of Auro, whose entire body tensed, vibrating with the same need. Alexios knew in that moment the maelstrom was one they shared. It had to be, not two people feeling something similar, at the same time—but them both sharing a piece of the same, singular thing. Sitting by the same fire, swimming in the same lake. Looking at the same stars, being blinded by the same sun.

Alexios's heart thundered in his chest, and he suddenly *had* to look into Auro's eyes—he had to see his sweet face. He could still give Auro this hard, aggressive fuck while drowning in his green eyes, couldn't he? His hips chased release even as he tried to pull back, off, out, and Auro cried out, desperate and lost and the sound pulled at Alexios's chest, but he wasn't planning on remaining separated for long. He pushed Auro onto his back, seized his ankles, and pushed his knees against his chest. Before he slid back inside, back home, Alexios took in the sight before him.

A fallen god, bent in half, staring at Alexios like *he* was the one from the heavens. Auro's hole winked at him, the skin around his rim puffy and red from the poundings it had taken, and they weren't even done yet. Alexios took a moment, steadied his breath, and reached for the oil on the side table. He added another glug to the palm of his hand, stroking his shaft a few times with a groan before plunging back into Auro. Auro's ankles were up by his ears, and his eyes were wide and vulnerable. Alexios grabbed Auro's hands, threading their fingers together as he pushed back inside. They groaned as one, and Alexios wasted no time stoking the fire between them once again. It had fallen to sultry, glowing embers and Alexios meant to bring on the inferno.

With his knees planted firm into the bed, Alexios pushed back inside as slow and as deep as he could, and Auro's cries dissolved into one, long, unbroken wail, his head thrown back, throat upturned. Alexios sank his teeth into the juncture of Auro's neck and shoulder, right where he found the cloud-shaped birthmark the first night they'd been together, and with his mouth full of Auro's flesh he began again, fucking into Auro with brutal, sharp thrusts. He could get deeper, in this position, and that's what Auro had wanted, needed—what both of them needed. The maelstrom was back, sucking them both in, and down, and down, and down, blackness pressing in on them from all sides, compressing the air from Alexios's lungs like he truly was drowning. Delirious, and drowning. He tried to kiss Auro again, to breathe into his lungs—to let Auro breathe into his, perhaps. Or both. The movement of their bodies prevented a true kiss, but their lips were close, they panted into each other's mouths, the tears finally wrung from Auro salty on Alexios's lips and tongue as he kissed Auro's cheeks, the tip of his nose, his forehead.

When Auro reached up to cup Alexios's cheek, staring into his eyes, the devastation there was startling, breathtaking, so raw that Alexios tried to look away, but Auro's strength held him fast—the strength in the small, soft hands that

Alexios loved so well, the strength of his heart. His grace, all of it.

It shattered him so thoroughly it was almost like he could *hear* it, or perhaps that was the clay pots housing all the plants Auro had filled his chambers with. They all burst even as Auro did, an explosion of leaves and petals that covered the entire room, falling and swirling around the bed as Alexios pumped his hips, fucking Auro through his climax, his weak moans spurring Alexios on until he too burst, his cock twitching as he filled Auro, his seed gushing out around the base of his shaft as they moved together, fitfully.

When the last leaves fell lazily to the floor behind them, Alexios finally stopped moving, still inside of Auro. Even as he softened, and the clenching of Auro's channel made his eyes roll, he wanted to remain. But he couldn't. His cock slipped free in a wet gush of oil and cum, and he released Auro's legs from his shoulders, letting him stretch out upon his back. He draped his arm over his eyes, chest heaving, body flushed. Alexios stared, and stared, and stared. He could stare at Auro forever and never tire, but the ruddy glow of sunset cruelly reminded him he didn't have forever. He didn't even have an hour.

"Fuck, Auro, I—" said Alexios, his voice breaking.

Auro pulled him down, wrapping him in a fierce embrace. "I know."

As the sun finally gave up its ghosts, they rode pillion through the forest, and Leofric followed on his own horse behind. He'd apologized, to be intruding on their farewell, but with Janus still at large, he refused to take any chances. He gave them as much space as he could while still keeping Alexios in his eyeline.

They didn't speak, but as he held the reins Alexios rested his chin on Auro's shoulder, breathing his scent in, a scent that smelled a little like him, now, after the day they'd shared.

They reached the lake when the moon was high and full above them, bathing the world in silver shadows. Auro led the way out to the island where his brothers waited, Alexios just behind, clutching his hand, and Leofric two dozen paces after.

Standing before Auro's empty plinth, Alexios seized Auro's face in both hands. Auro's fingers wrapped around his wrists, clutching at him like a lifeline. "I will tell them," Alexios said. "I'll wait right here, and I'll help your brothers. I *will*. When you wake up next spring, they'll all be here—they'll be waiting for you."

"And you?" Auro asked, his eyes swimming.

"Me, most of all," said Alexios fiercely. "I'll be waiting. For you."

Auro smiled weakly and pried Alexios's hands from his face. "It's time."

Alexios truly felt as though someone was shredding his heart, smaller and smaller ribbons of it falling on the ground at his feet. He could scarce breathe for the pain of it, watching Auro climb up onto his plinth.

With a final soft smile, Auro raised one hand to the heavens, waiting.

The silence was oppressive, and Alexios felt the only sound was the pounding of his shredded heart.

Nothing happened.

Auro had told him, what it was like, each year, the stone bleeding over his skin and enclosing him in a beautiful carved prison—but Alexios could not see even a hint of marble bloom on Auro's flesh. He was too frightened to feel hope, and the look on Auro's face was puzzled for half a heartbeat—until his eyes rolled up in his head, his legs buckled, and he pitched sideways off his pedestal to crumple, lifeless on the stone floor.

"*Auro!*"

uro. Auro.

Auro floated, his limbs leaden and groggy. It was spring, his time. For some reason, for the first time in four hundred years, he was afraid to open his eyes. Alexios had promised him, promised him that he'd do his best to help his brothers—to break the curse. Auro had a hard time believing it, but when he'd climbed up on his plinth and looked down at Alexios, he'd finally allowed himself to hope.

But what if he was awake now, and nothing had changed? What if he woke to see only the stone faces of his brothers' statues? What if Alexios was gone—what if his shining golden prince had married his princess and forgotten all about Auro? Better to remain stone, than to face that, he thought.

Oh, Auro.

That voice. He frowned, still refusing to open his eyes. That was a voice he hadn't heard in four hundred years—the voice of a ghost. And if it were the voice of a ghost, Auro must be dreaming.

Which was impossible.

As a statue, he never dreamed.

Not once, in all his centuries of imprisonment inside his statue, had he dreamed. He simply closed his eyes, and in the next heartbeat, awoke to the freshness of a bright spring morning.

Open your eyes, Apricot.

It was that, the name his mother called him as a boy, that pried open Auro's eyes. He blinked, a sparkling opalescent mist obscuring most of his field of vision. He realized he was lying on the floor of the temple, and he sat up, blinking around him. The statues of his brothers were gone, and a vague, shadowy form sat on one of the plinths. The mist seemed to coalesce around it, as if perhaps the form was the source of the mist.

Auro finally loosened his tongue. "Mother?" he croaked.

Perhaps, once, Apricot. But it's been a long time.

"I can't see you," he said, and to his ears, his voice sounded young and foolish—a lost boy's voice.

It's been a long time, the shadow said. *I never thought it would take you this long.*

"What?"

Why did it take you so long?

"I didn't know," he said. "I didn't know you—"

Didn't know I would never abandon my sons? She was angry with him. Her voice sounded fierce and terrible. Like a god's voice.

No, it said. *Just a mother's voice.*

Auro frowned. "You did leave us," he said.

Never.

"When I woke, the first spring after—after, you were already gone."

No.

"And when Ozias came to court, with his mother—you were never the same, after that. You left us then, too."

No. And it echoed, louder. The echoes were louder, but coming from farther away.

Auro flinched, and it seemed the shadowy form before him flickered, and for a second, he saw his mother's silhouette in the pearly clouds, but then she was gone again. "Help me," he said, plaintive as a child. "Help me understand."

I pulled away when Ozias came to court because I had to prepare.

"Prepare for what?"

For this, she said, as if that should be obvious. *I knew your father would fall. I knew he would destroy our family, Apricot. I should have known well before, but...*

"But what?" Auro frowned. His head ached, and he tasted something in his mouth like copper coins. He'd always felt it had been him and his brothers who destroyed their family.

I loved your father. But not as much as I loved you and your brothers. So, I prepared.

"Prepared *what*?" Auro repeated, frustrated. He licked his lips, trying to swallow around the taste of copper and salt.

I don't have much time, Apricot. You must hear me. I left you as many clues as I dared, but it wasn't enough.

"It was," said Auro. "I found Cedras's grace!"

You did, Apricot, and I am so proud. I knew it would be you, first. I knew it had to be you. But I didn't know it would take you so long, and I fade.

Even as she said it, it seemed to Auro her voice grew fainter the longer she spoke.

I held on, so I could see you. I had to see you.

"I don't understand this," said Auro. His tongue felt thick in his mouth, and the coppery taste intensified. He tried to spit discreetly on the floor, but it didn't help. "What is happening?"

I couldn't stop your father's curse. I tried, you must know that. You must.

Auro said nothing. He would never have imagined a mortal could stop a god's curse.

You're right. I couldn't stop it. But I could change it.

That brought him up short. "You *what*?"

I learned, I learned, I learned, I learned.

It seemed like the shadows and fog were dissipating. He could barely make out a human shape in the roiling clouds anymore. "No, learned—*learned what*?"

The arcane. I learned enough to alter the curse.

"Alter it how?"

You'll see.

Auro opened his mouth to beg her to stay, but all that came out was a choking, hacking cough. He turned over, spitting a mouthful of blood onto the floor, the red of it blinding and cruel against the muted whites of the misty temple. He didn't understand, his eyes flew open, it was dark, too dark, and hands grabbed his arms, slapped his face, he thrashed and pulled and all at once the sounds of the night came pouring back in, someone was breathing hard, someone calling his name, crickets, the splash of water—

"Mother?"

Big warm hands, safe hands, familiar hands, clasped his cheeks, steadying him. "No, Auro, it's me."

"Alexios?" Auro blinked, lights popping and spinning in front of his eyes. "What—?"

Alexios's face swam before him, pale and frightened. Dimly, Auro became aware of a third hand, rubbing his back, where Leofric crouched beside them both. "You fell off your pedestal—I think, I think you hit your head."

Auro rubbed his temple. "Yes, I'd say you're right. And near bit my tongue off, too." He spat another mouthful of blood on the ground. He became aware of something else. "I'm...naked?"

Alexios flushed, some color returning to his cheeks as he glanced away. "Your tunic...it disintegrated."

Looking around, Auro indeed found himself sitting in a small pile of disarticulated petals. Never had he felt this out of sorts when waking up at the dawn of a new season. He tried to summon his grace to reassemble the petals and dress himself, straining to reach for his power. His head gave a sickening throb, and he turned and retched bile and blood on the floor. Alexios pulled him closer, and he trembled, helpless, in the circle of Alexios's arms.

"Your hair..." said Alexios nervously. He fingered Auro's curls, tugging a lock from in front of Auro's eyes so he could see.

The color had gone out of it, leached away, leaving a pale, ashy auburn instead. "My grace," he said faintly. "I think it's... gone."

"But, Auro," said Alexios, cupping his face once more. "You're here—you're awake!"

He blinked. "Of course, I am," he said, confused. "Isn't it next year?" Auro asked, because, really, that should be the only reason he was awake. It felt wrong, though—Alexios still wore the bandage around his arm where Janus had bled him to create his clay duplicate. "It's spring, is it not?"

"Afraid not, little brother," said a voice, another voice Auro hadn't heard for four hundred years.

Behind Alexios, a shadow shifted, and Cosmo stepped down from his plinth with liquid poise. The moonlight shone on his freckled face, lighting up the fiery red of his hair, glinting off the dozens of golden baubles he always wore. "Now, can someone please tell me what the fuck is going on?"

Thank you for reading Bright Spring! Scan the QR Code below to access bonus content and join my newsletter!

Acknowledgments

While writing can often feel like a solitary pursuit, no story comes to life in a vacuum. There are a lot of people I want to thank, people without whom, Harmony of Seasons could never have been realized.

Thank you to everyone who has supported me along the way, and more specifically, thank you to the following beings who supported the Kickstarter campaign that allowed me to create this series. Thank you, from the bottom of my heart, to AK Faulkner, Alexis Winstanley, Ali Wolfe, Alice, Amanda Andrade, Amy, Andrew Singleton, Angela Wood, Asari Burk, Ashley Jarman, Audrey, Brenna Greenfield, Brianna Hall, Briar Elijah, Cecil Holloway, Chiara S., Dave Riedinger, Ed Hanscom, Eddie Joo, Elizabeth Noel Bennett, Emilie Rose, Emily P., Emma F., Erika West, Franchesca Caram, Gabriela Lopez Marecos, Heather M., Jade S, Jason Gray, Jen Garrett, Jennifer Robinson, Jess DB, John H. Bookwalter Jr., Jon Weaver, Joshua Furman, Kai'lee, Kala M. Bishop, Kat Shenton, Kaytea Grounds, Kenneth McKenzie, Kirsten, Kristie Redmond, Kyra Thrush, Kytarah Ikkin, Laura Edwards, Lulu, Luna Daye, M. Cosgrove, Mary Livingston, MayBunny8, Megan McGhee, Mercer Smith, Merit Burgett, Mitchell Adams, Morgan G., Mykah Wyatt, Nicolas Breton, Nicole Haarstad, Nikki K., Nimisha, Novak, Pepto, Philip A Perez, Phoenix R., Pip Walker, Rachel Emily, Rachiel R, Rasia159, Raychel Kill, Rinna, Rune, S. Taylor, Sam, Sarah Wallace, Scott Casey, Squiggs, Stephanie Dawley, Tammy S., Taylor

Nelson, Thai Huynh, The brilliant and extra spicy Jennifer Rhys., Toria W., Tosha, Victoria Edgett, Willow Stuart, Zenn Alvarez and everyone else who supported this campaign and the creation of this series!

Sincerely, thank you. Thank you all.

Emmaline Strange is the author of *Mighty Quill*, *Crown of Aster*, and *A Walrus & A Gentleman*. She loves to write and read about smooching. She lives in Boston with her husband, dog, and cat, all of whom she loves to smooch. When not smooching, she can usually be found doting on her plants, baking, or watching far too much television. Ms. Strange is a lover of all things nerdy, from *Dungeons & Dragons*, to *Lord of the Rings*, to the MCU.

She enjoys iced coffee, long walks on the beach, complaining about her feet after long walks on the beach, and long sits on the couch to recover from long walks on the beach.

For updates on upcoming projects, come say hello on Twitter (@EmmalineStrange) where she's always talking about writin', readin', and...well, not so much 'rithmetic.